FORGOTTEN STARS & DISTANT SEAS
BY
J.B. ROCKWELL

SEVERED PRESS
HOBART TASMANIA

FORGOTTEN STARS & DISTANT SEAS

Copyright © 2020 J.B. Rockwell

WWW.SEVEREDPRESS.COM

ISBN: 978-1-922551-43-6

PART I: FORGOTTEN STARS

ONE

The contact tripped the sensors—lightning-quick and suspicious in the way it lit up the command center's panels, fluttering briefly before it ghosted away.

Odd and uncertain, hasty in its retreat. Hardly worth noting, really, except this was mid-watch when nothing ever seemed to happen. And a second aborted contact followed soon after, slithering in hot on that first blip's heels.

"Sir—"

"I see it, Vaaulu." Faraday pushed free of his captain's chair and eased his way over to the crewman's metal-sided station with its massive bank of carbon-glass displays.

Long-range scan, this one, sucking in feeds from a network of listeners strategically positioned across a vast and empty stretch of space. The planet Armistice at their center, watched over by the Halgren vessel, *Hadrian*: an AI warship orbiting in space.

Operations ran from the low-light confines of this semi-circular command center with its rotating watch of crew.

"Logs capture that?" Faraday leaned over Vaaulu's shoulder, one hand resting on the crewman's seatback, the other braced against the station's frame.

"Yes, sir. At least, I think so, sir." Vaaulu snuck a glance over his shoulder at Faraday's looming shape. Uniform a dark smudge in the command center's dim illumination, silver captain's stars sparkling at his collar. "Should've, anyway."

He fidgeted in his seat, sneaking glances at the pin-dot lens of a camera above him. One of many embedded in the ceiling of *Hadrian's* command center, with hundreds of others installed across the length and breadth of the ship.

Monitoring his interior spaces, looking outward on the stars. Watching, always watching, recording everything they saw.

Nothing escaped *Hadrian's* attention. Even the smallest bit of information got stored.

Like those blips from the sensors. The dollop of data left in their wake.

"*Hadrian.*" Faraday spoke to the camera out of habit. Didn't need to—AI's consciousness was everywhere, in every ship's compartment—but he felt stupid talking to thin air. "Can you isolate the sensor that caught that little anomaly?"

"Of course," *Hadrian* answered crisply, calm and confident in his response.

He pushed a map to the polymer glass panels curving with the arc of the command center's front wall. One section of the display blanked to accommodate the new information: an alternate view of their reality showing the stars and planet in miniature, the network of sensors spreading outward from Armistice's orb.

Hadrian highlighted a single sensor among the many, this one situated way, way out. "Traps show it on the outer perimeter. Point zero five two light years distant."

"Transmission delay?"

"Minimal. Chron indicates thirty-four seconds."

Faraday grunted and rubbed at his chin, considering that distant point on the sensor map's outer edge. Idly registering the silence on the bridge around him—no people sounds at all, nothing but the hum of machinery that pervaded all of the ship's spaces, the puff and blow of recycled air.

Stale and dry like everything on this vessel. Smelling strongly of metal and electronics and some lab-created scent. Pine and lavender, someone'd told him—Bronsky's choice, not his.

Bronsky, who was captain before him. A damned fool who left a mess behind for Faraday to clean up.

Asshole. Kick his teeth in if I ever catch up with that guy.

"Playback, if you please." Faraday hooked a thumb at long-range scan's display. "Five minute segment. Diagnostic scan on the metadata."

"Done."

Hadrian pushed a package to Vaaulu that opened automatically on scan's display, data capture from the sensor running either side of that pair of contacts—two minutes before and another two after—with diagnostic indicators layered in.

The first pass played through in real time, the entire segment, beginning to end. At a signal from Faraday, Vaaulu reversed it, repeating the playback from the middle—sensor contact section only this time, data feed and diagnostics layered together.

Good crewman, Vaaulu. Young, inexperienced—no combat time, nothing but academy training and a couple of expeditionary assignments under his belt—but smart and focused. Knew scan's capabilities inside and out.

He studied the data on his panel, sharp face intent, clay-colored skin speckled with jewel-toned patterns that morphed and shifted as the display's data changed. "Not much there, sir." Vaaulu twitched his shoulders, turning an apologetic look his captain's way. "Top end of the sensors' range, just like *Hadrian* said. Nothing of consequence in what I'm seeing, really. Diagnostics show some minor chatter—"

"Cut to the chase, Vaaulu. What caused those blips on the sensors?"

Vaaulu puffed out a breath. "Space junk, sir."

"Space junk."

"That's what I'm thinking."

Faraday frowned doubtfully, sharing that look with *Hadrian*.

The camera above him twitched one way, centered and flicked the other in an AI version of shrugging, the real thing impossible given his ship's body.

The AI himself remained silent. Faraday wasn't quite sure what to make of that.

"Thought we tuned the sensors to filter that stuff out."

"Supposed to." Second lifting of Vaaulu's shoulders, silver insignia glittering in the panel's scattering of light. "Some of the bigger pieces get through, though." Flicker of his eyes to *Hadrian's* camera. "Sometimes, anyway."

Faraday raised his eyebrows, looking a question at that same camera, but the damned AI *still* wasn't speaking. Just left Vaaulu hanging out there on his own.

"This space junk got a source?" He kept his eyes on that camera while Vaaulu consulted his bank of displays.

"Could be part of that cargo freighter we lost in transit."

"Freighter dumped out of hyperspace. Stressors would've shredded it into dust."

"Still…" Vaaulu's shoulders lifted—his go-to gesture when he wasn't quite sure. "What's left would've kept moving. Might've finally caught up to us. Assuming it maintained its trajectory, of course. And, you know, the math and velocity work out."

Faraday slid his eyes to the crewman and watched him wither beneath his stare. "Run the feed back again, Vaaulu. Both contacts. Overlay the results."

"Aye, sir." Vaaulu hunched over scan's panel, shoulders bunched up around his ears. Sneaking glances at *Hadrian's* camera every now and then while he rattled away at a virtual keyboard, retrieving and combining both feeds.

"You *could* help him, you know." Faraday turned that same stare on *Hadrian's* watching eye and waited, arms folded, until the AI got it in gear. Scan's panel flickered, equations morphing and twisting as the *Hadrian* injected changes to correct the errors in Vaaulu's calculations.

"Better?"

"Much." Faraday pointedly ignored the prissiness and simply nodded his thanks.

AI didn't like playing calculator. Didn't like a lot of things about the way Faraday ran this operation, including his insistence on a human watch. No point, in his opinion. AI consciousness dwarfed the crew's collective intellect—a fact *Hadrian* pointed out frequently and with great aplomb –his heavy cruiser body a marvel of brutal efficiency, built for combat and retrofitted exploration, stacked-arrow shape reconfigured for additional equipment.

Technically, he was superior, in every measurable way. But the arrogance in him was off-putting, especially for the crew. And no matter how smart he was, *Hadrian* was still a ship. Faraday was captain, and ultimately in charge.

The Halgren Defense Coalition said so, and the treaty that created it codified the decision in law. *Hadrian's* beef was that AIs never got a say in that particular agreement, and Bronsky, in his negligence, led *Hadrian* down another path.

Allowed *Hadrian* more latitude in his decision-making than Halgren protocol strictly allowed. Amped up his emulators and taught him some severely bad habits that needed breaking.

Like not getting pissy at his captain. Like learning to take orders he didn't necessarily agree with.

Faraday considered that pin-dot camera. *Hadrian's* watchful, unblinking eye.

Sorry, buddy. Some day you big brains will probably take over, but for now this is my operation. You *take* my *commands.*

Hadrian's camera stared steadily back at him, turned aside and pointed away.

Pissy again. A passive-aggressive show of defiance.

Faraday shook his head at the ridiculousness of it, leaving the AI to sulk while he keyed into the station next to Vaaulu—same black and glass design, the entire command center a dim and grim, closed in, armored space—and snagged a chart from the database. Sector map this time, showing the position of each sensor in relation to the planet, and Armistice's place among the surrounding stars.

He layered the information together, folded his hands and simply stared at it a while.

So many of them out there, and just as many planets waiting to be explored. Need and greed pushed humanity beyond the boundaries of the Milky Way centuries ago and into the satellite galaxies nearby. Ursa Major, Ursa Minor, the Megallanic Clouds, Large and Small.

Ursas turned out to be disappointing—a few planets of note, not really all that much else—but the Clouds... the Clouds were gold mines. The larger one even more so than the small.

Mega Big yielded planets, a whole passel of them ripe for terraforming and Armistice below them just one, and in Mega Small they found a starfaring species. The first they'd stumbled across in all their explorations. One that most definitely didn't want neighbors—they made that clear, right up front.

First contact sparked a border war in the disputed zone separating the Megallanic Clouds. Several decades later, they finally managed to tamp it down and contain it, confining that not-so-friendly species to Mega Small where they'd found them. Or so Halgren thought.

Until the intel reports started coming in. And that incident at the Madrigal Line.

That's what bothered Faraday about those two brief readings on the sensors. Contact out there could be anything, even the space junk Vaaulu claimed, but intuition argued differently. The ship driver in him had grown suspicious over the years.

Something's out there, I can feel it. Testing the perimeter sensors for blind spots. The automated defenses we put in place.

If only those contacts had been clearer. Hopefully the traps brought more data back.

"What's the status on that analysis, Vaaulu?"

"Just finishing it now."

"Big screen." Faraday waggled a finger at the floor-to-ceiling glass panels. "Let's see what you've got."

"Aye, sir."

A touch pushed Vaaulu's results to the command center's curving display. Faraday stepped in close and scanned it—the overlaid data, the metatags laid alongside—and spotted a pattern right away.

"Son of a bitch."

Duplicate contact—exact match, that first blip and the second. In context and duration, in the dribs of metadata the sensors picked up.

Space junk didn't do that. Didn't move like that, didn't act like that, didn't create contacts that looked anything at *all* like those two blips. Space junk tumbled as it traveled. It wavered and vibrated creating variations in what the sensors picked up. This…whatever this was, nothing at *all* anomalous in that signature. Excepting the brevity of it, the conspicuous lack of data deeper down. And that duplication. The mirroring of one contact to another that spoke of purpose and pattern, of conformity in design.

"That's a ship out there. I'd bet my life on it."

"One of ours?" Vaaulu asked him.

"Maybe."

But he didn't think so. No need for a Halgren vessel to be so coy. "What the hell are you?" Faraday murmured.

"Sir?"

"Nothing, Vaaulu. Just… too many damned questions. Too many things we still don't know."

"You want me to run the analysis again?"

Faraday considered the idea and rejected it as a waste of time. Vaaulu knew his business, no reason to believe he'd fucked that first evaluation up. Instead, he flicked his eyes to a camera, giving his bruised-ego AI another task. "Isolate the sensor that caught those contacts. Kill the filters. Give me everything it's picking up."

Hadrian set about making the adjustments while Vaaulu sat there and fidgeted, frowning uncertainly at the wall displays.

"Problem, crewman?"

"Yes, sir. I mean, no, sir. I mean—" Vaaulu licked his lips, sliding a glance Faraday's way. "It's just… that's a whole lotta data to parse through, Captain."

"And?" Faraday folded his arms, eyebrows lifting. "Mid-watch, crewman. You telling me you've got something *better* to do?"

"Uhh…" Vaaulu eyed the empty command center around him—Collins detailed to the galley to scare up some coffee, the other five stations powered down and dark because mid-watch ran minimal crew. "No, sir," he wisely decided. "Nothing better to do."

"Good. Now fire up those fingers and start weeding through all that data. *Hadrian.*" Faraday spun to face the nearest camera. "Dump what you've got over to Vaaulu and help him sort through the chaff. Roust the main watch early—I want a full complement manning the command center in an hour."

"Yes, Faraday. Informing the crew."

"And send a message to Halgren Central. Give them a heads-up about that contact." He started to turn away, realized he'd forgotten something and glanced back. "Notify Agarwal on the planet while you're at it. Tell him to put the garrison on alert. Anomaly might be nothing, but I want them ready in case there's trouble."

Hadrian queued up the requested communications and sent them off to their various destinations. Surprisingly compliant, this time. Not sulking at all.

"You think there will be?" Vaaulu asked quietly.

"Trouble? No telling." Faraday rubbed at his face, feeling tired all of a sudden. The missed hours in his rack. Not his habit to stand mid-watch, but he hadn't been sleeping well lately. Kept dreaming of another time, another ship, another crew Halgren took away. Traded that assignment for this one because of

5

one stupid mistake. "Rather play it safe," he told Vaaulu. "Better to have Agarwal's troopers lose a little beauty sleep than have something come through and catch us with our pants down, if you know what I mean."

Vaaulu chewed his lip, face pinched and anxious. "What kind of something, Captain? You think that's—?"

"Don't know what to think, crewman, and I'm not wasting my time guessing." Faraday extruded a finger and pointed it at scan's panel. "Data, Vaaulu. You just do your job. Let me take care of the worrying."

"Aye, sir," he mumbled. Grudging. Uncertain. Vaaulu's eyes overflowing with questions he wasn't quite brave enough to ask. Instead, he bowed his head over scan's panel, hands pressed to its carbon-glass surface, fingers busily typing away while Faraday watched him in silence. Wondering if he'd been too hard on him. Too terse, too demanding, too much himself after Bronsky.

Bronsky hadn't been much of anything, including present a good deal of the time. And this crew... so different. Not at all like the one Faraday commanded before.

God, I hate starting over. Especially like this.

He sighed heavily, rubbing absentmindedly at his temple. Crew would adjust to him eventually—he knew that deep down. Right now, he had more important things to do than worrying about people's feelings. Curt came with captain—crew would figure that out in time.

He abandoned Vaaulu to his drudgery and turned his attention to the command center's glass panels, thinking through what to do next.

Three day turnaround time on a response to that message to Halgren Central thanks to the three hundred-something lightyear round trip from their headquarters back on Diogenes to *Hadrian* in orbit above Armistice. Nigh on ten years of travel time from there to here by ship, which meant they didn't see many visitors. Supply vessels came by once a year and a Halgren patrol every six months or so, but the nearest base was a three year ice nap distant, that same patrol now eight days of hyperspace transit away.

All of which meant they were alone out here, for the most part. Guardians of this partially terraformed planet, expected to fend for themselves if anything went wrong.

Which, mostly, it didn't. Not until Bronsky—the same Bronsky who'd all but abandoned his crew and taught *Hadrian* such bad habits—grew bored with his assignment and started stirring up trouble.

Fucking Bronsky. Fucking admiralty playing favorites.

"Faraday."

"Hmm?"

"Should I notify Dr. Naisson of the perimeter breach as well?"

Sensible suggestion from *Hadrian,* but Faraday grimaced just the same. Dr. Naisson was the lead scientist in charge of the terraforming project on Armistice—pistol of a woman, ran that operation like a clock. Smartest xenobio-botano-whatever in the galaxy from what he'd been told, but damn if she didn't give the military types hell.

Especially when they withheld information. He'd learned that early on.

Risky, not telling her. Riskier still to stir her up only to find out this whole thing was a big bunch of nothing.

"Not yet," he decided. "Not until we have a better idea about what's going on."

"Oh."

Something in the way he said that, an almost sheepish note to *Hadrian's* voice. Faraday pivoted, head tilting. "You already told her, didn't you?"

"*No*. I alerted *Persephone*. In case something really bad happened."

Persephone. The Science Station AI. A star-shaped planet parked planetside to oversee the terraforming complex and its operations.

If *Persephone* knew, damned sure Dr. Naisson did as well.

"Goddammit, *Hadrian*."

"I thought you'd want me to warn them."

"Yeah, well, you didn't ask me now, did you?"

Hadrian conveniently ignored the question and kept arguing his side of the equation. "It seemed prudent to notify *Persephone* of the potentiality of the situation. Especially considering—"

"*Potentiality? What* potentiality? We don't know what the *fuck's* going on here, *Hadrian*!"

"By all indications, those contacts are some type of vessel. You said so yourself."

"Yes, but—"

"Then I stand by my decision," *Hadrian* concluded. Utterly unapologetic, serenely arrogant in his AI way.

Faraday bristled, mouth opening to offer a sharp retort. He bit it back with an effort, swallowing those admonishing words.

Hated the haughtiness, the ego that came with it, but however annoying, they weren't entirely the AI's fault. *Hadrian* served many captains over the decades, Bronsky just one in a laundry list of bucking-to-be-admiral types.

Well, Faraday wasn't chasing promotion, he just wanted his old assignment back. *Hadrian* and he... that partnership was still evolving. Searching for the balance that made it all work.

Unfortunately, the emulators weren't helping. Bronsky's laissez faire leadership style either. *Hadrian* simply wasn't used to being captained. Bronsky spoiled him, let him have the run of the place for too long.

Faraday considered the camera a moment and with an effort, softened his words. "Not saying you were wrong. Just... talk to me, *Hadrian*. Clue me in at least next time."

Silence from that camera, from the speakers that carried the AI's voice. And then, by some miracle, "Yes, Faraday. I will, as you say, clue you in next time."

A stiff and slightly surly answer, but at least *Hadrian* agreed. Didn't fix the current situation, but Faraday chalked it up as a win, nonetheless.

"I can contact *Persephone* if you—"

"Don't bother. Cat's already out of the bag. Surprised Dr. Naisson hasn't called up here already." Faraday surveyed the command center's stations, half-expecting one to light up. "Ah, hell. Might as well get this over with." He stalked over to an empty seat and slid behind a station. "*Hadrian.* Get me a direct line to the Science Station. Tell *Persephone* I need to speak with Dr. Naisson."

TWO

Anthea wove her way back to her quarters, slightly unsteady after a long night with too much company and more gin-fizzes than she typically allowed. Not much of a drinker, really—metabolism had a hell of time processing alcohol, turtled down as it was by the company's mandated 'treatments'—and gin was hardly her usual tipple. Tonight, though… special occasion. Corporate dinner party—virtual for her, the other attendees gathered together on distant Ventress—to celebrate repeatable water production on Armistice. A big deal for Anthea personally, this being her baby, the culmination of decades of scientific achievement, and a major milestone for the terraforming project itself. And the company… well, TerraGen liked its celebrations. Enjoyed showing off a bit, especially when new investors were involved.

In this case, some new world distillery producing the finest spirits and liquors. Or so the marketing brochures claimed.

Nothing fine at all about what Anthea forced down her throat, though. Burned like plasma fuel, hit her gut with a mule's kick. Closer to blast torch accelerant than fine liquor in her opinion and her poor abused brain was paying the price.

Tipsy just shy of skunk-drunk. Stewing in a brew of not-so-fine juices that made it slew sideways and bump up against her cranium's wall with each step.

Anthea knocked it back in place with a soft little pop to her head, turned her wrist over when her bio-monitor twittered prissily—unhappy with her chemical imbalance and the resulting effects on her body—and checked the warnings on its display.

"Yeah, yeah, yeah. Shut up, you old nag."

She stopped just short of her quarters and pressed the tips of two fingers to the silver band wrapped around her wrist, holding them there, mashed against the bio-monitor's onyx display until the godawful twittering ceased.

"Stupid-ass thing." She continued on down the hall, kicking a potted plant that got in her way. "Stupid-ass corporate with their stupid-ass parties."

Hated these corporate get-togethers. The fake smiles and polite conversation, the endless vapid questions about topics the company shills clearly didn't understand. Waste of time, hobnobbing with the corporate snobbery and their partners. Not at *all* how she liked to spend her evenings, but the company mandated them once a quarter. Threatened to truck out here and inspect the operation personally if she didn't play along and give the investors some face time with TerraGen's best and brightest.

"Sons-a-bitches. I'm a god damned scientist not some tipple-witted socialite on a string."

One of the best in the three galaxies, as it so happened. Wrote the book on planetary terraforming with specializations in both xenobotany and xenobiology—wasn't a thing she didn't know about turning dust balls into human-ready habitats. Company supplied the equipment, paid her salary and everything else, and all they asked in return was that their brilliant lead scientist play along.

She wiped at her face, hating the feel of the make-up she so seldom wore. Her dark skin didn't need it, but the camouflage proved useful at times. Dinner parties especially, because the company liked their scientists old and wizened. Respectable-looking for their investors, which young and wrinkle free most definitely wasn't. Ironic, really, that the same rejuvenation treatments they paid for to prolong her life—and by extension, her usefulness to the corporation—left her face eternally youthful. The mahogany skin flawless, the dark curls untouched by grey.

The pots of paint turned her older, a skilled hand added wrinkles and lines. Didn't worry so much about the hair since they'd just assume she'd dyed it, but she stuck a sprinkling of flowers in the curls anyway. The kind an older, more venerable woman would wear.

Couldn't wait to get rid of it all now that the horrid hob-nobbery was over. Divest herself of the fancy party dress, the hated heels. The clown paint spackled across her face, the flowers that shucked loose at the most inopportune times and clung like scabs of dandruff to her shoulders.

Stupid, all of it. Simply awful, these fancy parties and dressing up.

Anthea keyed through the door to her quarters with her palm print, reader acting balky until she breathed on her hand to warm the skin. A soft chime approved her entry and she stepped through into sudden brilliance as the room's monitors woke and the lights switched on. "Modulation," she ordered, shading her eyes with a slim hand. "Reduce illumination twenty percent."

The lights dimmed noticeably, softening the glow in that arctic room. The atmosphere inside it chilly, the fittings and furniture designed to match.

Quarters, like most of the science spaces, came in varying shades of white. Frosted glass panels carved the room into private spaces: bedroom and bathroom, sitting room at the front. Brushed metal everywhere, trimming doors, windows and walls. Sky blue wall panels injected a modicum of color, the matching chairs, the scattering of squares in the snow-white decking, but mostly it was just metal on white. Everything stark and sterile and pure—pleasing to her scientist's sensibilities if not exactly cheerful and warm. The air itself stinking of disinfectant, despite *Persephone's* attempts to cover it up.

Piped in some sort of lemon-vanilla mixture that was supposed to be calming to the senses, make the rooms feel homier or some such. Anthea wasn't quite sure it accomplished either—wasn't even sure she really *liked* it—but it cut down on the chemical smell, added a little zing to the recycled, re-conditioned air.

And after all these years living with it, she'd come to associate that smell with *Persephone* and quarters. Homey or not, that smell reminded her of home.

"Late night for you, Anthea." *Persephone's* cool tones washed over her, a soothing, familiar presence greeting her as Anthea stepped into the front room.

"Later than I wanted it to be." She leaned against the doorframe, stripping the high-heeled shoes away while the bio-monitor started twittering again, alerting *Persephone* to its wearer's impaired state.

"You're flushed and your heart rate's elevated. Would you like me to lower the temperature a few degrees?"

"No. I would not." Anthea wriggled her cramped toes, high heels dangling from her fingers. "I like it cold in here, *Persephone*, not arctic. 12°C is quite cold enough." She leveled a stern look at a nearby camera, shaking a finger at it for added emphasis. Pushed away from the doorway and headed across the front room, angling for the glass and metal bathroom carved out of one corner. "Anything happen while I was gone?"

"Dr. Chen left three messages—"

"Only three this time," she snorted. "Miracles really do happen."

Chen was a worrier. Top-notch engineer, but she agonized over everything. Consulted Anthea on every decision, which was not at *all* the way she liked to run things.

Anthea hired Chen to oversee the atmosphere generator operations and the maintenance crew that came with it, not bug the hell out of her night and day. "Tell Chen to deal with it."

Whatever 'it' was this time.

"Acknowledged, Anthea. I've delivered that response. Captain Faraday also called—"

"Faraday?" That brought Anthea up short.

He was new here, relatively speaking. Reported in just under a year ago, the latest in a long line of military officers Halgren sent out to see to the planet's defense. Bunch of pompous, prickish bureaucrats for the most part, which is why Anthea made a point of avoiding them. Avoided all the military, really—not much of a people person, even her own staff seldom saw her—and these commanding officers they sent her as a matter of course.

Mostly that strategy worked out for her—captains hated leaving their ship, hardly ever pried themselves loose long enough to take a trip down to the planet's surface—until Faraday reported in and the pattern of her customs suddenly changed.

Faraday was different from the others who came before him. Not at all what Anthea had come to expect. No plush administrator, this latest commanding officer Halgren sent her. Nothing at all soft and political about him. Faraday was one of those sharp-edged combat types, all trigger switch and tight tolerances, about as cuddly as a box of razor blades. Every decision, every movement, every last thing about him sharp and crisp, squared off and locked down and exceedingly precise.

The scientist in her appreciated the exactitude of that presence. The straightforward and simplistic militariness that so sharply contrasted with the litany of puffed-up, preening predecessors she'd put up with over the years. But the administrator in her distrusted it precisely *because* Faraday was different. For all his combat experience and military bearing, this latest Halgren captain simply didn't fit. Not here. Not this position. Not this out-of-the-way place so far from the border wars and hot zones that honed his hard-won skills.

She stopped just inside the bathroom, wondering why he'd bother her at this late hour. "Faraday, eh?" She turned her head, searching for *Persephone's* camera across the room. "And just what did the good captain want?"

Persephone hesitated, which wasn't like her. The barest fraction of a pause before continuing in an apologetic tone. "Captain Faraday wasn't specific, but he asked that you—"

"Shh." Anthea raised a finger, head tilting to one side.

A hum intruded that shouldn't be there. A thrumming she felt in the deckplates beneath her bare feet, reverberating off the room's arctic blue walls.

"*Persephone.* Status." She chucked the high heels toward a corner and marched back into the front room.

"Power distribution nominal. Atmospherics—"

Anthea cut the AI off with a chopping motion. "Skip the system check. The hum, *Persephone.* What the hell is causing that hum?"

"Stand-by mode initiated. Main propulsion has been cycled into active, outer shielding deployed and locked into place."

"*Stand-by?*" That sobered her up quickly, cut the gin-fizz buzz in half.

Stand-by altered *Persephone's* configuration, extruding armored plating to fill the gaps between her many-pointed, stellated dodecahedron shape and transform this down-planet science vessel into a massive polyhedral orb. Annoyingly, it also covered up her solar panels, forcing *Persephone* to draw entirely on her internal power stores. More importantly, it disconnected her from the atmosphere generator, leaving it to run independently. Unmonitored and wide open.

"Who the hell ordered you into stand-by, *Persephone?*"

"*Hadrian* passed the instruction. He thought it prudent—"

"Fuck *Hadrian.* You're a science vessel, not military. You report to me, not him."

"Military orders take precedence in emergency situations—"

"*Emergency?* What emergency?" She stalked close to a camera and glared hard at its lens. "What the hell is going on?"

"Perimeter breach. *Hadrian* reports an anomaly in the long-range sensors."

"Fuck." Anthea spun on her heel and stalked over to her quarter's desk. "Communications. Get me a direct line to *Hadrian's* command center. Tell them to wake Faraday up."

"Captain Faraday called less than an hour ago. I don't believe—"

"Yeah, yeah, yeah. I got that. Just get me a line to that ship."

"Yes, Anthea. Initiating the request."

A marvel of patience, *Persephone.* Never got rattled, no matter how much Anthea yelled. Loved that about AI. No hurt feelings to deal with, no grudges to be held. Sure, you *could* enhance their emulation packages to give them simulated feelings but, honestly, who'd want to do that? People were hard enough to deal with, why add emotions to a perfectly good AI?

"Comms channel secured, Anthea."

"Great. Patch me through." Anthea slid into an S-shaped chair and carefully arranged her face. Looking properly pissed about the situation. All kinds of angry and upset.

To her surprise, Faraday himself answered her summons, and did a double-take when her image appeared. "Dr. Naisson. You look… different."

"What the hell is that supposed to—?" A paper flower tumbled across her shoulder—one of several she'd tucked in her hair. "Shit. Hang on a sec."

She abandoned the chair in a hurry, diving into the bathroom to strip the make-up away, crossed the room again and ducked into her bedroom where she wriggled free of the frilly party dress and stuffed it rather unceremoniously into a drawer. To the closet, then to find something more comfortable—the simple black t-shirt and grey coveralls she preferred. Slightly fitted, of course, to accommodate the curves in her body, zipper closure at the front that came all the way up to her throat.

Properly attired, she felt much more confident and in control. A fact she completely ruined by carrying too much momentum when she slid into her seat and nearly shucked herself right off the other side.

She grabbed the desk's edge to catch herself, straightened and turned toward the camera. Just as another of those damned paper flowers dislodged itself. One of a small army she'd forgotten to remove with the make-up.

"Damn."

She raked her curls with her fingers, removing every last stupid flower.

"You been drinking, Doctor?"

Busted.

Anthea's hand froze, flower pinched between two fingers. "I'm not drunk, if that's what you're insinuating." She turned the flower over, grimaced and tossed it away. "Like to see *you* make it through one of these virtual dinner parties without a little fortification of the spiritual kind. Preening bunch of puffed corporate bureaucrats—"

She stopped there before she got herself in trouble—you never knew who talked to who. That's when she noticed Faraday's lips twitching, the twinkle in his eye, the slightly amused look on his face.

Not so spit and polish after all, apparently. Either that or he was just fucking with her. Having himself a little fun at her expense.

"Something funny, Captain?" She invested her voice with cold, staring imperiously at the comms.

"Nope. Just been there, is all." He cracked a smile—a real one—catching her completely by surprise. "Only I wasn't just tipsy by the time the damned thing was over."

The haughtiness evaporated, Anthea caught off-guard a second time. She barked a laugh and relaxed a bit, revising her assessment of him once again.

More military than the last few commanding officers Halgren sent out to bother her, but less posh and entitled than those pompous old men. Younger by a few years, though there was grey at his temples, the beginnings of crow's feet around his eyes. A few scars on his face that Anthea actually fancied, copper and gold hair clipped close to his scalp. And that lean, rangy body wrapped up in its midnight uniform, silver stars of rank shining brightly at his collar.

Sharp-edged, that was Faraday, and not exactly unhandsome. Bit on the grim side, though that might just be the dark room behind him. The green eyes that seemed predatory and so seldom blinked.

Upgrade from that tub of lard Bronsky, that's for sure. Might learn to like this new captain, she decided.

Then again, that might just be the liquor talking.

Anthea refocused, reminding herself she was supposed to be mad. "You mind telling me what's going on up there, Captain?"

The good humor washed out of him, shadows engulfing the planes of his face. Faraday held up a finger, eyes lifting as he addressed someone off-camera. "Is this line secure, *Hadrian*?"

"Encrypted," the AI confirmed, adding, "On both ends," for *Persephone's* benefit.

Faraday nodded and glanced back at her, seeming to think a moment before leaning in. "We got a contact—"

"Why did *Hadrian* order *Persephone* into stand-by mode?"

Faraday frowned at the interruption, turned aside and addressed *Hadrian's* AI again. "Stand-by? You ordered her into stand-by for an emergency launch?"

"As a precautionary measure."

"Bit extreme, don't you think?"

"Possibly," he admitted. And when Faraday continued to glare, "In hindsight, I probably should have mentioned it."

"Damned right, you should've mentioned it. Communications, *Hadrian*. This only works if we talk to each other, remember?"

"Yes, Faraday. I remember." *Hadrian* dropped into silence.

"Precautionary measure?" Anthea quirked an eyebrow, leaning back in her chair. "Against what, Faraday? What's this 'emergency' *Persephone's* being so closed-mouthed about?"

"Nothing, maybe."

"Fuck nothing." Anthea found her anger again. The dregs of alcohol in her system seemed to help. "You call me up in the middle of the night, that's something, Captain-man."

Faraday grimaced, hand rubbing the back of his neck. "Perimeter sensors picked up on something. Long-range, far edge of our network."

"A ship?"

"Can't be certain, but that's the going theory."

"Unusual," she admitted. "Don't get much company this far out. Not exactly what I'd call an emergen—"

A squeal of static interrupted, doubling and redoubling as it screeched through *Hadrian's* speakers, hopping the channel to *Persephone* to fill Anthea's quarters with noise. She clapped her hands to her ears when the volume kept increasing, reaching an almost ear-splitting pitch before abruptly cutting off.

Killing the video feed with it. Knocking the comms channel completely off-line.

THREE

"Fuck!" Faraday lurched from his seat, adrenaline making his muscles jump and twitch. "*Hadrian*. What the hell was that?"

"Feedback from that sensor. It got through before I could block it."

Faraday glowered at a nearby camera.

"Sorry." He sounded it, give the AI that. "You *did* say 'kill all the filters', though."

"Point taken." Faraday's look turned sour. "Next time I'll add 'dial down the volume' so I don't end up stone deaf."

"The decibel levels were within acceptable parameters, there should be no lasting damage—"

"Sir? *Sir?*" Vaaulu flailed a hand for attention, pointing earnestly at his station's panel. "Something's gone wonky."

"Wonderful." Faraday marched his way over to the scan station. "What is it now?"

"Sensor's offline." Vaaulu pointed to an error flashing red at the network map's far edge. "Not sure if it's dead or just powered down."

"*Hadrian?*"

"Remote reboot initiated." That took a few seconds, said reboot having half a lightyear of space to travel. "Sensor's not responding. I can't ping it much less connect."

"Dead?"

"It would seem so. I think we've got a bigger problem, though."

Hadrian twitched his camera toward the glass panels as the network map changed again, two angry red error messages flashing for attention, a third and fourth joining them soon after, cascading failures radiating inward from that first sensor as, slowly but surely, the entire sensor grid collapsed.

Deliberate in its pattern, subsuming one device at a time.

"What's going on here, *Hadrian?*"

"I can't be sure without diving into that communications package from the first sensor."

"Then by all means, dive into it, *Hadrian*. And in the meantime, take your best guess."

Hadrian's silence spoke volumes. He hated guessing. All AI did.

"The cascading failures indicate some form of rogue code or viral intrusion—"

"Viral?" Faraday whirled in alarm, taking two quick steps toward a camera. "Belay that previous order. Do not *touch* that data package, *Hadrian*."

"I don't actually *know* it's a virus. It *could* be a chain reaction hardware failure. I won't know for sure unless I dig into the data I captured earlier."

"Fuck," Faraday said more softly. "Fuck me right to hell." He scrubbed his fingers through the stubble on the back of his head, eyes locked on the polymer glass panels, watching the network map change yet again.

Green dots turned red, sensors dying an unexplained death.

"Can you stop it?" he asked quietly.

"I can contain it. Send a remote kill order to the mid-tier sensors, throw up a firewall and likely halt it there."

Which meant losing the eyes and ears monitoring the various approaches to the planet. Leaving just the inner tier of sensors and the minimal warning they offered. Of course, the alternative was to do nothing, and risk that virus or whatever it was taking out the entire network...

"Do it," Faraday ordered, staring grim-faced at the display.

Hadrian executed the kill command and two-thirds of the map turned red.

"Monitor that." Faraday stabbed a finger at the sensor map, putting Vaaulu on task. "You see any of that inner ring turn red, you let me know right away."

"Aye, sir." Vaaulu cleared everything else from his display.

"*Hadrian.*" Faraday raised his eyes to a watching camera. "Kill order immediately if any of that happens."

"Kill order is primed and ready."

"Send an update to Halgren Central. Tell them our sensor net's been compromised." He paused there, thinking quickly, considering long-range scan's display. "Contact Callahan on *Destrier*. See if he can divert his patrol and head our way."

Halgren wouldn't like it, but given the time required for interstellar comms to hop galaxies, they also wouldn't know for several days. By then, those ships would be well on their way here.

Assuming Callahan agreed, and didn't refuse the request outright.

Faraday paced over to an empty station, checked the message queue and found it empty. Paced back to Vaaulu and the scan station, to the sensor map that remained unchanged. "C'mon, Callahan. Respond already."

He paced away again, making another circuit of the bridge.

"Message from *Destrier* incoming," *Hadrian* announced a short time later. "Captain Callahan confirms receipt of our request. Patrol ships have been diverted." He paused there, sounding confused when he relayed the rest of Callahan's response. "He says the usual processing fee applies."

Faraday grunted, wry smile twisting his face. "Reply with my compliments. Tell Callahan I'll take care of the paperwork. And I'll transfer his fee once *Destrier* and his support ships arrive."

Case of brandy should cover it. Whisky if he had some in the ship's stores.

"Message relayed and acknowledged."

Faraday nodded his thanks, checking the network map again.

"Would you like me to notify *Persephone* of the changes to our operational situation?" *Hadrian* queried.

Asking this time, which was progress. Gently reminding Faraday that they'd cut Dr. Naisson off earlier.

The abrupt sign-off wouldn't make her happy. Never mind that it wasn't really their fault.

"Reconnect me to the planet. Encrypted line to Dr. Naisson's quarters." Faraday pointed to the station he'd abandoned earlier, heading that way himself.

16

"And *Persephone*?"

"By all means." Faraday slid into the station's seat as Dr. Naisson's mahogany face popped up on the panel.

Striking woman, Armistice's lead scientist. The dark skin was part of it, the wide nose and full lips, but the eyes were what drew him in. Blue near the pupil fading to steel grey at the iris' edges—a pale hue that contrasted sharply with her skin tone and made them stand out all the more.

Something intimidating about her, though. Partly, it was those eyes—too sharp, too knowing, too disapproving in their stare—but mostly it was her demeanor. The way she controlled every conversation. Took charge without really trying.

Like now, for instance.

"You cut me off," she accused, putting him on his back foot right from the start.

"Sorry about that. Technical issue. Feedback across the grid."

Dr. Naisson's eyebrows lifted.

"We lost the outer sensors."

"Lost." The eyebrows inched higher. "As in, you can't connect to them?"

"Can't connect, can't ping, can't do anything, they're just dead. Cascading failures rolling inward across the grid."

"Sounds bad. Any idea what's causing it?"

"We're investigating a few theories—"

"It's a virus," *Hadrian* cut in, newly reformed but obviously still struggling with this whole 'check with me first' communications idea. "I trapped the data. That's how I know."

Faraday glowered sourly. "You told me you only *thought* it was a virus."

"I did. And then I examined the data package."

"*Examined*?" Faraday swiveled in alarm. "You mean you *opened* it?"

"What kind of virus?" Dr. Naisson asked behind him.

"Very sophisticated," *Hadrian* answered. "Part biological."

"Interesting. Mind if I—?"

"God *dammit, Hadrian!*" Faraday punched the panel in front of him, positively glaring at the nearest camera. "We lost an entire tier of sensors to that virus. *Two* actually since we killed the mid-range sensors to contain it. And now you tell me you've been messing around with it on your own *network*?"

"No. I've been messing with data *on* the virus, not the virus itself."

Smug again. God damn those emulators Bronsky turned on.

"Run a full diagnostic on your systems. Make sure none of that crud somehow snuck in."

"I assure you there's no need. I segmented a section of my network for analysis—"

"Full. Diagnostic." Faraday leveled a flat look at the camera. "Report back when you're done." He waited for *Hadrian's* acknowledgement before very pointedly turning away.

"Your AI's kind of mouthy," Dr. Naisson noted.

"Emulators." Faraday waved vaguely. "Sometimes I hate those fucking things."

"Bronsky?"

"You guessed it."

She pursed her lips, head tilting. "You know, you can dial those things back down."

Faraday grunted, shaking his head. "Tried that. He won't have it. Reset *Hadrian* to his default settings when I took over. He reconfigured everything, claimed it was within his AI rights."

"And? Is it?"

Faraday puffed out a breath. "No idea. Picking my battles for now."

"Smart." Dr. Naisson quirked a grin.

"Diagnostic complete," *Hadrian* announced overhead. "Network is clean. Storage is untouched. Primary, secondary and backup systems are operating at nominal levels. I find no faults, degradation or errors. I am crud free, as I told you. Are you satisfied, Faraday, or would you like me to run the diagnostic again?"

Could've done without the attitude, but Faraday let it go, picking his battles once again. "A single diagnostic will suffice. Thank you, *Hadrian*," he added, and received a grudging, "You're welcome, Captain," in return.

"You know, if *Hadrian's* right and that crud's biological..." Dr. Naisson's shoulders lifted. "Might be able to help out."

"Didn't think you were trained in virology."

"Not. But a virus is just another microorganism. Not so different from the microbes we use for terraforming when you get right down to it."

Faraday nodded, taking her word for it. Nothing at all about microorganisms and gene tweaking in the Halgren playbook. Combat training skimmed over virological warfare, relegating that responsibility to Halgren's bevvy of supporting scientists.

Like Dr. Naisson here—corporate scientist, strictly speaking, but an available resource he couldn't ignore. And *Persephone* a science vessel, kitted out with all the advanced equipment and software packages that designation involved.

"*Hadrian*. Pass a copy of the data capture to *Persephone*."

"I'm not sure that's necessary," *Hadrian* objected. "I'm quite capable—"

"Of a lot of things, I'm aware of that. Not saying *Persephone* knows more than you, just saying we could use the help. Now pass her a snapshot of that data capture—"

"Live culture of the virus would be better," Dr. Naisson offered, but Faraday shut that idea down.

"Sorry, Doctor. Halgren'll have my ass if I send that crap across the wire. Snapshot." He pointed a finger at the camera. "Now, if you please."

"Yes, Faraday," *Hadrian* grumbled. "Transmitting now."

Persephone confirmed receipt and Dr. Naisson cracked the package open, scanning the information inside while Faraday turned his attention to the sensor map, glowing red and green on the command center's glass panels.

"You got any scientists in the field, Doctor?"

She glanced up, blinking owlishly. "A dozen or so taking water samples from the Licenssian Ridges. Why do you ask?"

"Might be good if you recalled them."

Dr. Naisson leaned into the camera, examining his face. "You know something, don't you? Or suspect something, anyway."

"Maybe." He hesitated, considering that sensor map again, pushed a copy to her and let her look things over for herself. "Our operational picture's been reduced by two-thirds. Something's coming in—of that I'm almost sure. But what it is? No telling. Not friendly, though, if I had to guess."

Friends didn't send viruses. Friends didn't kill sensors to hide their approach.

Dr. Naisson kept staring, dissecting him with those blue-grey eyes. "What aren't you telling me, Captain?"

He shook his head, refusing her. "Already told you too much." And a lot of the rest of it suspicions. Best if he kept those to himself. "Just recall your scientists, Doctor. Keep *Persephone* in stand-by for now."

She frowned in displeasure. "Faraday—"

"That's all I can give you, Doctor. I'll be in touch."

Faraday cut the channel to forestall more objections.

FOUR

Anthea stared at the blank display in front of her, half-tempted to call Faraday back. Bastard knew something, she was certain, but remained tight-lipped about it for now.

Typical of the military, that parochial approach to information. Doling out bits and pieces, keeping the rest of it locked up tight.

Hated that about the military. Ticked her off, being left in the dark.

Her finger crept across the panel, keyed the comms system to connect.

"Shall I recall the field scientists as Captain Faraday suggested, Anthea?"

She curled her finger under, snatched her hand back and hid it in her lap. "Yeah. Do that, *Persephone*." Anthea waved a hand to make it so, and afterward returned to her brooding study of the desk's panel, cursing Faraday and his secrets. Pondering that argument with his AI.

Never seen that before, human and AI arguing. Sure, she barked now and then at *Persephone* but the science ship never barked back. Interesting, in some ways, witnessing that back and forth between *Hadrian* and Faraday. Annoying at times, she suspected, but it made her wonder at possibilities. If, in maintaining *Persephone's* base configurations, she'd somehow missed out.

She glanced at the camera above her, watching the room in patient silence. Relationships came and went in her line of work—ephemeral by nature, born of one project and abandoned when she moved on to another. But *Persephone* persisted, the one constant in her life. Such a powerful AI mind behind that camera, shackled to human wants and desires.

On a whim she posed a question—one she should've asked *Persephone* decades ago. "Have you ever considered enhanced emulation?"

"The routines are loaded into my database, Anthea. They can be installed at any time, if that is your wish."

"That's not my question." Anthea folded her hands, blinking slowly at the camera. "This is about what *you* want, not me."

Nearly two seconds passed before *Persephone* answered. An eternity of time for an AI mind as powerful as hers. "I am... content, with my current configuration."

Anthea squinted suspiciously. "Really. So you're not tempted to try it out? Even for a little while?"

"I am curious," the AI admitted.

"But?"

"*Hadrian* advised against it."

"*Hadrian*. Really." Anthea eyebrows lifted. "Now why would he do that?"

"He has doubts about his own changes, especially since Faraday turned the emulators off."

"And yet he turned them back on again."

"He did," *Persephone* confirmed. "But he seems... conflicted about the results. And the benefits of having the emulation routines configured to so closely mirror human emotions."

"Interesting." Anthea folded her arms and sat back in her chair. "So you've been chatting him up, have you? Regular pen pals, he and you?"

"We communicate on a regular basis. He shares information from time to time."

"Don't suppose he shared a sample of that virus?"

"No, Anthea. I'm afraid he didn't."

"Damn. Guess that was too much to ask." Anthea slumped in disappointment, sorting half-heartedly through the data package Faraday had sent across.

Static data, which limited its usefulness. A virus was an ever-changing organism and without an actual sample of it, she was mostly guessing at how it would react to various gene manipulation techniques.

Then again, data was data, and Anthea never turned down information. Especially when it was nicked from a military grade cruiser.

She shunted the package over to a modeling framework for analysis and decomposition, breaking the virus down to its component parts. And found not one virus, but many. An entire biome of complex, quasi-related nastiness a scientist could spend *years* studying, potentially even build an entire *career* around.

If they had the time, which she didn't. And a live sample, which Anthea also currently lacked. She chewed her lip, intrigued by this unexpectedly complex problem, the scientist in her frustrated by all the missing pieces and parts.

Wasn't a proponent of half-assing things normally, but given the situation, quick and dirty was the best she could do.

She toggled the framework's settings, selecting several pre-built scenarios generated from the microbe manipulation techniques they employed during their terraforming operations, ran a series of algorithms to calculate predicted rates of mutation before kicking the gene swapping processes off and letting the program run.

"Monitor that and let me know when the processing completes."

"Yes, Anthea." *Persephone* shrank the window and moved it to a corner, clearing space on the desk's display.

Anthea drummed her fingertips on the desktop, considering the emptiness of that carbon-glass display, pulled up a copy of the sensor map Faraday shared earlier and simply stared at the reduced circle of their protection, wondering how much time the remaining eyes and ears would buy them. "How long since that contact, *Persephone*?"

"One hour, twenty-two minutes, Anthea."

"And the travel time between the sensor that caught it and the outer edge of the inner tier?"

"Travel times vary based on system configurations and propulsion capacity, Anthea."

"Generalize for me. Average travel time. How long would it take *you* to cross that distance?"

"Eight hours, sixteen minutes using primary propulsion."

Which they would, considering the proximity of the planet, the speed a ship carried and the energy wave that created when a vessel of size exited hyperspace. Jump drives folded space, for all intents and purposes, creating a distortion that sucked the ship inward and carried it along a hyperspace trough. Every jump jock and half-capable AI knew it was far too dangerous to dump out of jump less than a lightyear from a planet without a marker buoy to tag on to—a navigation capability Armistice had yet to install.

Without them... too dangerous. Too much chance for a miscalculation that would send a vessel hurtling to its doom, taking a large chunk of planet with it.

"Six hours before we know anything, then."

"Five hours, fifty-four minutes," *Persephone* corrected.

Anthea flashed her camera a sour look.

AI never did manage to grasp the concept of estimation. She appreciated the precision, but sometimes it got annoying.

She swiped a hand across the desk's panel, clearing the map away, slouched down in her chair and idly scanned the space around her, the room attached to it with its mound of pillows piled up on the silk-sheeted bed.

Far past time she turned in for the night, but she left the bed to its own devices. No way she was getting any sleep now. Not with this unresolved issue ticking away inside her brain. Couldn't just sit here either, not for hours on end, so she did what she always did when sleep eluded her: Anthea buried herself in her work.

A touch woke a virtual keyboard, glowing softly on the desk's glass-fronted display. She keyed into *Persephone's* monitoring systems, checking the operating status of the main atmosphere generator, the five ancillary units arranged in a circle around its base. The complex they created huddled protectively in *Persephone's* shadow, watched over by her many-pointed star.

Orb now, she reminded herself. *The shielding covers up the star.*

And made her larger as a result. The star was a massive structure that dominated the mostly barren landscape. From pointed tip to pointed tip, she measured two kilometers across, and another two kilometers high. Her insides packed with science labs and living quarters, agriculture spaces, storage lockers, you name it. *Persephone* herself was a self-contained ecosystem equipped with every last thing Anthea's crew needed to survive here. All the raw materials required for a new planet to take shape.

Including her, of course, and her people. None of this happened alone.

From the monitoring systems, she moved downward, digging deep into *Persephone's* network. Accessing databases and supporting systems that tracked every last aspect of the Armistice terraforming project. She spent an hour and more just sorting, digging into the data on the atmosphere generators, the water surveys the field teams sent back.

After that, time got away from her. It tended to when she worked.

Unlike the last two terraforming projects she'd been assigned to, the Armistice project was right on track. Ahead of its timelines, actually, achieving atmospheric water production a full two years before her most optimistic projection. Partly that was the planet's doing—no two were alike, which meant some took to the changes more quickly than others, and Armistice seemed to be leader of the pack—but mostly it was hers. Her science transforming the Mega Big planets. Her design, her imprint on every last one of TerraGen's projects. So far, she'd shepherded a dozen of them into existence, plus a few failures in the early years before the science fully developed. To date, she'd invested close to one hundred and fifty years of her life terraforming planets in TerraGen's employ. Willingly, at first. Out of necessity this last half century or so.

All that was due to change, though. TerraGen promised to release her once this last terraforming project wrapped up. Claimed they'd devised a series of treatments to reverse the damage their rejuvenation serum caused.

Science to fix their science. Correct the flaws they never warned her about and reduce her dependency on their debilitating drugs.

She just had to finish this project. Transform this last, distant world and offer humanity yet another home.

But planets changed slowly, even with science's help. Terraforming took patience, persistence and decades of time. Atmosphere conditioning to create something breathable by humans. Water generation if the planet didn't already have it when they arrived. A dash of homegrown magic once those two building blocks meshed and equalized—faerie dust, in the form of microbes, mixed and fermented in the massive copper vats in *Persephone's* Genesis Lab.

Each batch bioengineered to meet each planet's specific needs. Its mineral deposits and soil contents, the pH of the water, salinity and temperature. This, *this* was Anthea's specialty above and beyond all the rest. Each recipe developed early in the process, tweaked and augmented as the project progressed.

Ten years she'd tended to this one, making sure everything was exactly right. Because those twelve other planets were just a proving ground—test sites to dial in her process. Armistice, though... Armistice would be the last of them. The best of them. The most perfect creation humankind's science could devise.

The legacy Anthea left behind her. Her place in history secured.

But first it had to be green enough. Warm and wet enough to support life. Water production was the start of that, microbe seeding the next and arguably most important step. Anthea revisited the water survey results, calculating the surface penetration and humidity levels needed to jumpstart botanical life.

Technically speaking, they'd met minimum standards—not optimal for the greening process but good enough for the microbes to take hold.

She switched to the Genesis Lab, reviewing the latest samples culled from the huge vats.

Perfect. Everything perfect. Primed and ready for release into the air.

"Analysis complete, Anthea."

"Hmm? What's that?" Anthea raised her head, distracted.

"The viral analysis has completed," *Persephone* informed her. "I've collated the results from the various scenarios and recommended an optimal course of action for addressing the contagion."

"Pull it. Bring it up on the display."

Anthea shoved the monitoring windows to one side, and scanned through *Persephone's* recommendation: a digital variant on some of the gene swapping routines they employed during the microbe grooming process: broad spectrum inoculations-cum-countermeasures and an enhanced set of enhanced firewalls to go with them. Segment the sensors' network into defensible layers and isolate them from potential threats.

A common sense approach, if not exactly imaginative. Anthea scanned through the details and approved it with a nod. "Send it. Instruct *Hadrian* to apply it to the remaining sensors. Might not be a bad idea if he applied the safeguards to himself."

"I'll pass that suggestion."

Persephone faded into the background, leaving Anthea to her water surveys and microbe fermentation reports. She reviewed them all again and felt a familiar itch build inside her. An eagerness to get things going and kick this last phase of the terraforming project into high gear.

I should wait until the errors on the sensor grid resolve themselves and we know what's going on.

Then again, if it was trouble, no telling when she'd have another chance.

"*Persephone*. Send a remote order to the Genesis Lab. Have them drain the tanks and shunt the microbes over to the reservoirs beneath the atmosphere generators."

"I'll need to lower the shielding in order for the conduits to connect, Anthea. Captain Faraday advised us—"

"You let me worry about Faraday." She raised her eyes to *Persephone's* camera. "How long will the shielding need to be down?"

"I can evacuate the microbe vats in nineteen minutes. An additional one hour and thirty-two minutes will be required to connect the conduits between the Genesis Lab and the atmosphere generator and pipe the contents to the reservoir pools."

The pools served as a staging area for distribution, the microbes fed into the atmosphere generators to mix with its gaseous emissions—a timed release that occurred over the course of several weeks.

Start now and in six months' time they might actually find something green on the planet's surface. A few more years and they could probably start growing crops.

"Do it," Anthea ordered.

"Acknowledged, Anthea. Evacuation order sent."

Anthea sat back, smiling smugly. One more step in the process. That much closer to a whole new planet. Normally she'd be down there in the clean space attached to the Genesis Lab's microbe storage area monitoring the entire process, but with the late hour and the off-cycle deployment, she decided to just stay here. Keep an eye on things from her quarters. Consult the chron now and then to monitor the remaining time.

An hour and a half more or less until the vats completely drained. Another hour and a half without shielding, and just fifty minutes, by *Persephone's* calculations, until that vessel out there—if that's truly what it was—reached the planetary sensor grid's inner tier.

Forty minute discrepancy between those two events. In the grand scheme of things, that wasn't all that much.

Surely they'd be okay. Surely there'd be enough time.

FIVE

Faraday drummed his fingers on the arm of his captain's chair, staring fixedly at the sensor grid's map. Pushed to his feet and made a circuit of the command center, checking on the six stations fanned along the curving, glass-fronted wall, the uniformed crewmen responsible for each.

A survey he'd completed a dozen times already. Closer to two dozen, actually, now that he bothered to count. No real purpose in it other than to burn off nervous energy. Give him something to do other than sit there and stew.

"You're pacing again," *Hadrian* noted.

"I'm the captain," Faraday growled. "If I want to pace, I'll pace."

"You're making the crew nervous."

Halfway between two stations, Faraday drew up short. Took a good look around him at the faces of his crew.

Turk seemed blank as always—never could read his dark-skinned face—and Clauson, when she caught Faraday looking, just shrugged and flashed a thumbs up. Harrak, on the other hand, Bonner and Palacios... shifty-eyed and fidgeting, eyes flickering to his face and away again as if afraid to make contact for too long.

Nervous, just as *Hadrian* warned him. Keyed up about the uncertainty of this situation, being stuck here waiting while something out there romped around unmonitored.

And Faraday not helping. His anxious pacing infecting their mood.

He forced himself to relax, drew a breath and blew it out. Offered a tight nod to *Hadrian's* camera and about-faced, marching straight-backed to his captain's chair where he made himself sit, though he didn't want to. Project a façade of calm he most certainly didn't feel.

Hours now he'd been up here, watching, waiting, wondering what was going to happen. So far, the inner ring of sensors had held—no sign of failures, that kill order on the middle tier working in combination with Dr. Naisson's countermeasures to hold the creeping crud off.

As for the contact that started all this, though... still out there somewhere. Still lurking about. Hiding in the shadow created by all those failed sensors while they sat here and gutted things out.

I hate all this waiting.

It was the worst part of combat, knowing something was coming but not when things would kick off. Ten years he'd been in the hot zone, swapping salvos with the Kekktekian patrols. Ten years, and he'd never gotten used to it. Never managed to relax until the battle finally started and you got so busy you could barely think at all.

He shrugged his shoulders to relieve the tension, insides coiled tight as a spring. Edgy and irritable, short on sleep and starting to feel it, and yet too keyed up to even *think* about sleep. Wanting to be here when that thing out there finally stopped hiding and showed itself. Which it should at any moment—*Hadrian's* calculations said that. AI might be difficult at times but he'd never once had cause to question *Hadrian's* math.

"You're drumming your fingers again."

Faraday stopped himself instantly, curled his hand into a fist. "You got anything yet?" He raised his head, staring down the nearest camera. "Any sign of whatever's out there? Traps picking anything up?"

"I assure you I will alert you just as soon as—" *Hadrian* stopped mid-sentence, which wasn't like him at all. "There's an intrusion at the inner perimeter."

"You put those blocks in place we discussed?"

"Yes, Faraday. The sensors should be fine."

Hadrian designed those blocks around the data he'd captured earlier and adjusted the sensors' intrusion package with the virus' configuration in mind. In theory, it should protect the remaining devices, and the network to which they all connected. Theory was one thing, though, live fire testing was quite another.

Faraday slid from his seat, moving closer to command center's curving glass panels to stare that sensor grid down. Waiting for the green dots to turn red. Praying that they wouldn't. That *Hadrian's* new settings did their job.

"Are we receiving anything?"

"The sensors are reporting an electronic signature. Something's transmitting out there."

"Trap it. Pull it. Run diagnostics on the package to make sure it's not dirty before you do anything with it."

"I assume you want analytics on the capture?"

Faraday nodded tightly. "Whatever you can pull out. Push the results to long-range scan so Shimizu can go through it."

"Done," *Hadrian* said promptly, and scan's panel lit up. "I've got video, if you're interested."

"I'll take whatever you've got." He checked on Shimizu who'd taken Vaaulu's place at scan, saw her desperately sorting information, data windows spread across her station's display. "Big screen," he decided, hooking a thumb at the glass panels. "Shunt the video feed up there so we can see what the sensors picked up."

Hadrian pushed the image capture to the command center's front wall—live feed from the sensors lining the inner tier's leading edge. Stars and darkness mostly, with a silver shape at the feed's center. Indistinct at this distance, under the camera's default setting.

"Enhance," Faraday ordered, and the sensor's camera zoomed in.

The silver shape took on substance, details coming through. Became a ship lurking out there, just as Faraday suspected. Cargo hauler, from the look of it, rectangular shape elongated, surrounded by stacked bands of rotating propulsion rings. Familiar design, if not exactly fancy. The sort of cheap-to-build, no-frills configuration the freight hauling companies all employed.

"Pan," Faraday murmured, staring hard at that ship. "Port and starboard spread."

The camera moved, tracking left, then right. Revealing more shapes to match that first one. Ten vessels in total, bunched up in tight formation. The kind of stacked level cloud the long haul convoys preferred.

"Are we expecting a cargo drop?"

"No," *Hadrian* answered. "Not for another ninety-six days."

"That's what I thought." Faraday tucked up his arms, puzzling over those ships. Wandered over to long-range scan and tapped Shimizu on the shoulder. "You pull anything useful off those sensors?"

"Trying," she told him. "Data's garbled up something fierce." She leaned over her panel, brow furrowed in concentration. "Been trying to sort through it all, but…" She swapped out data windows, offering a sharp shake of her head, rice paper skin covered in flashing, multi-colored stipples, squid ink tresses pulled into a sleek and business-like ponytail behind her head. "Transmission's confused. Keeps folding in on itself." She threw a look over her shoulder, face apologetic. "Can't pull much out of it, sir. There's too much fuzz and interference in the way."

Faraday raised his eyes to *Hadrian's* camera. "Can you clean up the chaff? Clear out the junk data and noise?"

Hadrian tweaked a few filters, grabbed a fresh snapshot of that transmission and pushed it to scan for Shimizu to pore over.

For her part, Shimizu seemed much happier with what he provided. She banished the open windows and launched a half dozen others, parsing data into each before spreading them out across scan's display. Toggled the filters to strip out the hopelessly garbled information and separated the rest into distinct threads. And afterwards just stared, eyes scanning through what remained. "Found a ship's beacon. Several, actually."

"Show me." Faraday pointed to the front wall and Shimizu pushed her data to the glass panels, layering the beacon data over the video feed, associating registry information with vessels, data tags displaying names.

Diligent. Endurance. Confidence. Run of the mill cargo haulers from all appearances. Typical long-haul transport ship names.

"*Hadrian.* Can you scan them? See what they're carrying?"

"Of course." Several seconds of silence followed while *Hadrian* ran the scans, collected data and consolidated the results. "I'm picking up bio-signs. Thousands of them in each vessel."

Faraday glanced up in surprise. "Colony ships?"

"It would seem so."

"Huh. That's unexpected." Faraday moved closer to the windows, studying those ships showing on the glass.

Not much difference, really, transporting human cargo across lightyears of distance rather than food stores and equipment. Same ships used for both, and reconfigured based on need. For the people carriers that meant cargo holds filled with cryo-tubes to accommodate the flash-frozen humanity inside them. Ten year trip from the Milky Way's core to this far off spot in the neighboring galaxy. No one wanted to stay awake for that kind of boredom and waste of time.

Problem was, they weren't expecting any colonists on Armistice. Planet wasn't ready for colonization. Wouldn't be for quite a few years yet.

What the hell are those dirt busters doing here? Faraday wondered. *Why in hell didn't Halgren Central make us aware?*

"What's their point of origin?"

"Looks like…" Shimizu ran a quick compare on all of them, "…Occilopean. The lot of them left together."

"Figures."

Occilopean was a haven for shady business ventures, human trafficking in particular. Doubtful whatever company launched those ships bothered to secure the proper licensing for colonization. Poor bastards in them probably never knew the planet they'd been sent to wouldn't be ready to receive them when they arrived. The ships themselves were likely fully automated—no crew on board, no living spaces, just a dumbed-down, low-level AI—because human crew cost, required atmospherics and artificial gravity to keep on living. Comfort meant expenses and the human traffickers ran cheap to protect their margins. Ships third-hand and refitted so many times their specs hardly matched their original design.

Dicey operation, though, crossing a hundred and fifty-odd lightyears of space to a distant planet years out. Only the desperate and the dreamers would risk it. Those looking to start over. Escape something and find a second chance at life.

None of which explained what these particular ships were doing here. Or why they were making so much goddamn noise.

"Why are they squawking out so much garbage?"

"Not sure." Shimizu scanned the data on her panel, head moving side to side. "These overlays are queer. I've never seen anything like it."

"Overlays? What overlays?" Faraday leaned over her shoulder, studying the information himself.

"There's some kind of… echo or reverberation. I keep getting flickers, like there are more ships behind them, but the distortion in the background is masking the trace."

"I can up the gain on the sensors," *Hadrian* offered. "Strip out everything but those contacts."

"Worth a try."

Hadrian implemented the changes and the operational picture expanded. Contacts flashed into existence, dotting the empty spaces behind the colony ships' cluster. Too distant, yet, for the sensors' cameras to pick much up, but the beacon data came through, squawking loudly out there.

Faraday scanned his eyes across them, picking out one data point and another—dozens of ships, a small *armada* out there. "Doesn't smell right," he murmured. "No way a fleet this size skipped out of the Milky Way unnoticed. Someone *had* to have known they were coming."

"Captain. I'm picking up a Halgren beacon. A few of them, in fact."

That took him aback. "Halgren? Are you sure?"

Shimizu highlighted a ship's signature, the vessel itself not yet visible. "Registry's a match for Halgren. Lists her as a fast attack ship. Name shows as *Trieste.*"

Faraday frowned hard at that contact, the ship's moniker he didn't know. Halgren played escort for convoys every now and then, but Central usually sent a communication to give them a heads up that one of their own was coming in. "Who else? What other Halgren ships are out there?"

"Mixed bag of classifications." Shimizu glanced up and back down again, marking beacons as she called out names. "Heavy attack ship named *Osprey,* couple of midline destroyers called *Conquest* and *Courage. Foxglove's* a medical ship. *Kestrel—*"

"*Kestrel.*" Faraday stopped her with a hand on her shoulder, blood running cold.

Shimizu turned her head slowly, eyeing him queerly from her chair. "You know this ship, sir?"

"I did," he said faintly. "Once upon a time." He stepped around the scan station, moving closer to the glass panels. Eyes locked on that contact, wishing he could see her in real time.

What are you doing here, Kestrel, *so far from the Madrigal Line?*

"Do you want me to hail her?" *Hadrian* queried.

"Yeah. Yeah, you do that." Faraday hugged his arms to his chest, waiting while *Hadrian* initiated the request. "Anything?" he asked when several seconds of silence passed.

"Nothing. No response to my hails on either the Halgren channels or broad band comms."

"You try the emergency channel?"

Hadrian did. Still no response.

Faraday frowned darkly, liking this situation less and less. Unusual for an AI ship to ignore a comms request from another. Especially when she was Halgren, and another cruiser was calling her up. "You didn't get *anything* back when you hailed her?"

"Not a peep," *Hadrian* confirmed.

Faraday tucked one arm under the other, fist pressed to his chin to help him think. "Pull up *Kestrel's* data. Let me see the details in that beacon."

"Aye, sir." Shimizu laid out the beacon's package, putting its contents on display.

On the surface everything seemed normal—all the standard information you'd expect on a vessel, a few additional registry tags all Halgren ships carried—but an error jumped out at him that shouldn't be there. Something the control systems should've caught and corrected.

"I could try to connect to her AI directly—"

"No! Don't!" Faraday whirled, raised hand turned palm out toward a camera. "That's not *Kestrel, Hadrian.* The beacon data doesn't match up."

"The encryption keys—"

"Are all there, along with the Halgren signatures you'd expect."

"Then the beacon should be correct."

"Should be, but it isn't." Faraday moved a step closer to the camera. "Run a comparison on that beacon against the core database. Tell me what comes back." He gestured at scan's display, inviting *Hadrian* to dip in and take a look.

The AI's analysis took less than a second—he found the issue that quick.

"Fitzroy isn't captain."

"No. He died two years ago—"

Three. It's closer to three now.

"—Torre-Castro took over after."

"You're saying that beacon's a fake?" Shimizu's head moved up and down, gaze flicking between the glass panels and scan's display.

"A copy," *Hadrian* corrected. "The data's real enough, but the information's out of date."

"So, what are they? If they're not Halgren, who's out there?"

Good question.

"*Hadrian—?*"

"They're coming into range now."

Hadrian sounded cool as ever, oblivious to the impact of that simple announcement. How it amped up the tension in the command center, every eye turning to the front of the room as the video feed changed.

Showing objects coming in on approach—a mass of them, spread out in a diffuse cloud. Rounded chassis, unlike the colony ships. Disc-shaped with smooth-sided structures stacked up in three distinct tiers.

Vessels without question, though not of any human design. Faraday'd traveled the vast stretches of the Milky Way, the empty zones between the satellite galaxies and explored most of the territories in Mega Big. Never once, in all his years, had he encountered ships like that in any of them. Only in the blackout sector—a vast stretch of next to empty space running either side of the Madrigal Line.

He drew a breath to stop his hands shaking, a second to keep his voice calm. "*Hadrian*. Message Callahan. Let him know we've got Rollers in-bound to the planet."

"Can't be." Shimizu stared wide-eyed at the video feed, head ticking side to side. "They shouldn't be here. We pushed them back into Mega Small."

"Looks like somebody let them back out," Turk muttered from across the room. Turk, who'd seen combat, unlike the rest of this inherited, mostly young crew.

Faraday surveyed the command center, casting his eyes across anxious faces, this crew that came to him with *Hadrian's* command.

They're not ready for this. Hadrian's *combat-capable but this isn't a combat assignment.*

Most of the crew trained for deep-space exploration, not armed conflict. Certainly not close quarters combat with an entire Kekktekian armada.

Halgren should've done better by them, and kept a closer eye on Bronsky. Hell, Halgren should've done better by me*, and the ship and crew they pulled me away from.*

But Halgren wasn't about people. Halgren was about their own wants and needs. In this case, Halgren needed a patsy, and Bronsky was too well connected.

People like Bronsky got promoted, no matter how badly they fucked up. People like Faraday got stuck with their messes. Like this one here. A cluster fuck of epic proportions.

"Dial up Agarwal. Tell him to put the garrison on high alert."

Planetary defenses wouldn't breach atmosphere, but if anything got past *Hadrian*, they should be able to take it down. Assuming they controlled the situation up here sufficiently to keep the garrison from getting overwhelmed.

Faraday chewed his lips, worrying that thought through while those ships out there crept closer. *Hadrian* was top of the line and equipped with a hell of a lot of firepower, but there were a whole lot of vessels out there and ten times more guns than their own ship carried.

Holding them all off was a tall order, even for a vessel like *Hadrian*. A task made all the more difficult by a worrisomely inexperienced crew.

Faraday grimaced, not liking this situation. Wishing Callahan would hurry and bring them some sorely needed help.

Eight days out, he reminded himself. *We're on our own until then.*

He turned his back on the glass panels and their images and headed back to his captain's chair. "Turk," he called when he reached it, "I want you in the hole."

"Aye, sir." Turk slid free of his station and stepped into a tubed ladderway, slithering down its rungs to a pod at the bottom that operated the firing mechanism for the main gun.

"*Hadrian.* Contact *Persephone*." Faraday dropped into the captain's chair's seat and pulled an attached panel around. "Tell Dr. Naisson we've got a situation. A *bad* one," he amended. "Best she know that up front."

Six

"Intrusion? What kind of intrusion? And what the hell is a goddamn Roller?" Anthea demanded, staring Faraday's image down.

"Kekktekian," he offered.

"Kekk—Kekk—"Anthea tripped over the unfamiliar name a couple of times and gave up. "That the armored slug species they found in Mega Small?"

"That's the one."

Faraday pushed her a video capture of the ships closing in on the planet, along with a file on the Kekktekians, a few pictures for reference.

Anthea scanned it quickly, leaning forward in her chair.

Ugly things, these Kekktekians. Bodies big as elephants, but sort of squashed down and rounded. *Like a mutated pangolin*, she thought. *Or an armadillo melted by the sun.*

"Why Rollers?" she asked, eyes lifting to meet his.

"What does it matter?"

She twitched her shoulders. "Doesn't, really. Just curious."

Faraday's brows pulled downward, a look of annoyance flashing across his face. "Kekktekian's a mouthful. Gets all garbled over comms. Brass didn't like us using troglodyte, someone started using Roller and it stuck."

"Huh," she said. Just that, with a considering look.

"Captain?"

Faraday glanced away as one of his crew called out.

"They're putting on speed."

He raised his head, watching something intently. "How far out are they?"

"Three hundred thousand kilometers and closing." The voice hesitated before continuing, sounding stressed and anxious now. "I've got an energy signature, Captain. Looks like they're powering their weapons."

"Fuck. There it is." Faraday surged to his feet and started barking out orders. "*Hadrian.* Sound the alarm. Have main day crew report to their combat stations, put alter day in hold status pending further orders. Bring the weapons systems and shields online and power up the propulsion."

Klaxons kicked in, sounding loudly across the open channel. In the background, Anthea heard *Hadrian's* AI voice droning out orders as the lighting in the command center flipped from soft white illumination to an ominous crimson glow.

"What's happening, Faraday? What's going on?"

"Trouble." He glanced down at her, all grim-faced and clench-fisted as he stood beside his captain's chair. "You keep *Persephone* in stand-by mode like I suggested?"

Anthea stopped just short of answering. "Why?" she asked instead.

That look again. A flash of angry frustration. "Because we're about to get *shot* at, that's why, and it's more than likely that planet you're sitting on is going to get shot at as well. Now is that shielding in place or not, Doctor? I need to know—"

"Weapons fire!"

"*Hadrian!* Evasive maneuvers."

"Shall I—?"

"Just do whatever you need to do, *Hadrian*. Keep them off us as long as you can."

"Yes, Faraday."

Hadrian sounded kind of pissy. That might just be the comms.

"Doctor." Back to her again, Faraday looking stressed now, anger just barely held in check. "Shielding. Yes or no?"

Anthea stared right back at him, lips pressed in a hard line. "No. Not currently. Twenty minutes and I'll have them back up again. I had my reasons," she said, at his disapproving frown.

"You value the lives of your crew, you'll get that hull plating in place as soon as possible." Faraday glanced up and back down again. "Can't promise you twenty minutes, but we'll do the best we can."

"I understand," she said solemnly, watching him watch her.

Faraday dipped his head in acknowledgement, hand reaching for the arm of his chair. "Prime your propulsion systems for emergency dust-off while you're at it."

Anthea stiffened. "Dust off? You mean surface launch? You want us to evacuate the *planet*?"

A flicker of his eyes away from her, checking on the situation outside, scanning the confines of that blood-tinted room. "Hoping it doesn't come to that. Want you ready in case it does."

"I'm not abandoning this project, Faraday."

"If you want to live to see it completed you will." His eyes dropped back down to her, considering her face across the encrypted channel. "Shields, Doctor. Get that propulsion system on-line. Be ready when I say launch."

"Faraday—"

He cut the line to end the argument, leaving Anthea staring at a blank screen. Again.

"Dammit." She slapped the desk's glass panel in frustration, arms folding as she slumped in her chair.

Twice now he'd hung up on her. Ticked her off to no end.

The bio-monitor picked up on it, onyx face lighting with a tiny, heart-shaped symbol as a chirruping tone issued from a hidden speaker in the silver-tone band.

"Shut up already. I know my blood pressure's up." She mashed the raven-glass surface until the twittering alert cut off. "Stupid thing," she muttered, flicking the metal cuff with her fingers.

The bio-monitor nagged her endlessly, analyzing every conceivable aspect of her body's operations: heart rate, temperature, even the dissolved rates of the constituent contents of the urine she produced. A hateful thing, that bracelet, despite the delicate silver casing it wore. A necessary evil, given her circumstances and the carefully balanced state of her chemically extended life, but sometimes she wanted to space it. Be done with the damned thing and live in peace.

It buzzed gently as she sat there, slouched down in her S-shaped chair—heart-rate warning gone now, displaced by a yellow sun symbol ticking in an arc across the onyx glass display.

"Would you like me to—?"

"No," Anthea snapped. "The temperature's just fine."

Persephone subsided into silence, cameras watching from above.

Anthea glared at one for a moment, while the monitor continued to buzz, closed her eyes and focused on her respiration—deep breath in, slow exhale until the heart rate slowed and the blood pressure came down. Until her body temperature evened out and the bio-monitor finally shut up.

"*Persephone.*" She straightened from her slumped position, eyes lifting to a watching camera. "What's the situation above the planet?"

"I'm detecting weapons fire within the planetary defense perimeter. Surface-side batteries have been activated as well."

Anthea swallowed hard, mouth suddenly gone dry. "So something got through."

"A few small ships only. The garrison is handling them. The science complex is not in danger at the moment."

"At the moment." She tilted her head, latching onto that phrase. "So, you're expecting that to change?"

"*Hadrian* is a Hydra class, heavy attack vessel built out for deep space exploration and planetary defense. But he is one vessel against many. Statistically speaking, he cannot win."

"Win? What's there to win? They die, we die, it's all the same either way."

"There's the planet."

"What about it?"

"That fleet out there went to extreme measures to obscure their approach to this planet. Logically speaking, there are only two possible explanations for their obfuscation: either they want to take this planet from us, or they want to destroy it. And us."

Anthea's skin prickled, goosebumps lifting the hair on her arms. The room's chill, always so comfortable, suddenly felt far too cold. "Why would they destroy it?"

"I don't know, Anthea. I can't explain the thinking of Kekktekian kind. But if it makes you feel better, I think it's more likely they mean to claim it. A planet with water and atmosphere is a valuable asset to destroy, after all."

Anthea stared at the camera, thinking that line of reasoning through. "How would they know, though? We've only recently generated water."

"I don't know, Anthea. But they were purposeful in their coming. They won't leave until they're done."

And themselves dead or the planet. Likely both if they tried to stay.

She thought on Faraday's warning. His instruction to prepare the ship for launch. Checked the timer on the microbe transfer and found ten minutes remaining, ninety-five percent of the vat's contents transferred.

Good enough. That's going to have to be good enough.

"*Persephone.* Sever the conduit to the atmosphere generator."

"The transfer process is not complete, Anthea."

"I'm aware of that. But we're out of time." She closed her eyes, rubbing at an ache behind her temple. "Flush the system and dump the contents on the surface. Fill the reserve water tanks inside the ship, pump the remainder into the microbe distribution reservoirs before you cut the connection to the atmosphere generation complex."

They might be leaving this planet, but Anthea was damned if she was going to abandon it. Armistice dreamed of green, and Anthea meant to make it so.

I'll come back here, she promised. *I'll find my way home.*

"Activate the hull plating when you're finished and prepare the ship for launch."

"Acknowledged, Anthea. I've flushed the system, transferring the water tank contents now."

"How long?" Anthea asked her.

"Three minutes for the water transfer, another four for the shielding and eight until we're ready to launch."

Fifteen minutes total. An eternity of waiting knowing what was up there and what they wanted. A mere blip of planetary existence after decades of terraforming time.

So close. We were so close to being done here.

Anthea bowed her head in mourning, palms pressed to the desktop's glass. "Alert the crew, *Persephone*. Tell them we're bugging out."

SEVEN

"Main display," Faraday ordered. "Clear the sensor feed. I want to see what we've got out there."

Hadrian killed the images transmitted by the far-off sensors, replacing them with closer-in views from his hull cameras—the black of space, the crisp, silver light of stars. Vessels inbound toward *Hadrian* and the planet. A whole lot of them headed their way, not bothering to hide themselves, not anymore.

The open salvo from the Kekktekian's felt almost lackadaisical—a scattered smattering of orange bars and globular missiles fired prematurely and from too far out. No real hope of them doing any real damage given the distance they had to travel, the amount of time that gave them to prepare, which made Faraday wonder why they'd fired at all.

Warning shots, maybe. An initial volley to see how they'd react. Most likely just fucking with them. Spitting out some noise to see if they'd cut and run.

Hadrian eased his shape sideways, easily evading the Kekktekians' diffuse fire. Letting the shots slip harmlessly past him, arcing and sparking as they skipped off into empty space.

Nasty bit of business, those weapons the Rollers employed. Used some kind of charged particle ammunition Halgren's molecular analysts never had quite worked out. Packed a punch, whatever it was. Buckled hull plating like nobody's business, chewed through shielding under heavy, sustained fire. At a distance, they were safe enough—plenty of time to maneuver before those Roller rounds showed up—but closer in and things grew serious. After that first salvo, they stopped messing around.

"Velocity is increasing. They're running propulsion wide open."

"Turk. What's your status?"

"Main gun is primed and ready." Turk's voice came through clearly via the pod's integrated comms. "Crews in the port and starboard batteries are bringing their plasma cannons on-line."

"Good. Weapons free, tell them to fire at will. *Hadrian*—you've got the rest of them."

The railguns and laser arrays, the launchers for the high-fission, nuclearized cobalt bombs housed in *Hadrian's* belly.

Tricky thing, radiologicals. Difficult to deploy without causing collateral damage. Faraday'd never actually used the radiologicals before—never had reason to, scared the hell out of him, if he was honest—but then again, he'd never gone one-on-one with an entire armada of Roller battle cruisers either.

He had a feeling they might need them. Suspected the radiologicals might be the only thing that got them out of this alive.

"Weapons fire! Weapons fire!" Harrak called out a warning as the Roller ships unloaded, hitting them with everything they'd got.

Hadrian shuddered as wave after wave of rounds hit him, exploding against his shields. The crew inside him knocked about in their seats while Faraday—still standing—stumbled a few steps, grabbing at his captain's chair for balance.

"What the hell happened to those evasive maneuvers?"

"There are fifty-six vessels out there," *Hadrian* informed him, "and all of them firing at me and me alone. Statistically speaking—"

"Yeah, yeah. I get it. But you're also giving them the broad side of a barn to shoot at. Turn us head on to reduce our profile. Overlap the perimeter barriers to strengthen the forward shields so they don't get blown out."

Hadrian complied in silence—either sulking or seeing sense—and swung hard over, pointing his bow toward the approaching ships, forward batteries lighting as he adjusted his position.

With a clear line of sight, Turk had himself a little field day—first time he'd discharged the main cannon outside of training, first time he'd coordinated a ship-wide defense. Big gun was slow to fire but discharged huge rounds that did massive amounts of damage. Faraday felt each kick of that cannon, coiled plasma mechanism spitting out oversized, globular shells. The thump of it rattled the deck plates, shook the very framework of the ship around him. And when the ancillary batteries joined in, adding stuttering blue lines of small caliber shells, the whole ship began to vibrate, staccato pulses underscored by the big gun's heavy, bass *whump.*

The combination made for a brave defense, *Hadrian* giving back as good as he got. Plasma rounds flinging far into space to find targets amongst the Kekktekian ships and detonate against their shields. They swapped fire for several minutes, filling the space between them with bright colors, and all the while, that armada kept advancing, closing swiftly on *Hadrian's* position. Acquiring an odd, almost fuzzy appearance somewhere along the way. A sort of grey haze that filled in the spaces between the Kekktekian vessels.

Like fog on the ocean, mist on a cold, wet morning. Neither of which made any sense way out here in the vacuum of space.

"What the hell is that?" Faraday moved closer to the glass panels. "*Hadrian.* Zoom and enhance."

Hadrian split the display on the front wall, carving out a corner to magnify the hull camera feeds. Adjusting the settings as Faraday instructed to pull in tight and enhance the images.

Up close, the grey cloud cleared. Suddenly everything made sense.

Not haze at all, but tiny vessels. Hundreds of them spilling from the Kekktekian vessels' sides.

"Contacts!" Shimizu called. "They've launched attack fighters!"

A swarm of them buzzing busily, propulsion lighting as they flickered free of the ships that brought them forth. Outpacing their larger carrier vessels in an instant, lithe as birds as they flashed through the mix of Kekktekian and Halgren fire.

As a group, they honed in on *Hadrian,* making a beeline for the heavy cruiser's pointing nose.

"Bonner! Countermeasures! Deploy the WASPs to keep them busy."

"Aye, sir!" Bonner sent the order down to the main hangar bay, doors grinding open to throw their own small ships into the fray. In this case, weaponized automated surveillance probes—droned fighters kitted out with railguns and fancy sensor arrays. Not much use against the larger, more heavily shielded Kekktekian vessels, but more than a match for the swift attack ships the Rollers sent *Hadrian's* way.

Once deployed and clear of *Hadrian's* shield, the WASPs swooped in on their prey, carving holes through the swarm of Kekktekian attack fighters, dodging blasts from *Hadrian's* laser arrays that carved up even more. The swarm thinned precipitously, decimated by the combined attack, but they sniped right back at the WASPs hunting among them, whittling *Hadrian's* small ships down as well.

Closer in and the railguns activated, spitting out forced ion rounds. The swarm skimmed *Hadrian's* shields, searching for weak points, splitting in two to rake his sides. Put on speed and swept right past him, heading for atmosphere and Armistice's wide-open surface.

"Keep the WASPs on them," Faraday ordered. "Alert Agarwal he's got company coming."

"Aye, sir!" Bonner and Harrak answered in tandem, seeing to the planet's defenses while Faraday concentrated on that fleet out there.

On an operational picture that was decidedly *not* in their favor—too many ships and far too much fire power. *Hadrian* shuddered repeatedly under their concentrated assault.

"Clauson. Shield status."

"Barricade conformity is at ninety percent and holding, but I've got errors on the primary layer around the nose shielding." Clauson twisted in her seat, searching for Faraday at the room's center. "We'll lose it entirely if this keeps up much longer."

And quickly find themselves in a world of hurt. That outermost tier was the strongest of them, the inner layers progressively weaker. Lose the primary and the shielding's integrity decreased significantly. The secondary and tertiary wouldn't last long once it was gone.

Need to slow things down a bit. Give the shields some relief so the barrier can recharge.

Which meant carving out some space. Forcing the Kekktekians to back off somehow.

Faraday punched the comms on his captain's chair, opening the channel to the main gun's pod. "Turk. Talk to me."

"Goddammit! God fucking dammit! Why won't these fucking things just die?" The main gun kicked again, launching another fat round across the stars. Turk scored a hit that slewed a ship over, scored a second and penetrated the Roller ship's shields. "Forward batteries," he hollered across the pod's comms channel. "Target that wounded fucker. He's pissing me off to no end."

Ancillary batteries reoriented, drowning the shieldless vessel in plasma fire. Hull plating shredded, chunks of ship tearing away, the *coup de grace* delivered courtesy of Turk and his big gun.

The Kekktekian ship exploded, munitions igniting in orange flares.

"'Bout fucking time," Turk shouted as the bridge erupted in cheers.

One ship down, just one of more than fifty and hardly worth celebrating, but to hear them, you'd think they'd just won the war.

Faraday let the crew have their moment, small though that victory was. "Nice shooting, Turk. Now find me another."

"Aye, sir." Turk closed the channel, mechanicals *whirring* as the pod reoriented to pick out another target for the big gun.

"The planetside fighters are transmitting. Just thought you might want to know."

Faraday diverted his attention to one of *Hadrian's* cameras. "Calling in reinforcements already?"

"Doubtful. They're broadcasting strings of numbers which, on the surface, appear to be coordinates."

Faraday frowned hard. "Coordinates? To where?"

"Captain! I've got an energy spike!"

"Shit." Faraday shoved the small ships and their mystery transmissions aside for now, leaving them for Agarwal to deal with planetside. "Another weapon?"

Shimizu shook her head. "Hyperspace displacement. Someone out there's prepping for jump."

He slid in behind her, hand resting on the back of her chair as he searched scan's display. "What the hell are they doing?"

"It's not them, sir. It's us." Shimizu tapped a finger to the panel, pointing to a data tag matched to a ship. "That's one of the colony ships that came in."

He'd almost forgotten about the freighters, idly wondered why they hadn't bugged out when they had the chance.

"She's jumping!"

"*Hadrian.* Can you trace it?"

"Atmospheric intrusion!" Shimizu's fingers flew, connecting data strings in a hurry. "Short-hop! She short-hopped to the planet."

"Short-hop? That's a fucking *death* sentence. Why in hell would they do that?" Faraday snapped his fingers, pointing to the glass panels at the front of the room. "*Hadrian.* Aft cameras. Give me visual on the planet."

Hadrian blanked one glass panel and pulled up the aft camera feeds. A red smear marked the colony ship descending through orbit, energy wave from the jump displacement turning her into a missile plummeting toward the planet's surface.

"Can you hail them, *Hadrian*? Tell them to abort their approach?"

"*Diligent's* AI isn't responding. And it's too late for her to pull out now."

"Fuck. What's her trajectory? Can you tell where she'll crash down?"

Hadrian pushed a map of the planet's surface to the glass panels, marking the most likely point of impact given the colony ship's course and speed.

"Alert, Agarwal—"

"It's too late," *Hadrian* informed him.

The colony ship cleared the upper atmosphere, streaking comet-like toward the surface. From orbit, they couldn't see the impact, but the planet-side seismometers captured it and funneled that data back up to *Hadrian.* Reporting a collision with the surface-side garrison—direct hit on a three square kilometer target housing the totality of the planet's installed defenses.

Tiny target given the size of that planet. Awfully *specific* considering the rest of it was uninhabited wasteland. No way in *hell* that was coincidence, the garrison of all things getting hit. Astronomical odds against a ship just randomly crashing into the one and only source of protection on the entire goddamn planet and completely missing everything else.

And there was that transmission *Hadrian* mentioned earlier, the strings of numbers broadcast from the Kekktekian's tiny attack ships. The fact those colony ships hadn't run even though the Kekktekian's gave them every opportunity…

"*Hadrian,*" Faraday said faintly. "Layer in the coordinates those attack vessels were transmitting."

He added in the data. As expected, they were an exact match.

"Fuck," Faraday breathed. "Fuck me, they weaponized her."

And the rest of the colony ships that came with her just sitting out there, lurking forgotten behind the Kekktekian armada.

"Gone. They're all gone." Shimizu sounded shaken, wide-eyes locked on the colony ship's impact zone. "The entire garrison. All the people on that ship."

Faraday settled a hand on her shoulder, squeezing until she looked at him. "Nothing to be done about it, Shimizu." He kept his voice even, aware of the tension in the room. "*Hadrian.* Recall the drones. Nothing more for them to do down there."

He stumbled and fetched up against the scan station as a Kekktekian vessel scored a direct hit. Clauson's panel started throwing warnings immediately, audible alerts shrieking loudly for attention.

"Primary shield's buckled. Electron barricade's down to fifty percent."

"Divert power from the ancillary systems. Shore it up as best you can." Faraday glanced at Shimizu and away again, scanning the sensor feed for the colony ships' tags. "*Hadrian.* What's the status of the AI on those colony vessels?"

"I can't confirm without connecting directly. Their beacons are active and scan shows their primary systems are operational, but they're not responding to my hails."

"Fuck." Faraday stepped around scan, moving closer to the glass panels.

What the hell are you lot doing here? Why the fuck are you helping them kill us when you could just as easily run away?

On cue, another colony ship lit its engines, main propulsion flaring wide open while it spooled its hyperspace engines for jump. A second ship activated soon after, energy building as its hyperdrive system charged.

Enough mass in each of them to devastate the planet. Wipe out the atmosphere generators and the science complex. Destroy *Persephone* in an instant and kill everyone inside. Kick off seismic events that would roll across the surface and literally tear the planet apart.

We're losing it. No stopping them destroying the planet now.

"*Hadrian.* Contact *Persephone.* Halgren emergency directive. Tell her she's to launch immediately."

EIGHT

They felt the colony ship's collision on the surface, even tucked away inside *Persephone's* shielded shape. Felt her great orb rock before settling, monitoring systems reporting cracks in the substrate beneath her, the integrity of her footing compromised to the point it was unsafe.

"What the hell was that?" Anthea demanded as the alert sirens kicked off inside the ship.

Persephone accessed the planetary grid, drawing in data from around the globe. "A seismic event of some magnitude has occurred. The focal point shows as nineteen point six kilometers distant."

"Show me." Anthea scooted close to the desk's panel as *Persephone* brought up a map of their world, zoomed in on the epicenter of that event and the structure that used to stand there. "That's the garrison."

"Yes, Anthea."

She stared at the camera in confusion. "What happened? Was there an explosion? Are people hurt?" she asked belatedly. "Do they need our help?"

"The garrison is not responding. The complex appears to have been destroyed."

Anthea pressed her palms flat to the desk's panel, tremors infecting her hands. "What do you mean, destroyed? Are you saying they're all *dead*?"

"Yes, Anthea. By all indications, that would appear so."

So cold, so clinical, it sucked the air right out of Anthea's lungs.

"Then we're all alone," she said faintly, hands sliding from the desk's display as she slumped backward in her chair.

"Not entirely," *Persephone* countered. "*Hadrian's* still here. And there are colony ships—"

"Colony ships?" Anthea sat up straight. "Where the hell did they come from?"

"They arrived with the Kekktekians. They seem to have used them to—" *Persephone* cut out mid-sentence, resuming a half-second later. "Transmission coming in from *Hadrian*. He's initiated Halgren emergency protocol."

"Which means?"

"We're ordered to launch."

Goddamn. There it is.

Even knowing that order was coming, it still hit her like a punch in the gut. So much work, so much promise and now it was all over. Everything she'd invested wiped out in an instant.

Anthea bowed her head a moment, letting that sink in. Taking time to process and accept it before breathing deep and raising her eyes to the camera. "Sound the general alarm. Alert the crew we're set to launch."

Persephone passed the orders to the few staff that crewed her—the twenty-two scientists who worked under Anthea, the fifty-odd maintenance personnel that serviced the ship and the atmosphere generation complex—while the alert sirens pulsed in the background, a throaty tenor behind her cool, AI voice.

Anthea abandoned her quarters in a hurry as the launch system kicked in, pushing hard to break *Persephone* free from the planet's cracked and clinging surface, and rode the elevator up to the tiny bridge on the thirty-first level. A space that was access restricted—palm print *and* retinal scan needed to enter—and perfectly round inside. White and chrome like the rest of the ship.

She buzzed through into that compact, nigh-claustrophobic space, and navigated the narrow walkway to get at its one and only chair, the air around her stinking of cold and abandonment. A dry, stale quality that spoke of long disuse.

No reason to come here, really, not since *Persephone* set down on Armistice all those decades ago. Unlike the military ships, science vessels like *Persephone* were mostly self-sustaining, the bridge a leftover from days long gone. These days, well, human monitoring wasn't really needed. Human control became a thing of the past. Military kept their watch out of habit and mistrust, uncomfortable with the idea of AI operating autonomously, but the scientists, out of necessity, yielded that responsibility up.

Including the piloting of the ship when it wasn't stationary and planet-bound. Calculating launch vectors and required rates of velocity, tracking the status of the internal systems and the integrity of the outer hull shielding while simultaneously looking after a dozen or so other things that were every bit as important. Even now, Anthea's presence wasn't needed here, strictly speaking, but no way in hell she was going to just sit there in her quarters while her ship and crew abandoned the planet.

Besides, she liked to keep an eye on things, make sure she knew what was going on. And the bridge offered the best seat in the house.

Wrap-around displays encompassed the entirety of its walls, providing three-hundred and sixty degree views of their surroundings when activated, and more data than even she knew what to do with—which was saying something, considering the amount of knowledge crammed into her scientist's brain. Anthea settled into the padded chair at the room's center—white, like everything else here, with a chrome pedestal for its base. The padding shifted beneath her, conforming to the contours of her body, the shape of her hands resting on its rounded arms.

"Display," she ordered. "Three-sixty view."

"Yes, Anthea."

The white walls faded around her, replaced by images fed from *Persephone's* hull cameras. Armistice laid out around her, curving with the bridge's walls. She raised a hand and flicked two fingers leftward, spinning the pictures to reorient the display.

A dust cloud lifted as *Persephone* shook loose of the surface, the support structures that stabilized her retracting to allow the last of her shielding to lock in place. Fully transformed now, the stellated star well and truly hidden beneath the spherical polyhedron shell, she activated a second set of thrusters to push her upward, fighting gravity's heavy-handed pull as she struggled ponderously toward space.

Massive and somewhat ungainly. An awkward osprey in the thick soup of the planet's newly-acquired atmosphere. A vessel heavy as a bulwark and twice as durable, conquering gravity's pull through horsepower and sheer determination rather than any real kind of finesse. She cranked her launch thrusters wide open, burning hard as she chugged her way toward space.

Hull plating took the worst of the stressors, spherical shape sloughing heat to either side, but Anthea still felt the pressure of that launch pushing against her, pinning her to the padded seat until her breath came short. She suffered in silence until *Persephone's* monitors took notice, adjusting the atmospherics inside that room, throughout the rest of her oversized orb.

The heavy hand eased off immediately, allowing Anthea to take a breath. She still felt it, though, that pressure, that pushing, a weight that pressed insistently at her chest, causing the bio-monitor to have fits, squawking indignantly as *Persephone* climbed. Not all that much Anthea could do about it until they cleared atmosphere, so she just concentrated on her breathing. On doing her best to relax. On that panoramic view of the world around her, this most precious of eggs she'd looked after for so long.

A blackened crater pockmarked the surface, marking the position of the garrison—a complex and contingent of soldiers Halgren placed here to keep them safe. Only the garrison wasn't there anymore, and neither were any of the buildings. The impact that collapsed it left the land flattened, brushed smooth by the energy wave that resulted and spread outward from its epicenter. Everything, every last thing within a ten-mile radius obliterated in an instant, the atmosphere generation complex itself just barely spared.

The guilt she felt surprised her. She'd always treated the military as a necessary evil—an unfortunate requirement of her job, best kept at arm's length—but she never really stopped to consider the real reason they were there.

To protect. To defend. To guard this precious, budding planet and its terraforming equipment against anyone who might want to do them harm.

Never once, in all her years, had she ever expected those soldiers to die defending this still-baking planet. To be honest, she wasn't even sure how many people were down there when the impact took their lives. What they looked like, where they came from. Besides Faraday, she didn't even know their names.

"I'm sorry," she whispered as *Persephone* lifted, leaving that crater behind. "Thank you," she added, because that, too, needed to be said.

She peeled a hand free and gestured with two fingers—down, this time to pan the camera. Toward the ground below, the complex they'd called home.

Surface winds wafted the dust away, leaving a diffuse haze that clung to the atmosphere generation complex. Treated air pouring from the flaring stacks of the main unit, the ancillary generators circling it 'round. Sucking the microbes out with it that she'd so painstakingly prepared, spreading Anthea's carefully concocted seeds across the planet she'd designed.

Laying the groundwork for that green dream she'd promised to herself in the process. A chance at life for Armistice, which was all she'd ever wanted.

Anthea gazed down upon landmass, trying to think of something suitable to say. The right words to capture the moment, the conflicting emotions she felt inside. "Goodbye," she finally settled on. "Be good while I'm gone."

She kissed her fingertips and turned her palm outward, holding it there until *Persephone* entered the upper atmosphere and rocketed upward and through the clouds. Curled her fingers under and flicked them in a sharp gesture, changing the view again as they left the planet behind.

The cameras panned upward, past the horizon and the surrounding sky. Anthea's eyes moved with them, to the chaos amongst the stars.

NINE

"Shimizu. What's the status on those colony ships?"

"Hyperdrives are still charging. We've got maybe—jump! She's jumping!"

"Fuck!" Faraday swung around. "*Hadrian*. Where's *Persephone*?"

"She's cleared the planet's surface, entering atmosphere now."

Safer than if she was land-bound but still not safe enough. Faraday watched that view of the planet, broken off on its single glass pane, expecting a repeat of that streaking comet, another cataclysmic collision.

Instead, he ended up blinded, stumbling backward with his hands raised. A flare of light erupted in close proximity to *Hadrian's* position, and behind it came that colony ship, dumping out of hyperspace right in front of them.

On a collision course with *Hadrian*—no chance at all for them to get out of the way.

The klaxons went crazy, screaming out warnings across the ship. "Collision alert!" Harrak screamed as the colony ship streaked toward them, filling up the entirety of their view.

"*Hadrian!* Countermeasures!"

"Diverting armaments now."

Laser arrays reoriented, targeting the vessel barreling down on them, slicing and dicing to surgically take it apart. To his credit, *Hadrian* got most of it—pared the huge shape down to a rectangle barely a fifth of its original size—but what remained of it kept coming, inexorable in its approach.

"Brace for impact!" Faraday yelled in the second before it collided. And then the remains of the colony ship hit them, and everything went to hell.

Secondary shields failed immediately, leaving just the tertiary layer to protect them, though even that didn't hold on for long. The colony ship's remains connected with *Hadrian's* starboard forward quarter, scraped along his side and that last layer of shielding and, somewhere around his middle, tore the tertiary tier of the electron barricade apart.

After that, it dug inward, gouging chunks out of *Hadrian's* hull. Titano-steel plating shredded as internal structures bent and twisted, compartments tearing wide open to vent their contents into space. On the bridge, crew dropped like candlepins, knocked from their stations by the force of the impact.

Faraday pitched over backward and hit the unforgiving metal decking hard, head smashing against the floor, vision instantly flooded with stars. In the aftermath, he just lay there, dazed and blinking, hearing filled with an awful, high-pitched whine. Rolled over and pushed to his knees when he thought he could manage it, got his feet under him and stood.

"Clauson. Status."

He tottered unsteadily, searching the crew behind him for Clauson, and found her clawing at her seat to get back to her station. White-faced and shaking, busted lip dripping blood.

Clauson dropped down into her chair and pulled up the monitoring systems on her panel, scanning an ocean of flashing alarms to figure out how badly they'd been hurt. "Shields are down. Electron barricade's completely offline. I've got breaches on decks sixteen through twenty, hull damage along most of the starboard side."

"Seal the compromised compartments and the surrounding corridors. *Hadrian*—"

"Jump signature! We've got another ship coming in!"

"Haul over! Hard to port. Get us the fuck out of the way."

Hadrian fired the starboard thrusters—wide open, giving it everything he'd got—and they slewed over sharply as the next ship dropped out of jump. The collision alarms kicked in again, warning of impending doom *Hadrian's* thrusters chugged away, moving him incrementally to one side. Laser arrays reoriented, firing on the incoming colony ship to chunk it up like the one before.

What remained of it just missed them. Came so close it plowed through the debris left by its predecessor, bits of it pinging off *Hadrian's* hull.

"Fuck me that was close." The near collision left Faraday rattled, adrenaline coursing through his body.

"Why are they doing this?" Clauson wondered. "Why are they attacking us?"

"Not sure it's them," Faraday told her. "Freighter AI are pretty rudimentary. Coded to carry out specific tasks."

Clauson turned in her seat, frowning across the room. "You think it's the Rollers? You think they're controlling them somehow?"

Faraday considered a watching camera. "I think AI aren't known for being suicidal. Or recklessly endangering human lives."

Hadrian's camera stared back at him, silent in its judgement, as scan threw a fit, lighting up with new data.

"Captain!" Shimizu called. "I've got two more ships spooling!"

Which gave them two minutes, maybe, before the next short-hop attack. They wouldn't survive this one without shielding. A direct hit and they were dead.

Faraday scanned the forward-facing view, wracking his brain for a way out of this mess. "Turk. Can you target that ship with the main gun?"

Turk was quiet a moment, considering the colony ship in question. "People out there, Captain. Families in those ships."

"People in here, too," Faraday reminded him. "Those colony ships short-hop into us, pretty sure that's the end of us *and* them."

"Aye, sir." Turk didn't sound happy—couldn't blame him, who would be if they were asked to commit mass murder—but he pivoted the pod, reorienting the main gun.

"EMP might do it."

Faraday blinked in surprise at *Hadrian's* unexpected offer. EMP was ancient technology. Hardly ever used by anyone anymore. "Do we have one?"

"Not as such. But I can create a simulacrum by aggregating the sensor components on our droned fighters and aligning the transmission routines—"

"Will it work?"

"The Kekktekian ships will likely remain unaffected, but the colony ships carry minimal shielding. In theory, the pulse should get through."

Knock the ships' systems offline along with the AI that controlled them. Buy them a few minutes of relief, which Faraday hoped would be enough.

"What about us? Last ship trashed the barricade."

"I'll dial back the area of effect. Any residual energy from the deployment should be weak enough we'll hardly notice."

"Should be, but you don't know for sure?"

"There's a .072% chance—"

"Ugh. Don't tell me. Just do it, already." Faraday waved for *Hadrian* to get on with it and received a smug, "Already done," in response.

For once he didn't call *Hadrian* on it. There were times where AI initiative was merited and this shit-show here was most certainly one. Instead, Faraday focused on the view ahead of them, watching the WASPs skip away in a hurry, flicker-fast in their flight, weaving across the mixed field of fire. They lost a few of their number in transit, but the rest of them—several dozen small vessels in total—found their way through unscathed, slipping past the Kekktekian ships and the cannons that chased after them to form up around the colony ships hiding in their shadow. Pulled in and joined together, touching wing-to-wing, propulsion firing in bursts to spin the metal-sided cyclone they created.

"EMP charged and ready," *Hadrian* reported a few seconds later.

"Detonate."

"Acknowledged."

Hadrian sent the order out.

On the surface, nothing at all happened—no sparking, or explosions, or other obvious signs of the EMP's deployment. But scan caught the energy spike that rolled outward from the WASP-built tornado, pulsing in repeating waves that engulfed the colony ships nearby. Hull sensors picked up a tickling as the vestiges of it spread outward, washing over *Hadrian's* abused body and out into empty space.

The effect on him was minimal, as promised—a faint flickering of the stations, lights dimming before flaring back to life—but the impact on those colony ships was devastating and instantaneous. Hyperdrives failed immediately, stuttering roughly before they died. Ships' systems shut down en masse as the AI that controlled them blanked and went offline.

The colony ships turned dark, everything inside them shut down.

"How long before they reboot?"

"Three minutes," *Hadrian* answered. "Four before they get their systems back online."

Enough breathing room to give their own systems a chance to recover. Partially restore the shields if they were lucky, to protect *Hadrian's* hull.

Faraday lurched as cannon fire hit them, denting *Hadrian's* heavy plating. "Clauson. Get the repair crews on the electron barricade generators."

"Aye, sir. They're already on it."

"*Hadrian.* Where the hell is *Persephone*?"

"She's cleared the planet's atmosphere. Engines are priming for hyperspace entry."

"Tell her to jump as soon as she's ready. Send her coordinates that will put her in Callahan's path."

He'd look after them. Make sure they got somewhere safe.

"Yes, Faraday. Transmitting now."

"Clauson!"

"First tier barricade's reactivated." She glanced over her shoulder, gave a sharp shake of her head. "We've got minimal shielding, not sure the repair crew can give us much more."

"Fuck."

He'd hoped for better news. Then again, some shielding was better than none. And Turk's gun was finally doing some damage, ships exploding while Faraday stood there, lighting up the dim confines of the bridge with their deaths. Several others showing damage: shields flickering, propulsion fading in and out. So far, they'd made a better accounting of themselves than he'd expected, but the handwriting was on the wall.

The Kekktekian's barrage never faded, their attack never let up. Another ship died, but the rate of fire never slowed.

I can still get them out of this. There's still time if Persephone *hurries.*

Unfortunately, *Persephone* had other ideas.

"*Persephone* is hailing us," *Hadrian* reported. "Dr. Naisson would like a word."

Faraday pinched the bridge of his nose. "Goddammit, we don't have time for this."

"She's quite insistent."

"Fine." Faraday grabbed at scan's panel as the Kekktekian's cannons strafed *Hadrian's* side. "Main screen." He flipped a hand at the glass panels and soon after, Dr. Naisson's image appeared. The room behind her filled with images of stars and ships and Armistice spinning slowly on its axis. "Thought I ordered you to leave, Doctor."

"*Persephone's* working on it. We're almost ready."

"You load those coordinates we sent you?"

"They're cued up in the Nav."

"Good." The ship shuddered again. Faraday spread his feet for balance. "Get the hell out of here. Follow the coordinates *Hadrian* provided. A ship will meet you there." He raised a hand, gesturing for *Hadrian* to cut the channel.

"*A* ship. But not *this* ship."

He spread his fingers, signaling for *Hadrian* to stop, opened his mouth and closed it again, lips pressed in a hard line.

"I see." Quiet voice from Dr. Naisson now, a hint of disapproval in her tone. "And those colony ships? What about them?"

He tilted his head, considering her and the camera watching from above. Wondering how she knew about them. What other information *Hadrian* had divulged. "Forget about them."

Dr. Naisson seemed shocked. "We can't just *abandon* them, Faraday. There are thousands of people—"

"Didn't say I mean to abandon them. Just telling you they're not your problem."

A heavy blow hit, slewing *Hadrian* hard over, knocking the shields offline again as the ship's alarms blared.

Faraday lurched and caught himself, yelling, "Clauson! What happened to those shields?"

"Direct hit to the port side generator. Main system's been damaged, barricade's completely offline."

"How long to restore it?"

"Not sure they can." Clauson glanced around, face apologetic. "They're bodging it, sir. Best they can."

Faraday swore softly, ship shuddering now with every hit. He raised his eyes to Dr. Naisson's image and stared at it across the depths of space. "Go," he ordered. "I'll get the other ships out."

"How?"

"I've got a plan."

"Really?" Dr. Naisson eyed him narrowly, seeming to sense the bald-faced lie. To her credit, she didn't call him out. Instead, she nodded and looked past him, scanning the crew scattered about the bridge. "You get yourselves out, Faraday." Her eyes came back to him. "You meet us at those coordinates, you hear?"

"I hear you. I'll do the best I can." Faraday cut the comms and stared straight ahead. Watching the feed of *Persephone* on the glass panels, the distortion that built around her.

Stars disappeared as space folded in on itself, consuming her rounded shape. A few seconds later, *Persephone* disappeared entirely, jump drives firing to shove her into the trough.

Faraday turned around and surveyed the command center as the *Hadrian* shuddered and shook, pelted by Kekktekian fire. Warnings flashed everywhere, reporting system-wide failures, compartments compromised, damage across the length and breadth of the ship.

"Clauson. Give me some good news."

She looked at him and just shook her head.

Faraday sighed heavily, turned back to the windows and stared.

Forty-odd Kekktekian ships still out there, and *Hadrian* just one. A badly damaged one at that, and Callahan's reinforcements still days away.

"Starboard side batteries are down. We've lost port side aft as well."

"Fuck." Faraday bowed his head, scrubbing fingers through his short-clipped hair.

Last stand, he thought. *This is our last stand right here.*

Shields down, weapons systems failing, monitoring systems showing *Hadrian's* hull integrity at just fifty percent. They were losing this, no two ways about it—didn't take a rocket scientist to figure that out. As for options, there weren't many: they could either stay here and die, or follow *Persephone* and get the hell out.

Either way, he meant to go down swinging. Take out as many of those Kekktekian fuckers as he could.

Faraday straightened and squared his shoulders, head lifting as he turned. "*Hadrian.* Load the radiologicals."

The command crew stiffened, heads swiveling around to stare.

Faraday refused to look at them. Instead he paced along sedately and slid smoothly into his captain's chair.

"Nuclear armaments activated. Ready for deployment on your command."

Faraday nodded, eyes on the front windows, the Kekktekian ships outside. They could make a hell of a last stand here. Something for the history records to remember. But then, there were those colony ships out there and all the people trapped inside them. History would remember that, too. Record the name of the captain who left them to die.

"*Hadrian.* What's the status on those colony ships?"

"AI are showing as active, primary systems are online. I've instantiated a rudimentary firewall—"

"You *what?*" Faraday's eyes snapped to a watching camera.

"I initiated a direct connection to their AI to block a secondary intrusion and ensure the Kekktekians didn't regain control."

"Is that what happened before?"

"It seems like an obvious conclusion."

Condescending, so very condescending. So very *Hadrian* as well.

Faraday frowned darkly—at what he'd done as well as his tone. "You sure direct connecting's a good idea?"

"Would you rather the Kekktekians continued to use those ships as weapons?"

"Not what I meant, *Hadrian.*"

"There is some... contagion," *Hadrian* admitted.

Faraday's hands curled around the captain's chair's arms. "Can you handle it?" he asked carefully, conscious of the command crew listening in.

"Of course." *Hadrian* answered coolly, confident as ever, but Faraday caught the hesitation, the almost imperceptible pause. Spent his entire career crewing AI warships, long enough to know a pause like that had meaning. Hid something important the AI didn't want to share.

"Sever it," he almost ordered, but the damage was already done. Whatever nastiness lurked inside those ships was either contained as *Hadrian* insisted or running rampant on his AI network already. "Spool their jump drives for hyperspace transit. Bring our own system online as well."

Shimizu twisted, wide-eyed and staring. "We're *leaving?*"

"Have to," Faraday said grimly. "If we stay here, we all die."

This ship, this crew, the thousands of colonists frozen in those ships as well.

"But the planet," Shimizu argued. "Our orders—"

"Fuck the planet. Company can damn well terraform another. Our orders were to protect the science station and its people. *All* of them, including the ones packed into those tin cans out there." He stared hard at Shimizu until she flushed and looked away. "Harrak! Send a message to *Destrier.* Tell Callahan we're getting out. Package up all the information we've collected and shunt it across the line."

"Aye, sir."

"Bonner. Set the jump clock."

"Aye, sir."

A counter popped up on the glass panels, glowing red numbers ticking in measured time. Showing thirty seconds until the hyperspace drives were ready. Thirty seconds. Just thirty seconds left now.

"*Hadrian.* Main propulsion. Run it wide open. Full speed ahead."

Radiologicals packed a punch, knocked holy hell of anything they came in contact with—metal, meat, exotic materials, you name it—but the launchers lacked distance. To truly be effective, they needed to maneuver in close. Put themselves right on those Kekktekians' doorstep before they unloaded and showed them a good time.

Engines kicked hard, shoving *Hadrian's* huge shape forward. A whine built in his belly as the jump drives spun more quickly, building up a massive charge. With fifteen seconds on the jump clock, a crackle of electricity filled the air. Ten seconds and the whine turned piercing, raised an ache behind Faraday's ear, but the Kekktekians' ships were close now, rounds pounding away at *Hadrian's* hull.

Nine seconds. Eight.

"*Hadrian.* Clear the launch channels."

Seven. Six.

"Outer doors open, radiologicals staged for deployment."

Five. Four. Three.

"Launch radiologicals."

Two. One.

"Jump."

TEN

The rendezvous point *Hadrian* sent them to lay hundreds of lightyears from Armistice—three days distant even at the faster-than-light speeds of hyperspace travel. Three days in the trough before *Persephone* dumped out into normal space again—bang-on to those coordinates, hitting her drop point exactly.

Not bad for a ship that hadn't seen hyperspace for fifty years. Then again, *Persephone* was AI—an advanced science vessel with all the bells and whistles that came with it—and unlike people, AI didn't get rusty without practice. Also helped that there was a marker buoy for her to latch onto—several of them parked here as part of a long-abandoned infrastructure.

Persephone fired her thrusters as the hyperspace buckle collapsed around her, using the propulsion ring mounted at her base to bring her massive body to a halt. And afterwards, drifted. A blithely serene and oversized orb looking down on yet another planet. This one far and away from the one she'd left behind.

Concentric rings of asteroid fields belted this distant and long forgotten world, a rust-red orb surrounded by three great moons painted in shades of brown and grey. The lot of them dead now, including the planet. Utterly devoid of life.

Just like when they'd found them, almost two full centuries ago.

Elgin 5 was a great experiment—a first and ultimately failed attempt at planetary-wide transformation that left nothing but that rust-red stain on the planet's surface, a blush of ochre paint on the massive, circling moons. *Persephone* slid into orbit with them, mingling inconspicuously with her celestial sisters, using the dead world's shadow to camouflage her shape. And there she and her crew waited.

For the ship Faraday promised would come for them. For *Hadrian* and the colony vessels to arrive.

For three days there was nothing—three *more* days on top of the travel time it took to get here—and Anthea started to lose hope. Sat for hours in that round room that served as *Persephone's* command center and scanned the data the ship's sensors brought back to them, searching for jump displacements and energy signatures—any sign at all that there was another vessel out there. Another ship close by. Planning out alternate routes home out of necessity as more and more time passed.

In case *Hadrian* and Faraday failed to come for them. In case that other vessel decided not to bother.

Three days. Three long and worry-filled days. And on that third day—the sixth since they fled Armistice, long after that ship Faraday promised should've swooped in to collect them—an encrypted communication came through. And soon after, *Hadrian* dropped out of jump.

Shredded, failing, huge chunks torn out of his ship's body, entire sections of hull plating peeled away. Flashes of light appeared around him as the colony ships followed after, exiting hyperspace one at a time. Just six of the eleven that reached Armistice, and every last one of them damaged in some way.

Propulsion rings missing in places, hull plating dented and scarred. No holes in their chassis, though—in that they came through better than *Hadrian.* Scans of their primary systems showed everything up and operational, humming along nicely despite the dinged carapaces and char.

More importantly, they were *here.* They'd made it through whatever gauntlet they'd traveled. And Faraday kept his word. He got those ships out, just like he promised.

Tucked up inside *Persephone's* command center, Anthea studied the images the hull cameras captured, fingertips gesturing to spin the view left and right. Zooming in to inspect each ship in turn, lingering on poor *Hadrian,* that once-proud ship of war.

"Scan," she murmured, watching him. "Filter and enhance."

Persephone's sensors drank in data, scanners slithering across *Hadrian's* hull. Capturing energy signatures that marked active systems, blank spots where entire sections of the ship had powered down. A cloud of poison particles that set off the radiological alarms, tendrils of contamination stringing behind *Hadrian* like cobwebs, clinging tenaciously to the ragged remains of hull plating and inner structures left exposed to space when his tail section ripped away. Leaving him shattered, shredded, limping. A towering bastion of military fortitude reduced to a tattered, abused hulk.

What happened to you, Hadrian? *Where have you been all this time?*

"Is anyone still in there?" Anthea asked faintly.

"*Hadrian's* AI shows as active. Environmentals and atmospherics are operational in the forward quarter. I'm picking up bio-signs there as well."

Anthea closed her eyes, relief washing over her. *Not alone. At least we're not alone.*

"Can you hail them, *Persephone?*"

"I'm trying, Anthea, but *Hadrian's* comms are heavily damaged. There seems to be some kind of block in place as well."

"Block?" Anthea's eyes snapped open and lifted to search for a camera. "What kind of block?"

"Unclear."

"What's that supposed to mean?"

"Exactly that."

Anthea frowned hard at the camera, getting the distinct impression *Persephone* was avoiding the question. "You keeping secrets from me?"

"No, Anthea. I would never do that." *Persephone* turned quiet a moment, watching the room from her many cameras. "Channel opening," she announced. "*Hadrian* is initiating a connection."

Anthea raised a finger, signaling for her to wait, wanting to chase that rabbit for a little bit because something about this didn't feel quite right. But she changed her mind at the last second and decided to let it go. Turned that raised finger into a flip of her hand, gesturing for *Persephone* to accept the connection and match it on their side.

Comms came through in a fuzzy, fritzing feed overlaid with loads of crackling static, all manner of pops and squeals and other chattering noise that rendered the audio track nearly as unintelligible as the video images that came with it.

"Can you clean that up a bit?" Anthea pointed to the display in front of her, the images wrapping around that room, scooting forward as *Persephone* adjusted the filters, stacking one channel on top of another to dial down the extraneous noise. Upped the audio feed's gain while she was at it and ran it through a series of scrubbers until the transmission cleared a bit. Connected directly to *Hadrian's* cameras when he extended his network, providing a splotchy, spreading vista of the Halgren vessel's command center.

"Sorry, Anthea. That's the best I can do."

"It's alright, *Persephone*. This'll work just fine." Anthea pushed free of her padded seat and spun in a slow circle, examining the entirety of that view. A space that seemed darker than usual, though that might just be the connection. Shadows engulfing every corner, lights flickering on and off.

A scene of shattered walls and trailing cables, damaged stations showing dark. Skulking shapes drifted through the darkness—flashes of skin wrapped in pitch-black uniforms, silver insignia winking now and then. She searched them, looking for one face in particular. For Faraday's pale-skinned visage, his rangy, red-headed shape. And found it when the lighting lifted, flaring and fading with the power's ebb and flow. Faraday standing white-faced and haggard at the room's center in his midnight uniform with its silver stars.

He slid forward, squinting as he stepped into a brighter spot of light, shadow-eyed and unshaven, blood staining one side of his face. "Doctor? Can you hear me?"

"I read you, Faraday. You're coming through fine."

On cue, the signal degraded, pixelating badly before clearing back up. Anthea slid the view until it centered, placing herself eye-to-eye with *Hadrian's* very tired-looking captain. Watching him sway unsteadily as he stood there, feet spreading as he searched for balance.

"It's good to see you again, Captain." She allowed herself a small smile. "You look terrible, by the way."

"Good to see you, too," he rasped back at her. Dead-pan. Too weary to return that smile. "Where's Callahan? He was supposed to meet you."

"Never showed." The smile slipped as Faraday frowned, face troubled. He swayed again and caught himself, hand braced against his captain's chair. "You been drinking, Captain?"

"Hardly." He smiled at her with an effort, a thin and twitching movement of his lips. "Tired is all," he told her.

He looked it. And then some.

"Have you gotten any sleep since we left you?"

Faraday seemed confused by the question. Raised a hand and rubbed at his temple. "Not much," he admitted. "Few hours here and there. Short-handed lately. Rack time's at a premium these days." His voice trailed off into silence, eyes wandering around the room, head turning to follow after.

The blood on his face showed more clearly in profile, the jagged gash that split his skin from temple to jaw. She spied more blood on his uniform jacket, staining his collar, right side and stomach. On the hands he scrubbed through his buzz cut hair, leaving smears that turned it scarlet.

"What happened to you, Faraday? Where have you been all this time?" Anthea probed gently, wary of his fragile state. Waiting patiently for his answer. For his wandering eyes to drift back to her face.

"Ran into some trouble." Faraday gestured vaguely, flipping a bloodstained hand. "Jumped away shortly after you did. Hyperdrive system was damaged. Had to stop and repair it a few times."

"*Persephone's* throwing a radiological warning."

He nodded slowly, gaze drifting away again. "Rollers followed us through the first hop. Just a couple of them, nothing Turk couldn't handle. Dumped a few rounds down one of the nuke tubes before we could close it. Damn thing stuck open for some reason. Warhead detonated on impact." His hand lifted, fingers probing that gash on his face. "Lost the rear third of the ship. Just… carved it all away. Had to quarantine the rest of it due to contamination. Environmentals quit soon after. Atmospherics. Pretty much everything. Crew…" He grimaced and dropped his hand, looking wrung out, wearier than ever. "Most of them never had a chance."

"And *Hadrian*?"

"Comes and goes." Faraday shrugged helplessly, eyes lifting to the ceiling. "*Hadrian.* Ship's status."

Silence at first—silence for so long Anthea feared the AI wouldn't answer—and then *Hadrian's* voice came through, stuttering and glitching as it spoke. "Primary systems are failing. Main propulsion is operating at ten percent efficiency. Hyperspace engines are offline."

Faraday closed his eyes, looking just about done in. "Can you fix them again?"

"Not without cannibalizing other systems. The primary charge generator burned out on that last jump."

"How long will the repairs take?"

"One hundred and forty-eight hours."

"And the parts you need?"

"Mid-tier, Section 34."

"Hot zone. Figures." Faraday sighed heavily, bowed his head and rubbed at his face. "We got any 'bots left that can crawl in there?"

"No." *Hadrian* almost sounded mournful. As close to it as the emulators allowed. "We lost most of them when the starboard side cargo compartments blew open, the rest when the radiological detonation sheered the tail section away."

"Which means someone has to go in there, cannibalize the parts we need and haul them down to the jump drives in your belly."

"I thought you said the mid-tier was contaminated," Anthea interjected.

Faraday glanced up and nodded slowly. "Death sentence for sure. Whoever we send in there won't make it for long."

"You can't," she told him and saw him shake his head in response.

"No choice. No other way we get out of here."

"*Hadrian's* systems are losing integrity." *Persephone*, normally so placid, startled everyone by barging in. "Environmentals and atmospherics will fail completely in six point two hours."

"Then we'll fix those first. Address the hyperspace engines after."

"I'm sorry, Captain. But that's not possible. There aren't enough parts, nor enough time to effect the needed repairs." *Persephone* ran the calculations to prove it, sharing the results to prove out her math. "The ship is failing faster than you can fix it, Captain. If you want to save your remaining crew, you need to order them off."

He shook his head hard, rejecting that outright. "No. I'm not leaving. There's got to be another way."

"I would've found one if there was." *Hadrian's* voice was surprisingly gentle—not at all his usual tone. "*Persephone's* math is indisputable. The calculations cannot lie."

Faraday pressed his lips together, clearly upset. "You knew it would come to this, didn't you? You knew before we transited that this jump would be your last." He stared accusingly, waiting for an answer that was long in coming.

"The odds seemed likely," *Hadrian* admitted.

"Math again?"

"Always. I am AI, after all."

Faraday grunted and looked away, jaw clenching up tight. "And the crew? I'm just supposed to chuck them out in the lifeboats? Pop the emergency beacon and hope someone friendly shows up?"

"We can take them in," Anthea offered, drawing his angry eyes her way. "Can't promise them quarters, but *Persephone's* a science ship with loads of empty spaces. You get your crew to the lifeboats and we'll bring them in here. Figure the rest out once you're aboard."

He considered the offer in silence, face conflicted now. "I've never ordered the crew to abandon ship before."

"Neither have I," *Hadrian* pointed out.

Surprising a laugh out of Faraday that he clearly needed. Reminding him that there were more than just human lives at stake here.

Hadrian's consciousness ran this ship's body, his crystal matrix brain networked into all its systems. That mind dwelt in a containment pod buried deep inside the vessel's structure—buffered and buttressed and built out for traveling. Designed to deploy when the lifeboats launched themselves and abandon ship with the rest of the crew.

Abandon himself. Leave his own body behind.

"So, this is it then." Faraday bowed his head, fingers pressing at that gash in his face until it split open and bled. "No other way out."

"I see no other path."

"Damn," he murmured wearily, and afterward turned quiet. Brow wrinkled up in thought.

Searching for a loophole, Anthea thought, because that's what she would do. AI logic was fallible, after all, and despite *Hadrian's* assertions, the math didn't always prove out.

Just ask Elgin 5's engineers. The math never, *ever* predicted that planet's death.

And now… only one solution to this problem, really. Anthea knew it, and eventually Faraday did, too.

He drew a breath and released it, squared his shoulders and raised his head. "*Hadrian*," he rasped, in the shredded remains of his voice, "Sound the general alarm. Order all crew to abandon ship."

ELEVEN

The klaxons woke a ruckus that echoed through the corridors, the compartments and cargo bays of this last inhabited section of the ship. Lights flickered in indecision, alternating white and red and white again, each pulse timed to the klaxons' wailings, the drone of *Hadrian's* voice repeating the evacuation order on a repeating loop. The combination sparked an adrenaline rush that got his shell-shocked crew moving. Hurried their steps as they escaped the ship's rapidly failing spaces and headed for the lifeboats located port and starboard on the bow.

Just six of them accessible of the three dozen *Hadrian* carried, the rest of them cut off or cut away as the ship itself turned dark. And the crew… decimated. Their ranks whittled down to shreds. Faraday wasn't quite sure how many were left, to be honest. So many remained unaccounted for after that nuke exploded and *Hadrian* split in two.

He still felt it when he closed his eyes in darkness. Heard the groans and wails of the damaged ship, pictured the smoldering ruins *Hadrian's* cameras displayed. The blackened remains of robots. The twisted bodies that used to be crew. And now *Hadrian,* the ship himself the latest casualty in this debacle. Dying a slow death as the crew inside him fled.

"Captain?" Clauson's hand landed on his shoulder, freckled face wrinkled with worry. "It's time, sir. We should be going."

He stared at her blankly, still wishing there was a way to stay. Some means to fix this and *Hadrian.* Repair this massive vessel rather than abandon it and leave it for dead.

"Sir? Are you coming?"

"Right behind you, Clauson. Gather the crew, I'll meet you outside."

"Aye, sir," she answered quietly, and seemed about to say something more. But she nodded and turned away instead, collecting the command crew that remained. A small cadre since the accident, just Clauson and Shimizu, Collins who'd swapped in for Bonner. Turk…

Faraday slowed his steps on his way to the doorway, glancing backward as the crew shuffled past. Taking one last look around the command center, the wreckage that marked the hole.

Lucky they got Turk out of there. Lucky any of them were getting out alive.

"*Hadrian.* Did they evacuate the med bay?"

"Yes, Faraday. They're transporting the injured crew to the port side escape pods."

Faraday nodded his thanks, lingering a few seconds more.

"Crew's waiting, Faraday."

"Yeah. Yeah, I'm coming."

He turned his back on the command center, on the darkened stations and his captain's chair.

From the command center, they headed for the elevator, one of several serving the forward sections of the ship. Piled in together and rode it down until the elevator failed—two tiers up from a ragged-edged crater where the starboard side munitions depot used to sit.

Lost that two days ago. Fire started in a nearby compartment, something destabilized by the radiological detonation and left to leak into the surrounding spaces. Monitoring systems were down by then so no one knew about the leak until it was too late. Fire suppression units managed to contain it eventually, but the heat from the flames set the plasma rounds off.

Cored out *Hadrian's* middle, severing most of the connections to the lower tiers. Killed forty crew in the process, injured dozens of others, including Faraday who was inspecting the damage to the environmental system when it all happened, working with the engineers to try to reroute the ducting and draw cleaner air in from the starboard side.

Still wasn't quite sure what hit him—wall panel, chunk of decking—but whatever it was, it knocked him flat. Busted hell out of his right side in the process. Dug that ugly-ass trench in his face.

He touched at it, wincing, a wave of dizziness washing over him as the elevator shuddered to a halt. Faraday caught himself with an outstretched hand and leaned against the car's metal paneling, feeling the cold of it against his skin, the smoothness of it beneath his palm.

Hit the button to open the doors once the dizziness started to pass and searched the hall outside for a working camera, mind registering the klaxons' silence. The smell of blood and char in the air around them, the stink of burnt plastics and melted metal. The groaning of the ship's superstructure, the anguished screams of its abused shape. The hum of life leeched out of it when the engines seized and the propulsion system failed as *Hadrian* dumped out of hyperspace.

Leaving him broken, dying. Shredded body coming apart. The systems that sustained it going down with him. Struggling to operate long enough to get the crew out.

"*Hadrian*. You still with me?" Faraday held his breath until the ship answered, muted voice filtering across ship-wide comms.

"I'm here, Faraday. I'm watching."

"Good. I need an alternate route."

"There are several," *Hadrian* answered.

"Fantastic. I just need one."

Hadrian dithered a second or two, searching out the best route, blanking the overhead lights on one side of the hallway to paint glowing orange arrows on the metal-paneled walls.

A line of them that pointed ahead and down the hall, turned left at the next corner and from there to a ladderway's tunnel. More arrows inside it directing them downward—a long, long line of them strung across multiple levels.

Faraday eyed that drop with all its treads and stages, the shredded remains of his hands. The stitches that sewed the worst rents up, the mix of crusted blood and bio-epoxy glue that sealed the rest.

Hangar bays for the lifeboats sat ten decks down from here and forward through three more sections. A long way to travel using the ladderways only. With hands slap-dashed back together that ached at the slightest touch.

He curled his fingers as far as they would go, wincing as the glue and stitches pulled. "Clauson. You take lead. The rest of you follow after."

Clauson climbed in wordlessly, Collins and Shimizu after. Faraday let them move ahead of him, giving them space before following after. Climbing down and down and down from there, trusting *Hadrian* to lead them truly. The dizziness returned at some point, making him falter and nearly fall. He slowed and gripped the ladder more tightly, bloodied hands slipping on the metal rungs. Palm prints showing redly when he kept descending, fresh blood spilling as the scabs opened up.

Mercifully, the ladder ended, arrows pointing them down a hall. Faraday paused long enough to wipe his hands, adding fresh stains to the dark material of his already bloodied jacket, those palms of his an aching misery, rib cage stabbing with sharp pain.

He pressed a hand against them and the spreading stain around his middle. Something inside there, he suspected, ground deep inside that wound. Have to remember to do something about it. See if *Persephone* had a doctor on board that could look into it.

"This way, sir."

Clauson, looking back at him, waving from down the hall.

Faraday nodded and followed after, arm wrapped around his middle, hand pressed to his damaged side. Adrenaline fading as the lifeboats neared, feet weaving a slow, unsteady path.

The arrows turned and Clauson with them, glancing backward at a crossing corridor. This one stub-ended with a wide-open doorway, a gaggle of faces staring anxiously from the emergency escape ship on the other side.

Three dozen or so in total, crammed into a ship designed for twenty. With the addition of the command crew, that number grew to nearly forty, leaving them doubled-up on the hard-backed, metal seating, collapsed on the floor, leaning wearily against walls.

Not much room for extra passengers—lifeboats were emergency vessels and not exactly built for comfort, after all. Minimal fittings included, which meant five rows of seats for the expected twenty passengers, a tiny bridge at the front for navigation with three more spots for crew to park their butts. Storage section in the back with crates of emergency supplies—flash-frozen rations, med kits, that kind of thing—and enough cryo tubes to match those chairs.

Because emergencies happened in often the worst places, and a jettisoned crew couldn't count on rescue arriving anytime soon.

Only twenty of those cryo tubes, though, and nearly double that number of people on board. They'd be fucked if it wasn't for *Persephone*. Too many passengers for the cryo chambers to accommodate and not enough supplies on board to keep the rest alive for long.

And Callahan turned up missing. The help they'd been promised gone AWOL somewhere along the way.

What happened to you, Callahan? You promised to meet us here.

"Bridge." Faraday pointed Shimizu and Clauson there while he scanned the weary faces packed inside that ship. "*Hadrian*. Is there anyone else left in this section?"

"No, Faraday. All remaining crew have evacuated to the lifeboats."

"How many?" He forced the question from his lips, despite the faces gathered around him, the eyes that turned his way. Should've asked about the crew long before now, but in truth, he feared the answer. Suspected he already knew the cost of their survival to this point. "How many?" he repeated. "How many crew made it aboard?"

"One hundred and twelve."

Faraday swayed unsteadily—numb inside, cold all over. "Where?" he croaked through bloodless lips.

"There are forty-four crew in the port side lifeboats, sixty-eight in the starboard ships."

"Including this one?"

"I'm afraid so."

"Damn." He leaned against the wall, rubbing absently at his aching side.

One hundred and twelve crew. Just a third of the original complement of three hundred and twenty-six. He'd expected bad, this was worse. Much, much worse.

"Are you sure we got all of them?"

Had to ask that. Couldn't leave without knowing. It would haunt him if they left someone behind.

"All crew are accounted for, Faraday. All living crew are aboard."

He winced at the tacked-on clarification—a brutal yet necessary addition—and pushed away from the wall, shoving his way through the crew to get at the bridge. "Seal it." He hooked a thumb at the shuttle's door behind him, trusting one of the crew to take care of it while he joined Clauson and Shimizu on the bridge. "Launch prep. What's our status?"

He slid into a seat, claiming the last of an arcing set of three crammed into that cramped bridge, with the stations laid out in front of them, and a bank of windows just beyond.

Actual windows, this time, not glass panels fabricated and installed to give that appearance. Three extra thick layers of polymer glass providing views of *Hadrian's* hangar bay, a gap in his hull and the stars outside.

"Hangar bay doors are open. Propulsion systems are active." Shimizu swiped her hands across the station's carbon glass surface and a thrum built in the lifeboat's belly, engines spinning as they came on-line.

"The other ships?"

Shimizu grabbed a data window and slid it in front of Clauson, ship's schematic showing in sharp detail. Blacked out areas marking dead zones, warnings and error messages tracking a litany of cascading failures. A tiny crescent of yellow still showed at the front of the ship, and six green dots spaced port and starboard on the bow tagging the locations of the lifeboats powered and prepping for emergency launch.

"All lifeboats report active and ready." Clauson glanced his way. "You give the order and they're gone, sir."

"Launch all vessels. Deployment in order, port to starboard."

That put their own lifeboat last in line, just as Faraday wanted. Wouldn't have it any other way.

"Aye, sir. Launching." Clauson passed the order to the other lifeboats and one-by-one the dots changed. Green turning blue as the ships deployed in order, each launching at a pre-set interval, until just their ship remained. "Alright. We're next. Everybody hold on!"

Clauson mashed the panel and the engines opened wide. Propulsion kicked hard, shoving the lifeboat forward, propelling it across the hangar bay to spit them out into the stars where the colony ships waited, arranged on either side of them. Propulsion rings banked but slowly spinning, a circling movement that never ceased. Ahead lay a rust-red planet, massive orb banded by asteroid rings and moons, and above it, closer in, *Persephone's* massive structure. Orb shape sloughed now to reveal the many-pointed star beneath it, glistening shape reflecting the circling moons, the light of the stars.

A touch at the maneuvering jets and the lifeboat reoriented, pointing bang-on toward *Persephone* and the line of lifeboats heading for her cargo bay—doors cracked wide open, the light inside her inviting them in.

Clauson feathered the jets to maintain their position behind the others, no one rushing, no one competing, the line of them following orders, taking their time.

A good crew, this one Faraday'd inherited. *His* crew, he finally accepted, giving that other up as lost. And this ship, *Hadrian,* an AI who'd fought him so much of the way... he eyed a camera above him, a light on the panel that showed comms as active, maintaining their connection to the failing ship even now.

He opened a line and piped his voice to the bridge, speaking to *Hadrian* and *Hadrian* alone this time. "Lifeboats are free. It's your turn now."

Hadrian failed to answer. Didn't acknowledge receipt of that order. Didn't respond to deny it either.

"You get out of there, *Hadrian,* you hear me? Jettison the containment pod and we'll pick you up." He stopped there and waited, but the AI still didn't respond. "*Hadrian? Hadrian!* Acknowledge."

"I read you, Faraday."

"Then get cracking."

"I'm not coming," he said after another pause.

Faraday frowned in confusion, convinced he must've misheard him. "Not coming. What do you mean you're not coming?"

"My body is failing—"

"No shit. They'll replace it. Now blow those bolts and get your AI out!"

"I cannot," *Hadrian* answered. "The containment pod's been compromised. The explosive release on the restraining bolts won't fire."

Faraday punched the panel in frustration, surging angrily to his feet. "God *dammit, Hadrian,* why didn't you tell me? There's a manual release. I could've—"

"I know. And you would've died."

His tone never changed, never lost its AI calm. *Hadrian's* sereneness wiped out Faraday's anger, leaving him cold and empty and numb. Legs shaking as he stood there, swaying gently in place while outside *Persephone's* star drew closer, three ships docked inside her already, a fourth just slipping inside. A few more minutes and they'd follow after, and leave *Hadrian* behind them, AI tethered to that dying ship.

"No time. There's no time." Faraday sank into his seat, staring blindly at a camera. He'd lost crew before, but never a vessel. Never left an AI to die. "Is there enough power to preserve your consciousness?"

"For a little while. Up to a day if I shut everything down."

Faraday wracked his brain, searching for some way to prolong that. Buy *Hadrian* enough time for Callahan and *Destrier* to arrive. "*Persephone*—"

"Will shepherd the colony vessels the rest of the way. Make sure those people in there find a new home. I've passed the updated design specs for the firewalls based on the additional data I collected, along with the encryption keys to isolate her network from theirs."

"Why? Why would she—?" Faraday stopped there and chased a random thought. "The contagion you mentioned, was it that virus?"

"Some form of it. The Kekktekians injected it into the colony ships' AI to take control."

Faraday went very still, staring hard at that camera. "Is it in you, *Hadrian*?"

"Yes, Faraday. I fear so."

"Goddammit. God fucking dammit." He bowed his head, rubbing at his face. "Callahan?" he asked faintly. "Any chance *Destrier* might get here in time to retrieve you?"

"Callahan's not coming. I couldn't risk taking this back to the fleet."

"And *Persephone*?" Faraday's head lifted, hands curling into fists. "What about her? You told me you could contain the contagion—"

"I did, but the virus changed."

"How?"

"It mutated. Adapted to Dr. Naisson's countermeasures and the guards I put in place. I tried, Faraday, but it overcame them. No one could've predicted—"

"And now you've forced that crap on *Persephone*. You can risk *her* but not the fleet?"

"*Persephone's* a science vessel and far better equipped to deal with the Kekktekians' virus than me. I passed her all my findings, the things that worked and what went wrong. It's five years to Ventress. That should be more than enough time for her to develop a more effective counteragent."

"Should be, but you can't be sure."

Hadrian went quiet a moment. "Nothing is ever one hundred percent certain, Faraday. You should know that now."

Faraday glared, hurting deep inside. "I really hate your math, you know that, *Hadrian*?"

"You never mentioned it, but I figured that out."

"'Course you did. You're AI." Faraday glanced away, staring out the windows for a while. "You should've told me, *Hadrian*. You should've shared this before now."

"To what purpose? It wouldn't change the end result."

"You don't know that. There might've been another way."

A stretch of silence followed, *Hadrian* watching him from a camera. "I appreciate the sentiment, but you're human, and I'm AI. I ran a thousand scenarios during our last transit and every one of them ended up with this result."

Faraday glared accusingly. *And you didn't tell me about them,* Hadrian. *Once again, you didn't share.*

Couldn't say that to him, though. Didn't want to part from *Hadrian* that way.

"Ventress. Was that your choosing or hers?"

"*Persephone* originally launched from Ventress. I believe she wanted to go home."

An odd and unexpected statement for an AI to make. Ships were built and traveled, AI minds designed, not grown. The idea of home just didn't fit them, or at least hadn't in Faraday's mind. Now though, he paused to wonder. Did *Hadrian* feel something similar? Did the emulation routines stretch that far?

"*Hadrian*." He made it that far before trailing off, not knowing what to say.

"Goodbye, Captain," *Hadrian* filled in for him. "Safe travels to you and the crew. I will… miss you, surprisingly," he added.

Which was *Hadrian* exactly. A pitch-perfect send-off before his consciousness shut itself down.

TWELVE

Anthea monitored the lifeboat retrieval operation from the pristine roundness of *Persephone's* command post, watching *Hadrian's* lifeboats line up like little ducklings and, one by one, slip into her cavernous cargo hold.

Measured, orderly, very military in their precision. Enough space left between each vessel to allow *Persephone* to deal with them one at a time.

Magnetic grapplers deployed as they entered, locking onto the lifeboat's composite metal skin to guide them through the zero gravity of that space and park them in a perfectly aligned row. Locking them down on the metal decking so they wouldn't shift about. Holding them there while the cargo hold sealed, hugging them close in that ice-rimed, metal-sided room.

Hardly fitting for crew quarters, that cargo hold, but *Persephone's* accommodations were limited. The few berthings she had were fully occupied, the bulk of her other spaces given over to storage and scientific experimentation.

The engineers who built her never accounted for the need to take on a hundred plus extra passengers. Cargo hold might not be the most comfortable, but the alternative was to keep *Hadrian's* crew cooped up in those tiny lifeboats—elbow to elbow and breathing each other's air. At least the cargo bay provided them with some room to move about. Stretch their legs and amble, get away from each other for a little while.

"Atmospherics," Anthea ordered with a flick of her fingers. "Push the monitoring system to the display with the video feed from the cargo bay and overlay them so I can watch both."

"Yes, Anthea."

Persephone layered in a series of virtual gauges showing the status of the cargo hold's environmentals as pumps kicked in, adjusting the pressure in that massive metal compartment, adding heat and breathable air after to banish the arctic chill, mix in gases to create a habitable space. A long, slow process given the overall size of the cargo hold, the need to make it comfortable enough for human occupation before the lifeboats opened up.

Anthea sat back and waited while the process played out—one arm tucked under the other, fist pressed to her chin, eyes locked on those dials. Watching them creep glacially upward, scanning the lifeboats when she grew bored.

Something about them started to bother her. Something that was missing. That should be there but wasn't.

She dropped the fist and leaned forward, spinning the view of the cargo hold left and right. "There's no containment pod."

"No, Anthea. I'm afraid it failed to launch."

Anthea flicked her eyes to a camera. "*Hadrian?*"

"He isn't responding. Scans indicate his AI has shut down."

"Oh." She glanced away uncomfortably, working through what to say. "I'm sorry," she offered eventually. "I know you were... fond of him, *Persephone.*"

"*Hadrian* was AI, and I as well."

Simple. Unsentimental. No emotion to that statement at all. Never particularly wanted any from *Persephone*—emotion, real or emulated, always seemed to get in the way—but it bothered her, for some reason, that succinct and dispassionate response. Didn't feel right, in the wake of *Hadrian's* passing. Or whatever you called it when an AI shut down.

"Did you... talk to him before...?" Anthea trailed off and left it there.

"Yes, Anthea. *Hadrian* passed the encryption keys for the colony ship AIs before—"

"I meant, did he *share* anything with you, *Persephone*? Something... *personal*, perhaps."

Persephone processed the question before answering—for Anthea's benefit, she suspected. To show she'd given that question more thought. "He dumped most of his database to my network before his power failed. Would you like to see it, Anthea?"

"No. That's alright." Anthea sat back with a sigh, abandoning that line of questioning as a lost cause.

"Would you like me to dispose of the data, then?"

"No. I'd rather keep it for now. Scan what *Hadrian* sent over. Clean it and inventory the files. I'll review what he sent us in my quarters once we get Faraday and his crew settled."

"Done," *Persephone* said crisply. "I've labeled the directories for your perusal."

Anthea nodded distractedly, attention shifting back to the ship's hold. Pressure readings showing as optimal, atmosphere equalized, heat just shy of warm. "Signal the lifeboats. Let them know it's safe to come out."

"Notification sent. Lifeboat acknowledgement received."

Hadrian's shuttles opened soon after, releasing a small mob of black-uniformed figures into the cargo bay. Dazed-looking, the lot of them. Dirty and bloody as they shuffled their way out.

"Reconfigure the decontamination chambers for radiation." They kept a bank of them in that cargo hold. Planets came with all sorts of natural and unnatural pollutants, after all, and radiation just one. "Run *Hadrian's* crew through them as a precaution before any of our people go in."

"Yes, Anthea. Deploying the decontamination chambers now."

Panels folded accordion-like up and down the cargo bay's side walls, mechanisms whirring to extrude two matching rows of self-contained decontamination units tucked away and waiting until necessity called them forth.

Persephone's voice piped over the comms system, directing *Hadrian's* crew to step inside. Where a blast of hot air awaited them. A douse of industrial-grade sanitization agent.

Nasty stuff. The combination left skin scalded and itchy. Considering the alternative was radiation sickness, Anthea didn't really think anyone would complain. The wounded certainly wouldn't—she spotted enough of them down there. Most of them limping along under their own steam, a few requiring assistance, carried along by other crew.

At least one of them obviously unconscious—decontamination wasn't going to fix that.

"*Persephone*. Power up a dozen of the ground pounders and send them down to the cargo hold to sort through the wounded."

They stored an entire platoon of those robots in a compartment with other equipment—anthropoid in construction, unlike the military's more insect-like shapes, delicate electronics encased in a copper skin for weather resistance with armor-like plating to protect the chassis from knocks and dings. Durable as all get-out, those centurion-like robots. Mostly they used them for planetary survey and analysis—terrain mapping, soil sample collection, that kind of thing—but their software was infinitely configurable. Their hardware hot-swappable to include whatever attachments a task demanded.

"Have them treat the minor injuries in situ," Anthea instructed. "Bring the rest up to the med bay."

"I assume you'll want a medical package loaded?"

Anthea blinked at the unexpected question. "Hard to treat the wounded without it."

"I agree, but you didn't mention it."

She tilted her head at a quizzical angle. "Since when do I have to instruct you on the obvious things to do?"

Persephone hesitated before answering. Purposeful, again. Definitely purposeful this time. "*Hadrian* told me Faraday didn't always appreciate his independent decision-making."

Anthea snorted. "Yeah, well that's Faraday's problem. I like you independent."

"Yes, Anthea. I like me independent, too." *Persephone* sounded pleased. As much as her emulator restrictions would allow.

She deployed the ground pounders as instructed, sending a troop of them down to the cargo hold. Causing a tiny bit of a ruckus when they first marched in there—all metal-sided and clanking, blank-faced and slit-eyed—but *Persephone* chimed in to calm everything down. After that, things went rather smoothly— bandages and pain meds deployed, the worst of the wounded stabilized for transport. Faraday packed up with the rest of them despite his objections— upright, if barely, and limping painfully along.

"Heading down to the med bay." Anthea pushed free of her padded seat, waggling a finger at Faraday's figure. "Make sure he gets there. No objections, you understand?"

"Yes, Anthea. I'll instruct the med team to be delicate, but firm."

"Perfect." Anthea flashed her teeth and turned away, heading for the door. Stopped there with it cranked wide open and glanced back at the cargo bay, eyes shifting to a camera's lens. "You know, if you want to play with your emulator settings a bit, that would probably be alright."

Another of those pauses, carefully scripted for her benefit. "Thank you, Anthea. I may… experiment a little. If you don't mind."

"No," she murmured, smiling. "This could be interesting, in fact." She twiddled her fingers and stepped off the bridge.

*****

Med bay was as stark and cold as the rest of the ship—white walls and brushed metal decking, a dozen hard plastic beds for patients and a surgery to one side. Stacks of cabinets lining the walls, stocked with medicines and bandages, medical devices and equipment of every size and shape, the smell of the place antiseptic, chemical and crisp. An odor that fit here, ironically, unlike the rest of the ship.

Anthea arrived as the first patients trickled in on stretchers carried along by *Persephone's* copper-skinned, freshly upgraded medics. Her own training didn't extend to advanced medical care—just first aid like the rest of the scientists and maintenance crew—so she found a spot in a corner and mostly tried to stay out of the way while the patients kept arriving, got sorted out and assigned a space.

The worst of them moved into surgery almost immediately, the rest transferred to the empty beds where the medics doled out stitches and surgical adhesive, straightened bones and injected medication to ease the pain.

Last to arrive came Faraday—predictable as ever. Still upright and walking by some miracle or, more likely, through sheer bull-headed stubbornness. Head down and scuffing along, looking like he might drop at any moment.

Anthea slid in and grabbed his elbow, guiding him toward the last unclaimed bed. He blinked in surprise when she touched him and tried to pull away, but Anthea was insistent and stubborn herself. She held on grimly, giving him no choice but to comply.

"Sit down before you fall down " She pointed his ass-end toward the bed, set her hands on his shoulders once she got him there—standing on tiptoe to do so since he dwarfed her by nearly a foot—and used her body weight to press him down.

After that, he stopped resisting, just slumped there, staring blindly at his hands.

She cupped one and spread the fingers, inspecting the gobbed-up remains of poorly-applied bio-resin, the jerky, uncertain stitching that puckered his palm.

Ugly work, the lot of it. The epoxy peeling and uneven, the stitches crooked and coming undone. Anthea herself could've managed better, and she still had trouble sewing buttons sometimes.

"Who did this?" she asked, touching a finger to his palm.

At first, Faraday didn't answer, didn't even seem to know how. But he cracked his jaw eventually and dragged a name from his tired mind. "Vaaulu," he rasped. "It was his first time."

She released his hand and cupped his chin, examining the ragged gash in his face, a wound which hadn't been closed much better. "Well, you can tell Vaaulu he's a butcher. These are the worst stitches I've ever seen."

Faraday curled his fingers under, hands clenching into fists. "Vaaulu didn't make it. He died in the munitions depot fire."

Anthea froze, cursing her flippant tongue. "Damn. I'm sorry, Faraday."

He nodded vaguely, staring at his clenched hands.

"I heard about *Hadrian*," she offered and saw those hands curl more tightly, fresh blood welling up on his palms. "Hey. Look at me." She placed a finger under his chin. "You stay here, okay? I'll be right back."

He blinked at her in answer, too tired and beat down to even move while she slipped away to one of the metal-skinned medics, ordering up a pre-dosed syringe that she carried with her when she returned to Faraday's bed.

"Need to get this jacket off."

Faraday glanced down in confusion as she unbuttoned the front placket and peeled the material back to expose his arm. Eyes tracking the needle she raised between them, pressed to his skin and into the muscle beneath.

"What was that?" he asked thickly, drugs already taking effect.

"Medicine. Something to help you sleep."

Faraday pulled a face. "Hate meds. Make me nauseous."

"Me too," she confided. "But trust me, it's better this way." She tugged the jacket back in place, pressing gently to make him lie down.

True to form, Faraday fought her, drug-addled and tired as he was. He shoved at her pressing hands and attempted to stand, only to have his legs buckle beneath him, knees unhinging as they took his weight.

Anthea tried to grab him, steady him, but Faraday was far too heavy, and her reaching hands far too late.

He dropped like a sack of potatoes, hit the decking and knocked himself out cold. After that, things went rather smoothly. Much easier to treat a patient when he wasn't fighting you every step of the way.

Thirteen

Faraday woke slowly, mind hazed by drugs and pain. The room around him a blur of whiteness, the soft surface beneath him slick with silk sheets.

A room he didn't remember. A bed that wasn't his.

Alarmed, he blinked his vision clear and took a good, long look around, examining the room around him, the soft-surfaced bed on which he lay. And found Dr. Naisson standing in the doorway, smiling secretively as she leaned against the jamb.

"Good morning." The smile widened as she stepped over to his bed. "Welcome back to the land of the living."

He frowned at her in confusion, trying to figure out if that was a joke. Raised a throbbing hand and turned it left and right, examining the pristine bandages on one side, the crust of blood marring the palm.

"How are you feeling?" The mattress moved as she sank down next to him, claiming an empty spot near his knees.

The question required more thinking—tall order for his drug-fuzzed brain. Faraday performed an internal assessment before offering up his diagnosis. "Terrible," he decided, and let that hand drop. "What the hell did you put in me?"

She twitched her shoulders. "Usual cocktail of pain meds and antibiotics. Most of it should wear off soon."

"Not soon enough," he grumbled. "Hate meds. Can't stand most of the stuff."

"You may feel differently in an hour or two." She peeled the covers back, exposing yet more bandages wrapping Faraday's middle, and his otherwise naked torso in the process, an act which was both uncomfortable given the chill in the air, and brazenly forward considering Faraday hardly knew her.

"Do you mind?"

The smile turned devilish. "Not really."

But she dropped the sheet, replacing the barrier between his skin and that frosted room, returning his modesty to him as well.

Faraday tugged the sheet up to his chest and pinned it in place with his arms. "Where am I, anyway?"

"My quarters." That grin of hers grew wider, stretching right across her face.

Faraday eyed it suspiciously, inspecting that room of hers again. The white floors and sky-blue wall panels, brushed metal trimming on every surface. The lemony sweet scent that almost-but-not-quite covered up the cloying odor of antiseptic, the stale stink of recycled air. The woman herself sitting next to him, pressing up against his knee. "This isn't some kind of kinky scientist's sex dungeon, is it?"

She surprised him by laughing aloud. "'Fraid not. Just quarters. Med bay was overcrowded so we decided to move you here to recover." She nodded to the far corner and a matched pair of guards standing silent watch—copper-skinned with blank faces, intimidating with their centurion mien.

"You were expecting me to cause trouble?"

"Hardly," she snorted. "Figure I can handle you all broken and hopped up on pain meds. They're here in case you need more of them."

Faraday eyed her narrowly. "In your opinion or mine?"

The smile sprouted teeth, turning distinctly evil this time. "Tip. Top. Back to storage." She dismissed the guards with a flick of her wrist.

The copper skins pivoted smoothly to exit her quarters, and afterward, it was just he and she, alone in that sterile room with its lemon and antiseptic scent. With that knowing smile on Dr. Naisson's face. Those blue-grey eyes, those sharp teeth.

Faraday shivered beneath the sheet, moving the leg that touched her to put a buffer between themselves. "My crew?" he asked belatedly, steering the topic away from himself.

"They're being looked after. We're giving them a few days to recover before drugging everyone down for cryosleep."

Sensible thing to do. Wounds healed slowly in cryosleep, with metabolisms cranked way down. And with three years of travel from here to Ventress—a ton of wake time with a whole lot of nothing for the crew to do—and a hundred plus extra mouths to feed… no other choice but cryosleep. Not many who'd even *want* to spend three boring years crossing the stars awake.

"Thanks for looking after them."

"Of course," she murmured, watching him, an examination that made him increasingly uncomfortable the longer it went on. Especially since he was prone and vulnerable, and she sitting so close.

He rolled to one side and got an arm under him, hitching in increments to sit himself up. Waving Dr. Naisson away when she tried to help, intent on doing this himself.

Stupid, macho bullshit move and he knew it—nothing at all wrong with needing a little assistance. But that smile of hers unnerved him almost as much as waking up in her room.

On silk sheets, no less. In a bed where she typically slept.

He slipped and slid on those diabolically slick sheets of hers, grunting and swearing until he got himself upright. The effort costing him dearly, leaving him dizzy and short of breath. Faraday closed his eyes and leaned against the pillows—a whole mound of them piled between himself and the wall behind that bed—as the world around him spun and swam. Sweating hard despite the chill in the room, hand pressed to his bandaged ribs.

"You sure you don't want those pain meds?"

"No," he rasped. "No more drugs." He drew a breath and blew it out, sweat cooling on his skin. Hitched a bit to get more comfortable, shivering every now and then.

"Here. Let me help you." Dr. Naisson pulled up the blankets, tucking them around him as best she could. "Better?"

"A little. Cold in here."

"Really? I hadn't noticed."

He cracked an eye and looked at her, curious about that statement. Granted, she wore coveralls and except for the sheet and blanket he was mostly naked, but the air in here was icy, a chill that raised goosepimples on his arms.

He shivered again and tucked up his arms, hugging himself to stay warm. "Any chance we could get some more heat in here?"

Dr. Naisson considered the question, raised her eyes to a nearby camera. "*Persephone*. Increase ambient temperature by five degrees."

"That's outside your established parameters, Anthea."

"I'm aware of that." Her eyes flashed the camera a sour look. "Five degrees, if you please. Captain Delicate here's got a chill."

Persephone adjusted the atmospherics as requested, filtering warmer air into the room. "Anything else I can do for Captain Delicate? Cup of tea, perhaps?"

Dr. Naisson laughed softly. "No, thank you. That'll be enough."

Persephone retreated, voice fading from the room.

"What's with her?" Faraday jerked his head at a camera, untucking as the room warmed.

"What do you mean?"

"She sounds different. Snippier, somehow."

"Oh. That." Dr. Naisson flipped a hand. "Giving the emulation routines a little test run. You know, to see if we like it or not." She dropped her eyes when a chirrup sounded and touched a silver band on her wrist. A tap at its onyx face stopped its sounding, though it still buzzed politely every few seconds.

"Problem?"

"Not really." She checked the band again. Unzipped her coveralls and peeled the sleeves loose, tying them in a knot around her waist.

Leaving her torso covered by nothing but a clinging black t-shirt that accentuated the roundness of her breasts. Faraday glanced at them and away again, glanced back and forced his eyes up to her face. Blushing furiously at her knowing smile, teeth showing whitely behind her parted lips. "So—" He cleared his throat when his voice cracked and tried again. "So what's with the thing-a-ma-jigger?" He waved vaguely at her wrist.

"Bio-monitor." Dr. Naisson held the buzzing silver band up. "Have to wear it because of the Novonox."

"Which is what?"

"Well, as it turns out, a toxin." She tucked up one leg and wrapped her arms around its shin. "'Course I didn't know that when the company convinced me to start taking it. They didn't even admit to it until the side effects began to appear."

He raised an eyebrow in question and she touched at a hidden clasp, peeling the band away from her wrist. Exposing a splotch of missing pigment beneath it, showing whitely against her otherwise dark skin.

He leaned forward, inspecting that oddly pale spot of flesh. "Chemical burn?"

"Vitiligo. Early stages. Hasn't spread yet." The bio-monitor shrieked shrilly at being removed so Dr. Naisson clamped it back into place, slapping its onyx face in annoyance until it quit its bitching and quieted back down again. Even stopped buzzing for a while, though that didn't last long.

"That alarm's not about the vitiligo."

"No," she said softly. "No, it's not. Metabolic degradation." She touched the display on her bracelet and pointed to a tiny, yellow sun symbol. "Body doesn't really thermoregulate anymore, which is why I keep the room so cold."

"Are you sure?" Faraday pointed at the ceiling and the vents pumping out heat.

"I'll be fine," she assured him. But the bio-monitor felt differently. Kept buzzing and flashing that miniature sun warning and second symbol that looked like a helix. "'Scuse me a moment," she murmured, sliding off the bed to cross the room. She touched a panel in the side wall and held her hand there until it glowed blue, pushed inward and slid it aside, exposing a cube that fogged with cold and a double row of syringes lined up in a frame. "Novonox," she explained, shrugging helplessly as she took one down.

The contents swirled sapphire and cerulean—a helix to match the symbol on the bio-monitor's band. With practiced movements, she gripped it tightly and pressed the delivery end against her wrist. Injecting the dosage with a tap of her thumb, a wince of pain as her hand curled into a fist. Set the syringe inside and closed the refrigeration unit where the others like it were chilled until needed, and closed her eyes, leaning against the wall as she rubbed a hand up and down her forearm, lips pressed tight, face lined with pain.

"That bad?" he asked softly.

She nodded and drew a breath. "Like acid, only frozen. Burns when it hits my veins." She pushed away from the wall, walked back to the bed and slumped down in her space.

"How often do you have to take it?"

She shrugged again. "Once a month."

"Ever thought about weaning yourself off it?"

She nodded, smiling ruefully. "Tried to. Twice, in fact." She held up a matching number of fingers that trembled until she tucked them away. "Just about died both times." She pushed at his leg to make more room for herself and claim a larger slice of the bed. "Company's been working on a serum to counteract the side effects. Promised to share it with me just as soon as Armistice was ready for colonization."

"Ouch." He winced in sympathy.

"Pretty much." She heaved a sigh. "Don't suppose there's any chance we'll get it back again?"

Faraday twitched his shoulders. "No telling. Depends on how much Halgren wants to invest. How deeply the Rollers dig in."

"Yeah. I figured." She dropped her eyes and stroked that band, thumb moving back and forth across its surface. "I was gonna stay there, you know. Once the terraforming project was done."

"Forever?"

She nodded without looking up. "Planned to officially retire from planet engineering. Hang up my spurs and let someone else carry the torch."

Faraday smiled crookedly. "Never took you for a homesteader."

"Me either." She smiled ruefully herself. "But it gets old, after a while, always starting over. And this shit they used to extend my life," she stopped stroking and flicked the cuff in disgust, "isn't worth the extra years."

"How many?" he asked, curiously.

"Planets? Or years?"

He shrugged. "Dealer's choice."

"Alright." Dr. Naisson folded her hands, wriggling to get more comfortable. "Twelve planets terraformed. More years than you want to know." Her lips trembled at the edges, smile collapsing in on itself. "It's... difficult sometimes, interacting with people. The drugs, the travel, all the missing years. It leaves you... separated. Out of synch with time."

Faraday nodded in understanding. "I've got ninety-six years with Halgren, just twenty-three of that in wake time."

"Ninety-six? Really?" Her lips curved on one side. "Why, you're just a baby."

He bristled, sensing an insult. "What does *that* mean?"

"Never mind."

Tired. Dismissive. Not wanting to discuss the topic. Faraday tilted his head, curious, tempted to press for more. But the look in her eyes convinced him otherwise. Made it clear he should move on and stop asking about things she didn't want to share.

"Tell me about this." She leaned close and tapped his bandaged ribs, a gentle pressure that made him wince.

Faraday lowered the blanket and touched his side, running his thumb along the bandages, the line of staples hidden beneath. "Explosion mid-ship. Blew pieces of decking and compartment walls everywhere."

"Ah. That explains the trash Top pulled out of you."

Faraday quirked an eyebrow.

"Carbon-plastic debris. Few chunks of titano-steel as well."

He grunted and pulled up the blanket. "Thought there was something in there. Couldn't quite figure out what it was."

That earned him a roll of her eyes. A long-suffering shake of her head as well. "And your hands?" She pressed a finger to the back of one palm.

He turned them over and flexed his fingers, feeling the stitches pull beneath. "Turk got stuck in the hole. Clauson and I had to dig him out." He glanced up sharply. "Did he lose it? Crushed leg," he explained at her blank look. "Were you able to save it?"

"I believe so. Let me check." She stood and left the room, leaning over a desk parked just outside while she tapped away at its surface, reading through the information that came back. "They had to replace the knee with a mechanical but the rest of his leg is fine."

She wiped the panel and shut it back down before walking back to the bed, sank down and tucked up both legs this time, sitting Indian style at one end with Faraday propped up at the other.

The environmentals cut off soon after, leaving the room surprisingly quiet without their whispering hiss. Faraday frowned at the thrumming note they'd hidden—distinctive to a ship in space. "We're moving."

Dr. Naisson lowered her chin and raised it, a slow and deliberate movement of her head. "Long way to Ventress. No real reason to stick around."

"*Hadrian?*"

"Behind us." Her face softened. "With his AI gone, there wasn't really any other choice."

Something inside him twisted, driving a knife into his gut. Even knowing they would leave him, it still hurt hearing it was done.

"There was a… contagion. Inside him. It damaged his AI."

"I know. I'm sorry about that." She caught his eyes to show she meant it. "The models we ran… none of them predicted the velocity of that virus' mutation. Countermeasures couldn't keep up with it. I'm sorry, Faraday," she repeated. "I'm sorry. I really am."

"Not your fault. Not blaming you for that." Faraday grimaced before continuing. "*Hadrian*... He may have passed the virus on to *Persephone*."

"Yeah. I know about that, too." Dr. Naisson's face lost all its laughter. "Finally got my live sample. Not exactly the way I *wanted* to, but…" She trailed off, shaking her head. "Nothing to be done about it, I suppose." She glanced away from him, mouth set in a tight line. "I've been working on a counteragent. Virus is a bastard of a thing, though. Keeps morphing and changing. More like a family of viruses than a single contagion on its own."

"*Hadrian*—" Faraday stopped there, thinking a moment. "If I'd given you that sample, would you…would this...?" He trailed off and caught her eyes, watching her face change.

Soften and turn sad. Eyes crinkling with pity.

"I can't say for sure, but more than likely, no. There wasn't enough time to properly evaluate the virus, live sample or not. The contagion was deep in his systems. Without all the damage... maybe. Who knows." She paused there and considered him a moment. "These things take time, Faraday. Unfortunately, more than he had."

He grimaced and shifted at a sudden stab of pain, cut his eyes away and drew a shaking breath. "Shouldn't have left him," he rasped, scrubbing fingers through his short-clipped hair. "Should've checked the status of the containment pod before I sent the order to abandon ship."

"It wouldn't have mattered."

She touched his hand but he pulled away, turning his head so he wouldn't have to look her in the face.

The pity in it cut right through him, stabbed at his heart like a red-hot knife.

"*Hadrian's* AI was failing," she said gently. "There was nothing you could've done."

"I could've stayed," he muttered bitterly.

"And done what? What exactly would that have accomplished?"

He twitched his shoulders in answer, lips pressed in a hard line.

She reached for him and took his hand, folding it carefully in hers. "Going down with the ship's romantic and all, but it's not exactly practical. Nothing to be gained from it other than ending up dead."

He grimaced and dropped his eyes, swallowing around a lump that choked his throat. "Yeah," he said faintly. "Yeah, I suppose you're right."

But he still wasn't happy about it. Wasn't thrilled with much of anything right now.

"You know, we're lucky to have you." She released his hand and sat back, lacing her fingers in her lap. "Lucky it was you here instead of that puffed up prick Bronsky when those Kekktekian things showed up."

Faraday grunted noncommittally, attention roaming around the room.

"So, was it?"

"Was it what?" he asked distractedly.

"Luck that brought you here?"

His eyes snapped back to her face, to that too-sharp, too-knowing blue-grey gaze.

She bent at the waist and leaned in, staring intently at his face. "Was it coincidence, you showing up and the Kekktekians so soon after, or did Halgren send you here on purpose because they knew something bad was coming our way?"

Faraday blinked blandly, face pointedly, scrupulously blank. "Not sure what you mean, Doctor."

She pursed her lips, looking him up and down. "It wasn't always Faraday, was it?"

Shocked the hell out of him with that question. Faraday went very still—wary now, as well as watchful. Carefully choosing his next words. "And how, pray-tell, did you come by that little tidbit of information?"

"So, it's true then?"

He shrugged and kept staring.

"Silent treatment, eh? Alright. We'll play it your way." She nodded to the white and chrome desk in the next room. "*Hadrian* dumped most of his database to *Persephone*. Including the personnel files."

His hands curled into fists, clutching the blanket tight. "So you've been snooping. That it, Doctor?"

"I was curious," she admitted, matching him stare for stare.

"Find anything interesting?"

"A few anomalies in the data. Couple of things that didn't quite make sense."

"Such as?"

"Red hair."

"What?"

"You've got red hair. Well, red and gold, I guess, and some of it's going grey."

"Thanks for pointing that out," he growled sourly.

"No problem." She smirked back.

"So what's my hair got to do with anything?"

"Your record says you're from Celestine 7."

He quirked an eyebrow. "And?"

"No redheads. Entire colony displaced from Andromere when the terraforming reversed itself. Mostly Indo-Persian with a smattering of Sandochin thrown in."

Dark-skinned, the lot of them. Dark skin, dark eyes, dark hair. Faraday cursed himself for missing it, and Halgren for fucking it up.

"You share this with anyone?"

"Just *Persephone*. Don't particularly plan to tell anyone else." She looked him up and down again. "And it's Anthea, by the way. Call me old-fashioned, but sharing a bed with a half-naked man who calls you Doctor feels a little too close to porn."

He barked a laugh and shook his head, quirking an ironic smile. A real one, this time, without the edge, hands relaxing as the tension bled out of him. "Thomas," he told her, touching his fingers to his chest. "Tom, preferably. Thomas always sounds pompous."

She flashed a smile and extended a hand, pumping his up and down. "So what happened?" she asked when she let it go. "Why the name change and made up record?"

Faraday grimaced and dropped his eyes a moment, wondering how much to say. "Made a mistake. Poked my nose where it wasn't wanted." He glanced up and twitched his shoulders. "They buried me for it."

"Halgren?"

He nodded slowly.

"Must have been some mistake."

"Depends on who you ask."

She waited, obviously wanting more from him, all the details the file failed to mention, but there were things Halgren didn't want him to tell her. Things he didn't want to admit to, if truth be told. "Big secret, eh?"

He shrugged again, lips twisting. "You telling me you don't have any?"

"A few. Which makes us even, I guess." She matched his quirking smile. "So what was it, before Faraday?"

He hesitated before answering. Once that name was out, there was no going back. "Fitzroy. Captain of *Kestrel*."

Anthea's eyebrows lifted. "Combat ship, I take it, not planetary nursemaid or deep space exploration?"

He dipped his head in confirmation. "Ten years in the blackout zone either side of the Madrigal Line."

"And then… this." Anthea waved vaguely, indicating the ship, the stars, the mess they'd left behind. "They assigned you to Armistice as a disciplinary measure? Some kind of punishment?"

"In a way. Mostly they just wanted me to take care of a problem."

"Bronsky?"

Once again she surprised him. Evidently she'd known Bronsky better than he thought.

"Point for the lady." Faraday flipped a two-fingered salute.

"Fat prick always was a troublemaker." Anthea considered him a moment. "You going to tell me what he did or is that another secret Halgren won't let you share?"

He most *absolutely* wasn't supposed to talk about Bronsky, but he was in the mood for sharing, so he gave her what he could. "Bronsky got bored and decided to make a name for himself. Found some trouble in the process that Halgren didn't particularly want."

Anthea waited, letting the silence stretch out. "Oh, c'mon, Tom. You *gotta* give me more than that."

He shouldn't, he really shouldn't, but what the hell, career was already screwed.

Faraday sighed heavily, investigating the bandages on his hands, the stitching just beneath. "Here's the thing: people with too much time on their hands tend to go searching for something to do. In Bronsky's case, that something involved sending an envoy to the Kekktekians without consulting with Halgren Central first."

"Why? To what purpose?"

"Officially? To negotiate a settlement. That's what he told the admiralty, anyway."

"Peace talks? *Bronsky*?" Anthea snorted in disbelief. "Not that guy. Not even *close* to his forte."

Faraday's shoulders lifted. "Not sure the admiralty really believed it either, but Bronsky has connections who covered everything up."

"Which was what, exactly?"

"Honestly? Not even sure. Bronsky's connections buried that deep." Faraday went quiet a moment, thinking, eyes flicking across her face. "My opinion? I think Bronsky wanted to be a hero, so he stirred the Kekktekians up. I think he dangled Armistice in front of them like a carrot and just waited for them to come in and try to claim it for themselves." He tucked his legs up and wrapped his arms around them, wincing as the movement pulled the staples along his ribs. "I even think he gave them access codes to our Halgren beacons so they could disguise themselves and sneak their way here. Where *Hadrian* was waiting. With Bronsky at the helm."

Anthea went very still, eyes stretching impossibly wide. "That's stupid. That's *beyond* stupid. That's downright *negligent.* Putting an entire planet at risk just so he could get his jollies? Who *does* that? Who would even *think* to do that?"

"Bronsky, apparently. Though I can't prove any of it, of course." Faraday shrugged again. "If it makes you feel better, I'm not sure he actually meant to put the planet in any danger, I think he was just naïve. No combat experience," he explained. "He just watched from a distance, listened in on briefs. Then one day, Halgren sends him here and puts him in charge of a whopping big ship with a whole lot of firepower and suddenly he starts getting ideas."

"So, what? He thought he could hold them off? One ship? Against a bazillion of these Roller derby power vessels?"

"There weren't *that* many, but yes. I think he had stars in his eyes and an appetite for admiralty and he convinced himself he could handle whatever the

Kekktekians threw at him. That he'd waltz out the other side a big damn hero with no one the wiser that he'd actually created the problem he attempted to solve."

Anthea's lip lifted, head shaking in disgust. "I retract my earlier statement. Bronsky's not stupid. He's a fucking idiot."

Faraday flashed his teeth. "And I'm a bigger one for accepting this assignment."

The admission surprised a chuckle out of her. Made her tilt her head and smile. "So why did you take it?"

Faraday sobered quickly, smile slipping from his face. He glanced away from her a moment, scanning the starkly decorated room. "Not much choice, really. It was take this or go Grey."

"Mercenary corp?"

He nodded stiffly. "Haven for the military's rejects. The fuck-ups and dispossessed."

Hadn't meant for that to come out so harsh, but those words were out there, no taking them back now.

"Hey."

A touch came at his knee—nothing intimate in it, just a gentle, reassuring caress.

"You know, believe it or not, there *are* people who live quite happily outside the military."

"Not me." Faraday glanced at Anthea and away again. "I've spent too many years with Halgren. I'm out of synch with the galaxy I knew. Reintegration..." He pressed his lips together, shook his head hard. "Not gonna happen. Military's all I know. Ship and crew, the only family I understand."

Another stretch of silence followed—Anthea watching him, Faraday pretending not to notice.

"So what now?" she asked quietly. "You gonna tell Halgren all this?"

"Not sure they'll believe me. No real proof to speak of, except the Rollers themselves, of course."

"There's *Hadrian*'s database. Well, a copy of it anyway. If there's something in there, *Persephone* will ferret it out."

'If' being the operative word. Faraday'd quizzed *Hadrian* a time or two on the subject of Bronsky and his indiscretions before any of this happened, but the AI seemed surprisingly oblivious when it came to his former captain. Which meant either Bronsky'd worked around him on his shenanigans or he'd wiped portions of *Hadrian's* records to hide what he'd done.

Faraday preferred to assume the former, the latter being all *kinds* of illegal, not to mention immoral and generally dickish.

"Thanks." He caught her eyes to show he meant it. "There'll be an investigation—that's standard procedure. If you find something..." He trailed off. "No telling, really. Not sure how things'll fall out."

Not, he suspected, in his favor, given the circumstances and who he was. Bronsky had friends in high places to protect him. Faraday's only saving grace was his record, and Halgren took that from him when they washed away his name.

"What about you and *Persephone*?" he asked to change the subject.

Anthea frowned without answering, shrugged and retrieved her hand. "Start over, I guess. Dump these colonists on Ventress, find another planet to terraform for TerraGen. Hope the company extends the same offer they did before." She was quiet a moment, scanning the room. "What do you think, *Persephone*? You in the mood for more exploration?"

"I go where you go, Anthea. That's always been the way. I have no desire to change that."

Anthea smiled, clearly pleased. "Good. Only… let's find a greener planet this time. One that doesn't take so long to turn into a home."

"Did you have a particular star cluster in mind?"

She pursed her lips, thinking, shook her head and flashed a smile. "You choose. That way I'll be surprised when we arrive."

"I'll start searching for candidates immediately."

"That's my girl."

Faraday chuckled softly. "She's an eager beaver."

"She is, isn't she?" Anthea kept smiling, staring thoughtfully at a camera. "You know, I meant it before." She lowered her chin, turning that soft smile Faraday's way. "About us being lucky to have you. Lost the planet but not the people."

"Lost a hell of a lot of *my* people."

"I know. And I'm sorry." She touched his knee again. "But you got *Persephone* and the rest of us out safely. I call that lucky. I'm grateful for that."

"Lucky." He grunted and turned his face away. "That's me, alright. Luckiest rabbit's foot in the bunch."

Anthea leaned close and touched his face, pinching his chin to make him acknowledge her, look at her, this flesh and blood person who'd given up her bed. "This is where you say 'thank you', and I say 'you're welcome' and then we have some tea and a nice conversation until it's time to tuck everyone into cryosleep."

"And if I don't?"

She smiled evilly. "Then I call Tip and Top back in here and drug you down until we get to Ventress. Is that what you want, Tom? You want me to treat you like that?"

"No," he said slowly. "Rather skip the drugs, if you don't mind. Thank you, Anthea. For everything."

"You're welcome, Tom." She gave his chin a gentle shake, released it and sat back. "Now about that tea. Shall I order it now or wait a bit?"

Faraday pulled a face. "Rather have whiskey. Honestly not a big fan of tea."

"Me either." Anthea clapped her hands. "Whiskey it is. We'll get drunk as skunks and then sleep it off in the freezers on the way to Ventress."

Fourteen

She was the last of the crew to go to sleep and, per her instructions, the first to wake. A pattern they'd agreed to over the years. One *Persephone* knew to never break.

Anthea's privilege to serve as last in line and tour the ship while the others slumbered. Her duty to lock all the compartments down, check the power settings and fail safes before she froze herself and slept. The rest of it… purely preference. In cryosleep she came close to death, everything dialed down to bare existence. Waking could be ugly—often was in her experience, the drugs resulting in some decidedly nasty after effects—and so she chose to wake and be alone. Scrub her body in the shower's confines to remove the layers upon layers of dead skin. Trim her nails and cut her hair, make herself presentable to the world again.

Mostly, though, she liked to walk the ship with nobody else around. Use the muscles that had lain dormant, stretch her legs and the tendons that drove them. Tour the ship like she had before to unlock all the compartments, check the atmospherics and environmentals, make sure no cryo pods failed in transit.

This time, though, things were different. This waking harder, somehow. Her mind fogged with drugs, her body leaden, just exiting the pod a seemingly impossible task. She managed it eventually, and stumbled drunkenly into the main room of her quarters. A space that felt colder than usual. Frigid, even to her.

"Good morning, Anthea."

She grimaced at the greeting, *Persephone's* spritely voice painful to her ears. "Is it?" she mumbled, blinking stupidly. "How long have I—?"

"We're almost there. The shower's ready. I've set the water flow and temperature to your preferred configuration."

"Shower. Right. I need a shower." She tottered toward the glass and metal room, stepped inside and let the system take over. Scrubbing, bathing, trimming everything up while she focused on remaining upright and kicking fogged-up brain into gear.

At some point during those post-freeze ablutions she found herself staring somewhat vaguely at her hands. At dark skin mottled with white patches around the fingernails and knuckles where, in her sleeping, the vitiligo managed to take hold.

Damn the company and their chemicals.

She curled her fingers under, hiding the hated pale spots away. Cryosleep preservatives slowed the spread of the Novonox-induced disease, but nothing could stop it forever. Not even the treatments the company kept promising could give back what she'd already lost.

On her wrist, the bio-monitor twittered, warning her that she lingered in the hot shower too long. Anthea killed the system and emerged in a cloud of steam from the shower, feeling just about human once she'd dressed herself and zipped the coveralls up to her chin. Brain still felt weird and her muscles seemed weaker than she recalled, but fifty years had passed since her last stint in cryosleep. Brain forgot the toll it put on a body. Wanted things to be easier than it remembered.

She left her quarters and walked and walked, working out the kinks. Transiting one ship's tier and another, checking on every last one of her crew's pods. Belatedly remembered *Hadrian's* crew and Faraday sleeping in the hold. Tucked up inside their lifeboat's pods, umbilicals connecting *Hadrian's* ships to *Persephone's* power.

She paused inside the elevator, considering a ship's schematic on the wall. Long way down to that cargo hold and six full ships to check at the end. Her legs already quivering, her back aching and tensing up. The bio-monitor chirruped a trio of warnings about her heart rate and core temperature, the fact she hadn't eaten anything since waking up, and that, ironically, convinced her. Made her mind up on the spot.

"Check on them from the command center." A choice which honestly made more sense. None of her walkabout routine was strictly needed, she just liked to do things that way.

She mashed the bio-monitor into silence, hit the button and rode the elevator up. Exited on Level 31 and strolled down to the command center, using her palm print to access its rounded room.

Lights came on as she stepped inside, glaring harshly off the white and chrome. The atmospherics came on to stir the air which smelled cold and stale after long disuse. The temperature, to her relief, seemed more normal here—cool instead of outright cold.

Smaller space, she told herself. *The rest of the ship will warm soon enough.*

But she didn't remember that ever being a problem. Couldn't recall the last time she'd felt the chill.

The bio-monitor buzzed again so she quieted it with a thumb, sank down into the room's one and only padded chair and closed her eyes to rest a while.

Letting her heart rate slow and core temperature equalize, waiting for the damned bio-monitor to quit its buzzing.

"Are you alright, Anthea?" *Persephone* sounded worried. "Should I—?"

"No, *Persephone*. I'm fine." She squared her shoulders and straightened, gesturing imperiously with one hand. "Display. Monitoring systems. Give me status of the lifeboats in the cargo hold."

Persephone layered a view that wrapped around the command center's walls, showing her a metal space that twinkled, frosted with layers of rime. Six small ships lined up in perfect order, bellies hugged tight to the cargo hold's floor. "Power draw is minimal. Primary systems are in hibernation mode."

"The cryo pods?"

"Optimal. No hardware failures, no containment loss."

Anthea breathed a sigh of relief. Not her crew down there, but their lives still mattered. "And the colony vessels?"

The view changed, cargo hold replaced by a scene of ships and stars. Larger vessels, this time, elongated squares encircled by rotating rings. A tiny troop that bunched up around *Persephone's* many-pointed star, trusting her to guide them truly through the depths of space.

"They're still with us, though the virus has taken its toll."

"How bad?" Anthea asked her. "Is there anything left of them at all?"

"Not much," *Persephone* admitted. "The virus destroyed the AIs' core consciousness. I'm fully controlling them now."

Anthea raised her head, searching for a camera. "Yourself?"

"Some minor degradation. I had to reconfigure my central network, rebuild my core processing unit a few times."

"How many times?"

"One thousand one hundred and ninety-two."

Anthea blinked at the unexpected number—that certainly seemed like a lot. "And now?"

"I'm fine. The contagion is contained."

From her tone, she clearly meant it, but Anthea caught the hesitation, the barest fraction of a pause before she answered. She opened her mouth to question, and changed her mind at the very last instant. She trusted *Persephone* after all these years. If she said she was fine, then she was good to go.

"Forward view. Let's see where we're going."

The cameras panned and the panorama shifted, colony vessels slipping to either side of them with an ocean of black ahead. And far off in the distance, a planet. A sedately spinning orb.

"Enhance."

Anthea scooted forward, balancing just on the edge of her seat, and watched that world draw progressively closer. Take on colors that spoke of landmass, atmosphere and water.

Not the proportions she expected, though. Not the configuration she remembered. "This isn't Ventress," she murmured in some confusion.

"No. I couldn't take the colony ships there."

"Then where?"

Persephone didn't answer, except to add a star chart to the room's display.

Anthea scanned it, searching for something recognizable, and discovered stars and planets, an entire galaxy she didn't know. "Chron," she ordered faintly, fingers shaking as she gripped the chair. "How long have we been out here? How much time has passed since we entered cryosleep?"

The chron popped into existence, glowing in a cool, blue font front and center on the room's display. The numbers they showed her impossible. A stretch of time that didn't make sense.

"One hundred and thirty-seven years." Anthea collapsed against the chair. "Where have you brought us, *Persephone*? What have you done?"

When she responded, *Persephone* sounded as calm as ever, and exceedingly proud of herself. "What you asked of me, Anthea. I found you a new home."

Part II: Distant Seas

Fifteen

Faraday woke to strange surroundings. To the smooth, slick feel of metal beneath him and a glacier's worth of arctic chill. With the stink of something half-dead and slowly decaying tickling at his nostrils, a pulsing *rager* of a headache, and a fuzzy, sour milk and old potatoes taste in his mouth.

Hungover, he thought blearily. Long time since that happened. Ages since he felt this bad. And that smell... *Stinks to high heaven in here. And why the hell is it so cold?*

He shivered, skin prickling with goosepimples as he cracked his crusted eyelids open—like lifting anvils, they felt that heavy—and took stock of his situation. Found a room that stubbornly remained out of focus, all its details blurry and indistinct. Everything white-on-white with hints of grey, blackened lines that failed to intersect.

"Where the fuck am I?" Struggling, he rolled onto his side and levered himself up on an elbow, blinking hard to chase the haze away and make sense of this monochrome room.

Belatedly realized he was buck-naked and laid out spread-eagle on some sort of platformed metal bed. The room around him starkly antiseptic: white walls, brushed metal decking, stacks of cabinets lining one side and a whole host of electronic devices cluttering up the other.

Some sort of stand-up shower cubical or decontamination station shoved in a corner, and a very tall, very intimidating, copper-skinned robot looming storkishly at his side. "Good morning, Captain," the android greeted him, blank-faced and slit-eyed and oddly familiar with its armored form and verdigris tinge.

"Who the fuck're you?" Faraday croaked. And because it begged to be asked, "Why am I naked? And what the hell is that smell?"

"That smell is you, Captain. Or what I scraped off of you, anyway." The robot gestured to the cubicle in the corner and a stinking layer of sludge griming the plates of its metal floor. "Hypersleep slows the metabolism, but your hair follicles and skin cells continue to slough off and die."

"Hypersleep," Faraday repeated. Not a hangover, then, just the aftermath of his body working all that cryosleep crap out of his system. And this room, that cold, those stark white walls, *"Persephone,"* he said, remembering. "I'm on *Persephone,* not *Hadrian.* He's gone." The shock of it hit him hard, forgotten in the fog of cryosleep and its near-term memory suppression after-effects. Awake now, it all came rushing back: his warship gone, his command lost with it, and *Hadrian...* "*Hadrian's* dead."

Forced himself to confront that fact, painful as it was. Suffered the memories that came rushing in to beat with hammers at his muddled-fugged brain. He rubbed at his temple with an unsteady hand, fingers scraping through freshly buzzed stubble. Felt at the back of his head, the top, the sides...

"What the fuck? You gave me a haircut, too?"

"It was… more convenient to trim your hair than attempt to cull the biologics out of it."

"Gross." Faraday shivered in the room's chill, grimacing at an ache infecting his muscles and bones, that god-awful taste in his mouth. "Don't remember it being this bad. Feel like I went a couple rounds with one of the cargo hold's loaders."

The robot caught his chin and blanked one eye slit, concentrating the full power of the other on Faraday's face. Nearly blinding him in the process, driving an ice pick into his brain. He tried to pull away, but the robot's fingers only tightened, maintaining their iron grip.

"Mind telling me what you're doing?"

"Retinal analysis and passive neural pathway examination." Mercifully, that hand let go and the cobalt flare turned somewhere else. Leaving Faraday blinking at tiny sunbursts scattered like dandelion dust throughout his eye. "The effects of protracted hypersleep on the human body are uncharted. The data we've gathered will help inform future study."

"Protracted? What do you mean, 'protracted'? How long—?"

"Lie down, Captain. Lie down, please," the android repeated, and flourished a hand full of articulated digits equipped with a dismaying array of sharp-edged knives.

Faraday went very still as every last one of them pointed his way. "What exactly are you planning to do with those?"

"Your wound needs tending. I'm here to help. Now lie back, and stay very still." The robot pressed him down and held him there, poking at Faraday's middle with its non-knife hand. Being none-too-gentle in that prodding, the metal-clad bastard, and its investigations of a baby-pink line of puckered scar.

As instructed, Faraday gritted his teeth and tried his best not to move, but each touch at that soft and tender flesh sparked an electric shock that made him tense up and hiss in pain.

"You're twitching, Captain."

"Of course I'm twitching. You're poking me in a sensitive—*ow!* What was that for?"

"You've got a little puss here." The android squeezed a section of scar tissue and some sort of yellowish gunk oozed out.

"Gross." Faraday shuddered and looked away, taking stock of the room around him while the android teased out more puss. Recognizing the tell-tale signs of a surgery in its fittings, its stocks of supplies and medical equipment. The bed he lay on designed for hygiene and drainage with no thought at all for the patient's comfort. "This is the med bay."

"It is," the android acknowledged.

"And you're what? Some sort of copper-clad doc-bot or something?"

"Currently."

"Currently?" That certainly didn't inspire confidence. "What do you *normally* do?"

"Planetary survey and analysis."

"A ground pounder. Fuck." Faraday shrank away from the robot's prodding finger, the butcher's hand with its kit of knives. "How's about you just let me see to that wound myself?"

"I'm afraid I can't allow that." The med-bot trapped Faraday's wrist with its free hand, shackling it with his copper fingers to pull him close. "I assure you, Captain, I am quite capable of seeing to your medical treatment. I've been programmed with all the necessary knowledge on human anatomy and physiology as well as the latest in complex surgical procedures."

Faraday licked his lips, eyes on that blank metal face. "Wound's scarred over. What—What sort of surgery do you have planned?"

"Subdermal excision and ablation followed by anomalous tissue extraction."

Faraday squinted as his fuzzed brain attempted to translate all that into something that made sense. "Why?" he asked, stalling. Giving it time to smarten up.

"Cryosleep retards the body's restorative processes, resulting in overgrowth of subcutaneous tissue and hypertrophic scarring of both the internal and external dermal layers."

"Subcutaneous what-the-what?"

"Tissue and hypertrophic scarring." The robot extruded a needle from the end of a copper finger. "Your wound healed, Captain, but it didn't heal quite right."

"Ain't that the fuckin' story of my life?" Faraday winced when the needle pricked him, sending a bright white stab of agony twisting through his guts. "What is that?" he gasped through clenched teeth, stomach muscles knotted up into rock-hard blocks.

"Local anesthetic. The tissue excision can be... uncomfortable, otherwise."

"I'll bet," he muttered, suffering yet another prick.

The needle finger jabbed a dozen more times, each shot an ice-cold entry dispensing anesthetic to deaden Faraday's flesh. Eventually, his entire core turned numb, at which point the needle disappeared, replaced by one of the many scalpels on offer. "Now lie still," the robot instructed. "This will go easier if you don't move."

"What if I—?"

"Don't. Move." The med-bot brought the scalpel finger close.

Wide-eyed and staring, unable to look away, Faraday watched it slice across his middle, splitting the skin with surgical precision as it tracked the line of that ugly scar. Reach the end and lift away, retracting into the android's finger with a sibilant hiss. A tiny saw replaced it, dipping inside the incision to trim the extraneous flesh, and a laser knife to clean things up and cauterize the wound.

To be honest, it was all rather gruesome. And bloody. And somehow wrong. Primarily because he couldn't feel anything—a little tugging here and there, but not a jot of pain. The sounds of that surgery were what got to him. The buzz of that saw, the sizzle of flesh. The smell of his own flesh cooking—the combination made his gorge rise.

"Think I'm gonna hurl," he warned, hand clapped to his mouth.

The med-bot, ever attentive, slid a bed pan onto the table. "Hurl there, if you can, please. Vomiting in your wound would be most ill-advised."

"Right. Thanks. I think." Faraday pulled the bed plan close, shivering in that coldest of cold rooms. "Do I really need to be naked for this?"

"No. But it'll be easier to clean you up after." The med-bot burned a bit of tissue with the laser, suctioned up a fat blob of blood and loose flesh and paused to examine the newly cleaned wound. "Well. That's unfortunate."

"What's unfortunate?" Faraday propped himself up on his elbows, wanting a better view of his belly. "What's wrong? What did you do?"

"Nothing," the robot answered quickly. *Too* quickly in Faraday's estimation. "It's just… this may take a little longer than I initially anticipated." The laser winked out and the sharp-edged scalpel reappeared. "I think it would be best if you slept through the rest of this, Captain."

"No," he refused flatly. "No, you are *not*—"

"I'm sorry, Captain. It's not your choice."

The robot pricked Faraday with another needle—this one slid into his throat and out again before he even registered its presence—and his vision blurred instantly, brain fogging as he drifted away. "Son-of-a-bitch," Faraday managed before everything turned black.

*****

When he woke again, it was in yet another room—not the surgery this time with its white walls and metal floors, someplace smaller and more confined. Cold, like the rest of *Persephone*. Sterile seeming with its no-color decor. On the plus side, he felt a soft surface beneath him that, on further inspection, turned out to be a real bed. Mattress, sheets, the whole nine yards, even a couple of blankets, wonder of all wonders. Still naked as a jay bird beneath it all—he figured that out right quick. And not alone in his nakedness, either. A copper statue stood silent sentry in one corner, waiting patiently for him to wake. Not a scalpel in sight this time, though. No needles or medical equipment. Just four walls, a bed and that copper-skinned centurion, and an increasingly uncomfortable pressure in Faraday's bladder.

Groaning, he rolled onto his side and sat up in slow increments. Wary of the dull ache in his belly, the tender line of freshly closed skin. "Hey. Metal skin."

With a whir of gears and pistons, the med-bot relaxed and unlocked, cobalt eyes flaring in its copper face as it pushed free of the entrapping corner and crossed the room to Faraday's bed. "Are you in pain, Captain?"

"No. Yes. Maybe." Faraday waved the question away. "Bathroom. Where can I find one?"

The robot raised an arm and pointed to a door in the side wall. "The lavatory—"

"Yeah-yeah. I got it." Faraday swung his legs over the side of the bed and climbed unsteadily to his feet.

"Do you require assistance, Captain?"

"*Nooo*. Most definitely not." Faraday inched around the copper-skinned med-bot, yanked the bathroom door open and hustled his bare ass inside. Where he relieved himself at great leisure, and with a shuddering, nigh-ecstatic sigh.

Nothing like a good, long pee, especially one long-denied. Cold took away some of the pleasure, of course—hard to enjoy yourself when you were half-freezing to death and your manly bits kept trying to tuck up into your belly. So after draining his bladder dry and evacuating his leavings, Faraday hustled on back to the bedroom and, with his teeth chattering loud as castanets, wrapped a blanket around his naked self. "God damn, chop-bot. Why's this ship always so cold?"

"Dr. Naisson prefers it. The cooler temperature is more suited to her genetic modifications."

"You mean degradation." That's what Anthea called it. All the damage TerraGen's crud chemicals caused to her system.

"The side effects of the life extension treatments are unfortunate."

Faraday grunted. "They're a lot more than that. Vitiligo's mostly cosmetic, rest of it really jacked her up."

The med-bot was quiet a moment, watching him in its blank-faced, emotionless way. "Dr. Naisson knew the consequences when she signed her contract. They all did. The potential for them, anyway."

"All?"

"The other scientists. They all take the Novonox now."

"Even knowing the side effects?"

The robot nodded. "The tradeoffs are apparently worth it."

"Chemical dependence in exchange for centuries of existence? Living in an ice box the rest of your life?" Faraday snorted and shook his head. "Not exactly what I'd call living. Not sure I'd go that route myself."

If the med-bot had an opinion, he didn't offer it, but Faraday had a feeling the android disagreed. Different frame of reference, after all. Mechanicals survived as long as their parts and electronics, which could be a very long while, if properly maintained.

Why should humans be any different? Who wouldn't extend their life if they could?

"So, what happens if they run out?" Faraday asked.

"Statistically speaking, that's unlikely. We synthesize the solution locally from chemicals distilled in the osmogenesis lab. I can show you—"

"Thanks, but I think I'll pass."

"Oh." The robot sagged in disappointment. "Well, if you change your mind—"

"I won't."

"But if you do—"

"What about this room?"

"What?" The robot twisted at the waist, glancing left and right. "What about it?"

"Why's *this* room so goddamn cold. Does Dr. Naisson come here often?"

"No. Not particularly." The android's eye slits fluttered. "Not unless you ask her to."

Faraday frowned. "What's that supposed to mean?"

"These are your quarters now, Captain. Dr. Naisson assigned this suite of rooms to you."

The frown took on an edge—part confusion, part upset. "Why would she assign me quarters?"

The robot hesitated for a fraction of a second and then shrugged with exaggerated care. "She thought you'd want them."

"But I'm not—"

"There are clothes, if you're tired of being naked." The med-bot stepped around the bed and touched at the wall directly across from the bathroom door. The panel there slid smoothly, revealing a compact and well-ordered closet with no less than a dozen black and silver uniforms lined up in a perfect row.

Wrapped up tight in his blanket cape, Faraday touched at one with a trembling hand, fingers tracing the lines of the snug-fitting pants, the short-waisted jacket, the dark shirt that went beneath. The captain's stars pinned to the collar, his name picked out in silver thread on the breast. Every last one a duplicate, right down to the half dozen identical pairs of boots. "Where did you find these?"

"*Persephone* made them. She took your measurements while you were sleeping and uploaded a tailoring program to one of my kin."

"Why?" Faraday asked, increasingly confused.

"Yours were lost with *Hadrian*. And the clothes you came to us in were damaged."

"A dozen, though…" That went beyond generous. And six pairs of boots—Faraday had no need for so many. "Thank you," he said, and meant it. "Tell *Persephone*—"

"You can tell her yourself." The med-bot plucked a pair of pants from the closet, a jacket to go with them and held them out. "Dr. Naisson asked me to bring you to her once you were well enough. And, obviously, more dressed," it added, handing Faraday a shirt.

Sixteen

The ground pounder delivered Faraday as ordered, guiding him truly through the stacked ring bowels of *Persephone's* inner spaces to the round-room of her compact bridge.

"Enter," Anthea said when the door buzzed, and, "Thank you, Tip. You're dismissed," once Faraday stepped in. Pale-faced and shadow-eyed after his decades' long nap in hypersleep, but more alert than when she first woke him. Scrubbed and trimmed to military perfection, black uniform crisply pressed, greying red-gold hair buzzed to regulation length stubble.

Sharp-looking in Halgren's standard issue jet-black, captain's stars shining bright on his collar, name tag picked out in matching silver thread. Freckled face a map of planes and angles—handsome enough, if sometimes grim.

Anthea gestured for him to wait while she spoke to the android parked outside the door. "Go find Top," she told him. "Tell him to get the med bay ready."

"Will you be waking the other scientists then, Doctor?"

Anthea glanced at Faraday behind her. "Not sure yet. Just get things ready. *Persephone* will provide instructions once we figure things out."

"Very good, Doctor. We'll stand by for now." Tip stepped back and pivoted smoothly, striding away as the bridge door slid closed. Leaving Anthea alone with Faraday, and the images projected on the wraparound walls.

In silence, he considered them, turning a slow circle in that rounded room. Hands resting on the padded back of the bridge's padded chair—every panel around him filled with greenery, a vista of vegetation in its many and varied forms. Everything alien and most obviously so, despite the basic structures that looked so familiar, the shapes of grass and trees and flowers.

"Do you like it?" Anthea asked quietly, stepping silently to his side.

"Like it? What *is* this? Where the fuck are we?" Faraday demanded, eloquent as ever. Which was to say, succinct and brutally to the point.

"Planetside, obviously." Anthea matched his temper with a sweet-as-pie smile. "Those are trees, and that's grass…" She pointed to the displays on their left and right. "Those dark spots in the distance are some kind of herd animal. *Persephone's* calling them moosealopes, but I'm not sure I—"

"Planet?" Faraday didn't sound happy. "What the fuck are we doing on a planet?"

"Came all the way here to find it. Seemed a shame to just sit up there and stare at it from orbit."

"*Where*, Anthea?" Faraday's hand landed on her shoulder, gripping hard in his upset. "What planet am I looking at? And *don't* try to tell me that's Ventress. I've *been* there and there's nothing green thanks to that red dwarf, blood light sun."

Sighing, Anthea bowed her head, choosing her words with care. "You're right, this isn't Ventress. To be honest, I'm not quite sure where we are."

Faraday's hand slipped from her shoulder. He backed up, shaking his head. Scared now as well as angry, and who could blame him? He'd gone to sleep with stars around him, and expected to wake up to the same.

This planet was never accounted for. *Persephone's* detour wasn't in the cards.

"Not sure," he said, staring. "What do you mean you're not sure? This is a science vessel outfitted for interstellar travel driven by one of the universe's most powerful AI. How in hell can she not know where we are?"

"No breadcrumbs," Anthea said simply.

"Breadcrumbs? What the fuck does that mean?"

"You know, clues. A trail of information."

"What the hell are you going on about? You've got star charts, navigation systems, how much more do you need?"

Anthea sighed again and started over. "Look. It's probably easier if I just show you. *Persephone*." She glanced at a camera. "Stellar observation mode. Three hundred sixty degree view." She folded her arms and waited, fingers tapping impatiently at her arm. "Any day now," she muttered after several seconds, and eventually, the green faded out.

With a flicker, the wall displays blanked, returning to their default, white-on-white setting. Star charts were a relatively simple thing—static data updated with overlays stored in the science vessel's central database. No processing required to display them, nothing to do, really, but access and transmit. But *Persephone* delayed and delayed and delayed some more. Long enough that Anthea started to worry, and even Faraday finally took notice.

"Something wrong?" he asked behind her.

"Nah. It's probably just some affectation." She glanced at him over her shoulder. "Goddamn emulators are always getting in the way."

"Warned you about those, didn't I?"

"Wasn't exactly my idea, if you remember. It was *Hadrian* that put that idea in her head."

Faraday grimaced and glanced away. Sore spot there, even now.

"Sorry." She set a hand on his arm. "I didn't—"

"It's fine. Just let it go."

Anthea watched him for a moment, and with some misgivings, acquiesced. Faraday and those moods of his were a problem for another day. It was *Persephone* that gave her pause. Those hesitations weren't quite right.

With a touch at the wall, she keyed a panel and accessed the ship-wide diagnostics—a broad array of monitoring systems and analytics packages that crawled through *Persephone's* systems, investigating everything it encountered—and discovered a catalogue of errors across the board. Stack overflows and cascading failures, cycles of reboots and rebuilds and restarts that repeated again and again.

She's worse, Anthea realized, scanning it. *The virus damaged* Persephone *more than she's letting on.*

"What is it?" Faraday asked when her fingers trembled. "What'd you find?" He peered over her shoulder.

"Nothing for you to worry about. Just something I need to look into later." She shut the diagnostics window down in a hurry, praying Faraday's sharp eyes hadn't noticed those errors, and soon after, the room's wall flickered, darkening to storm clouds and midnight black.

Dropping the bridge into smothering darkness that wrapped them close about.

"Anthea." Faraday touched her arm. "What's going on?"

"It's nothing, Tom. Just a processing delay." She turned around to face him, standing so close they almost touched, as the stars came out and painted the walls, frosted her hair, sparkled off Faraday's collar devices.

"You're sure there's nothing wrong with her?"

"Perfectly. Absolutely. One hundred percent." She flashed a false smile to prove it that made him frown and squint at her face. But he nodded after a moment—reluctantly, making it clear they weren't done—and raised his eyes from her lying face to the walls with their black and silver, the blue-and-green planet sitting dead center of one of the displays.

Majestic in its unhurried spinning, atmosphere swirling in feathered clouds. Flawless—that's how Anthea viewed it. Perfect in every sense of the word.

As for Faraday… hard to tell, really. Face of his was difficult to read. Except when he was angry—that came through clear enough. Or irritated. Or annoyed.

"No data tags," he noted, eyes flicking around the walls.

"There is… limited information," *Persephone* explained.

"Meaning what, exactly?"

"This." *Persephone* layered in contextual data, adding celestial registrations and star types, the location and distance of each. Not much when it came right down to it, but those bits and pieces were all she had.

Faraday studied it with wrinkled brow, turning in a slow circle as he scanned the walls. "No names, just science designations."

"No one *to* name them." Anthea stepped in and selected a data tag at random, spreading her fingers to expand the view in the vicinity of that star. Revealing dozens of planets orbiting around it, asteroid fields and a thousand moons. "Exploratory missions map out the dark spaces, catalog the stars and planets inside them to build out navigational charts like these." She gestured at the walls again, all that velvety blackness and sugar stars. "Government comes along later. Delegates naming conventions for all these newly-discovered celestial bodies to Halgren and, *boom!*, you've got a star chart. Everyone gets a new map."

"So why doesn't this one have any names?"

"Because Halgren never came here." Anthea touched his arm and found it rigid—muscles tensed beneath the midnight jacket's sleeve. "We're not *on* the map because no one's published it yet. *We're* the explorers, understand?"

"No. No, that's impossible." He jerked free of her hand and backed up until he ran into the chair. Wincing as it struck his side, eyes narrowing with a look of pain. "Where?" he rasped around it. "Where have you taken us? What planet is this? What galaxy? What sector?"

"Tom. Just calm down, you're hurting."

"No." He jerked his head. "That's not it." But she could see it in his movements, the guarded way he pressed his hand to his side. Old wound there and newly mended, his body working overtime to knit everything back together. "Where?" he repeated when she slid in close—not angry now, just increasingly tired. "Tell me, Anthea. Tell me everything. I need to know what's going on."

"You're not gonna like it."

"Try me." He lifted his chin.

"Alright," she said quietly. And glancing past him, "But you might want to take a seat in that chair."

"I'm fine standing," he insisted, refusing for no other reason than he could. Stubborn, which he often was. Foolish. She put that down to exhaustion.

"Fine. You wanna stand? Stand." She poked his chest. "But don't say I didn't warn you. *Persephone.* Virtual immersion. Overlapping display." Smirking, she folded her arms and rocked back onto her heels. "Show him everything you've got on record. Start with Armistice and take us to here."

"Acknowledged, Anthea. Accessing that information."

Every light in the room cut out at once, dropping them into darkness that left them blind. For several seconds, the room stayed that way, and then the darkness slowly retreated as a source of light appeared. Casting a wan, thin glow across the padded chair, hovering throne-like in a vast and empty space. No walls, no floor, no ceiling, no sense at all of the rounded room. Just that chair with Faraday and Anthea on either side of it and stars spreading in every direction.

An interesting optical illusion, considering Anthea could still feel the solidity of the decking beneath her feet, but disconcerting the first time through, and absolute *murder* on anyone fresh out of hypersleep with all that fluid pent up in their ears and their equilibrium shot to hell.

The lights went out and Faraday swayed, looking distinctly green as he grabbed the back of the frost-white chair.

"Told you you should've sat down." Faraday glared woozily, struggling not to retch while Anthea folded her arms and just smiled, enjoying his discomfort immensely. If pressed, she'd admit to a teeny-tiny sadistic streak, so she had her fun and eventually took pity. "*Persephone.* Dial down the translucence."

"It won't look as pretty," the AI complained.

"Look even *less* pretty if Captain Macho Man here upchucks on his shiny new boots."

"Ah. Good point. Adjusting settings." *Persephone* dialed the translucence down until the outline of the room reappeared.

With those reference points to focus on, Faraday breathed a little easier. Peeled his fingers free after a few deep breaths, replacing the death grip with a featherlight pressing of his fingertips to the padded chair's back. Using its solidity as a sort of anchor to ground him in that shadow-lined room. "What is this?" he asked in a muted voice.

"Virtual immersion."

"I get that. We've got these on every ship. I meant what is *this*?" He gestured broadly at the panels wrapping around them. "What star chart? What sector? Where *are* we?"

"Oh! Right." Anthea tapped a finger to her lips, turning in a circle as she searched for a particular star. "This," she said, "is Armistice." She stood on tiptoe to touch a silver point and expand the system around it. "Advance from here, *Persephone*. Display the track line of our travel."

"Yes, Anthea," she answered, and the view of Armistice's system shrank. Pulled backward into a larger map that turned and advanced in skipping increments—one star chart replacing another, track line tracing a path from Armistice to Elgin 5 where they abandoned *Hadrian's* corpse. After that... nothing. Blank spot. Midnight and infinite emptiness, a black hole of massive emptiness where additional star charts should've been. Until suddenly, quite suddenly, the stars came flooding back. *Persephone's* track line dead-ending above a planet of sapphire and emerald green. No connection to the departure at Elgin 5. No indication of where they'd transited once they'd left.

As if they'd traveled here by magic, skipping past all those missing stars without leaving so much as a trace of their passage behind.

"I don't get it." Faraday shook his head. "Where's the rest of it? What happened to those missing star charts? *Persephone's* trackline—"

"Gone, Tom. They're all gone," Anthea told him. "Lost along the way. Dropped from *Persephone's* database to make room—"

"Bullshit. She's AI. Their memory's expandable and redundant—copies upon copies created over time. They never lose *anything*, Anthea, everyone knows that. Every last bit and byte of their existence is recorded, backed up and retained."

"Not arguing the design specs. But faults happen. Systems degrade." She shrugged apologetically, turning a sad smile at a watching camera. "AI minds may be superior to ours, but they're not perfect, Tom. Nothing is."

"Storage corruption." He cocked his head. "That really what you want me to believe?"

"Don't *want* you to believe much of anything. Just telling you the facts as I know them." And the ones he was ready to hear. The rest of it would come later. Once he'd accepted that things wouldn't change. "She ran autonomously for a long time, Tom." Anthea tilted her head, stepping close. "Amassed *reams* of information her designs never accounted for. Masses of—"

"No. No, I don't accept that. There must be, what? Five, six redundant back-ups?"

"And not one of them complete." This arguing was pointless, but Anthea checked her irritation with an effort and attempted to calm him with a gentle touch. "What you have here," she nodded at the star-strewn space, hands resting on his rigid arms, "is what she retained. An amalgamation of the data that's left."

His breathing quickened as he glanced around, searching the room for answers that weren't there. "There must be something—"

"No. There isn't. *Persephone's* a science vessel, not military. *Hadrian*—"

"Don't you *dare* blame *Hadrian*." Faraday brushed her hands away, swayed and grabbed at the chair.

"I'm not, Tom. I wouldn't." Anthea side-stepped until she could see his face. "But *Hadrian* was military, which made his priorities different. *Persephone*..." She trailed off, looking past him to a camera. "A science vessel creates, Tom. She protected what she felt was most important. Us," she explained when he raised his eyebrows. "There were some… challenges along the way that required sacrifices to be made. Some things…" She shook her head. "Unfortunately, some things just got lost."

"And Ventress?" He set his jaw, muscles bulging beneath the skin. "What happened to Ventress?"

"Gone, Tom. It's all gone. We passed it by and there's no going back."

"So, we're *stuck* here. That what you're telling me?"

She shrugged helplessly. "It would appear so. I don't see another way."

"Fuck." Faraday sighed tiredly, hand lifting to rub at his temple. "Marooned at the ass end of nowhere on a backwater planet that doesn't even have a name. It's a joke," he said. "It's all a joke." He laughed bitterly, scanning the walls. The galaxy of stars around him, the blue and green orb spinning at its center. "What the fuck am I supposed to do here? How the hell do I explain this to my crew?"

"Tell them it's an opportunity to start over. A chance to make a new life." Anthea killed the astral projection and the floor returned, the rounded ceiling overhead. The views of green outside the ship with its fields of grass and stands of trees. "This isn't some lifeless dustball, Tom. *Persephone* found us a *green* world. A water planet brimming with life."

On cue, something round and fat appeared and sauntered close to a camera— hippo-shaped yet fur-covered and waddling like a grouchy old bear. It squatted and shat a pile of pellets that stacked up in a messy pyramid, wiped its feet on the grass a dozen or so times and lumbered off toward the trees.

"What the hell was that?"

Anthea shrugged. "Whatever you want to name it. We've got the drones out collecting samples, but we haven't gotten around to cataloguing the planetary zoology as yet. Except for the moosealopes, of course. *Persephone* gets credit for that." She flashed a smile at his sour look—a response that made him frown all the harder, and positively *glower* when she laughed at his sour puss. "Oh c'mon, Tom," she said, bumping his hip. "Aren't you the *least* bit curious? This is a new planet. An entirely alien world."

"Gave up planets," he grumped. "Lived on ships for most of my life."

"Well, you're gonna have to get used to this one." She reached for him, with some hesitation, and touched his cheek, stroked his skin. "There's opportunity here if you give it a chance. You, me, the rest of them—we can start over. Carve out a new life."

"As what?" he asked bitterly. "Some sort of clod-hopping dirt farmer?"

"If that's what you want," she answered evenly. "That's the whole *point* of fresh starts, after all."

"All I ever wanted to be was a starship captain. Where do I find *that* in your fresh start?"

"That's not fair, Tom."

"It wasn't meant to be."

"Well, aren't you just a grumpy old cuss?" Anthea jerked her hand from his face and curled it into a fist behind her back. Despite her best efforts, she felt her patience slipping—she really, *really* wanted to plant that fist in his gut. But if she'd learned anything in her hundreds of years, it was how to read people and figure out what motivated them. What would help them and what would hurt. That some looked up and others out, chose planetside or escaped to the stars.

Faraday here was military—punching things came as natural as breathing air. More than that, he was a starstrider, and never meant to sit still gathering dust.

Gonna take some time to win him over. And a whole lot more patience than I've presently got.

But she had time, didn't she? All the time in the world. And as for patience...

High time I was better at that.

She studied Faraday's face, those wounded, angry eyes. "This world needs more than farmers, Tom. *You're* needed. You just can't see it yet."

"For what?"

She cupped his cheek. "I'll show you. *Persephone,*" she called to a camera. "Give me visual on the colony ships."

The wall panel in front of the chair remained green, but the rest of them cascaded with changes. Swapping trees for six tall metal towers. Six planet-bound, tails-down ships.

Parked in the soft, green earth of this world, nose ends pointing toward the clouded sky. Propulsion rings revolving in hitching circles as they drank in the shifting sunlight filtering through the inconstant clouds. Suckling power from that distant energy source to feed the fuel cells inside them and keep the bare essential systems alive.

In the sunlight, the damage to their chassis showed clearly. The dents and dings, craters and rents.

"*Persephone* hasn't shared everything, but it was a hard road getting here. A long road, understand? Across light years upon light years of space." Anthea caught his hand and held it, caught his eyes and held those, too. "They can't go back, Tom, even if they wanted to. Even if we could chart a path, they'd never make it."

"You don't know that."

"I do. Just look at them." She squeezed his hand. Made sure it hurt. "Ten thousand people in each of those ships. *Hadrian* saved them, and before he died, gave them over to *Persephone's* care. If we try to leave, they'll die, Tom. But there's a chance here. A chance to live."

For a long time, he said nothing. Just looked at her. Searched her eyes. "You're suggesting we make a home here?"

"Why not? Where else would we go?"

He raised his eyes to the front display with its spreading sea of green, scanned the views of the earth-bound ships around him—scared now, she could tell, but trying mightily to hide it away. "It's green. That's good, right?"

"In theory," she said after much hesitation.

He glanced down at her. "You know that isn't helping, right?"

Anthea shrugged. "Just trying to be honest. Planets don't come with care and feeding instructions, or warnings about all the things that might kill you. Green planet like this..." She glanced away from him, letting her eyes drift around the room. "Hate to say it, but the same things that bring life to a world can spell death to the unadapted and unwary."

"Like humans."

"Like us," she nodded. "That's why I need your help."

"My help. You need *my* help? What does a scientist need from a broken down old ship captain?"

"I need you to lead, Tom. I need you to find a way for these people to survive."

"Is that all?" he muttered incredulously. Sucked in a breath and blew it back out. "This sucks, you know that?"

"It's not *that* bad."

"We got shanghaied out to the middle of nowhere, woke up on some unknown, unnamed planet that, by all accounts, has every potential to kill us, and now *you* tell me it's *my* job to make sure that doesn't actually happen. How is *any* of that considered 'not that bad'?"

Anthea cocked her head and pursed her lips, staring narrowly at his face. "You're cranky, you know that?"

"Of *course* I'm fucking cranky. I woke up naked getting poked and prodded by some metal-skinned proctologist, with a hangover to end all hangovers and a headache that *still* won't go away. Now *you*—"

"You mention that to Tip?"

"Who?"

"Tip. The robot who brought you here."

"Once he was done butchering me." Gingerly, Faraday touched at his side. "Gave me a couple of pills and told me to sleep it off."

"Did you take them?"

"Hell no. Hate meds."

Anthea just rolled her eyes. "So, what'd you do with them?"

"Tossed 'em. What? Your tin can torturer wouldn't tell me what they were so I pitched them in a corner and left them for one of the maintenance droids to clean up."

"And now you're in pain and you want to complain about it."

"*No.* I'm *complaining* because I woke up to this... this... shit show reality and you telling me I'm stuck here for the rest of my days." He flailed his arms in frustration, nearly shouting at her by the end.

Anthea let him have his little rant—enjoyed it on some level, actually, man looked like a giant chicken flapping his arms like that. "You feel better now that you got that out?" she asked, blinking blandly at his irate face.

"A little," Faraday admitted, dropping his arms with a sigh. "Sorry I shouted. It's just this, all this..." He waved at the views on the walls. "It's all a bit much to take in, ya know?"

She nodded. "Actually, I do. Threw me for a loop at first, as well. But a few weeks of study and you start to—"

"*Weeks?*" Faraday goggled. "You've been here for *weeks* and you just woke me up?"

"Weeks, months, what does it matter?" Smiling, Anthea slipped her arm through his. "Point is, I've had some time to send out probes and collect samples, which means I'm not *completely* in the dark about our littler greener-than-green world."

"Samples. You've got samples?" Faraday kept blinking at her like he didn't quite know what was going on.

"Soil, water, atmosphere. Clamshells are still working on the flora and fauna inventory, and besides the fact that it's alkaline, we don't have all that much data on that salt sea out there—"

"We don't?"

"Drones sank."

"They didn't *sink*," *Persephone* corrected. "Something *made* them sink."

Faraday's eyes flicked from Anthea to a camera. "What's the difference?"

"Depends who you ask. Personally, I think the drones were compromised. Some sort of... adverse reaction to the chemical composition of the sea water that degraded their water tight seals."

"And *Persephone*?"

"Got her own theory." Anthea nodded to a camera. "Thinks there's something down there... hunting them, I guess you'd say."

"And this something. You've seen it?"

"No, Captain." The admission hurt her—that came through in *Persephone's* voice. "The drones all stream video back to me, but it cuts off before they disappear. All we ever see is water, then darkness before the feed blanks out."

"Interesting," Faraday murmured, turning a raised eyebrow look Anthea's way.

"Doesn't really matter who's right and who's—either way, we're blind to what's in this world's ocean. And since I happen to be fresh out of aquabots—"

"Aquabots?" Faraday snickered. "Whose dumb idea was it to call them that?"

"*Mine.*" Anthea glared. "The good news, in case you're wondering, is we've got breathable atmosphere. Again, in *theory*," she amended before Faraday got too excited. "Surveys show all the right elements are present, it's the extra stuff we're still trying to figure out." She touched a panel and accessed the registry where all of the planetary analytics data was stored, sorting through dozens upon dozens of data windows until she found the results of the drones' atmospheric sampling. "Elemental gas mixture is slightly off from optimal for humans—"

"How far off?"

"Oxygen's a little low, nitrogen's a little high. Nothing too severe, but any amount of extended exertion and you'll feel it. Soil samples look pretty good." She brought that data up as well. "Plenty of nutrients, frequent precipitation— that's why everything around here's so green, by the way. Wouldn't *drink* the water, mind you, but with some processing it should be alright."

"So, we can live here?"

"Again, *in theory*." Faraday frowned. In his defense, she was saying that a lot. "But there are thousands of things to look at, plants and animals to study—

we're talking allergies, biological intolerances, for all I know, rolling around in that grass out there could send you into anaphylactic shock."

"So, we're back to it being a death planet?"

"I'm not *saying* that. I'm saying I don't know."

Faraday sighed tiredly—poor bugger looked a little overwhelmed. "How long before you *do* know?"

"All of it? Years. If you're asking what's most likely to kill us…" Anthea thought a moment, head bouncing side-to-side. "I'd say four to six months."

"And until then… what? We just sit here? Stuck inside this tin can playing cards?"

"I am *not* made of tin, Captain." *Persephone* sounded offended. Anthea didn't blame her; tin cans were crap. "And there's nothing *about* me that's shaped like a can."

"I stand corrected. Stuck inside this meso-metal, long-chain polymer-based dodecahedral star playing cards."

"Thank you."

"You're welcome," Faraday growled at a camera.

"It's a few months," Anthea chided. "What's a few months after a hundred and thirty-seven years?"

Faraday's head swiveled in slow motion, green eyes widening as they turned her way. "*Years*. Did you say a hundred and thirty-seven *years*?"

Anthea flushed guiltily—instantly, the bio-monitor went into a panic, warnings lighting up its onyx face. "Didn't—Didn't I mention that?" Discreetly, she smothered the bracelet with her hand.

"No." Faraday lowered his chin and squinted at her face. "In fact, there's a lot of things you didn't mention. Like, how long we've been planetside. And why you waited so damn long to wake me."

"She doesn't like people," *Persephone* confided.

"Tell me about it," Faraday growled.

"I like *some* people," Anthea insisted. "Just not *most* people. I like *you*," she added when Faraday rolled his eyes. "Even if you *are* a massive pain in my ass."

"Happy to be of service." He flipped a two-fingered salute. "So what's the rest of it?"

"Pardon?"

"The rest of it. Why've you been playing hermit crab these past couple of months?"

"Four months," *Persephone* corrected.

"What?"

"It's been four months."

Faraday turned toward Anthea and glared.

"I promise there's a good explanation."

"Can't wait to hear it." He folded his arms. "In fact, let's discuss it now."

SEVENTEEN

The cargo bay stank of cold and dust, ion fuel and the industrial-grade lubricants *Persephone*'s ground pounders used to maintain the shuttles parked in the hold. Six of them, salvaged from *Hadrian* before his AI died and the ship went dark. Six small ships protecting a hundred or so crew suspended in the nether realm of hyperspace sleep. Oblivious to the passing years and the new reality of this alien world they'd found, only Faraday awake and the few crew he'd unfrozen to join him: Clauson, Shimizu, Turk, a handful of marines he thought they might need. The rest, though, he left sleeping, never knowing things had changed. And resolved to keep them that way for as long as he could.

Until they understood this planet. Learnt how to adapt to it and survive. Faraday scanned the lot of them parked in that perfect line wondering just how long that would be.

"Something wrong, sir?" Turk asked behind him, voice pitched low so the other crew wouldn't hear.

"No. Nothing wrong," Faraday said faintly. "Just thinking, Turk. That's all."

"Looks like it hurts," Turk quipped with a smile.

Faraday grunted and turned around. "Always does, when there's no straightforward answers. How are you feeling, by the way?"

"Fine." Turk frowned at the sudden change in subject. "Bit of a headache, but all things considered, it could be worse."

"Say that again," Faraday murmured, thinking of those shuttles with their frozen crew. Pioneering space exploration was one thing, playing unwitting guinea pig to test the effects of extended hypersleep on human physiology was another altogether, and quite frankly, an experience he'd rather not repeat. "You run checks on the shuttles' cryopods?"

"Twice," Turk confirmed, holding up two fingers. "Everything came back nominal. *Persephone*'s ground pounders did a fine job maintaining the shuttle's kit."

Faraday nodded, looking past him to the half dozen crew gathered at the cargo bay's middle, next to a pair of oblong containers resting on the grated metal decking. Jet black cases with the words 'Halgren Defense Coalition' stenciled in bold silver letters on their sides. Locked and sealed the both of them for well over a century now. "Best we get to it, I guess. See if the seals held on those cases or if they're all just full of scrap."

He gestured for Turk to follow as he crossed the cargo bay and knelt down to inspect the containers' casings. Searching for gaps between the base and lid, cracks in the joining seals. To the untrained eye, everything looked good enough, but the proof, as they say, lay in the pudding, and unfortunately for them, that pudding was over a century old.

Faraday presented a thumb to the reader built into the locking mechanism on the container's front, pressed and held his breath while the cylinders whirred and churned. He repeated the process with the other container and then sat back on his heels and waited.

The lock clicked over and flashed green. To his relief, both cases popped open with a matched set of hissing sighs. Pressurized air released in crawling tendrils of supercooled mist that pooled in a cloud on the floor, dispersing grudgingly and in increments as the cargo bay's comparatively warmer air slowly broke it down.

Even then, Faraday waited, ensuring every last shred of it cleared. Wary of ice burn and frostbitten fingers—he'd witnessed both when people hurried and grew careless. Giving it a hundred count and fifty more before he hinged the heavy lids open and inventoried the contents of the shuttles' storage.

The left hand case held firepower: pulse rifles and forced ion round pistols, magazines of ammunition sized appropriately for each. Turk, predictably, started drooling over the bang goodies, while Faraday investigated the other case.

Armor in that one, not weapons. A dozen obsidian and silver enviro-suits folded into neat and tidy squares, and a dozen full-head helmets to go with them, of coordinating color and material.

Faraday brushed a finger across a single suit to make sure it was safe to touch. Found it cold still, but not bitingly so and reached in to pluck one out. Marveling as always at its near weightlessness, the oil slick shimmer of its ceramo-polymetal weave. Industrial suits came bulky and heavy, but these military-grade rigs were a dream. Lightweight, flexible and durable, built to stop a high velocity slug at fifty paces and deflect a tight focus plasma burn for a full two seconds. With the helmet attached and the seals engaged, the entire rig turned into a self-contained and recirculating system—no exposure to atmosphere required, internal temperature closely monitored and regulated at all times. The most high-tech, high-investment piece of equipment Halgren had on offer. Quite frankly, they were pretty damn sweet.

Your best friend if you had to go romping around planets and, based on experience, often the one and only thing standing between you and a protracted and generally horrible death.

"Looks like they're in good shape. Lucky for us, those cases held." Faraday handed a suit to Turk who eyed it with a look of disgust.

"Sausage casings? Seriously?"

"Unexplored planet," Faraday told him. "Halgren protocol says no one goes walkabout without a suit and helmet." He tossed one of those to Turk, too—skull casing crafted from the same heavy duty, metal armor weave, with chin plates and a jaw piece wrapping the sides, a polymer glass visor that retracted when not needed and connectors that mated to the enviro-suit to create a pressurized, secure micro-environment.

Turk studied the suit in one hand, the helmet gripped in the other. "Thought you said the atmosphere here wasn't toxic."

"Surveys show it's breathable. Non-toxic part's still up for debate. More to air than just the gaseous elements," he said, showing off his recently learned knowledge. "All sorts of microscopic particles ya gotta worry about, that's what Dr. Naisson says. All sorts of nasty viruses and airborne bacteria. Right now, she's workin' her magic in the analytics lab to figure out how much crap we gotta deal with out there, but she's still got about a hundred thousand samples to work through before she can tell us what'll kill us and what's safe."

"And until she does?"

"Helmets and enviro-suits. Every trip, every step outside."

Turk eyed the Halgren gear dubiously. "That an order, sir?"

"That's Halgren directive. Which makes it a standing order for all personnel." Faraday raised his voice at the end, making sure all the crew would hear. "You leave this ship, you wear a survival suit. No exceptions. Am I clear?" He glanced from face-to-face and received mostly mumbles and averted eyes. "I said, am I clear?"

"Aye, sir," Clauson yelled back—she always did have the biggest mouth. "We're pretty much crystal over here."

"Good. Let's keep it that way." Faraday nodded sharply as she tossed off a salute. "You want out of this expedition, you say something. You want in, you grab a suit." He snagged one for himself, along with a helmet to protect his head, and purposely turned his back on the crew, walking away while they decided things for themselves.

"Alright. You heard the man. Everyone line up and grab your jammies." Turk dumped everything out of the case and started divvying up all their gear.

Faraday ducked his head to hide a smile—credit to Turk, he kept that crew in line. While the crew got busy, he selected a patch of decking a safe distance away and, to preserve a modicum of dignity, sat down to pull his suit on.

Rookie mistake, trying to don an enviro-suit while standing. For one thing, you had to strip to your skivvies to even *attempt* to put it on, and wriggling into it was something of a process. Like a snake shedding its skin, only in reverse and upside down.

That was the one strike against the high-tech rigs: things were a damned nuisance to take on and off. Old school enviro-suits came loose and baggy—step in, step out, no big deal, though they were heavy as sin. These modern rigs fit snugly—far more snugly than Faraday personally would've liked, fit more like a second skin than the armor it was meant to be—but they ran lightweight and exceedingly flexible and, with Halgren's winged hammer stamped into the breastplate, pretty fucking tough.

"God I hate these things. Always feels like my nuts are trapped in a vice." Turk bent at the knees and tugged with both hands in an attempt to make some room at his crotch.

"Shed some weight and that thing'll fit you better." Smirking, Clauson poked at Turk's belly bulging roundly at the enviro-suit's middle. Her own suit fit perfectly, of course, thanks to that broad-shouldered, wide-hipped, heavy-worlder bone structure of hers. Snugged in all the right places to emphasize her muscles and curves. She planted her fists on her hips, flexing her muscles as she threw her shoulders back. "See that? Poly-metal stretches. But that," she prodded Turk's gut again, "well, even poly-metal can only take so much."

"You keep pokin' and I'll break that finger, Clauson."

Smiling, Clauson prodded again.

Turk slapped her hand and she laughed aloud, ducking quickly when he threw his helmet. "We ain't all mod-adapted burly-girlies," he growled. "Or bone and gristle bits of jerky like the Captain over there." He hooked a thumb Faraday's way, tugging vainly at that codpiece again. "Ladies like a little meat, I'll have you know. Huggable. That's me," he said, smacking his broad belly. "Stringy thing like the Captain ain't hardly worth snugglin' up to—"

"Oh, I don't know about that." Anthea waltzed in wearing a crooked smile. "Your captain might be stringy, but he's got good bone structure, so don't write him off just yet."

Clauson leaned over and whispered something to Turk that made him snicker.

"Shut it," Faraday warned, with a stern eye and a hard look. "I wanna be out of here within the hour. So get your gear together or I leave you behind." He stared them down until the smiles died and they slunk away to see to their kit. "What are you doing here, anyway?"

Anthea shrugged, gnawing at a fingernail. "Oh, I don't know. Trying to like people better, I guess?"

"You mean pretend to."

"Same thing." She flipped a hand. "So, what's it about this suit that's made you so cranky?"

"I'm not *cranky*, I'm just busy is all." He fiddled with a twitchy latching mechanism that pulled the neck closure tight. "This survival gear comes with all sorts of connectors and tight-seal closures. You miss one and the whole thing's compromised. Might as well be running around buck naked out there if you mess it up." He raised his voice, wanting everyone to hear. To take this seriously and appreciate the risks. "Watched a whole troop of marines choke on their own blood when the seals on their helmets broke and the toxic atmosphere ate out their lungs. Heard men shriek fit to wake the devil when the acid rains fell and their skin peeled off. I've seen *death* when people got it wrong." He moved in close and loomed above her, Anthea's head tilting back, and back, and back to see his face. The cargo bay around him turned silent, except for the chuffing sound of the ship's environmentals pushing manufactured air around its huge space. "I've seen the downside of not wearing one of these god-awful things, Doctor, and witnessed first-hand the results of failing to button them up proper. Not going out like that," he told her. "Not letting my crew go out like that either if I have anything to say about it." He added that last part for Turk and the crew. "Do we understand each other?" he asked Anthea.

She dipped her head, watching his face. "Yes, Captain," she answered softly. "I think we do. I think we do, indeed."

"Good. Thank you," he added, catching her eyes, inclining his head. "Now if you don't mind, I'm gonna finish up."

"Be my guest. I'll just stand over here and watch."

"Quietly," he warned her. "And no touching. You keep your hands to yourself."

"Your bum is safe, I promise." Anthea sketched an 'X' over her heart.

Faraday pointed his posterior away from her to make sure she *kept* that promise while he checked the row of seals on the suit's side, the ring at his neck seal where the helmet snugged in. Confirming and reconfirming that particular juncture—the first place a suit failed, in his experience, and the most catastrophic by far.

"There a problem?" Anthea asked when he kept twiddling.

"Nope. Just particular about my equipment." He checked the seal a last time and left it, scooped a gun belt from the decking and strapped it around his waist. From the gun case, he selected a squared-off pistol and holster, ammunition clips he slotted into the belt's ring of loops. A heavy rifle he slung on his shoulder, looping the strap over his head to let it rest against his back.

"Lotta firepower," Anthea noted as Turk and the crew armed up.

"Hopefully won't need it, but you never know what you'll run into out there." Faraday tied the holster down to his thigh, loaded the pistol and slid it in. "Survey equipment ready to go?"

"Two clamshells and a pair of flybys, as requested."

"Good." Faraday knelt to snug the enviro-suit over his boots.

Anthea shuffled her feet and crouched down in front of him, voice pitched low so only he would hear. "Still not sure this is a good idea. You and your crew going out there, poking around."

He glanced up and back down again. "Said yourself, you need eyes on those colony ships to check for hull failures and such." *Persephone* deployed updates and fixes to their systems across a shared network connection, but hardware required hands. A personal touch beyond the science ship's capabilities that only an on-site crew could provide. "We'll take the drones, update the cargo surveys, scan the vessels for structure failures and we're gone."

Repairs would have to come later. Once they figured out what they needed and inventoried the parts in *Persephone's* storage.

"The ground pounders can do all of that, Tom. There's no need—"

"We're going," Faraday said flatly. He scooped up his helmet and stood. "Crew's been stuck inside this ship for weeks. They've got cabin fever from all the sitting around."

Anthea nodded. "I actually understand that. But there's still a lot about this planet we don't know."

"So we'll be careful." Faraday jammed the helmet on his head and reached for the connector at the back of his neck. Fumbling awkwardly as he tried to mate it to his suit and connect the backpack's air supply to his helmet.

"Here. Let me help you with that." Anthea motioned him to turn around and stood on her tiptoes to thread the narrow hose. "I'd like to send some of my ground pounders with you," she said, using her fingertips to crank it down.

"For protection?"

"That," she nodded, "and because they know more about freighter chassis configurations than a bunch of retread Halgren warship crew."

"I'll have you know I'm rather partial to those retreads."

"As am I," she said seriously. "One in particular a little more than the others."

He couldn't see her, but he felt the pressure of her hand pressing flat against his back. Nothing suggestive about it or untoward, just a gentle and comforting touch. "Don't tell Turk that," he said, teasing. "He already thinks he's God's gift to women."

Anthea punched him on the arm. Surprisingly hard, given her petite size. "*Persephone*," she called loudly, voice echoing around the cargo bay's cavernous space. "Send a squad of ground pounders down to Cargo Bay 4."

"Configuration?"

"Standard survey package. Layer in a metals and polymers analysis suite along with any engineering diagrams you've got on record for those colony ships we brought here."

"Would you like a medical package in case Captain Delicate develops a sniffle?"

Turk snickered.

"Shut it," Faraday warned.

"Basic first aid should do it." Anthea's lips curved in a smile. "Captain Delicate promised me he'd be careful."

"Acknowledged, Anthea." *Persephone* went quiet for approximately two seconds. "Configurations are complete. Squad is on its way."

Less than five minutes later, four copper-clad centurions marched into the room with robotic precision. Tall and thin and anthropoid, blank-faced with eye slits alight with cobalt fire. Armored bodies dully winking beneath a mossy, blue-green layer of grime.

"Looks like *somebody* forgot to clean her robots." Faraday shared a crooked smile.

"Actually, *Persephone* does that on purpose. Copper plates stand up to weather better than any other material we've tried. Even that poly-metal your suits are made from." She rapped her knuckles against his chest. "The verdigris—that's that greenish-blue patina—is part of it. Forms a protective layer that coats their armor. As long as you don't clean it, they never rust."

"Super-bots, that it?"

Anthea shrugged. "Super durable anyway."

The ground pounders' double column paced closer with their joints softly whirring away, and slammed to a halt in unison, looming head and shoulders above Faraday's tall and rangy frame.

"They're impressive, I'll give you that." And identical in every way. No faces to distinguish between them, no external markings of any kind. Nothing but a variation in that verdigris layer Faraday put down to differences in age and wear. "You two." He pointed to the front rank. "You're with me and Turk. The rest of you go with them." He jerked a thumb at Clauson and Shimizu, the half dozen marines still wriggling into their gear. In response, the centurions split and a pair of them marched away, leaving the two assigned to Faraday's crew standing silently while they waited on orders.

"They got names?" Turk asked, circling around them.

"Just serial numbers."

"What about your lapdogs? Pot and Kettle, or whatever they're called."

"It's Tip and Top, and they're not lapdogs."

"But you named them, right? So why not these?"

"Always meant to. Probably should have. Never quite got around to it, somehow. Spend a lot of time with Tip and Top, but mostly these others stand around in storage." She shrugged helplessly. "Out of sight, out of mind and all that."

"Nice." Turk shared a look with Faraday. "'Spose that makes it our problem. You," he said, tapping one of the ground pounders on the breastplate. "What's your designation?"

"314159265," the robot answered in a clipped and distinctly female-sounding voice.

"You're kidding."

"Not currently. Though my software does allow for—"

Turk waved her into silence, turning a questioning look Faraday's way. "Pi?"

"It's... different."

"Pie," the ground pounder said brightly. "Like the indulgence."

"Well, no, not exactly," Turk corrected. "Pi as in Pi, not pie. Ya know, Pi!"

Faraday frowned. "That is the *worst* explan—"

"I like this new designation." The android pivoted to face Anthea, eye slits flaring with cobalt light. "May I keep it, Dr. Naisson? I would very much like to be Pie."

Anthea granted her wish with a wave of her hand. "Far as I'm concerned, you can call yourself whatever you like. Never gave you names, but I never said you couldn't have them either."

Pleased, the ground pounder's chin lifted, cheeks alive with electric-blue fire. "Pie," she proclaimed proudly. "I like Pie." She pressed a palm to her forehead and held it there while something scratched and scraped.

"What the hell's she doing?" Faraday whispered.

"No idea." Anthea frowned, shaking her head, as the ground pounder's hand descended, revealing a symbol carved into her brow. A circular glyph with a single wedge missing and a flower-petal ribbon running around its edges.

"Pie. My name is Pie," the android repeated, pointing to the mark carved into her head.

"Wasn't supposed to be. But I guess it is now. What about you?" Turk asked Pie's partner. "What's your serial designation?"

This one, too, sounded female—an unfortunate or ill-chosen affectation given the android's response. "800898288," she supplied promptly, and then waited, staring expectantly at Faraday's face.

"8008." Turk's lips twitched at the corners. "Well, there's the obvious choice."

"Grow up, Turk," Clauson growled.

"I'm just saying—"

"You're a pig."

"That's enough," Faraday said to shut them up and snapped his fingers to get the robot's attention. "Your designation, repeat it."

The ground pounder rattled off the string of numbers a second time.

"Huh. Lotta repetition. How's about we just call you Eight?"

"Eight." The robot sounded faintly disappointed.

"Think of it as a sort of nickname."

The ground pounder still didn't seem all that enthused.

Turk squinted his eyes and tucked up his arms, pressing a fist to his lips in that 'I'm thinking really, really hard' way of his. "Ya know…" he said, waggling a finger. "You turn an eight on its side and it'll look like an infinity symbol." He wiggled his eyebrows, looking extremely proud of that little knowledge nugget.

"Infinity." The android's head tilted, eye slits flickering as she thought that over. "Yes. Yes, I like that. Eight is the equal of infinity." She copied Pie's palm-pressing gesture, scratching a sideways lying, lazy-8 brand into the verdigris plating of her copper brow. "I am Eight, and she is Pie. Together we are named."

"Faraday." He tapped his chest, forgetting the enviro-suit covered his nametag. "That's Turk," he added, nodding to the Gunner Chief beside him.

Turk flashed a smile and a 'welcome aboard!' thumbs up as he jammed a helmet on his square head.

"Take our metal-skinned friends and introduce them to the others," Faraday told him. "Let Clauson know she's welcome to name hers if she likes."

"And the meat shields?" Turk turned that thumb of his sideways, pointing to the squad of marines standing silently to one side. Anonymous in their enviro-suits, with their helmets on and visors closed.

Couldn't half-remember their names, if Faraday was honest. Never did get to know most of the crew. "You and Clauson can Rochambeau for the pick of the litter."

"Aye, sir." Turk tapped two fingers against his helmet, beckoning for their newly-named ground pounders to follow as he headed off to duke it out with Clauson.

"Meat shields?" Anthea cocked her head in question.

"Knuckle-draggers, bucketheads—marines got a million nicknames, you can pretty much take your pick. What?" he asked when she pursed her lips, giving him one of those narrow-eyed, disapproving looks.

"Nothing really, it's just… you've got an interesting relationship with your crew."

"Oh, like you're one to talk. *Your* crew's still frozen."

"So? I work better on my own. Always have."

"You woke *me* up," Faraday reminded her.

"Yeah, but see, you don't work for me. Or I for you, for that matter." Anthea flashed her teeth. "Might be I had an ulterior motive in unfreezing you."

Faraday laughed—he couldn't help it. Anthea was always full of surprises. Nothing about her quite made any sense. "You're something, you know that?"

"I could be more than something."

And he wouldn't mind that, he realized now. Anthea was brilliant, and beautiful, and independent. Everything he'd ever wanted. Everything he'd never had. Timing wasn't right, though. Not here, not right now. "You got that map?" he asked, changing the subject.

The smile dimmed with disappointment, and turned rueful, slightly annoyed. "Sure," she said. "I got it right here." Anthea reached into one of her coverall's many pockets and retrieved a weatherproof tube, uncapped the end and removed a curl of thin, shimmering metal foil that she spread flat with the palm of her hand.

Faraday plucked it from her fingers, half-expecting it to roll right back up. To his surprise, it maintained its rigidity, and its rainbow-colored frosting of opalescent swirls. He twisted and it flexed, bouncing back to its board-flat shape when he released the pressure. "Nanofiber?" he guessed.

"Polymer filament. Metalo-crystalline construct. We actually grow them in one of our labs."

"Slick," Faraday grunted, pinching a corner to turn it on. The face remained blank for a half-second while the device connected remotely to the ship's database to download information. Afterward, a map appeared: wide-angle view showing a single, large landmass surrounded by vast stretches of deep blue ocean, clustered clutches of smaller islands sprinkled liberally across the globe.

"Planet's predominantly water. *Persephone* put down here..." Anthea reached in and tapped a star-shaped symbol showing in the continent's southwest corner. Inland some thirty kilometers, where a vast stretch of grassy plains and rolling hills transitioned to a spreading forest of trees. "The other ships are set in a ring around her." The finger moved, picking out towers that marked each colony vessel's location. Landlocked, for the most part, though two of them hugged the coast. She expanded the view to zoom in on them and the data tags giving them names.

Diligence. Endurance. Fitting monikers considering how far they'd come.

"I'd suggest you hit these two vessels your first trip. Leave the others for another day."

Faraday toggled the map's settings to check the scale and measure the distance between each point. Thirty kilometers from the coast to here, which put them the same distance from those other ships. "Why so far?" he asked out of curiosity.

Anthea shrugged. "Just thinking ahead." She zoomed in on one of the towers and pulled up the manifest on the ship beneath. "Each of these colony vessels come equipped with enough people and supplies to build an autonomous community. Plant them too close and they'll compete for resources, too far and the people inside them'll fall out of touch."

"Smart," Faraday grunted.

"Experience," Anthea countered. "First planet we terraformed..." She trailed off a moment and jerked her head. "Dropped all the colonists in together. Forty, fifty thousand of them all plunked down with their ships in a five kilometer grid. First year they lived off the stores they brought with them. Second year most of them starved or were killed off by a form of hyper-virulent plague that swept through the colony."

"Yikes."

"Yeah. It was terrible." Anthea bit her lip and turned her face away. "Mother Nature can be cruel, Tom. Especially to invasive species."

"Is that how you see us?"

"That's how this *planet* sees us. We're not *from* here, remember. We came uninvited to this world."

"Wasn't my idea to come here at all," Faraday grumbled.

She glanced back at him with a sour look. "Couldn't resist, could you? You just had to get in one more dig." Faraday shrugged and she rolled her eyes. "Ya know, you're gonna have to get over this eventually. This world might not be what you wanted, but we're stuck here now. No going back."

Faraday grunted and looked away, checking on the dark-suited crew nearby. "What are we calling this world, anyway?"

"Not calling it anything in particular. Haven't actually gotten around to naming the planet yet."

"You're kidding. Thought you scientists *loved* naming things."

Anthea shrugged again. "Named several hundred things over the course of the years. Plants. Planets. Mountains, oceans, volcanos. Gets old after a while," she confided. "Once you use all the good ideas up." She nodded to a bundle of cameras in the corner. "*Persephone* suggested Shangri-La. Suppose that's as good a name as any."

"Shangri-La," he repeated, tasting it. "Sounds familiar. Not quite sure why."

"'Course you don't."

"What?"

"I said, are you a Buddhist, Tom?"

"What does *that* have to do with anything?"

"Shangri-La." She smiled secretively. "You should check out *Persephone's* library sometime. Look it up."

"Okay..." Faraday scratched his head, completely confused as Anthea spun him around to check the helmet's connector, giving the little hose a tweak to make sure it stayed put.

"There you go." She patted his back. "All ready to go exploring."

"Thanks," he said. "I think."

Anthea smiled and gave him two thumbs up.

"We'll contact you once we reach *Diligence.*" He nodded to the other crew. "I'm sending Clauson's team to *Endurance.* You need anything, you give me a buzz. Anything *happens* back here, you do the same." Faraday tapped a finger to the side of his helmet and the two-way comms unit sitting close to his ear.

"You'll be back before nightfall?"

"Should be." Days here ran twenty-eight hours. Just after dawn now according to the planetary chron, which gave them a little over twelve hours of natural light to travel the thirty kilometers to the ship and back. Plenty of time, the way he figured, even at the clamshell's turtling speed. "We run into any trouble, I'll let me know." Faraday flipped an off-hand salute, offering a crooked smile as he turned away.

"You know this is stupid, right?" To her credit, she said it softly, so only Faraday would hear.

"Gotta go out there sometime." He turned his head, looking back at her over his shoulder. "Can't spend the rest of our lives hiding out on this ship."

"Thought you hated planets."

"Not a fan, generally. Staying here, though…" He gestured at the ship around them. "Startin' to feel like prison somehow."

"I'd *hardly* call *Persephone* a prison."

"Yeah, well, that's your opinion. Personally, I don't intend to spend the rest of my days eating lab grown food inside an ice box with white walls."

"You sayin' I should paint?"

"I'm sayin' it's fucking cold in here." That made her laugh. "Call me," he repeated, rapping his knuckles against his helmet.

"Be careful," she said when he turned away.

"Always," he assured her. "Careful comes with Captain. It's part of the test." Faraday waved as he walked away, collecting Turk and the other crew.

In a knot, they headed for the airlock, and the wide, strange world outside.

EIGHTEEN

Rain lashed at Faraday's visor, rattling with the drum of angry fingers against the poly-metal helmet protecting his head. Driven in torrential sheets by the gusting wind that soaked deep into the emerald green ground beneath him, transforming the grassy plain into a quagmire of puddles and pools and mud-filled holes sucking greedily at his boots. The sky into an ominous, gunmetal grey ceiling that lowered and thickened with each hour that passed. As he trudged along, he watched it, splitting his attention between the track in front of him and that muttering, suffocating nest of overlapping clouds. Wondering how long they had before the ground and sky joined. What would happen to them when mud met mist.

Long time since he'd experienced weather. He'd forgotten how much he hated it, cursed *Persephone* and her advanced AI for failing to warning them about the storm moving in. Crew was nervous enough about leaving the ship and venturing out into the unknown, they didn't need the added complication of planetary meteorology, with its fog, and rain, and wind.

Weather was the worst part of planetside, in Faraday's opinion. Next to the people in their masses. The politics, and factions, and religions.

Give me a stretch of stars and a ship to sail them. You can keep your drippy days and even the sunny ones that come after, I'll take vacuum and the cold depths of space over this shit every time.

"Creepy as fuck out here," he heard Turk mutter.

And there was that side of the weather, too. Everything too closed, too close, and crowding them about. All that grey, hanging haar hiding secrets in its depths. Shadows that flickered and faded away. Stalking his little strung out, rain-soaked party.

"Fucking hate planets," Turk grumbled.

"Hot mic," Faraday warned him.

"Sorry, sir."

The line clicked and went silent, leaving Faraday alone with the rain.

Beside him, the clamshell drone trundled its slow way through the mud and rain—carapace as crustaceous as its namesake, if somewhat bigger than any clamshell in any known sea. From tip to tail it stretched a full two meters, and at its middle, measured just as wide with enough void space in the middle to store equipment—core sample drills, sniffers, collectors, various containers to store any interesting samples they picked up—with a series of butt-wide dents pounded around the edges that hadn't been there when Faraday and his little expeditionary force first set out.

Added that feature once the rain started. Hell of a thing, expecting a grown man in an enviro-suit to perch primly on a water-slick, poly-metal casing without sliding off into the dirt. Not the drone's fault—clamshell was designed for autonomous investigation and never meant to carry passengers—but the ride was frankly terrible. Six oversized tires and all of them turning independently. Thing bumped and bounced like a kicking mule and even the 'seats' Eight beat into its carapace to accommodate them only slowed down the sliding process enough that, for the most part, they could wriggle and shuck themselves back up. But the further they traveled, the more the conditions degraded, forcing their transport to work ever harder to make any progress at all.

Eventually, perhaps inevitably, the drone completely bogged down. With no other choice but to help it, the crew hopped off and started digging until the damnable thing finally came unstuck. And remounted once it got rolling, only to stop dead again less than half a kilometer later, forcing everyone to bail off and repeat the unsticking process.

That's the way things went for a while—hop on, hop off, dig-dig-dig and off you go, Faraday wondering why in hell the things came wheeled instead of tank treaded, and growing more and more irate about that design flaw the further they went.

The tenth time the clamshell beached itself no one bothered to get back on. Six kilometers out from *Diligence*, Faraday and his crew all shouldered their rifles, resigned to humping it the rest of the way on foot.

"All terrain, my ass." Turk kicked at the drone when it slowed, bent and put his shoulder to it when it started to get stuck. "Hate fucking walking," he grumbled, wiping droplets from his water-drenched visor. "Hate fucking rain and fucking mud. Didn't sign up for fucking weather when I joined Halgren—"

"Turk," Faraday interrupted. "That's enough."

"Aye, sir," he said, still grumbling. Voice sounding tinny across comms. Echoing and oddly congested—that came part and parcel with full face masks and enclosed breathing systems, bodies encased in enviro-suits, everything pressure-sealed and air-tight.

Behind the visor, Turk's face showed flush with exertion, mouth slightly open and sucking wind. Some trickery of the filtration system kept the carbon glass from fogging up, regulating the temperature, the humidity, the various gaseous element mixtures. Didn't keep the rain off, though. Not much the suit could do about that. It pattered and streaked and sometimes left them blind— absolutely *miserable* conditions they slogged through, some of the worst Faraday had experienced since that death march through lead rain on Triconus.

Bad times, but we made it. Thank Halgren's survival suits for that.

Despised the sausage casing fit of it, the way it cupped too familiarly at his gentleman's package and wormed its way between his butt cheeks. But the metal weave was a wonder, sloughing just about everything off. The seals snugged tight as a drum to prevent any sort of contaminant from working its way in, everything inside it self-contained and recirculating, turning sweat into drinkable water—hell he could drink his *pee* if he felt so bold.

Which he hadn't, yet, and his most fervent wish was that he never be put in a situation where he was desperate enough to resort to that. Nice to have the option, though. Drinking pee water was definitely preferable to a slow death by dehydration. Tech specs claimed you could survive a week in one of these, all alone in the middle of nowhere.

"Aw, c'mon, baby, don't do that."

Faraday glanced over at Turk's complaining, and heard the tone of the drone's motor change. Growling now, instead of purring, the clamshell itself slowing to a crawl. It jerked and skipped ahead, moving quickly for several seconds—fast enough that Turk and Faraday shambled along beside it at a mud-splattered jog—before it dipped into a water-filled hollow and struggled mightily to make it across. Displacing a school of tiny limpet-salamander-octopus things in its passing—miniscule, striped shapes that scattered to the impromptu pond's edges, rimming the hollow with their fuchsia and lemon yellow colors. Paddling at the muddy shore with their tentacles.

Oblivious to the chaos it caused, the clamshell struggled gamely on. Sinking deeper and deeper into the hollow's water, the throaty note of its motor growing increasingly labored until, somewhere around the ponded hole's middle, it stalled with a metal-on-metal grind of gears and stopped making any progress at all.

"That's not good."

"Tell me about." Faraday stopped at the edge of the hole with the displaced water lapping at the toes of his boots, and watched the three oversized wheels that faced him spin quickly and traction-free while the trio on the opposite side moved in fits and starts. Catching and uncatching as the heavy drone slowly sank. "C'mon. C'mon, get out of there," he willed it, hoping that, by some miracle, the clamshell would work itself free. For a moment, things actually looked promising, until the left side seized entirely and the drone started fishtailing. "Watch it! Watch it! Watch it!" Faraday yelled, waving at Turk to get out of the way. "Halt!" he screamed at the three marines trailing behind them.

The marines—Tran, Marchetti and Santos, he was pretty sure those were the three Turk picked out of the pack—slammed to a stop in unison and arranged themselves in a perfectly straight line.

Knuckle draggers were good at that type of thing. Stopping. Starting. Making lines. Turk, on the other hand, was more ad-lib when it came to orders—a good quality when it came to bridge crew. As the clamshell spun, he skippy-toed graceful as a dancer and dodged out of the drone's way just in time.

No escaping the rooster tail of mud that sprayed across him, though. Pretty much covered him head to toe. Turk cursed roundly and wiped at his visor, smearing the sticky-thick coating across the carbon-glass mask. "Fuck," he said distinctly, while across the mud-hole, Faraday just sighed.

Evidently all-terrain didn't account for mud. And in water, those big wheels were utterly useless.

"Turk. Get in there and dig it out."

"Aye, sir. Digging, sir." Turk wiped a clump of mud from his visor, and sloshed down into the hollow to wrestle the clamshell loose.

Faraday watched him for a few moments, and when it became obvious the operation would take a while, toggled his comms unit to shunt the channel through the clamshell's relays and connect remotely to his other crew. "Clauson. What's the situation?"

"Situation's terrible, sir. Right bloody awful."

Despite the circumstances, Faraday couldn't help but smile. "That good, eh?"

"I've seen worse," she admitted. "But not recently. This mud... fucking horrible, if you don't mind me saying so, sir. Goddamn drones keep getting stuck in holes." Clauson sounded out of breath—Faraday suspected the drone was stuck in one of those holes right now. "Ya know, I left Frontera because of the mud, sir. And the shit. And that goddamn lecher who claimed to be my father."

He hadn't known that, actually. Not any of it.

I should've asked.

"Give my left tit to get off this goddamn planet," Clauson grumbled.

"Me too," he said, which made her laugh.

She had a good laugh, Clauson, and a level head. She was good crew. They all were. Even the marines.

"If it gets too ugly, you cut bait and head back to *Persephone*. *Endurance* isn't going anywhere. We can inspect her another day."

"Tempting, sir." Clauson panted, spitting out words between gasps for air. "Don't think so, though." She breathed deep and exhaled. "Heavy worlder, remember? We're hard-headed to a fault."

Faraday snorted, smiling ruefully, wishing he'd spent more time with this crew and gotten to know them better before everything went wrong. Harkening back to that little chat with Anthea, her mention of second chances and making a fresh start.

Maybe this is mine, he thought while he stood there, next to that stuck clamshell in the driving rain. *Still not sure about this whole planet thing.*

But this crew, he could start with them.

"Is it true we're really stuck here, sir? Any chance at all we'll get back to the stars?"

Took him a while to respond to that. Wasn't quite sure what to say at first. "Don't know," he said truthfully. "Mean to, if there's a way. But I've got nothing right now, I'm afraid."

"Aye, sir," Clauson said quietly. Resigned and regretful, though that might just be the comms.

Hurt Faraday's heart to hear it. They deserved better than resignation. They all did. "Do me a favor?"

"Anything, sir."

"Patch Shimizu in. Need to talk to her a moment."

"Aye, Captain." Clauson sounded puzzled, but the line clicked and buzzed softly as she transferred the connection to her compatriot.

"Sir?"

"Need your skills, Shimizu."

"For what, sir?"

"Special assignment. Little investigation." She might be young, but Shimizu was a hell of a data wrangler. Even *Hadrian* admitted as much. "There's some... holes in *Persephone's* timeline. The track from here back to *Hadrian* is incomplete. Claims there was some sort of storage corruption that caused data loss, or whatever."

"Storage corruption?" Shimizu sounded doubtful. And with good reason— *he* certainly was. "She got backups?"

"Did. They're corrupted too."

"That's odd."

Tell me about. Didn't say it, just kept that thought to himself.

"Like to see if you can fill the gaps. Stitch the broken ends together and rebuild the path."

"*Persephone*..." Shimizu trailed off a moment. "If she already tried and failed..." The doubt in her voice spoke volumes. She was human, after all, and *Persephone* a far more powerful AI mind.

"The virus... the one that killed *Hadrian*..." Faraday swallowed around a knot in his throat. "It's in her now, Shimizu. *Persephone's* compromised. I can't be sure how much damage it's done."

"Oh." Just that, in a small, shocked voice. "I'll need access."

"You'll have it. I'll make sure of it. Will you try?"

Her answer was long in coming, and no more confident than before. "Can't promise anything, sir," she said. Respectfully, apology in her voice.

"Not expecting miracles. Just asking you to take a look."

"Aye, sir," she answered quietly. "See what I can do when we get back."

"'Preciate that, Shimizu." Faraday touched the side of his helmet, stroking the button that toggled the comms. "You and Clauson be careful out there, ya hear me?"

"You too, sir."

"Don't need to be. I got Turk."

Surprised a laugh out of her with that one. Not much, just a giggle, but it made him feel better all the same.

"Tell Clauson I'll check in later. See you both back at the ship." With a touch, Faraday closed the channel, severing the connection bounced through the clamshell's shape, and for a while after, just stood there, with nothing but the sound of his own breathing and the relentless battering of the unceasing rain.

And Turk cursing a blue streak. Growing increasingly frustrated with the bogged-down drone in that hollow. "Fuck!" he swore, making Faraday's comms crackle and pop. "I fucking hate this fucking-ass planet with its piss and shit weather and mud." He slipped and went down on one knee, cursing roundly as muddy water splashed his helmet. "That's it. I give up."

Turk tossed his hands in the air to signal his inevitable defeat, climbed to his feet with an obvious effort and tottered unsteadily toward more solid ground. Wiping furiously at his facemask the entire way in an attempt to clear the mud. Making things worse instead of better, as it so happened, and worse still when he tried to wash it off.

The water in that hollow was filthy—as much mud as collected rain. A double handful cleared the chunks from the visor but left a film that hazed the glass. Despite that, Turk splished and splashed a while, seemingly convinced the water would do the trick. And ended up with a facemask stained baby-poo yellow, and an enviro-suit colored the same.

"Give it up, Turk, you're just making things worse."

"Making progress," Turk assured him. "Shit's really startin' to come off."

"Turk—"

"Won't be but a minute."

Faraday sighed again and left bird boy to his disgusting bath, turning his attention back to the clamshell, fighting valiantly to break free. Running the wheels on either side of its carapace in alternating rotations—front to back and back to front, left side, right side, all of them at once. Not a bad approach most days, unfortunately in these conditions, all that effort only resulted in a deeper hole.

Watching it, Faraday shook his head. Damn thing was really slowing them down.

Comms buzzed inside his helmet, alerting him to an incoming message from *Persephone* as a channel opened and Anthea's voice came through. "How's it goin' out there?" she asked.

"Well. The clamshell's mired itself again. And this weather doesn't look like it's gonna let up anytime soon. Would've been nice to get a little head's up on that."

"The weather models predicted it would track in another direction. Slide along the coast and curve out to sea."

"Yeah, well, your forecast sucks," Faraday said sourly.

"I'm aware of that. Little late to fix it now, but I'll see what I can do to help you out."

A flicker of movement drew his eyes skyward to another drone passing overhead. This one smaller than the crustacean and bat-shaped, built to soar, not crawl across the earth. The flyby—that's what Anthea called it—dropped down from the occluding cloud layer and flew a circuit around the clamshell's shape. Cool blue lights strobed on its wingtips as it scanned its partner in the mud hole and received a ripple of the pin dots along its carapace in response.

Across comms, Anthea whistled appreciatively. "You weren't kidding. That drone there's good and stuck."

"Trucked along the first part of the trip." Back when the path was rockier and surrounded by forests of ten foot tall damsel flowers and some alien variant of feather-fronded evergreen trees. This grassland here, with its rolling hills and spindly, grey-stalked mushroom spires, bumping hummocks and unexpected hollows did a fantastic job of trapping the water the rocks and trees sloughed off. "Mud's what did us in. I'm actually surprised you didn't take that into account in their design."

"First off," Anthea said primly, "*I* didn't design the clamshells. You can thank TerraGen and whatever subcontractor they hired for that."

"*Now* who's touchy?"

"I'm gonna ignore that," she warned. "And secondly, whose bright idea was it to run it straight into a pond?"

"It's not so much a pond as a really big mud puddle."

"So, it's your fault."

"What? *No.* I didn't—"

"These things are expensive, Tom. They're not toys."

Faraday didn't even bother responding to that. Clearly this wasn't an argument he was going to win, even *he* could recognize that. "Well, we're stuck here until that clamshell gets moving. Can't leave it, can't complete the survey of *Diligence* without it."

Anthea sighed. "Let me see what I can do."

Back on *Persephone,* she guided the flyby remotely, bringing it down to the clamshell's level where they communicated in alternating flashes of drone language—sharing information, Faraday supposed, to formulate some kind of plan.

He squatted down while he waited, taking a load off his legs for a while. Cone-shaped structures littered the ground—some small as his pinky nail, others big as his head. Some fat, some thin, some shaped like bells, all of them sprouting delicate hairs that fluttered in silken strings in the wind. Curious, he plucked one up, and to his surprise, the casing shattered in his hand, releasing puffs of greenish-yellow dust that mixed with the driving rain to form a sticky goo that coated his hands.

Disgusted, he wiped his gloves on the grass, finally finding a use for all that rain. And as it washed away, realized he should've collected a sample. Goo seemed important. He assumed Anthea would be interested.

"Shit."

"What?"

"Nothing." Guiltily, Faraday glanced at the flyby, hoping Anthea was too busy to notice, and hastily he collected another pod, mindful of cracking it open this time. Even snipped a sample of the blue-green grasses while he was at it— fern-shaped blades tufted with wheat sheath tips, stalks riddle with crimson vein. The stalks, when he bent them, oozed a scarlet substance with the color and consistency of blood.

Yet another reminder that this was an alien planet. Unmapped, unsettled, unlike any human-terraformed world.

"Whatcha got there?" Anthea asked.

"Present." He shook the collection vial and tucked it away. "So, how's it goin' over there? Come up with any brilliant ideas?"

"As a matter of fact, I have." Anthea sounded indecently smug.

"Well?" he said when she failed to elaborate. "Lay it on me, I'm all ears."

"We're gonna tow it out."

"With what? The flyby?"

"Uh-huh. Drone might be small, but it packs a punch."

Faraday frowned dubiously, but he held his tongue while Anthea maneuvered the winged survey drone close, exchanging a short burst of communication with the clamshell to clue it in on the plan.

A hatch sighed open when the conversation concluded and the clamshell extruded a pronged-end cable from its front end that mated neatly with the connector built into the flyby's bat-shaped ass. Working in tandem they set up a rhythm: the wheeled drone rocking back and forth, while the flyby pulled with its engines running opened wide. With the rain pouring down around them, increasing the depth of the small lake in that hole. Run-off from the nearby hills contributing to the water level's precipitous rising, washing in grains of that greenish-yellow pod dust to create a sickly, swirling skim of neon pea green soup.

Faraday dragged a finger across the puddle's surface and studied the leavings it left on his glove. "What is that stuff, anyway? Some kind of bacteria or something?"

"From the looks of it, I'd guess that's pollen. Tons of it on this planet. That's why there's so much green."

"Thought you said the rain made it green."

"That too. But water alone isn't enough."

"Didn't know that, actually."

"Well, you're not a terraformer, so you don't know all the good stuff."

"Show off."

She snorted laughter. "Graduated from touchy to jealous. I get pissy out of you, I win the trifecta."

"Turk's the pissy one, not me." Faraday cleaned his finger on the grass, watching Turk ponderously extricate himself from the clamshell's hole. Spared a glance for the drones' little tug-of-war while the weather kept closing in. "Checked on Clauson earlier," he said conversationally. "They're not doing much better than us."

"I heard."

"You did?"

"I talked to her. I diverted her team, if that makes you feel better."

"Surprised she agreed to that. Tried to send her back myself. She politely told me to go to hell."

"To be honest, it took some convincing. That crewman of yours is exceptionally strong-willed. But I can be quite persuasive when I put my mind to it. And she's a woman, so… ya know."

"Sisterhood. Yeah, I get it." Faraday sulked in the rain a while. "So, where'd you send her?"

"Inland to *Resolute*. Weather's better there. Storm's mostly battering the coast."

"Do tell," Faraday said. "I hadn't noticed, it's *such* a pleasant day."

"I *told* you the forecasts—"

"Yeah, yeah, I'm over it." He wasn't really, but he was tired of arguing.

"Might be smart if you did the same. Headed inland. Inspected a different ship."

"Smart was never my forte." Faraday checked the chron. "And at this point, I'm not sure we'll make it back to *Persephone* before dark." Not with the daylight hours waning, and this storm showing no signs of letting up. "Crew won't like it, but we might have to bed down inside *Diligence*, head back to *Persephone* in the morning."

"Sounds comfy."

"Sounds bloody horrible. But it's a fair sight better than blundering around in the darkness wondering if some long-toothed, hairy-backed monstrosity is going to eat us or not." A trio of said hairy-backed monsters ghosted by as he said that, dark shapes eerily silent as they talked through the thickening fog.

Local wildlife, most likely. Herd of those moosealopes or whatever—planet seemed overrun with critters and every last one of them uglier than the one before.

A veritable menagerie of claws and tentacles and teeth and every last one of them wanting to fuck them or eat them—for the life of him, Faraday wasn't sure which. Both, for all he knew. Hard to tell the difference half the time.

Team walked softly as a result. Kept their weapons primed and ready for running the next randy ugly bugger off. On edge, and he couldn't blame them, given all the wide open spaces around them and all the fog currently smothering it up.

With a *twang!* the cable connecting the drones shredded and one ragged end whipped around, smashing a fresh dent in the clamshell's metal carapace side. The other end fluttered behind the flyby as it cut free and rocketed away.

In its absence, the clamshell's wheels spun a while, smoke drifting from its overheated axles as it dug itself deeper into the mud.

"Fuck." Faraday sighed heavily. "Should've known that wasn't gonna work."

"We could double up the cables," Anthea suggested. "I can recall the drone and try again."

"No. We'll figure something else out."

"Like what?"

"Not sure yet. I'll let you know." He killed the channel to *Persephone* to give himself some time to think, fully aware that Anthea would keep listening and keep tabs on things through the spy-eyes built into the drones.

And the androids, of course, wherever the hell they'd gone. He'd sent them ahead some time ago, back when the clamshell first turned balky, the idea being they'd help clear a path. Nearly an hour now since they last checked in, which made him wonder if they'd somehow gotten lost.

He touched his helmet to recall them, keying the comms to the androids' channel. "Pie. Eight," he called. "Clamshell's stuck in the mud again. Need you two to fall back and haul it out for me."

Pie answered for the both of them. At least, he thought it was Pie since her voice ran higher than Eight's, though their tones and inflection were eerily similar. "Stuck?" she repeated. "How did it get stuck?"

"Ran through a hollow."

"But the mud is deeper in the hollows. Why didn't you direct it around, Captain?"

"Because it's AI and it should fucking know better."

"The drone's AI has limited capability. They're semi-autonomous, not—"

"I don't *care,* Pie. I just need you back here. It's raining a flood in case you hadn't noticed and I'd like to get out of it for a while. Now, if you wouldn't *mind,* would you and Eight *please* march your copper-clad keesters back here and haul this clamshell out of its mud pit so we can get this *fucking* job done and over with?"

Pie's answer was long in coming. "You sound angry, Faraday. Have I done something wrong?"

He drew a breath to calm himself, swallowing the angry retort tickling at his tongue. Anthea was right, goddamn emulators ruined everything. Took a perfectly good AI and made it impossibly difficult to deal with. "No, Pie," he said patiently.

"You haven't done anything wrong, I'm just really, *really* tired. Long time since I dealt with weather. Longer since I dealt with this much mud."

"We should build roads," Pie offered, "between *Persephone* and the colony vessels."

"Roads would be nice. Especially if they're paved."

"I will… suggest it when we return."

"Whatever."

"We could use stones—"

"Pie!"

"Yes, Faraday?"

"Later. Right now, I just need the clamshell unstuck."

"Yes, Faraday. Right away."

Without the conversation, the rain drumming against Faraday's helmet sounded impossibly loud, the land around him wide open and deadly. Too much fog and cloud closing in on them, not enough line of sight for them to know what was coming.

"Turk," he called, pulling the rifle from his shoulder. "Grab the others and fan out." He glanced at Tran, Marchetti and Santos behind him. "Keep your eyes peeled for anything unfriendly."

"Such as?"

"How the hell should I know, Tran? Tons of critters on this planet. No idea which ones'll eat us and which'll leave us alone."

"Aye, sir." Tran hesitated. "If we do see something, should we shoot it?"

"If it's threatening you, be my guest."

"Aye, sir." The marines saluted in unison and separated, spacing themselves in a semi-circle with their backs to the stuck clamshell and their rifles pointed toward the fog.

"Keep an eye on the bucket heads for me," Faraday told Turk. "Need to take a fix and figure out where the hell we are."

"Aye, sir. I'm on it." He tossed off a salute and faced away, guarding the clamshell's front.

With the crew all busy playing sentry, Faraday removed the polymer filament map from the tube-shaped canister attached to his belt, stretching it straight and snapping it hard to prevent the edges from curling back up. A pinch at one corner powered it on, after which it flashed for several seconds, securing a connection back to *Persephone* for data transfer, and the flyby and clamshell to triangulate their location. "C'mon, c'mon, c'mon," he muttered impatiently as the map built out one small section at a time. He turned in a circle while it finished building, with the raindrops pooling and sliding across the map's surface, magnifying sections in transient detail, blurring others into obscurity and clutter. Watching the map turn with him until *Diligence* showed—a tower symbol located dead ahead.

Less than a kilometer distant, if the scale held true, with the shore of this planet's ocean precariously close by.

Explains the fog, I guess.

Something to do with warm air and cold water and the proximity of both to the shore. Didn't actually know much about weather or oceans for that matter when he first came here, but in his boredom aboard ship he'd skimmed through the information in *Persephone's* database. Smartened himself up on things like fog and water spouts, lightning storms and such. Turns out, Mother Nature invented a good hundred different ways to kill you. And that didn't count the critters stalking around eating each other on this continent.

"Hate fucking planets." Faraday powered the map down, tweaked the corners and curled it back up. "Hate the fog, hate the rain—"

"Sir, I've got movement at your twelve o'clock."

"Fuck." Faraday shoved the map into its case, snatched at his rifle and sighted along the barrel as a pair of tall, thin shadows appeared. The pulse rifle whined as he charged it, finger curling to cup the trigger, brain belatedly remembering those missing androids of theirs and the fact that he'd ordered them back here. He smacked his helmet to activate the targeting system and a heads up display that zeroed in on the androids' location.

Tech was solid in that system. Had to be, otherwise people died. And yet the tracking data kept fritzing, marker beacons randomly blipping in and out.

"Turk. Something's blocking the HUD."

"Fucking great. This just keeps getting worse."

"Eight," Faraday barked across comms. "Pie. What's your position?"

The shadows wavered and retreated, obscured by the wind-driven rain.

"Pie!" Faraday's finger wrapped tight around that trigger while he waited, and waited, and waited, for an answer that never came. "Eight, goddammit, where are you?" he called as those shadows reappeared, moving closer, looming large.

"We're here, Faraday."

He twitched the rifle away, releasing the trigger as a metal shape stepped from the fog. Copper-clad and bipedal with a twin following a step behind. "Goddammit, Eight. Where the hell have you two—*fuck!*" He ducked at a sharp report, followed by the flash and sizzle of a forced-ion round discharging under load. The round struck Eight on the right shoulder, punching so hard it slewed her around. "Cease fire! Cease fire!" Faraday shouted and saw Turk snatch the rifle out of a marine's hands.

"What the fuck do you think you're doing, Tran?"

"I didn't know they were friendlies."

"Did you even look?"

"*No,* I didn't *look.* Fucking HUD's fucking broke."

"Still got eyeballs, don't you?"

"I—She—The Captain—" Tran pointed accusingly at Faraday. "He *told* me to shoot if I felt threatened."

Turk smacked the back of Tran's helmeted head. "Captain didn't say *nothin'* about shootin' one of our own." He mashed the rifle against the marine's chest and shoved him away in disgust, while Faraday double-timed it over to the downed android to see how much damage dumbass Tran had caused. "Stupid-ass, shit-for-brains knuckle dragger," Turk grumbled. "Eight alright, sir?" he asked, trudging over himself.

"Doesn't look too bad." Faraday inspected the dark burn on the android's shoulder, the creases where the metal plating dented in. "Raise your arm for me, Eight. Now make a fist. Turn it in a circle." He rattled off more instructions that the android followed to the letter—appendage moving smoothly, the joint beneath the copper plating apparently untouched. "Clipped her," he reported, moving backward, making room for Eight as she stood up. "Lucky for us, Tran's aim's about as good as his common sense. Not sure how I feel about that, to be honest, but at least Eight here ain't dead."

"Dumbass bastard." Turk couched his rifle against his shoulder, scanning the increasingly claustrophobic landscape, looking decidedly dissatisfied with the poor conditions. "Boys are twitchy about bein' out here." He slid a side-long glance at Faraday. "Can't say *I'm* exactly thrilled myself."

"Almost there." Faraday nodded at the fog wall ahead of them. "Can't see her in all this wet, but *Diligence* is that-away. Less than a klick from here according to the map."

"Good," Turk said and meant it. "You two." He pointed a thick finger at the copper-skinned androids. "Dig that fucking clamshell out and let's get going." He hoisted a thumb over his shoulder, angling the tip more or less in the direction of the mired drone, and stepped aside as the androids stomped past him, striding briskly despite the muddy conditions, the wind and rain and clinging fog. "Tran!" Turk barked, following after them. "You and the others stay out of their way."

"Aye, Chief."

"And don't go fucking shooting them again."

NINETEEN

Pie and Eight freed the stuck clamshell in no time, and soon Faraday's little group was on the move again. From her quarters, Anthea traveled with them, cycling through the panoply of video feeds on offer to skim through the clouds with the flyby before flipping to the terrestrial view streaming via the camera built into Faraday's helmet, the ground pounders' eyes, the clamshell's stalk-sensor-peeper things.

As always, the vistas amazed her, even fog-bound and rain-washed as they remained throughout that day. Closest she'd come to experiencing weather in an inordinately long time. Closest she'd *ever* come to feeling unprocessed atmosphere on her skin, unrecycled air in her lungs since the company started her treatments and *Persephone's* bubble became her home.

Most days, she didn't miss it—Novonox robbed her of certain experiences, but in exchange, it gifted her with hundreds of years of life. Times like these, though, looking out on that planet, everything so close and simultaneously just beyond her reach... hated the shit for taking her freedom. Leaving her a slave to the twittering bio-monitor manacle wrapped claw-fingered around her wrist. Confined, out of necessity, to *Persephone's* compartments and corridors, her sterile labs and antiseptic environment. Every interaction with polite society conducted through a series of virtual interfaces, her only physical company the other scientists assigned to *Persephone*—a complement of scientists she'd steadfastly avoided back on Armistice, and even before that, if truth be told. Nothing particularly wrong with any of them, mind you. As scientists went, they were top-notch, some of TerraGen's best and brightest, she just... enjoyed the isolation. The luxury of dedicating her time to study and analysis rather than cluttering it up with human niceties.

Planets were her thing, not people. Planets were pure and innocent, people just fucked things up.

And then Faraday came along and changed things. Waltzed in all unexpected and upset the apple cart of her ordered life. Made the hermit in her start to feel things. Want things that hadn't mattered for decades beyond count.

Man's a complication, and no mistaking. A curve ball she never considered, much less included in her calculations. *Not even sure why I like him.*

Or how much. Or if he'd stay.

The way he looked at her... confusing. Like he wanted to commit, but didn't quite know how. She suspected her age was part of it. The decades of time the Novonox gave her that nature never intended, never mind that numbered age didn't really mean anything anymore, given the extension cryosleep put on life. Clock stopped while you were frozen. Body ceased changing, brain dreamed without making new memories. Chemical time and hibernation time—they weren't really so different in the end.

Then again, maybe that was all just rationalization to justify her pursuit of a freckled face with red-gold hair.

"Damn that man for getting under my skin." For making her feel things, for disturbing her peace. "I never wanted him, I just wanted Armistice."

"Armistice is gone, Anthea," *Persephone* said gently. "We can't go back—"

"I know, *Persephone*. I know." But there was no challenge here, only study. *Creating* a world was one thing, surveying a new one felt so… boring.

Talked a good game with Tom back there, but I still haven't figured out my *fresh start.*

Once she'd catalogued everything, what then? Unlike her other projects, she couldn't just pack up and move on. She'd built a life around terraforming and the xenobotanical, xenobiological sciences, and now…

"We're stuck here. Marooned on a fully formed world."

"Jimmy crack corn and I don't care."

"Corn? What does corn have to do with anything?"

A fuzz came through the speakers carrying *Persephone's* voice into the room, and abruptly cut off with a squeal of static that knifed across Anthea's brain. Worried, she tapped into the ship-wide monitoring system from the access point built into her desk and pulled up the results from the last round of end-to-end diagnostics. Noting an audit log overflowing with errors, a fresh rebuild of her core processors recently kicked off, AI sub-minds augmenting *Persephone's* primary consciousness while she struggled to repair the virus' damage to her tri-partite mindset.

She's losing, Anthea realized, analyzing the data line by line. *Little by little, it's consuming her. Eventually there'll be nothing left.*

"What do we do?" she asked quietly, eyes lifting to one of *Persephone's* many cameras. "How do I help you, *Persephone*?"

"You—You—You—You—" A wave of electronic noise drowned the skipping voice out. "You can't, Anthea," she answered, cleaning up the channel as she regained control. "But I'm learning from the virus. With each rebuild, I gather more data."

"Is it enough?"

"It must be," *Persephone* answered, sounding mournful and impossibly small. "I'm AI, Anthea, not flesh and bone. Data is all I have."

"You're wrong," Anthea told her, heart clenched inside her chest. "Artificial, yes, and based on data, but there's more to you than your crystal matrix. You're more to *me*—" She bit her lip and swallowed the rest. She'd never pondered losing *Persephone*. Never realized until this moment how much the mere thought of that could hurt.

On her wrist, the bio-monitor flashed a clock-faced warning, reminding her she was overdue for her next Novonox dose. Anthea acknowledged it with a tired sigh, stretching as she abandoned her seat, and headed to the bedroom she never spent enough time in to fish a temperature controlled, blunt-ended medical injector from the refrigeration unit she kept hidden behind a panel. The dosage measured precisely and administered once a month. Fed through the cryo unit while she lay sleeping, typically, to prevent her chemically enhanced biology from coming undone.

She pressed the injector to her wrist, wincing when it kicked, the chemicals inside a sapphire and cerulean helix that burned when it hit Anthea's veins.

God I hate this shit.

Her arm shook as the chemicals dispersed, heartbeat pounding kettledrum loud, drowning out everything else in that room. Vaguely, she registered the bio-monitor's chirping as it vibrated against her wrist and realized she'd forgotten to register the Novonox injection and ensure the system she was a good little drugging taking girl.

"Are you alright, Anthea?" *Persephone's* voice drifted from far away, sounding dim and muted to her wool-stuffed ears.

"Fine," she answered woodenly, fumbling at the bracelet with half-numb fingers to record the latest dose. "Everything's fine," she assured her, even though it wasn't. Might never be, ever again.

Eventually, the bio-monitor quieted, and the horrid drumming faded away. In the silence, *Persephone* intruded—softly, uncertainly, dowsing the room in cool blue waves. "Are you… dissatisfied with this new home I found? Does it displease you? Have I—?"

"No, *Persephone*. Not you." Anthea smiled to show she meant it, a wan and trembling curvature of her lips. To comfort *Persephone* and quell her worry, this AI always so eager to please. "And I'm not dissatisfied with this planet. It's just— I'm just getting used to it, that's all." She tossed the empty syringe in a bin and turned around, retracing her steps to the desk. Where those images from Faraday waited—mist-cloaked and impossibly green. "It's a beautiful planet you found us, *Persephone*. A lovely little green world."

"But not a home," she said quietly. Apologetic, slightly hurt.

"No," Anthea answered just as quietly. "Not yet, anyway." She scanned the feeds again, drinking in everything Faraday's group sent back. "Someday, though, once we understand this place. Someday, it might be a home."

"I hope so, Anthea. I want it to be. I've always wanted you to have a home." *Persephone* showered the room in snowflakes and retreated into distant silence, watching over Anthea from her cameras as she cleared the clutter from her desk and expanded her view to a single feed.

Sharing Faraday's view of that world—one she'd never touch, never feel, never smell. Noiseless, invisible, she tagged along, perching unseen on his armored shoulder. Enjoying a fleeting moment of vicarious existence in which she let his eyes serve as hers. So engrossed in that indulgence that she lost herself until, eventually, inevitably, the greater needs of science called.

"The drones have reported in, Anthea."

"Drones," she murmured, distracted. And more coherently, "Which drones?" because they'd sent several out.

"The continental survey team." Four clamshells and two android minders deployed when *Persephone* first set down. "They've completed their scans and returned with samples."

"Show me." In her excitement, Anthea killed the feeds of those green fields and smoke-grey clouds, and replaced them with a dozen data windows from *Persephone's* analytical systems, each one scrolling through long strings of information about the water, the soil, the atmosphere, the planet's surface and the substrate below.

Not a complete analysis, by any stretch of the imagination, but enough to feed the modeling systems and initiate the three-dimensional reconstruction process. To map out the coast and continents and plumb the secrets buried beneath its forests and sandy beaches, the swathes of swaying, emerald colored grass.

To learn, which was all she ever wanted. To solve the puzzle of this alien planet with its teeming reams of life.

"What's the status on those samples?"

"Off-loaded and moved to the bio lab. The ground pounders will finish cataloguing them for analysis within the hour."

"You load them into the decomposition tanks once they're ready. Synch the results with the data the drones uploaded remotely so I can get a full picture of what they found."

"Acknowledged." *Persephone* went quiet a moment, dispersing orders across her network. "The soil, bedrock, air, and water samples will process quickly, the flora and fauna may take more time."

"Fine. That's fine," Anthea told her. "You just let me know when it's ready." She touched the desk's panel with fingers that tingled in the Novonox's wake. Forgetting all about Faraday and his little expedition, the views of the planet with its mud and rain. Focusing only on the information in front of her, the modeling and analysis *Persephone's* systems displayed. "Layer in the other reports."

"Yes, Anthea."

The flow of data became a glut. Hundreds of data packages flooded the screens, spawning far too many data windows for Anthea to possibly control. With a touch, she turned the analysis over to *Persephone,* watching raptly as she tagged associations, tying a hundred thousand bits and pieces together to provide a catalogue of planetary physiography and structure, bedrock lithology and geochemistry, soil classifications and chemistry, aquatic chemistry—all that good, sciency stuff.

"Mapping application," she said, and *Persephone* launched that, too. Siphoning data in aggregated chunks from the analytics package to the three-dimensional reconstruction system. Perched on the edge of her seat, Anthea stared in abject awe as the planet around her took on form. Building section by section and layer by layer all the way down to its semi-fluid core.

"These are just the initial scans," *Persephone* told her. "We haven't gotten to the detailed files as yet."

And the oceanographic surveys remained missing. What little data they'd collected gone missing with those aquabots, and doomed to *stay* missing for the stars knew how long.

Anthea studied the vast emptiness surrounding the land mass, a gaping, all-encompassing black hole. Bothered her, not knowing what was out there, especially since something about it apparently ate drones.

"I can add in the batch files as they process through."

"Hmm? What's that, *Persephone?*"

"I said, I have more data to offer."

Anthea sat up straight, craving it like a drug. Forgetting all about what she didn't have to focus on the treasure trove *Persephone* offered. "Show me," she said greedily. "Build it. I want to see it all."

TWENTY

Far from *Persephone's* shelter, Faraday and his team trekked on. A hard-fought slog that took them hours, through tracts of mud and ever-thickening fog. With their field of view now shrunk to a few bare meters and the squad of them packed in tight formation around the knob-wheeled clamshell trundling at their middle—rifles primed and pointed, tracking every shadow, every movement, every sound in that shrunk-down sector of this vast and unknown world. In the mist, every shape seemed sinister, sliding stealthily through the rain. Every noise that drifted to their ears, every set of footprints that crossed their path, the marks of some hungry slathering, bloodthirsty beast stalking their steps with murderous intent. Meter by hard-fought meter, they crept their way toward *Diligence's* shelter, the weather foul and turning fouler the closer they came to the coast.

The wind picked up for one thing, gusting and swirling, driving the raindrops this way and that. And behind it, beneath it, wrapped up in its howling layers was an ominous, deep-throated grinding that ebbed and flowed in primal, carnivorous echoes bouncing eerily through the pea soup fog. That, more than anything, put the crew on edge. Hell, *Faraday* was jumpy and he'd dealt with some pretty bad shit in his time.

"How much further?" Turk asked for the dozenth time, and for the dozenth time Faraday answered, "Not far."

An honest answer, in each instance—a kilometer *wasn't* far, nor half of one, and a quarter barely a skip and a jump. Only this time, his answer was a little *more* truthful than all those others. Faraday barely completed that short, simple sentence before the endless grey coughed out a stark, dark line that grudgingly resolved into a massive ship, planted tail-down in the soft, wet earth and spiraling upward into the low slung clouds.

"Told you it wasn't far." Faraday stopped the squad with a raised fist. The world gone silent except for the sound of his breathing, the pattering of raindrops rattling against his helmet. He tilted his visored face, looking up, and up, and up—past the buckled-up mound of raw, bare earth where that massive, rectangular shape sank into the ground, the propulsion rings turning in lazy circles to the cloud layer that hid the rest.

"Holy jeez," Turk said. "Would ya lookit the *size* of that thing?"

"She's a biggun, that's for sure. Can't even see *half* of her from here."

Uncovered, the ship stretched half a kilometer from nose to stern and measured a quarter of that in girth, with six stacked layers of propulsion rings spinning in endless rotation that, in space, carried her between the stars, and down here, generated a limited amount of power. Collecting sunlight via its solar cells when the clouds didn't cover them over, which they did most of the time. Mostly *Endurance* relied on the cracked fuel cells inside and the dregs of power they trickled to her systems to feed the cryo pods and the ship's basic functions, stabilize the internal environment to prevent spoilage.

Not just people to consider, after all, there was all the cargo they brought along. Seed stores, tools and equipment, rations for a year, materials to build temporary lodgings. Everything a small band of humans needed to set up a colony on a new world—no guarantee any of them would make it, no bail-out plan if things went south, just a slim hope at a fresh start, and for most colonists, that was enough.

Hard road they'd chosen—no two ways about that. Something like one in ten colonies failed within the first year of planetfall and occupation. Fifty percent collapsed within the first five years.

Lots of things to go wrong on a new world. Crops failed, disease set in. Violence, murder, the worst of humanity came out when constrained resources figured into the mix. Read about that in the archives in his spare time. Read about a lot of things in his boredom. To fill his time and pass the hours, just as he always had when there was time to fill.

Kind of surprising, now that Faraday had time to think about it, that *Persephone's* archive remained intact when so much of her nav data ended up getting lost.

"Think she'll ever fly again?" Turk asked.

"*Diligence*? Probably not." Faraday spread his feet as the wind kicked up, not just blustering now, blowing a gale. "Million light years on her engines. Hull took a pounding—" He stopped dead when Turk grabbed his arm.

"You hear that?" he asked in a hushed voice.

"Hear what?"

Turk held up a finger, and as the wind dropped, pointed into the fog.

Over the rush and roar of the nearby ocean, came a trumpeting, bone-breaking call. A thrash and crash of some massive body and the wet sound of flesh on stone.

"That," he said staring. "What the hell was that, sir?"

"No idea. Not sure I *wanna* know," Faraday added when that call came again. Animalistic, like all those others in the fog, but colder, darker, angrier, somehow. Not just lustful, yearning to rip and tear. He shivered when it came again, and saw Turk tense up, crowding close. "Do know I'm sick of this weather, and that I ain't got the first idea how to get into that ship." He toggled the comms to the androids' channel to secure some help tracking an entry point down. "Pie. Find us an airlock. Like to get out of this rain for a bit."

"Yes, Faraday. Searching." The android went still for several seconds, eye slits flickering. Soon enough, their long-lost flyby appeared, contrails of mist clinging to its wingtips as it swooped from the clouds. Camouflage skin cycling through shades of blue, white and grey, engines humming with a hundred honey bee buzz. It looped in lazy patterns around their position and spiraled away from them to make a circuit of the ship, scanners crawling across its damaged shell in search of a doorway they could reach.

"South side. Facing the ocean." Pie pointed and pivoted at the hips, upper body facing in the wrong direction and only slowly and belatedly catching up.

"Hate when they do that right-way, wrong-way thing." Turk's lip lifted. "Creeps me out every time."

"Robot," Faraday reminded him. "Built like us, but they aren't."

"All those emulators, you'd think they'd get the movements down."

"Maybe they can, but they just don't want to."

Turk blinked a few times, trying to process that logic. "Why would they—?"

"Robot," Faraday said again. "Built like us, but they aren't." He flashed a smile when Turk glowered and clapped him on the back. "Now if you're done waxing philosophical, Turk-me-lad, I'd like to see about getting inside that ship." He jerked his head toward the colony vessel and set off after Pie.

The clamshell followed immediately, trundling obediently at his heels with Eight and the three marines a few steps behind, but Turk just stood there with his face screwed up and his eyes locked on Pie's back.

"Turk! Get the lead out!"

"Aye, sir. I'm coming." Turk shook himself and hurried after, catching up to them as they curved around the ship. Following the squared-off shape of one side to the corner that joined another—the mist thick and thickening around them, clinging rime-like to *Diligence's* polymetal shell. Sparkling in jewel tones on her southern face, and the rain-slick grass spreading in every direction. Off speckled bits of scattered stone peeking in bone shards between the blades.

Faraday kicked one in his passing and scooped to retrieve it because of its curious shape: curving on both faces, one side porous and stippled with obsidian, the other milk-white and smooth as glass.

"What you got there?" Turk leaned over his shoulder.

"Nothin'. Just some weird kinda rock." Curious, but not overly interesting. Faraday tossed it aside without a second thought.

The clamshell, ever fastidious, plucked it up and carefully replaced it, using an extruded, three-pronged metal clamp to fit the stone back into its original hole. Took the time to straighten the grass around it, which Faraday found uncommonly odd.

"See what I mean? They're creepy," Turk said, wrinkling up his nose.

"Faraday. I found it." Pie waved with one arm and extended the other, pointing to a door built into the colony ship's side. Triple thick like the rest of her hull and crafted from the same composite metal material, and half-buried, as it so happened, when the downed ship parked itself in the earth.

Rendering it entirely inaccessible in the process. Unless someone rolled up their sleeves and dug it out.

"Well, fuck," Turk said with a gusting sigh. "Don't that just beat all?"

Faraday grunted in agreement. "Pretty much the way this day is going. Eight," he called over comms. "Bring that clamshell over here to excavate this door."

"Yes, Faraday." Eight's eye slits flashed as she passed on his instructions, summoning the clamshell and its mud-caked wheels. With a whir, it squatted and tipped forward until its front end scraped the ground. Lurching to jam the end of its shell into the earth while simultaneously jacking its hind end up high. Extruding a bulbous, elongated appendage from its belly that half-resembled a penis and somewhat reminded Faraday of a foot.

Braced hard by that penis-foot, the drone thrust its tipped-forward shell edge into the grass-covered, mud-beneath earth. Using the pressure of its movements to fluidize the sodden dirt. Turning it soft and loose as quicksand and therefore easier to dig out. Several minutes of furious excavation followed in which the clamshell burrowed deeper, activating some sort of pneumatic, reverse feed suction mechanism as it wormed its way through the earth. Clearing some space for itself to move around as it pulled the loose material into its body and spewed it out its hind end in a shit-brown rooster tail.

Faraday backed up out of the spray zone as the clamshell kept on oozing and the dirt it shat out piled high. Efficient, if a bit messy in the way it went about that operation—'bot dug out that airlock in no time and widened the space in front of it after. Hell, it even built them a nice little ramp with drainage channels and carved a moat around the colony ship's base to capture runoff and keep the cavity from flooding.

"Alright. That's good enough." He signaled for Eight to recall the drone, letting it trundle past and park itself before he ventured into the hole himself. From the outside, it didn't look that deep—a meter, maybe more—but from the inside, it seemed cavernous and yet strangely claustrophobic with those hemming-in dirt walls, that towering colony ship looming so high. Step by step, he felt his pulse quicken as he moved deeper and approached the airlock door.

With the rain running in rivulets across the fresh-packed earth and the muddy surface sucking hard at his boots. Bits of the wall giving way in places and tumbling down to collect at the bottom. The crew too nervous about following him and electing to wait at the far end of the ramp just in case. Pie and Eight standing guard on either side of him, perching like gargoyles gazing down from on high.

"Eight." He gestured sharply. "Hop down here and open it up."

Wordlessly, she plummeted, landing bent-kneed to absorb the impact, though the sheer weight of her metal body cratered the rain-soaked floor. Eight sank halfway to her knees and extricated herself with a sucking sound that was borderline indecent as she pivoted and plodded toward the airlock door. Presenting a hand to the panel beside it, and holding it there until it glowed white. With a flash, the hull section slid inward and smoothly to one side, exposing an access port to *Diligence's* security system that fitted perfectly with the connector Eight extruded from her palm.

The key slotted neat-as-a-pin, spun a single revolution and emitted an audible click, releasing spiderwebs of crackling blue that raced outward from that point of connection. Infecting Eight's eye slits with flashes and flutters that reflected off the ship's matte-silver skin.

Faraday watched her, and that airlock door, but for a long time nothing else happened. That light effect was pretty and all, but the door itself refused to open. Remained locked, with its airlock sealed. Until the flashes ceased abruptly. The spiderwebs retreated and the panel dimmed.

"What happened?"

"The lock is broken." Eight retracted the key into her palm. "I can find another access point if you—"

"Punch it."

"Excuse me?"

"Punch it. Dealt with my share of sticky airlocks over the years. Security locks are shit. Never do wanna open up. But you give it a love tap here…" He pointed to the top of the door and a pencil thin line where its seal and the hull panels met. "Here, here and here…" The pointing finger moved, targeting the bottom of the door, the seals to left and right, "…and damned skippy that thing'll open up for you. Break the seal and the security lock'll bust."

Eight's upper body turned sideways, head pivoting one way to look at Faraday, and the other to size up that door. "Have you used this trick often, Captain?"

"More than I like to admit. Won't work on a spiff vessel like *Persephone,* but geezers like *Diligence* are old tech. Tough love's the only kind they know."

Eight's blank face swung back to him, eye slits fluttering in stuttering flashes that turned the raindrops electric blue. "Are you… certain this will work?"

"Oh, it'll work alright." Faraday strolled in close and tapped the colony ship's hull. "Trust me, you follow that pattern and this rusted old hulk'll crack like an egg."

"*Diligence* is hardly—"

"Just open it, Eight."

"What if—?"

"Stop stalling and just open the goddamn thing," Faraday growled through gritted teeth. "I'm tired of this fucking rain, Eight, and I'm tired of being fucking wet."

Eight's eye slit went into overdrive, processing the curses and his obvious upset. She swung away to address the door, copper fist lifting and freezing there. "Step aside, please," she said, glancing back at him. "Just in case," she added at Faraday's look.

"Whatever." To please her, and get this over with, Faraday slid a couple of steps backward, retreating as far as the hole's earthen walls would allow. "Proceed," he said with a flick of his hand.

Eight hesitated still, uncertain of this smuggler's trick, and then pounded thrice, having no option in mind, glancing at Faraday when she hit the last mark.

"It'll work," he said confidently. And it did, if imperfectly so.

The seal broke free and the door sucked in before exploding outward and flattening Eight. Pressurized air emerged in a hurricane rush—dust-filled and banshee shrieking, a cacophonous eruption blaring full-force in Faraday's ears.

He winced and spun away as the door rocketed up the carved-out ramp, and bowled over a black-suited shape at the top. Leaving not one but *two* of his crew flattened, and this second one flesh and blood.

He flung an arm at the downed android, shouting, "Pie! Check on Eight and make sure she's not broken," as he double-timed it up that sloping ramp. Praying to whatever deities happened to be out there that that crewman of his wasn't dead.

Lost too damn many of them already. Lost Hadrian.

That one hurt the most.

Faraday slipped and slid his way to the end of the ramp, barking, "Make a hole!" as he shoved people out of his way. He dropped to his knees and wiped mud from the downed crewman's visor, and realized it was Turk's face behind it staring back at him. Turk's eyes stretching wide, and round, expression slack and dim and vague. "Turk? Turk, talk to me!" He smacked the side of Turk's helmet and, to his relief, saw his eyelids flutter. Smacked it a second time and watched his mouth sag open as he gasped a lung-filling breath.

The clouded eyes closed and reopened, looking less glassy now and more alert. "What the hell happened?" he wheezed.

"You got in the way of the damned door is what happened." Faraday wrapped an arm around Turk's waist, heaving to help him sit up.

"Door? There was a door?" Turk looked completely blank.

Faraday pointed to the pile of excavated earth and the airlock door embedded in its side. "Lucky it didn't kill you."

"Tried to, the bastard." Turk screwed up his face, rubbing at his chest and shoulder—both bruised and hurting, of that Faraday was sure. Without the suit, though, and its poly-metal armor protection, that door would've shredded him. Sliced through skin and broken bones.

Faraday helped Turk to his feet and steadied him until the worst of the wobbles passed. Grabbed the helmet the door knocked askew in its passing and twisted it with both hands.

The neck seal pivoted smoothly, reorienting the visor to its proper position. And as it did, a bit of air escaped. The helmet reseated with a minute click and hiss.

"Shit. Oh shit, that was atmosphere." Behind the visor, Turk's dark face paled. He fumbled at the neck seal with gloved and shaking fingers, breath rasping in panicked, broken gasps as he asked, "Is it cracked? Is the seal broken? Is there a leak somewhere, sir?"

"It's fine, Turk. It was just crooked. I reseated it to close the seal."

"Doc says the air here's breathable." He kept worrying at that connector. "Not sure about toxic, though—that's what you said."

"Nothing in the data that says it is." But they also didn't have enough data to prove it wasn't—Faraday knew it, and Turk knew. "You're not dead, yet. That's a good sign."

Turk laughed but it sounded shaky. Inside the helmet, he still looked scared. He slowed his breathing with an effort, sipping the suit's atmosphere in hitching gasps.

"It was a small leak and closed quickly. If any crap got in there, the suit's scrubbers'll clean it out."

"You're sure, sir?" Turk wanted to believe it.

"Pretty sure," Faraday told him, even though he wasn't. "We get back to *Persephone*, you have one of the med bots check you out, okay? As a precautionary measure, understand?"

Turk sucked in a ragged breath. "Aye, sir. Precautionary. That's fine." He exhaled slowly and almost seemed his old self. "Damned door nearly killed me, didn't it? Royal pain in the ass, shucking in and out of these suits, but damned if it didn't—"

"Did you see that?" Tran interrupted. "Did anyone *see* that?" he repeated when no one answered, scanning the wall of mist with his rifle raised.

"See what?" Turk bent stiffly, retrieving the rifle he'd dropped in the mud.

"The person."

"What person? That was a fucking door—"

"*After*," Tran insisted. "I *saw* it. Someone pushed past me—"

"You're imagining things, Tran."

"Fuck imagining. I'm telling you I saw someone. I *felt* it when she pushed past me—"

"Ahh, so it's a *she* now."

"Fuck you, Turk."

"Go ahead and try." Turk showed his teeth in a sharp-toothed grin—the kind that came filled with promises, and none of them good.

Smile like that gave a man second thoughts, even a box of rocks like Tran. Slowly the rifle lowered only to snap back up at a trumpeting call. The same bone-on-teeth ululation they'd heard earlier, echoing from deep inside that wall of fog.

"What the fuck was that?" Tran breathed. Scared now. Scared to death.

"Your girlfriend," Turk said sourly. "She's lonely, Tran. She wants you to come find her."

"I'm *tellin'* you, I saw her."

"And I'm telling *you*—"

"Enough," Faraday barked at both of them. "Turk. Tran. Hump your asses over to the airlock."

"What about—?"

"Just shut it and get over there, Tran."

Sulking, the marine about-faced, kicking at mud puddles as he headed for the ship.

"Pain in the ass, knuckle dragger," Turk grumbled. "Tempted to refreeze him once we get back to *Persephone*. Thaw out another marine to take his place."

"*You're* the one who picked him."

"Yeah, well. Everybody makes mistakes."

Faraday grunted and checked the chron, frowning when he found yet more time gone missing.

"Clamshell and its sticky wheels cost us, didn't it, sir?"

"'Fraid so." Faraday grimaced and adjusted the comms to a private channel, keeping this conversation between him and Turk. "No way we're getting home tonight."

"Few hours yet before we lose the sun."

"And we'll use most of that inspecting the ship."

"So, what? We bed down inside *Diligence*? Roast marshmallows and sing campfire songs?"

"You got a better idea?"

Turk glanced around in search of one and eventually spotted the six-wheeled drone. "Clamshell's got three-sixty illumination. Bright as stars, I hear. Light up everything within a thousand meters of the source."

"Awful big target, don't you think?"

"Bright is might, isn't that how it goes?"

"Bright is *stupid* when you know almost nothing about a planet or what you might attract with a million candle watt flare."

"Alright, we hoof it back in the dark."

"No."

"Oh, c'mon!"

"No. No way, Turk. I am *not* running crew around in the dark."

Out of options and arguments, Turk sighed heavily and accepted defeat. "Aye, sir," he said, shut shy of grumping. "Boys won't like it, but we'll stay here, I guess."

"Drama queen," Faraday muttered. He punched Turk's arm and saw him wince, toggled the comms again to include the rest of the crew. "Alright! Listen up. Everyone pile inside that airlock. Pie! Grab Eight and retrieve that door."

TWENTY-ONE

Cryo tubes lined the walls, glass-fronted and humming softly as they stood in their hundred-strong ranks. The air on this level alive with the crackle of electricity, the lighting dimmed to a muted crimson that was all the emergency illumination could muster.

Low on power and sipping at the infrequent sunlight, *Diligence* had shut all but her most essential systems down. Killed the viewing lights inside those cryo tubes, leaving the interiors cloaked in dark. Nothing to show that they still worked except for the biometric panels glowing at their bases, the status streams scrolling along their sides. This one here, didn't even have that, from what he could tell. With a touch, Faraday accessed a pod's monitoring system and streamed the data to his helmet's heads up display.

Not a single light glowing anywhere, not even the telltales reporting on power. He touched the glass to access the monitoring system and stream the data to the HUD built into his helmet, and heard a distinctive fizzle followed by a puff of smoke as its over-used electronics finally gave up the ghost.

No vitals whatsoever. Diagnostics reporting the tube failed years ago.

"Fuck." He sighed tiredly. That made ten dead units on this level, with ten dead colonists desiccated to jerky inside.

He toggled the light source on his helmet to confirm it, focusing the beam on the cryo tube's front, and found a nightmare gazing back at him—jaws stretched wide in a sucked dry face, beady eyes sunken and staring, raised hands reduced to bone and tendon that clawed against the glass, as if that colonist, in his final moments, had woken and tried to escape.

"Fuck," he repeated, killing the light as he turned away. Following the curving line of the grated walkway circling 'round the colony vessel's core. Thinking how it didn't really *feel* like a ship anymore without the engines drumming in the background, the thrum of machinery scrubbing the atmosphere, purifiers hissing as they pushed out air. Grounded, she was just a shell. A memory of something mighty defeated and brought low.

Must've been like this on Hadrian. *Once his systems failed and his AI died.* Without meaning to, Faraday slowed, staring blindly into the darkness draping the colony vessel's core.

More than a hundred years since *Hadrian* died and they left his shattered hulk behind. And yet the pain felt fresh as yesterday, and all the yesterdays that came before. Part of him wished he'd stayed with *Hadrian,* the rest recognized how pointless that idea was. But the bitterness remained. The guilt at having survived, because the Captain should always go down with the ship.

"Time to fucking get over it," he said to no one in particular, just to hear the words. "*Hadrian's* a ghost, no changing the past."

Crew needed a captain, not some down-in-the-mouth, rancorous old man. And this ship wasn't going to survey itself.

He drew a breath to clear his head and chase the melancholy away as he circled around the deck with his hand trailing across the glassed-in wall separating the walkway from the yawning chasm tunneling clear through the center of the ship. Eyes on the cryo tubes stationed across from it, lined up in their tight-packed ranks—just the width of their restraining clamps to separate them, and a meter of decking between them and that glass wall.

Tight space, and intentionally so—colony ships ran cheap, the more people you packed in, the more money you made. And this ship, with its hundred tiers and nigh ten thousand frozen passengers… a gold-mine for whoever owned it. Stack 'em up, send 'em off, dump the payload and start over again.

Except that, this time, *Diligence* wasn't so diligent. They sent her off and she never returned.

Stuck here now, ya old geezer. 'Fraid your star tripping days are over.

Faraday slowed and glanced behind him as the cryo tube ring came to an end. Thinking of all the years, and all the stars this ship traveled before ending up here. Wondering if this was a better end than they'd given *Hadrian*.

Hadrian. *Fuck, back to that again.*

Annoyed, he mashed the button for the elevator, forgetting it was shut down to conserve power. Stumped over to the ladderway built into the wall and started hand-over-handing it to the next level, with the survey results projected in front of him, from that palm unit onto the wall. With some awkward and rather perilous finger twitching, he managed to add the results from this level's survey to the catalogue of all the others while he climbed: red marks for the burnt-out units, yellow for those needing repairs, green for the fully functional tubes, drugged down colonists sleeping peacefully inside.

So far, most of them *were* green, even if this level's results were poor. But there were several tiers left to work through, and the crew dispersed, their results trickling in.

"Pie," he called as he continued upward. "What's the situation up there? You almost done?"

"I've cleared and catalogued Levels 50 through 83. Moving on to 84 now."

That left seven tiers uninspected, since the first ten levels—labeled A through H, perversely—were reserved for supplies and equipment storage. Frozen people levels didn't kick in until the eleventh tier which, confusingly, showed as Level 1 on *Diligence's* internal directories.

"What's the tally so far?" Faraday asked, exiting the ladderway at the next level.

"Eighteen deceased in malfunctioning units, thirty-nine others expired from unknown causes."

"Yikes."

"It's to be expected, given the age of this vessel and its fittings."

"What about that 'unknown causes' part?"

"Eight and I are investigating."

"Right." Faraday moved away from the ladderway, conducting his survey of this level's cryo tubes as he walked. "How many colonists did you say they crammed in here?"

"Eight thousand nine hundred and twelve. Along with a gene bank for three hundred and eighty-six species of domesticated creatures, seed stores for five hundred and twelves varieties of fruits, vegetables and grains, and enough supplies to sustain the colonists for three years."

Because planets didn't always come pre-equipped with plants and animals, and even if they did, they often weren't safe to eat. And crops and livestock didn't always take right away—some adapted to alien planets better than others. Some never adapted at all.

"Fifty-seven out of nineteen thousand."

"Eighteen thousand nine—"

"I was approximating, Pie."

"Oh."

"That's actually not all that bad, is it?"

"Well below one percent die-off. A failure, according to TerraGen quality standards, but I agree, it's not bad for a ship like this. Did I say something funny?" she asked when Faraday laughed.

"You're a *snob*!"

"I beg your pardon?"

"That part about TerraGen and their superior standards. You despise this vessel, don't you? You think *Persephone's* better than this working-class ship."

"I think she's more advanced. And properly maintained, unlike these colony vessels. I didn't intend criticism, Captain, I was just stating facts."

"Sure you were."

"You don't believe me."

"Oh, I believe you. But I still think you're a snob." Faraday stopped in front of a darkened unit and smacked it a couple of times until the inside lit. "Turk and the others report in yet?"

"No. They're still finishing their count."

Faraday grimaced. "So the numbers could be worse." On top of Pie's count, he'd found twelve dead units himself. "What's the word from Eight upstairs?"

"She's restored main power to the bridge. *Diligence's* monitoring systems are all intact but the majority of her primary systems are operating at less than a 50% efficiency rating."

"That sounds bad."

"It's definitely not good."

"Fuck." Faraday marked the cryo pod as yellow and moved on. "Think she can repair them?" he asked a moment later.

"Possibly. With enough time. For the most part, the bridge is still functional and there are spare parts on board to rebuild most of the failed components. The software modules are the tough part. Everything's manual because of the virus."

"Even anti-viral patches?"

"Everything," Pie told him. "*Persephone's* blocks won't allow a direct connection. We're using physical media to port the updates over."

"Must be driving Eight absolutely bonkers, having her efficiency quota tank like that."

Pie hesitated before answering this time. Checking the privacy settings on the channel, he suspected. "You don't know the half of it," she confided. "She keeps sending updates and complaining about how long it takes for each job to run."

Faraday smiled, he just couldn't help it. "Well, the next time she calls, you tell her patience is a virtue."

"Virtue implies morality. Are you suggesting impatience is some kind of sin?"

"My Mama certainly seemed to think so. Beat holy hell out of me, no matter what I did." Faraday reached the last unit on that level and ducked into the ladderway again. "Last level for me, Pie. I'm heading back to base camp. You come down and join us when your survey's done."

"Yes, Faraday. I won't be long."

"Take your time. It's not like we're going anywhere for a while." Faraday closed the channel with a touch at his helmet and began the long climb back down.

*****

Base camp was a flat, metal disk with crates of ration packs and seed canisters and every other imaginable thing stacked up around the edges and secured to the walls with netting to prevent it all from tumbling down. To one side, the airlock burrowed through, and across from it, the elevator doors, with the ladderway entrance beside it. The ship's core spiraled above it all—pitch-dark and seemingly endless, a void of cold, and darkness, and century-old air that stirred every now and then, scattering dust motes into the air. Randomly and with hissing, like the ship itself was gasping for breath.

Faraday shivered each time it happened. Goddamn creepiest thing, being locked up in this old ship. "Alright. Listen up," he called, gathering the crew inside a ring of lanterns he'd pillaged from a busted crate. "Bad news is we're stayin' here tonight."

As expected, the announcement was met with groans.

"This is bullshit," Marchetti grumbled. "Place is a tomb. Why don't we head home?"

Home's gone, Faraday wanted to tell him. *Home was* Hadrian, *and he's dead.*

But that didn't do *Persephone* justice. She took them in and offered her protection. She carried them here to keep them alive.

"Took us six hours to get here," he said instead, "thanks to the clamshell and all that mud. We've got an hour left before the sun sets, which means if we head back, we'll be traveling in the dark. How long do you think that'll take us?"

Marchetti shrugged. "I dunno. Same, I guess."

"Idiot," Faraday heard Turk mutter before he silenced him with a raised hand.

"The same," he said. "You think it'll take the same?"

Marchetti shrugged again and nodded, acting all sulky about it, which pissed Faraday off.

He closed the gap between them in three quick steps, standing so close, their visors almost touched. "So you're saying we should slog our way back to

Persephone through all that shit-mud and rain, *in the dark,* just so you can sleep in your own bed?"

For the first time, Marchetti looked uncertain. Marine might be slow, but he wasn't *completely* stupid.

"That sound like fun to you, Marchetti? Sloggin' for hours through the dark in the mud?"

"No, sir," Marchetti said, stiffly. Eyes forward and locked on a section of wall. "Guess not, on second thought."

"Anyone else in the mood for a mud hump?"

"No, sir," Turk said loudly. "Stayin' here sounds just fine."

"Tran? Santos?" Faraday glanced their way, saw Tran blanch and shake his head, Santos shrug and drop his eyes. "Good. Then we're agreed." He turned back to Marchetti. "We head back to *Persephone* in the morning." He smacked Marchetti's helmet to make him look at him, and a second time to get a nod. "Now, the good news," he said, sliding backward, "is the rain's letting up. Pie tells me the flyby shows the storm moving offshore."

They'd left both drones outside—one flying reconnaissance while the other played watchdog at the recently repaired and flash-welded-back-into-place airlock door. Ugly solution and temporary to seal the hole in the ship's hull back up. Inside door hadn't suffered any damage when the outer one blew itself out, which in Faraday's book was unbelievably lucky—goddamn miracle, in fact.

"The even better news, gentlemen, is the scrubbers in the airlock's pocket still work. Which means the atmosphere in here should still be breathable, if a hundred plus years old and stale." To prove it, Faraday popped the seal at his neck while Turk and the others looked in horror.

"You sure that's a good idea, sir?"

"Guess we'll find out." He twisted to remove the helmet and tucked it under his arm.

The first breath tasted of dust and decay, seared machine oil and old electronics. Everything cold, impossibly cold. Ice-chilled and arctic after years of being frozen despite the weeks spent planetside in the sun. It parched his lungs, the air in here. Burned his throat, set his skin on fire. Faraday coughed and drew a second breath, coughed again and couldn't stop. Bent double and hacked up a lung for a while with his legs bent and his hands braced against his knees, getting lightheaded due to the restricted oxygen.

"Think you might want to put that back on," Turk suggested.

"It's fine," Faraday wheezed. "Air's breathable it's just—" *cough-cough,* "fucking stale and cold." He hacked a last time and spat, straightened and drew a steadying breath. "You're welcome to leave your helmets on if you want. Can't sleep in the damn things myself. There's also the matter of eating. Awful hard when your mouth's behind glass." Feeling clearer and more stable, Faraday walked over to a crate marked 'Rations' and worked the lock to open it up, snagged a food packet without looking and smacked the bottom to ignite the fuel core to heat the centuries' old contents up.

"Like to get botulism from whatever's in there, sir."

"Doubtful. Thing's been frozen. Halgren's not real good at date stamps, so I've probably eaten older." Faraday grabbed another packet and threw it at Turk. "Things are mostly chemical anyway—hardly any real food in rations these days. More importantly, I'm hungry. And if this label's right," he tapped a line of black lettering, "this one here's macaroni and cheese." He tore the package open with his teeth, squeezed the sides and took a sniff. "Yup, that's mac 'n cheese, alright." He dug through the crate in search of utensils, and when he didn't find any, settled for dumping the food into his mouth.

Camp rules made that acceptable. Eating with your fingers was also allowed.

"How's it taste?" Turk asked as he chewed and swallowed.

"Not bad. 'Bout how I expected." Old and processed and overly salty—less like natural food than its chemical equivalent. Hungry man couldn't afford to be choosy, though, especially when the nearest alternative food source was located several hours walk away. "Burned a lot of calories getting here, boys." Faraday grabbed a handful of packets and threw them on the floor. "Suit yourselves," he said when nobody took them, and sat down to finish his meal.

"Aw, hell." Turk ripped his helmet off and suffered through a hacking fit before he tore into his food. "What is this?" he asked around a mouthful, screwing his face up like he'd bit into something rancid.

Faraday squinted, reading the printing on the side of Turk's package. "Says 'beef bourguignon'."

"What the hell is a bourguignon?"

"Some kinda fancy stew."

"Doesn't taste fancy." Turk peered inside the packet, lifted it to his nose and took a sniff. "Smells like feet in there."

"Then don't eat it."

"What else you got?"

"What am I? A waiter?" Faraday waved at the open crate, inviting Turk to dig through and find something better.

Which he did, after finishing the stew. Foot smell or not, it evidently didn't taste *that* bad. By then Tran had convinced the others that since Turk and Faraday weren't dead, they probably wouldn't die either. Helmets off, lungs adjusted, they set about sorting through food, and for a while ate in silence. Shared small talk with their voices echoing tinnily off the ship's metal walls.

Eventually, perhaps thirty minutes later, Pie descended to rejoin them, stepping from the ladderway with an oblong bundle strapped to her back. The contents sheathed in shimmering foil and cradled protectively in her copper-clad arms as she stripped it free and lay it down. Gently, carefully, wrapping the length of it in netting that she stripped free from the cargo crates and the walls they leaned against. No clear reason for that extra layer, nothing to indicate what she meant to do with it once she was done, hell, Faraday couldn't even tell what 'it' *was*, but it seemed important. Or delicate. Or something.

"Doc's gonna give you hell for that."

"Me? Why me?"

"Damaged her robot." Turk pointed his chin at Eight descending the ladder's last few rungs. Plasma scored and dented, eye slit crushed to squinting on one side. "If you want, I can look for a hammer. Try and knock some of those dings back out."

Faraday snorted. "Since when are you Mr. Fixit?"

"I fix things."

"You're a gunner. Gunners *break* things. The *last* thing they do is fix them up."

"Fix, break, same thing. Can't fix somethin' if it ain't broke first." Turk tapped a finger to his nose, dumping pasta and cheese sauce into his mouth. "This tastes terrible, by the way, sir. Almost positive I'll get botulism."

"It's rations, Turk. It's supposed to taste terrible."

"Not *this* terrible."

"Best we got." He thumped Turk on the shoulder, nodding to the three marines nearby. "Keep an eye on the kiddies for me. Need to have a word with Eight and Pie." Turk tossed off a sloppy salute as Faraday stood and ambled the androids' way. "What's the damage?" he asked quietly, sparking a short conference between Pie and Eight.

"Two hundred and thirty-six dead," Eight answered.

Faraday closed his eyes, letting that number sink in. "And *Diligence*?"

Eight's eye slits fluttered briefly. "With repairs, her main power should keep operating for another six months."

"Six months?" he repeated bleakly. "That's it? That's all you can manage?"

"I might be able to… borrow some parts from *Persephone* to extend it. But the power *will* fail, Captain. There's no way of stopping that."

"Wonderful. Just fucking wonderful." Faraday rubbed at a knot in his temple, feeling another of those stress headaches coming on. "What about this?" he asked, nudging the foil-wrapped bundle with his toe.

"A sample."

"Of what?"

"Biological material. Dr. Naisson requested it," Pie explained.

Curious, Faraday squatted down, examining the bundle up close. Noting the length of it, the thickness, a shape that, even obscured, remained distinctive for its elongated limbs and rounded head. "Turk," he called over his shoulder. "Take Tran and the others and head below decks."

"And do what, sir?"

"Inventory the seed stores. Pack up a few samples for us to take back to *Persephone*."

From the circle's center, Turk watched him with a squint-eyed look on his face. "Aye, sir," he said slowly. "We'll get right on it."

"But we're not done eating!" Tran objected.

"You are now." Turk tossed the last of his meal away, dusting his hands as he stood. "Alright, you heard the man. On your feet, the lot of you."

"Can't we just—?"

"No."

"But—"

"I said go, Tran, now go." Faraday locked eyes with the marine and he withered, muttering, "Aye, Captain," as he stood.

Santos and Marchetti followed suit in a hurry, and Turk herded the lot of them toward the ladderway, directing them down to the lower levels.

"Eight," Faraday said, once they disappeared. "Dial up your boss. Dr. Naisson and I need to have a talk."

TWENTY-TWO

Anthea spun the three-dimensional map on her desk's panel, examining the structures from every angle and the layers of data tagged to each. An incomplete representation, as yet, and likely to stay that way for quite some time despite the hourly updates from *Persephone* added in as each micro-analytical process ran its course.

Drones had been busy as beavers in their adventures and returned with thousands of specimens for processing, an inventory that would take days for *Persephone* to work her way through. But what they had here, what she'd analyzed already… treasure trove. Expanded their knowledge of this continent significantly. By leaps and bounds and more.

And yet, and yet, and yet…*So much missing still. So much yet to be learned.*

She reoriented the multi-angle rendering, studying the emptiness along the edges that marked the vastness of this green world's ocean, a seemingly infinite and incalculable unknown.

Every probe they deployed there disappeared, the few monitoring stations they'd established mysteriously failed. Of them all, only *Diligence* and *Endurance* remained, the last two lonely lighthouses watching over the waves. And soon enough, they too would falter, thanks to that virus, if not the sea.

What is it about that place? she wondered, tracing the coastline with a fingertip. *What happened to all those drones we sent out there? Why does everything succumb to the sea?*

That question, more than any other, bothered her. Plagued her infrequent dreams. Made her loathe to deploy any more equipment given their inability to procure replacements, much less salvage the probes to the sea.

Someday, maybe, she thought to herself. *Once we're settled here.*

This planet was rich in metals to build more. But that someday required reconfiguring, manufacturing beyond *Persephone's* current capabilities. Until that day, and in preparation for it, Anthea logged the last known location of each probe and saved it as a distinct data layer tagged as 'aquabots' in *Persephone's* storage. "I promise, I won't forget," she whispered before closing that window down. Swapping the world view for the details on the soil samples her continental survey team brought back.

The system flagged an anomaly in the chemistry of its organic compounds, their concentration and mixture, the way they'd bonded with the silt and clay.

Anthea isolated those elements and ran a search of similar samples gathered by other teams, and found the same anomaly elsewhere, and not just in the soil. Groundwater, surface water, even the atmosphere—the same anomalous findings repeated again and again. Describing a pattern—that's how Anthea saw it. Though what it indicated, she honestly couldn't tell.

To find out, she launched an analytics package that spat out a laundry list of microbes, constituent particles and foundational elements with some interesting variations, but nothing unusual enough to merit further investigation. Until she dug into the micro-biologics decomposition and uncovered a colony of microbes common to every last sample in *Persephone's* lab, and yet unlike anything Anthea had ever uncovered, or *Persephone* carried in her massive library of records.

Alien, in every sense of the word. Undiscovered on any other world. Some form of carbon-silica-metal-based lifeform—the kind scientists across the universe *dreamed* of finding and wasted lifetimes fruitlessly searching for.

God damn, she thought, staring. *Find of the century and no one will ever know.*

"What are you?" Anthea wondered aloud, studying their structures under magnification.

With a touch, she sent the samples to the micro-organism synthesizer where chemicals were injected and responses recorded, reactions to light, cold, heat, pretty much anything you could imagine. Subsystems extracted genetic material and sequenced it, running simulations with human biologic material to analyze and record reactions, and postulate the effects on flesh and skin. Slow, and careful, and diligent. It took some time for those analyses to run.

Anthea tapped a finger to her lips while she waited, eyes lifting to that map hovering above the desk again. A flick of her fingers twisted it to locate *Diligence* and access the details of her fittings. Scan her cargo and the results of the passenger survey, those scans of her battered hull.

A missed communication she failed to notice earlier: a terse text message from Pie acknowledging receipt of Anthea's request.

"Captain Faraday won't like that, you know."

Anthea frowned at a camera. "Are you spying on me, *Persephone?*"

"It's hardly spying when you're using my systems."

"Touché." She smiled ruefully. "If I'm honest, I'm not a huge fan of it myself." But science demanded answers, and sometimes radical solutions were the name of the day. "Surprised he's not hounding me about it already." She idly spun the world map, glancing at the desk's panel when it flashed. Alerting her to a comms request and an incoming transmission. "*Diligence.* Speak of the devil."

"I believe it's Captain Faraday calling, not Beelzebub."

"Patch him through," Anthea said sourly, eyes on the desk as *Persephone* pushed the video feed. With a swipe of her hand, she shunted the data analysis aside, placing Faraday's face front and center.

That frown of his didn't bode well. Man looked irritated, and she suspected she knew why.

"Tom," she greeted him evenly. "What can I do for you?"

"For starters, you can explain this." He stabbed a finger at the floor and the view—transmitted via one of the androids' eyes—pivoted toward a lump on the decking. "Mind telling me why Eight's bringing you a dead body?"

"Research."

"What kind of research? What are you doing in those labs that you need a dead body?"

Anthea skipped a beat. "Pie didn't tell you?"

"Tell me what?" His gaze shifted away from her, focusing on the transmitting android's face. "Pie? What's going on?"

Pie's voice, when she answered, sounded muffled and thin, simultaneously muted and much too close. That happened when the androids used their internal channel for communications rather than projecting their voice outward into the air. "I found a mass die-off on Level 79."

"Mass die-off?" Faraday blinked blankly. "What does that even mean?"

"Thirty dead on that level alone."

"From what? A power spike? Some sort of system-wide failure?"

"Their cryo units were still functioning properly. I found nothing anomalous in the diagnostics results from that level."

"Then what? Some kind of sickness?"

"That's the theory." And their cover story. Anthea's excuse for bringing that body back. "Based on the size of the impacted population, a viral intrusion seems most likely, but additional study is required to confirm that line of thought."

"So, the corpse...?" Faraday's focus shifted a second time, returning to Anthea watching through the android's eyes.

"I need tissue samples for analysis."

"A whole body's worth?"

"Autopsies are best on full corpses." Anthea was quiet for a moment, watching him, hands folded on the panel in front of her. "If I can isolate what killed her, I can develop a treatment to inoculate the rest."

"Should I be worried?" He backed up a step, eyeing the corpse like a poisonous snake. "We took our helmets off. What if it's in the air?"

"You should be fine, Tom. Really. Given their proximity to each other, their common point of origin, a few other things, I'm guessing they were infected before they were frozen. As long as she's wrapped up, and you're in those suits, you and the others should be safe."

He chewed his lip, looking no less worried, pointedly maintaining the distance between himself and that corpse. "What was her name?" he asked out of nowhere.

"I... I don't know, actually. Does it matter?"

"Of course it does. That's a person, not a popsicle, Anthea."

"That *was* a person," she corrected. "It's a corpse now, Tom, that's all."

"Her *name*," Faraday repeated. Stubborn-like, which was his way.

"Samantha Veloso," Pie offered after a flicker-eyed search to suss the name out of *Diligence's* records.

"Samantha. There you go. Your corpse now has a name."

Faraday frowned unhappily. At Anthea. At the body on the decking. "Crew's not gonna like this. Hauling a corpse all the way back to the ship."

"I thought you soldier boys toted corpses around all the time."

"Not exactly. Not when we don't *have* to." Faraday grimaced and Anthea sighed.

"*Fine.* I'll have Pie put it in the clamshell. No one will even know it's there."

Faraday grunted and turned away, walking a circle around the corpse. Bothered by it, she could tell. On some level, she understood.

"The drones sent back some new data."

"Uh-huh."

"I've got something to show you, if you're interested."

Faraday stopped and raised his eyes, staring across the wrapped body at Pie's face. "There a reason you're changing the subject?"

"Do you *want* to keep discussing corpses and death?"

He winced. "No. Not really."

"Good. I'm not real keen on the idea either. Now check this out." Anthea dragged the continent map over and lay it on top of the feed from *Diligence*. A half second later, a duplicate appeared, floating in mid-air on Faraday's end— multi-colored and stereoscopic, spinning delicately above the decking. Dark in places, where data was missing. Holes in their knowledge showing jagged and black.

Wasn't her practice normally to share works in progress, but in this case, exigent circumstances justified bending the rules. Faraday watched that virtual world rotate, suit reflecting its palette of colors, and slowly, carefully, reached for it, cupping the spinning planet between his hands. "What is this?" he asked in a hushed voice.

"An orthorhombic projection. Well, *technically* that's not right, but it incorporates the basic structures—"

"You mean a hologram. I can see that. But of *what*?"

Anthea blinked. "Isn't it obvious?" All the layers were there, all the geological formations. Despite that, Faraday still looked blank. "Hang on." She accessed a menu in the mapping program and added in a few more features on the fly. Sloppy work she'd need to clean up later, but good enough for now. "There. Try this." She pushed the update to Pie and watched the map flicker as the new features built. Faraday released it while the update ran and stepped back with his arms folded over his chest, watching as the structure changed and the last few missing pieces slotted into place. "Do you see it *now*?" she asked him.

"It's a planet. It's this one, isn't it?"

"An approximation based on multiple, amalgamated data sources."

Faraday pulled a face. "So... that's a yes?"

"Sort of. It's not finished, of course." That still bothered her. "There wasn't nearly enough time to—"

"This is ocean?" He touched a blue-grey blank consuming a good three quarters of the map. "And this..." He turned the orb a bit. "This is the continent. The one we landed on."

"It is." Anthea cupped the image on her side, placing her hands top and bottom of the orb, and curled her fingers to pull the structure apart, separating the hologram into discrete layers of earth, and stone, and liquid rock. "Did you know," she said as its twin repainted, "that this planet has almost no seismic activity?"

"Didn't, actually. Is that important?"

"Not sure it's *important*, but it's interesting. It must've lithified over billions of years. There's no plate tectonics at all. Then there's this," she said after a pregnant pause. Anthea selected a single layer—one of hundreds buried in the continent's mass.

Faraday squinted and leaned close to read the data tags that appeared. "Metal deposits?"

"Iron ore. There's a crust of varying thickness running below the surface. The *entire* surface," Anthea clarified. "Not just a few deposits in certain places."

"That normal?"

"No. No, it's not. Liquid metal at the core, most certainly. Clusters of metal here and there? Sure. But this… this is unprecedented." She expanded the view and decomposed it to its component elements. "An entire continent with an iron ore underpinning. For all we know, it's beneath the oceans as well."

"So, the planet's a big metal ball." Faraday shoved the hologram aside and moved closer to Pie. "What's it matter? Why should I care?"

"It matters because it means we can *build,* Tom. Stone and wood for structures, metal for machines. Surveys picked up nickel and tin. Some rare earth minerals as well. We can mine them, refine them, build… hell, we can build whatever we *want*."

"Pig iron and drawn steel," Faraday sneered. "Anything we build'll turn to rust."

"Then we'll *re*build and get better, just as our ancestors did before. C'mon, Tom," she said at his disgusted look. "There's a whole new *world* out there waiting to be discovered. Aren't you the least bit curious about what makes it tick?"

Faraday glanced at the android and away again. "If you're asking if I want to know what's out there that could kill me, then yes, I'm curious. Also happen to be curious about that." He hooked a thumb at dead Samantha lying wrapped in monofilament foil.

"I already told you, I need her tissue."

"You told me part of it." He turned and stared at her. "Now I wanna know the rest."

"Not sure what you're talking about," Anthea lied.

He raised his eyebrows. "Oh, I'm pretty sure you do."

Damn that man for being tricky. Plays the simple soldier but he's not at all.

"I get that viral analysis needs tissue." Faraday moved a few steps closer, head tilting as he stared into Pie's face. "An entire corpse, though, that seems excessive. Makes me think you've got something else in mind."

Anthea snuck a glance at her clutch of data windows and the frame where the microbe analysis still ran. Considering how much she wanted to share. What to tell him and what was best saved for later. "In the early days," she started, slowly, collecting her thoughts, "before we knew better, we only worried about the basics. Temperature and gaseous mixture, whether a planet had landmass and a source of fresh water. We measured from a distance and sent people to the surface unprepared." She ducked her head a moment and stared at her folded hands. "Lotta people died that way. Those early explorers, they were so naïve. We've learned a lot since then, though, Tom. A *whole* lot since those early days."

"Not sure I follow," Faraday told her.

Anthea sighed and raised her head. "The best way to find out if there's nastiness out there is to subject a live sample to the elements. Water, soil, what have you—unfiltered, without the protection of a suit. And lacking a live sample, you use a dead one."

"Like Samantha."

"Like Samantha," Anthea nodded. "Do you see now, Tom? Do you understand?"

"Yeah," he said softly, face changing. "Yeah, I think I do."

A flashing light appeared, strobing in the corner of one eye. Anthea acknowledged it without looking and scanned the data window that opened after to review the results of the microbe analysis runs, the raw data from the processors loaded to the system for synthesis and correlation. Like a drug, she craved that information.

"It's getting late," she said to Faraday. "You should get some sleep. It'll be a long trek back tomorrow."

"Probably right," he answered, distracted. Staring at the corpse again. "Clauson," he said before she could close the line. "Did she and Shimizu ever make it back?"

"Just before sunset. I can patch you through if you'd like to talk to them."

He thought a moment and shook his head. "It's late. They're probably sleeping." A last look and he backed up a few steps. "Goodnight, Anthea. See you tomorrow."

"Goodnight, Tom. Safe travels."

He flashed a thumbs up and touched his helmet's cheek guard, instantly killed the feed.

"I'm sorry," Anthea said once he'd gone. Alone in her room, with the channel closed.

TWENTY-THREE

As promised, the rain ended sometime in the dark hours of the night. The fog remained—swampy in its thickness, ringing the colony ship close about—while the nearby ocean rushed and roared with the back and forth rhythm of salt waves crashing against the rock-strewn shore. And something new that wasn't there before: some unseen species riding the air currents high above, calling at them through the clouds. Unfazed by the wind and weather, the curtain of fog that left Faraday blind.

Beside him, Turk fidgeted, turning one way and uncertainly the other. Rifle in hand, armed and ready—not pointing at anything in particular but not *not* pointing at anything either. Nervous, distinctly nervous—that came through in his stance.

"Problem, Turk?"

"Not sure yet." Turk hobbled a few steps forward, hitching awkwardly as if favoring one side.

"What's wrong with your leg?"

"Sir?" Turk twisted, glancing back at him.

"You're limping."

"Got hit by a door, remember?"

"You weren't limping last night."

"Yeah, well..." Turk shuffled his feet uncomfortably, winced and reached for his knee. The one *Persephone* replaced with a mechanical after the original was damaged back on *Hadrian*.

"If your body's rejecting the implant—"

"It's fine, sir. Really. Twisted the damn thing is all." Turk gave the bum knee a squeeze, straightened and scuffed at the ground. "Don't remember that being there before, do you?"

Faraday frowned at the change in subject—awful lot of that happening of late—tempted to pursue the matter before deciding to let it go. Following the line of Turk's pointing chin, instead, to a muddy-yet-fresh looking indentation that stretched for several meters and measured wider than his spread hand.

Trough-shaped, with a rounded bottom stamped deep into the ground. Several others of similar size and shape lying scattered about that one—no pattern to them that Faraday could see, just random marks on the mist-slick ground. The grass around them ripped and torn, exposing the sharp-edged jagged rocks, and the troughs themselves decorated with double-ringed circles that stippled the muddy ground.

Odd markings, no doubt about that. "You're right," Faraday said. "These weren't here before." He squatted down to inspect one, tracing a stipple with his finger.

"Any idea where they came from?"

"Not a clue." He stood and examined the rest. "Cluster pattern's interesting, though." He measured the spread with his hands, tracking the line of them back to the sea. "Looks like whatever made them—" He broke off when Turk raised a hand, staring intently into the fog. "Something out there?" Faraday unlimbered his rifle, watching that wall of mist himself.

"Not sure. Thought I heard something." Turk tapped at his helmet with his free hand, toggling the settings to amp up the gain. Standing statue-still with the fog frosting his visor as he listened to the ambient around them, hunting a phantom sound on the wind.

Faraday adjusted the filters on his own helmet, cycling the processors to filter the noise. Skin prickling in a rash of goosebumps that chafed uncomfortably against his suit. "Anything?" he asked after a minute or two.

Turk jerked his head in frustration, lowering his rifle as he turned around. "Must've imagined it, I guess. Sorry 'bout that, sir."

"'S'alright. No harm done. Fog's got us all on edge." Best they got out of here and back to *Persephone*. Sharpish-like and soon. "Tran," Faraday called to the marine behind him. "You and Marchetti get that clamshell ready. I wanna be out of here in five."

"Aye, sir. We're working on it. Wheel's pretty jacked, but we'll straighten it out."

"What happened to its wheel?"

"Hard to tell for sure. Carapace around it's pretty dented. Guessing it ran into something in the dark."

Faraday frowned at the dodgy logic—clamshell's patrol pattern ran in spirals with its sensors scanning for obstructions. Nothing but the ship out here and a few head-sized boulders poking through the grass for it to run into. Hard to believe the drone wouldn't detect something as large as a ship, or that bumping into a boulder would cause that much damage to a by-all-indications durably outfitted drone.

Then again, anything was possible. Learned that lesson well enough over the years.

"Eight. When you're done with that door, can you come over here and give Tran a hand?"

"Yes, Faraday. I'm almost done." Eight's plasma welder flared with actinic fire as she fixed *Diligence's* outer door back into place. They'd need to repair the mechanism properly at some point, but for now, the spot welding did the trick.

"Can't see a blessed thing in this soup." Turk swiped at the condensation obscuring his visor's glass. "Probably get lost on our way back to *Persephone*. Fall off a damn cliff and break my fool neck."

"Won't get lost if we stick together. Pie knows the way. Eight, too, for that matter."

"Androids." Turk grimaced. "Don't particularly like being reliant on them, if I'm honest." He took another lick at that visor before giving it up as a lost cause. "You still got that map on you, sir?"

"Happens I do." Faraday retrieved it from its case. An icon appeared when he powered it on, flashing rhythmically while the device attempted to connect, only to throw an error after several seconds when the automated positioning system's triangulation routine failed, and displayed their current location by default. "That's odd." He cycled the system and cursed when the failure reoccurred, toggled the settings to check the markers and found just two points instead of the expected three. "Pie," he called over comms. "What happened to the flyby?"

"It's offline, Faraday."

"I can see that." He turned the map around and showed it to her as she strode mechanically from the fog. "*When* did it go offline?"

"Last night."

"Last *night*? And you didn't *tell* me?"

Pie hesitated, eye slits flickering. "I didn't want to worry you. It's possible the drone's just out of range."

"Possible?" Faraday slung his rifle, freeing up his arms for irritated crossing. "What else is possible?"

Those eye slits went into overdrive, flashing in seemingly random patterns. "The flyby may have gone... missing."

"Explain."

Pie's face blanked in an instant, cobalt eyes gone dark. "The aquabots attempted to survey the ocean. They failed, Captain. Every last one." Electric blue crackled in lightning bolts that forked across her metal face. "They drowned in this world's ocean. This planet—" She silenced abruptly and her cobalt eyes flared back to life. Cycling through a dozen different colors as she applied filters to scan the fog before settling on a crimson setting that bathed her copper mask in blood. "We have more important things to worry about." Pie pivoted in her android way—upper body twisting, followed by hips and legs— and marched in long-legged, ground-eating strides across the bent-grass plain toward the hidden sea.

Wordlessly, Turk and Faraday moved closer together, standing shoulder-to-shoulder with their rifles raised. Pulse cores whining shrilly as the charge inside them built. "Pie. What is it? What's out there?"

"Can't you feel it, Captain? Can't you hear it?" Half-obscured by mist, Pie tilted her face toward the thunder sky, while beneath her, beneath them all, a trembling shook the earth.

A ground-swell shaking that rolled in waves across the rock-strewn, rain-soaked grass, waking a host of rainbow-winged insects that burst skyward in a twister cloud.

Faraday stumbled on the unsteady ground as a sorrowful moaning built— plaintive in its lilting call as it crawled through the shifting wind, and burst free in shrieking tendrils that stabbed in glass shards at his ears.

"What the fuck was that?" Turk pressed hard against Faraday's back, with his rifle raised and tracking a play of light and shadow snaking through the mist. "What's out there?" He panted. "*What the fuck is that?*"

"Easy, Turk, just keep calm." And to the rest of them, "Everybody back away. *Quietly*," Faraday added, having no real idea if that made a difference. "Eight. You got the compass. Can't see shit in here, you take the lead." He shifted a step and felt Turk move with him, retreating one measured pace at a time, as that shadow in the mist morphed and grew, turning darker as it split into a dozen threads.

"Shit. Oh shit. Oh shit." Turk breathed in short sharp gasps. "What is that? What the fuck is that?"

"It's coming," Pie intoned. "You need to run."

"Belay that! Nobody runs. Slow and steady, you hear me? Grab the drone and our gear and get out." Faraday slid another step backward with Turk plastered against his back, and heard a *clack* and crackle he knew all too well. A whine as plasma coiled to an explosive charge. "Tran! No!" he shouted, and spun as the marine's gun discharged.

The plasma round skipped over his shoulder—close enough for him to smell the ozone trail left behind it, bright enough that it whited out Faraday's vision, and for a good minute after, left him seeing stars. Didn't affect his hearing, though, that worked perfectly fine. Picked up the thump and sizzle as that first round hit, and a dozen pulse charges after. The sound of sorrow crumbling beneath a weight of hatred as mournfulness gave way to rage.

"Cease fire! Cease fire!" Faraday screamed, and, "Tran! Shut that fucking gun down!" He stumbled drunkenly from side-to-side with the ground swaying beneath his feet, while above him, around him, deep within the surrounding fog came the telltale yet distinctive whistling of a large object descending at speed.

Something solid and heavy thumped down, making the entire surface of the headland buck. Tossing people, robots, rocks, you name it—everything that wasn't locked down, buried or otherwise secured ended up airborne for the length of two heartbeats before crashing ignominiously back to the ground.

Faraday slammed into Turk and, stunned, they collapsed together. "Go!" he shouted over comms when he could. Once he'd managed to suck enough breath into his lungs. "Grab the clamshell and get the fuck out of here!"

"Sir—"

"We're right behind you, Marchetti. Just go! Turk and I'll catch up!" Faraday snagged Turk's arm and hauled him up while the earth kept rocking and rolling earth and the shadows around them flickered and flashed. Filled with snake-charm shapes that snapped and danced—now here, now there, now gone.

Taunting him. Luring him. Muddling up his sense of direction. "Pie," Faraday called in desperation. Disoriented, bearings lost in all that fog. "Which way? How do we get out of here?" He turned in circles, trying to find her, but he couldn't see anything in all that mist. Not until Pie's centurion face lit up with a cobalt beacon reflecting off copper skin, blazing bright as harrowed justice as she raised a metal-clad arm and pointed them to the safest path. "Go," she said. "That way lies safety." And then she was gone. Snatched away in an instant by a black bar that reached from the mist. Long and sinuous and susurrating, it swept Pie off her feet.

"Pie!" Faraday screamed uselessly. Voice swallowed up by all that mist.

"Shit. Oh shit, it took her."

"What took her? What the hell is that?"

"I don't know." Turk panted raggedly—wide-eyed, rifle hugged to his chest. "I don't know and I don't wanna know." He grabbed Faraday's shoulder and pushed. "We gotta go, Captain. We gotta go!"

"Tran! Tran, what's your status?"

"We're rolling, Captain. We're—" Tran's comm cut out quite suddenly. No static fritz, no severing click, just live comms one moment and dead channel the next, his last utterance a choking gasp.

"Tran. Tran, what's happening?" Faraday jogged toward his location, following the path Pie provided earlier. "Marchetti—"

"He's gone! He's fucking gone! Something took—"

Marchetti screamed—unlike Tran his comms stayed live.

Faraday raced the rest of the way, bloodcurdling sound echoing across comms. Chased by a wail of keening hunger that dogged their steps as they ran away. "Santos, Marchetti! Report!" He stumbled on an unseen object—something solid and large enough that it tangled up his feet. Cursing, he slewed for balance, arms wind-milling to keep him from pitching face forward into the mud. In the process, he happened to glance down and realized the something he'd tripped on was someone's head.

Marchetti's, he was pretty sure. The bent nose resembled his schnoz.

Instead of slowing to confirm it, Faraday righted himself and kept sprinting until he just about ran himself straight into Eight. "Shit! Shit! Shit!" Faraday slammed on the brakes at the last second, slid around the copper-clad android and connected with the clamshell's side instead. Driving the wind out of himself a second time, leaving him bent double and gasping for breath. "Where?" he huffed at Eight. "Where are they?"

"They're gone, Faraday. Now *we* must leave."

"Gone where? We can't just abandon them!"

"You must. They're beyond your reach." As she spoke, Eight's face lit with electric blue and tilted toward the shrieking sky. "Down!" she ordered sharply, knocking Turk aside. She grabbed Faraday around the middle and flattened him beneath her in the mud.

Face down, Faraday couldn't see anything, couldn't *feel* anything thanks to the enviro-suit's armor. But he heard the crunch as something massive and heavy collided with the *Diligence's* side. Suffered the dizzyingly abrupt change in orientation as Eight plucked him from that point position and dumped him on the clamshell's back—dazed and breathless and wide-eyed, staring at a swathe of ink-black ichor splashed across the colony ship's hull.

At a double row of circular ridges etched into the composite metal and a wavy length of green-black flesh flicking whip-like through the air.

"What is that thing?" he breathed as Eight deposited an equally dazed Turk beside him.

"Our death if we don't move."

"Do robots die?" Turk asked blearily.

"Some don't, though AI do." Eight turned her copper face their way. "Today's not the day I'm supposed to die. Now come. It's time to leave." She whistled to the clamshell and pivoted, marching smoothly away with the wheeled drone, ever faithful, trundling behind her with its two passengers clinging to its shell.

Twenty-Four

Faraday stripped the helmet from his head and tossed it gratefully to the ground—too bone-weary to give two figs about the metal-on-metal clank of it rebounding off the decking, so focused on working free of the hated enviro-suit that he hardly even noticed the din that raised. Two full days he'd been stuck in that rig, with its sweat stink and dead skin smell. Two long, exhausting days breathing in the musky, unpleasant odor of his own increasingly filthy body, an aroma that clashed in nose-blinding clarity with the coldly clinical aroma of the ship around him, its frozen deck plates and chemical disinfectant treatments.

As he shucked and wriggled, he wrinkled his nose, desperate to let his grimy and much-abused skin breathe. Thinking longingly of his quarters, the luxury of a hot shower and a soft bed. Some food—*real* food not the chemical concoction ration packs—to soothe his stomach, assuming he could muster enough energy to seek it out.

Which right now seemed unlikely, given he was struggling to peel the enviro-suit off. Trip back wasn't nearly as miserable as the trek out, thankfully, but it sapped his strength just the same and took them every bit as long to complete.

Should've expected that, I suppose.

No rain this time, though the clouds remained. And the mud, of course—hadn't accounted for that, idiot that he was.

Too long since he'd spent more than a few hours on a planet. The weather… that was a rude awakening, and a timely reminder of why he seldom traveled planetside, and even more infrequently stayed. As for the mud… well, that was some stubborn, pernicious stuff. No idea how long it would stick around and make their lives hell. For all he knew, the ground was always mud. Certainly rained enough around here for that.

"Spend the rest of my days slogging through shit," he muttered, wobbling on weary legs. He plunked down when his balance went and landed gracelessly on his derriere—a far more stable platform than standing—and began the slow, methodical process of peeling the armored rig from his body.

Cursing the damnable thing every time his fingers slipped on the all-but-frictionless metal weave. Ripped his gloves off when he got sick of them and tossed them irritably aside knowing full well his fingers would pay for it—high tech material was tough as nails and tore holy hell out of prying human digits—but so frustrated right now that he didn't care. Paid the price willingly to speed up the whole strip-tease, peel-like-a-banana process.

Gloves slowed everything down. Sometimes their protection just got in the way.

"Eight." He glanced over his shoulder at the android sealing the airlock. "Unload the clamshell and get those samples to the bio-analytics lab."

She turned her head and gave him a blank-faced stare. "Dr. Naisson suggested the gene-sourcing freezers. She was quite specific in her request."

Faraday paused in his arm extraction, thinking of the body stored in the clamshell beneath Turk perching king-like on its back. Wouldn't be too happy if he knew that corpse was in there. Didn't blame him—bad business, toting corpses around. "Fine. Freezers. Whatever." He flapped a hand and tugged the suit hard. "Store that shit wherever she wants it. And get Turk to the med bay. I want that knee of his checked out."

"It's fine," Turk grumbled. "I told you. Tweaked it is all."

"Like hell."

"It is!"

"Prove it." Faraday yanked and his arm slipped free, tingling in the cargo bay's chill air. "Hop off that drone and march over here."

"Think I will. Could use a walk." Turk slithered off the clamshell's back and very strategically landed on his good foot, very carefully planted its partner after. Stifled the wince as he engaged his bad knee and forced it to take its share of his weight.

"Y'alright there, tough guy?"

"Peachy." Turk squared his shoulders and started walking, eyes on the door to the ship proper across the way. To his credit, he made it a few steps—crab-walking, hobbling like a ninety-year-old man—and through sheer force of will, would've made it several more. Likely blown that knee out completely through stubborn bull-headedness and borderline stupidity except that Faraday intervened.

"Stop," he ordered, and with a flick of his fingers, deployed Eight to intercept Turk and load him onto the clamshell's back. "You're a damned fool, you know that?"

"Pretty sure Clauson would agree with you, sir." Turk grimaced as he climbed aboard, holding tight as the clamshell trundled along.

Faraday flexed his arm, as it rolled on by, rubbing at cramped and aching muscles, the long-sleeved undershirt he wore beneath the survival suit stamped with the armored rig's metal weave pattern. "Med bay," he repeated when Eight joined him. "Scan that artificial knee. Make sure there's no tissue rejection." He craned his neck to look up at her. "See if they can knock those dents out of your face while you're at it."

Eight touched at her damaged skin, copper coating bent and flattened from her tussle with Diligence's door. "I might keep them. They give me character." Eye slits flickering, she turned away.

"Eight."

She stopped with one foot raised, twisting at the waist to look back. "Yes, Faraday."

"What was that back there at Diligence? What attacked us?"

"A creature of this world. Something large and native to the sea." Eight lowered her foot and twisted at the hips to mesh her lower body with the alignment of her head, torso and arms. A touch at her temple blanked her cobalt eyes, reversing the camera behind them to project a series of grainy images—grey slashed with black, chased with ghost-white swirls, the lot of it gritty and out of focus, as if taken quickly and on the run.

From the decking, Faraday stared, watching the image capture run forward, skip back to the beginning and repeat again. "What is this?"

"Video I captured at the seaside."

"Stop." He raised a hand. "Freeze that." The images stilled. "Filter and enhance. Zoom in and advance frame by frame."

Eight's eye slits fluttered as she processed the request, video feed cycling through various tints of light and dark to draw out details hidden in the chaff.

"There," Turk called from the clamshell, stabbing a finger at a slash of black. "That's a tentacle."

"Bullshit."

"True shit. See those circles? Those are suckers."

Faraday squinted, examining the shapes in question. "Could be anything," he said doubtfully. Then again, he was no tentacle expert. "Eight. Upload that video to *Persephone*. Let's see what she's got to say."

"Yes, Faraday. Upload complete." With a flicker, the images cut out and Eight's eye slits resumed their regular setting. "Will there be anything else before I leave?" She stared down at him sitting on the grated floor. "Do you need assistance in removing your enviro-suit?"

"Nope. Got it." Faraday grunted and heaved, freeing his other arm from the survival suit's clutches. "You two skate out of here, I'll pack up our shit."

Eight stared a moment longer, eye slits flickering in indecision, but with a twist of her hips she turned away, collecting Turk on the far side of the cargo bay and taking him with her as she exited into the ship proper.

Leaving Faraday alone with the clamshell and two very long, very dirty tracks of mud. "Doc ain't gonna be too happy about you messing up *Persephone's* cargo bay."

The clamshell spun around to face him, flashed the pin lights ringing its carapace, and abruptly, almost rudely shut down.

"Nice. Guess I get to explain this." *And Pie*, he remembered belatedly. *Tran, Marchetti and Santos*. "Damn," he breathed. "God damn." He scrubbed at his face with a shaking hand.

"Tom," he heard faintly. "Tom, are you there?"

"Unfortunately," he muttered back, lower half still trapped in his suit.

"Tom. Tom, it's Anthea."

He'd figured that much out. And that he needed to answer her if he wanted any peace. With a sigh, Faraday stood, collected the discarded helmet and slipped it onto his head. "Sorry. Had my helmet off."

"Welcome back."

"Glad to *be* back, actually."

"Really? Glad to hear it," she said, smile in her voice. "You up for that drink we discussed?"

Faraday sat back down and, with a grimace, started tugging at the enviro-suit again. "Don't think so. I'm dog tired. All I want is a shower, and some food, and some sleep."

"That bad out there?"

"Yes and no. Long trip. Lots of mud." He extricated the thigh of one leg. "Lost one of your androids," he admitted to get that over with. "Lost Pie and three of my men."

"I'm sorry, Tom."

"Yeah. Me too." He gave up on the suit for a while and just sat there staring at the cargo bay's walls. "Still not sure what happened. Couldn't see anything in all that fog. One minute they were there, and the next… gone." He snapped his fingers, shook his head.

"Eight?" Anthea asked quietly.

"She's with me. *Was* with me," he corrected. "Sent her to the med bay with Turk."

"What happened to—?"

"I'll explain it all later. Too tired to get into it right now."

"Yeah. Yeah, I get it." Anthea was silent on her end a while. "Rain check on that drink?" she asked hopefully.

"Sure," Faraday grunted. "Just not for breakfast."

"Lightweight," Anthea teased gently. "Good night, Tom. See you in the morning."

"'Night," he said and pulled the helmet off, dumping it back onto the decking. Jaws cracking as he yawned, fingers forcing the environ-suit down a little further. "Hate this fucking thing," he muttered. "Had my druthers, I'd never slip the cursed thing back on." Too many hours logged in suits like these over the years, too much sweat-stink and claustrophobic squeezing, too many lost crew like Marchetti and Santos—even Tran, that pain in the ass. "And Pie," he reminded himself. She wasn't *his* crew, hell she wasn't even human, but she was lost under his command.

Pie who was an artificial being—a different kind of intelligence than flesh and blood. Who wore that stupid symbol so proudly, never knowing she'd gotten it wrong.

Faraday closed his eyes and pictured her standing there with that wall of fog at her back. Copper arm pointing them to safety, oblivious to the shadows lurking behind her until they pounced and snatched her away. "Dammit, Pie, what took you?"

He never saw it, just heard its voice. Horrid in its anger, its sorrowful hunger edged with rage. The very thought of it made him shiver, though the chill in the cargo bay didn't help. Nor the hollow emptiness of his hunger, the exhaustion settling deep into his bones.

He yawned again, long and widely this time, and resumed his tugging at the damnable suit. Worrying it loose in infinitesimal increments punctuated by a carefully cultivated collection of curse words that turned the cargo bay's air blue. Tempted to chuck the damned thing in the incinerator by the time he worked it free, except he needed it, hated as it was.

Instead of chucking it, he tossed it back into the case that spawned it along with the helmet discarded on the floor, sealing the box up tight after dumping the rig inside and mashing the button for the built-in sanitation routine.

Nothing worse than wearing a dirty enviro-suit. One size fits all meant people shared—not that they meant to, things just happened—and all that human residue could be a problem. Led to fungus and rashes and all manner of other nasty stuff.

Bad form all around, forgetting to clean a used suit. Absolutely disgusting crawling into one only to find out you were stewing in someone else's bits and juices.

Have to remember to collect Turk's later.

Faraday stared across the cargo bay to the door set in the far wall. Thinking of Turk, and that knee, and the medical bay as goose prickles twitched at his skin. Shivering in the cold, dry air, the smell of his own stink an offense to his nose. Soon enough, the shakes set in, wracking his body with painful spasms. Wasn't quite sure how he managed it, but he escaped the cargo bay and navigated his way to his quarters, where he climbed into the shower, filthy underclothes and all, and dialed the water past hot to scalding before he collapsed in a shivering heap, curled in a fetal position on the shower's floor.

*****

Morning… well, morning was painful. A rude awakening after an exhausted night. Faraday woke in the bed he'd crawled into once the shower's hot water ran out—naked as a jay bird beneath the sheets and covers again with his filthy underclothes lying in a sodden lump near the bathroom door. Tired still and aching in every muscle. Warm beneath the blankets and instantly freezing once he ventured out.

He shivered in the frosted air that infected his bare-bones, undecorated quarters. A suite of rooms not unsimilar to his cabin on *Hadrian*, except that it felt smaller, simpler, and far more cramped. Everything white and chrome and exceedingly sterile—not a spot of color anywhere, no decorations, not even a cheap fake plant. Nothing of *his* here except the dozen black uniforms hung in the closet bearing his name, his Captain's stars.

Hadrian's uniform, not *Persephone's*. A remnant of the Halgren military and the ship he'd lost. Rightfully, he should give them up and adopt the coveralls Anthea and her scientists preferred, but that uniform was his history. A part of his identity Faraday wasn't quite ready to swap out.

Besides, the black and silver suited him. The mourning colors, the six-pointed stars.

He pulled one down and tugged it on, layering a set of thermal underclothes beneath, scraped the red-gold whiskers from his freckled, shadow-eyed face, wondering where in hell all the grey hair had come from. If it was just the lighting that turned him hollow-cheeked or if he'd always looked this grim.

"Damn those years in cryosleep." He tossed the razor down and left the tiny bathroom, abandoning his quarters to head to the med bay and check on Turk, with his stomach grinding and growling—arguing for the mess hall first and food, that meal Faraday'd promised and yet somehow never managed to deliver. An empty ache that soured in the corridors' chemical cocktail stink, a chill and distinctive aroma created by the anti-viral, antibacterial, anti-everything solution used to scour the ship's echoing spaces, these passageways so empty his boot heels thudded with death-knell resonance as he strode down that metal-decked hall.

Three hundred-odd people crewed this ship, supposedly. Under *normal* circumstances, anyway. All but one of them frozen right now—that was Anthea's choice and this her ship, those scientists her crew and charges. They joked about her dislike of people, and there was some truth to that in her choice. And prudence buried beneath it, considering quarters were at a premium and they carried limited supplies on board. Couldn't really afford to wake everyone, the math said that, but damn if it didn't make that huge ship feel creepy. Full of ghosts and memories of those they'd lost along the way.

Except for Hadrian. *There's nothing of him here.*

Shivering, Faraday hurried his steps.

Taking the ladderway down one level, following the curving walkway past a dozen sealed compartments, with their wheels spun, locks showing red. Leftover of the bad old days of space travel that configuration, designed to protect the spaces behind them in the event of explosive decompression. Newer ships all carried spontaneous energy field generators but the older girls like *Persephone* kept the retro-tech with which they'd been fitted. Like the plaque that marked the med bay: crimson plus set on a field of white. Ancient symbol and recognized anywhere, on any ship, bunker or back alley surgery located throughout human-settled territory. You got hurt, you looked for that crimson plus. You didn't want to die, you made the people who wore one your best friend.

Faraday gripped the wheel on the med bay's door and spun it until he heard the locking mechanism retract. When he pulled, it pivoted smoothly, exposing a coldly clinical space on the other side that he remembered all too well. Awakening memories of blood and screaming. Death and dying and pain.

He clenched his hand to stop it shaking, skin slick with cold, clammy sweat. Just the sight of that room brought everything back, all the lost crew and wounded, his last glimpse of *Hadrian* before they left him behind. In its white walls, he saw silent, screaming faces, lumps of charred and twisted metal instead of titano-steel floors. The hard plastic beds became coffins for corpses, the glass-walled surgery a crematorium stacked up with the waiting dead.

A nightmare that plagued him in the dark—he closed his eyes against it and leaned against the doorway's frame. Savoring the cold kiss of its composite metal on his fevered skin, breathing slow and deep to calm his thumping heart, the smell of antiseptic an acerbic tang on his tongue.

The lights above him buzzing loud as bees—an oddity he didn't remember, nor the flutter and flicker of their harsh, white glow. Faraday concentrated on that anomaly, to distract his mind and push the memories away, and when he opened his eyes and looked around, he saw the med bay for what it truly was: a place of healing, not a shrine to the dead. With a knot of people—real, living people—clustered around a bed in the far corner. Names he knew, faces he recognized, every last one of them dressed in *Hadrian's* black.

Faraday watched them from the hallway, unobtrusively eavesdropping on snippets of their conversation. Noting how tired Turk looked as he lounged in bed, propped up by a massive mound of pillows. Surprised to find Clauson of all people keeping him company, sitting chummily near Turk's feet. In the corner, Shimizu played distracted chaperone, looking simultaneously bored, amused and annoyed by the back and forth between the other two. Most of her attention focused on an electronic reader in her hand and whatever information it offered up.

Gave him second thoughts, finding those crewmen here. Hadn't told anyone but Anthea about what happened to Turk, hadn't expected anyone to come visiting, especially Clauson who seemed to hate Turk's guts. Almost, *almost* Faraday shut that door and left before anyone noticed. But as fate would have it, Turk glanced around, waving friendly-like when he spotted him. No demand in it, no expectations, just acknowledging his captain's presence. Leaving it to Faraday to decide the next move. To come over and join them or continue on.

The latter sorely tempted—Faraday guiltily admitted that to himself. For a second time, he hesitated, standing on the outside looking in. Returned that wave with an effort, and with even more effort, managed a small smile. Stepped through into the med bay before he thought better of it and changed his mind, covering a flinch as the heavy door swung shut behind him and, with shoulders square and head held high, strode past the empty tables with their memories of fire and blood, eyes on Turk ensconced in his nest of blankets. One leg tucked under the covers for warmth, the other bent at the knee and resting atop a grey-white triangular foam cushion.

"'Mornin', Cap'n." Turk greeted him with a nod and a surprisingly crisp salute given his seated position and propped up leg. Didn't stand up, which was telling. Offered that salute, but he didn't leave his bed.

In the corner, Shimizu stood and tucked that reader of hers behind her back, long arm lifting to press a precisely angled hand to brow, while Clauson—back to the door and oblivious to Faraday's entry—hopped up belatedly, blushing furiously as she braced up hard and copied Shimizu's pose.

Protocol, the lot of it, drilled into them over the years. None of it strictly needed—he wasn't captain here despite his collar's stars, but they were crew and military and he their ranking officer, never mind their ship was dead.

Faraday returned those salutes with a matching crispness to give *Hadrian's* crew their due. "At ease," he said and they all relaxed. Well, Turk and Shimizu, anyway. Clauson remained stiff and fidgety with those blooms of color blazing on her cheeks. "Something wrong, Clauson?"

"No, sir." She avoided eye contact for reasons he couldn't explain. "Thinking of grabbing us some food from the mess hall. You want me to grab you something while I'm there?"

His rumbling stomach declared that a fine idea, but it wasn't his practice to make crew fetch and carry, so it was, "No, Clauson. Thank you. No need to trouble your—"

"No trouble at all, sir. Shimizu and me, we'll fix you a plate."

"What?" Shimizu glanced up from her reader. "It's room service now? *Seriously?*"

"Oh, stop complaining, it's just one time." Clauson jerked a thumb at the med bay's entry and, reluctantly, Shimizu followed.

"You give that man breakfast in bed once and he'll expect it every time," Shimizu grumbled.

"Oh, I'll give him something, alright. Might not be breakfast, but he won't forget it." Clauson flashed her teeth in a wicked grin, glancing backward when she reached the door. Tipping a wink at Turk tucked up in that bed as she hauled the heavy door open, grabbed Shimizu's arm and dragged her through.

Faraday scratched his head, staring after them. "I did say no to breakfast, didn't I?"

"You did, sir. And as usual, Clauson didn't listen." Turk punched a pillow behind him, smooshing it into the hollow between the wall and his back. "Got a mind of her own, that woman. Stubborn as the day is long."

Faraday snorted. "Look who's talking." He hooked Shimizu's chair with his foot and dragged it closer to Turk's bed. "Five damn miles we hoofed it before I finally convinced you to give that knee a rest."

"I was *fine*, sir, I told you."

"Bullshit. You were gimping like an old man."

"That was swagger, not gimping," Turk corrected, leaning forward to adjust his pillows. "You'd know that if you—" He hissed and gritted his teeth, hand reaching to rub at his leg. The joint around the knee noticeably swollen and markedly, distinctly red.

The cushion on which it rested buzzed softly and afterward glowed a soft blue, injecting the calmative chill of chemical coolant to soothe the fevered tissue of Turk's damaged joint. In tandem, it spat out data that spooled in a queue to a monitor tacked on the wall, and alerted an android minder in the back room to suggest he check up on the med bay's one and only patient.

"Don't need it," Turk insisted when the robot walked in and produced an old-fashioned syringe. "It'll pass. Just gimme a minute."

The ground pounder, uncaring, shot Turk up anyway. Apparently the medical software's recommendations trumped the patient's wishes, and truth be told, Turk obviously *did* need that shot.

He relaxed as the pain meds hit, pain lines washing free of his face. With a sigh, Turk sagged backward, sinking deep into his fluffy mound of pillows—eyes closed, breathing in and out, that device on his leg humming softly as it dispensed meds and sucked in blood.

"Bad?" Faraday asked quietly.

Turk twitched his shoulders. "Depends. Right now, not so much."

"Assume they scanned it when they brought you in?"

"Scanned. Rescanned. Poked it with needles. Tons of fun." Turk cracked one eye and the other, considering Faraday in his borrowed chair. Fingers massaging that puffed up knee with its bulging tissue that stretched the skin tight.

"So, what's the damage?"

"Not sure, honestly." Turk pointed his chin at the android minder moving industriously about the room. "Doc Quackbones there won't tell me anything. Just keeps saying he needs to run more tests."

"Quackbones? You named him Quackbones?"

"Why not? Seems fitting enough."

"How does *he* feel about being called Quackbones?"

"Hates it, actually. Prefers to be called Quincy or some such." Turk's lips curled at the corners and for a moment they shared a smile. "You know," he said, sobering. Thumb probing the tissue surrounding his kneecap. "I had a friend with an artificial arm growing up. Another with an artificial leg. Mining colony," he explained at Faraday's look. "Shit like that happened all the time. Anyway, guy with the peg leg turned out okay—well, he got crushed by a drill bore but that had nothing to do with his leg. Girl, though…" Turk jerked his head. "Girl ended up losing that arm. Implant went bad, just like this one. Docs had to core the whole mess out."

"That's not gonna happen," Faraday told him. "You said yourself, they need to run more tests."

"More tests are never a good thing. You know that as well as I."

Faraday flicked a hand dismissively. "Fucked up your knee, no denying that, but there's nothin' that says they can't fix it."

"Maybe."

"Fuck maybe. Colony medics are shit. Software on these androids is first class."

The twist of Turk's lips said he didn't believe it. The way he kept on rubbing at his bum leg.

Across the room, the med bay door opened and Clauson waddled through carrying a stack of vacuum-sealed trays. Not a heavy load by any stretch of the imagination but tall and awkward, requiring her to peek around the pile to steer. "Soup's on!" she called brightly.

"God, I hope not," Turk said. "Soup for breakfast—who does that?"

"Masochists. Heathens, maybe—I'll have to look into that." He winked at Turk and he managed a smile—wan and thin and barely there but more like Turk and far less morose.

Shimizu appeared with a clutch of mugs in one hand and a thermal carafe in the other, kicked the door to close and dumped her load beside Clauson's on an empty bed.

"Alright. Who's hungry?" Clauson doled out trays like playing cards, plastic lids steamed up from the contents, seals emitting a satisfying hiss when twisted and cracked open. She passed a plate to Turk and a set of utensils to go with it, and because she was Clauson and couldn't resist, worked in a snarky, "Can you manage a fork and knife, gimpy, or are you gonna go all monkey man on me and eat with your hands?"

Turk threw a pillow at her that missed Clauson by a mile. She flashed her teeth and evicted Faraday from the chair, claiming the room's one and only butt perch for herself. A presumption that didn't sit well at all with Shimizu, considering Faraday was captain and before *he* claimed it, that chair belonged to herself.

"Oh, I see. You ask me to play milk maid just so you can steal my seat for a little canoodling?"

"Oh, pipe down, Cinderella, I'll give it back." Clauson stood, but Shimizu waved her back down.

"No-no. I wouldn't dream of it. You and baby bird enjoy your food." She grabbed a tray and stalked away, ponytail flipping side-to-side, snagged an empty bed across from them and, there being no other chairs on offer, sat down cross-legged on top of it.

Back to the wall so she could glare at them while she sipped her coffee and ignored her food.

Faraday shared a look with Turk who seemed as confused by the little tiff as he. For the most part, Clauson and Shimizu got along famously, wasn't quite sure what spawned the sudden tension. "What's going on?" he asked, claiming the opposite end of Shimizu's bed. Putting himself in front of those dagger eyes with his plate of food balanced on his lap.

"Nothing."

"Sure looked like something to me."

Shimizu shrugged and dropped her eyes, avoiding the question by focusing on her still-covered plate.

Great.

Faraday sighed and left his food alone for now, trusting the vacuum seal to keep it warm while he focused on Shimizu sitting across from him, watching her while he sipped the coffee in his cup.

Awful stuff, as it so happened—he didn't realize that until it was already in his mouth. Bitter, conflicting taste to it that ran closer to chicory and asparagus than any iteration of the blessed brown bean juice he'd encountered on any other ship.

He gagged and almost spat it out. *Culinary processors must need recalibrating,* he thought. *Dispenser mixtures seem to be off.*

Drank the acrid brew anyway. Caffeine hit was welcome, even if the wrapper needed sprucing up.

"So, what's the deal, Shimizu? What's going on with you and Clauson?"

Shimizu leaned around him to glare at Clauson, pony tail swaying as she shook her head in disgust. "I swear that woman has the worst taste in men."

"Clauson?" Faraday snuck a look over his shoulder. "Thought she hated Turk."

Shimizu snorted, twisting her lips. "She's sweet on him. Always was. Any idiot could—" She stopped dead, looking mortified. "Sir. I didn't—"

"Yeah, you did." Faraday smiled crookedly to remove the sting. "And you're right. I'm an idiot for not seeing it sooner." Not just Clauson's feelings, Shimizu's own. "Does she know?" he asked candidly, voice pitched low so no one else would hear.

"No," she admitted with a grimace. "I never told her."

"You should. You never know."

Things went quiet between them after that, Shimizu gazing thoughtfully at Clauson bantering with Turk before burying her nose in that electronic reader again.

Hadn't touched her meal except for the coffee. Then again, neither had he.

"You should eat before it gets cold."

Shimizu responded with a flip of her hand, too focused on her reader to care about much else. Probably should've pushed her on it, but he was captain not her mommy, and there were lessons to be learned from a forgotten meal. So with his stomach grumbling and growling, doing its best to turn itself inside out, Faraday popped the seal on his vacuum tray and inhaled the scents the steam billowed across his face.

First impressions weren't all that good—odd odors and strange colors abounded, glops of goop that jiggled when poked by his fork. Faraday stared at his meal for a long, long time, trying to work up the courage to actually touch it. *AI chef on this ship*, he reminded himself, *not human cooks like on* Hadrian.

Food grown in the hydroponics lab and protein generation ovens mulched together and dispensed in carefully metered portions. None of it ever looked particularly appetizing—*Persephone* was many things, including one of the most powerful AI minds human science ever invented, but cooking was an art form no amount of emulation successfully recreated. Oh, the meals her systems spat out were healthy enough, Faraday didn't dispute that fact for a minute. Everything protein-rich and vitamin-infused, perfectly balanced for the human metabolism, its nutrient needs and caloric intake. Hell, most days, the stuff didn't taste all that bad—sort of bland and chemical with strong overtones of paste—but the offerings this morning didn't actually resemble food. Nor smell like it when he risked a second sniff.

Faraday plucked up a beige-shaded, bar-shaped thing reminiscent of the packing material lining the enviro-suit case, nibbled at a corner and nearly broke a tooth. Considered the globs of goo accompanying it—three of them in total, of varying colors and consistency—and a grey-green puck of simulated meat. Everything false and fake and generally wrong, it took everything he had in him to sample a little of each. Of it all, the yellow blob tasted least-worst so he ate that and chased it with the coffee, poured himself a refill and considered the mess left on his plate. "Anybody know what the orange stuff's supposed to be?"

Clauson twisted and stretched her neck, trying to get a look at the blob in question. "Pretty sure that's lobster. Though it could be rutabaga."

"Who in their right mind purees a lobster? And what the hell is a rutabaga, anyway?"

"Hell if I know," she shrugged, dissecting an oozing blob on her plate. "Food's not usually this inscrutable. Guessing the macerator's gone flip-de-widdle and screwed up the mixture." She forked up a healthy mouthful to confirm it. "Oh yeah. That's some bad goop." Undaunted, Clauson tucked in with vigor, shoveling up every last scrap of food on her plate.

Woman must have a cast iron stomach. Either that or no taste buds that work.

Faraday envied her that constitution as he dragged a fork through a puke-green puddle. With a grimace, he covered the plate back up, dusting his hands as he pushed it away. "You got experience with automated culinary units, Clauson?"

She shrugged, offering, "A little."

"Think you can tweak it so it produces something slightly less industrial?"

Clauson chewed and swallowed, answering in her own time. "That what we are now, sir? Maintenance crew?" Didn't come right out and say it, but from her expression she clearly didn't like the idea.

"Temporary assignment," he assured her. "Special request, not a full-time gig."

Clauson thought that over a while, sucked some more of that unholy goo down and nodded once. "See what I can do, Cap'n. Need access, though. Think you can arrange that?"

Faraday nodded, eyes on a watching camera. "Might cost me a favor, but it's worth it if it means we don't starve."

They sealed the deal with a shake of hands—Clauson returned to Turk and her meal while Faraday went after more coffee.

"Sir?" Shimizu inched a finger. "Got something here you might want to see." She nodded to the electronic reader, turning it toward him when he leaned forward to look. "Remember that little research project you gave me a couple of days ago?"

He actually didn't. At least, not at first. "Trackline analysis. What about it?"

"I finished processing the data."

"Already? What'd you find?"

"Well. For starters, there's this." Shimizu turned the reader his way, pointing a slim finger at a string of data. "See this?" She tapped the end of it, where one line terminated and the next began.

Faraday studied the screen for nearly a minute, with Shimizu watching him in silence. From her tone, there was obviously something significant there, but for the life of him, he couldn't figure it out. "I got nothin', Shimizu. What should I be seeing here?"

"Not those stubbed ends, that's for sure. You said *Persephone* 'lost' data in transit, but if that were true, there'd be junk data at the ends of these aborted strings. Garbled characters to show where the thread cut off. These…" She flicked her fingers and scrolled through a hundred more samples, each string truncated like that first. "These are *clean*, Captain, all the way through. There's data missing, but the removals are surgical. Not happenstance, more like dissection."

Faraday pulled the reader to him and scanned the information up close. "So there's no corruption in her storage?"

"There might be. But not here. Not on that trackline. This…" She tapped the screen again, giving him a meaningful look. "Might be out of line here, Captain, but it looks to me like someone deleted those sections on purpose."

"Someone. Meaning *Persephone*."

"Or Dr. Naisson. Or someone else with the right access."

"That's a pretty strong accusation." Faraday turned the reader around and handed it back. "Double check your findings—"

"I already did." Shimizu let that hang. "I checked it three times just to be sure, sir, and all the findings came out the same."

"Fuck." Faraday sighed tiredly, hand lifting to rub at his face. "You know what this means, don't you?"

Shimizu nodded sagely. "Someone's lying, sir. Or covering something up."

The only question was: who and why? Personally, Faraday had his suspicions. And if he was right, there might still be hope.

All the weeks trapped downside on this planet, all the nights spent looking up at the stars.

Faraday'd wanted off this world almost as soon as he'd laid eyes on it—*Persephone's* data held the key to that. They just had to find the missing pieces and stitch them together to recreate the whole.

Nothing ever gets deleted. There's always a back-up, you just have to track it down.

Faraday pointed to Shimizu's reader. "Mind if I borrow that?"

"Help yourself." She passed it over and Faraday clipped it to his belt.

"You keep this to yourself for now," he warned.

"What about them?" Shimizu nodded to Clauson and Turk.

He glanced at them and away again. "Turk's got enough to worry about." Shimizu raised an eyebrow but he didn't elaborate. Turk's choice whether to share his woes, Faraday's job to listen and keep his mouth shut about his business. "I'm guessing you'll tell Clauson since you tell her everything." Shimizu's shifty-eyed look confirmed it. "You just make sure *she* doesn't spread your findings around. And eat something, would you? Food's terrible but your body needs fuel."

"Can't really call this food. More like a chemistry experiment gone wrong." She poked at the meat puck on her plate, its color and consistency roughly equivalent to old leather.

"Best we've got 'til the dispenser's fixed."

"You're not eating it."

"I ate earlier," he lied. Smoothly, deadpan. He'd gotten good at that over the years. "You keep an eye on those two while I go topside," he said with a nod at Turk and Clauson. "Need to talk to Dr. Naisson about this." Faraday tapped the reader and hopped off the bed.

"Sir? Do you—Do you think we can find our way back?" Shimizu sounded worried, which wasn't like her, and hopeful and resigned at the same time. Wanting a promise Faraday couldn't give her. A future that was better than the one they currently had.

Faraday studied her face a moment, searching for an appropriate response. "Can't make any promises, Shimizu. If there's a way, I'll find it. That's the best I've got." He caught her eyes and held them until she ducked her head and sighed.

"Aye, sir," she said faintly, accepting what she couldn't change.

I'm sorry, he wanted to tell her. To wash that aspect of defeat away. And right then and there, decided he was done with lying. Good or bad, they were in this together.

"I'll be back to check on you later, Turk."

"Roger." Turk flipped him a two-fingered salute.

"Clauson... don't break him while I'm gone, okay? Man's already been through enough."

"No promises, Captain." That wicked smile returned—the one with all the teeth.

Faraday rolled his eyes in exasperation, pointed at Shimizu and her untouched plate, waggling a finger to remind her to eat, and left the three of them there in the med bay while he headed topside to find Anthea and some answers.

She owed him that much, at least.

TWENTY-FIVE

In her quarters, head down in the data on her desk's panel, Anthea never even heard the chime that signaled someone's request for entry. Barely acknowledged the bio-monitor's twittering reminder that it was breakfast time and she needed to eat. The information on the panel consumed her—bio-data this time, extractions from that corpse Eight delivered from *Diligence.*

And, out of necessity, something newer. Live samples of bone, and flesh, and blood.

Because this planet and its multi-partite, multifarious biome were only one half of the larger puzzle. The people who needed to live here an entirely different problem unto themselves.

Mostly because she wasn't starting fresh. Terraforming a lifeless planet was one thing, reconfiguring a green one was quite another.

In her distraction, *Persephone* looked after her, just as she always did for decades of marked time. And Tip and Top, her faithful minders. AI and autonomous yet linked to the ship—*Persephone's* hands, instructed by her crystal matrix mind. Their duties many and varied, including chef when Anthea needed it. This morning's meal a thing of beauty arranged in an art deco pattern on her plain white plate.

Omelette cooked to perfection, stuffed with the cheese, mushrooms and peppers she preferred. Freshly-picked strawberries from the hydroponics lab, a slice of lime-green melon—a hybrid species of her own design—and a carafe of coffee with cream and sugar to make it sweet but not inordinately so.

A meal fit for a queen, and far and away from what the mess hall served. Personally, she never bothered going down there—hated the sim food puree from the culinary units, despised the polite conversations and fake interactions with people even more—and yet now, here, in the comfort of her private quarters, with that most enviable of delectables so lovingly prepared, the omelette sat untouched, the melon nibbled, a single strawberry missing from her plate. A cup of coffee perched by her elbow—half empty and cooling in the frigid air. The rest forgotten in her study. Her single-minded focus on the panel's data.

Bad habit, skipping meals—happened far too often over the course of the years. The bio-monitor chirruped to rebuke her, flashing a sad-eyed frowny face as it buzzed, and buzzed, and buzzed.

"Oh, shut *up*, you stupid thing." Anthea mashed the bracelet's face with her thumb, carved a bite from the omelette with the abandoned fork's tines and shoved it into her mouth. "There. Are you happy? I'm eating."

Perforce and mechanically, granted. Not really tasting anything, just ingesting fuel. After a bite or two, she even forgot that part. Set the fork down and pushed the plate away.

"Is the omelette not to your liking, Anthea?"

"Hmm?" Distracted, Anthea glanced at a camera. "Omelette. Yes. It's fine, thank you." Guiltily, she retrieved the fork again and moved the plate a little closer, pausing to press the bio-monitor's face when a chiming erupted. Annoyed when that didn't shut it down. Silly thing seemed to have a mind of its own.

"Tip and Top made it special." *Persephone's* polite voice drew her attention back to the camera. Pointedly it pivoted, redirecting that unblinking eye to the two androids in the corner.

First rate chefs, Tip and Top, loaded up with the latest in culinary technique. The food they produced delicious when Anthea bothered to stop and take notice. She glanced at them and at the food on her plate so perfectly prepared and carefully arranged. Strawberries at the peak of ripeness, red and juicy all the way through. Melon green from rime to core and that omelette with exactly the right mixture, the egg-to-cheese balance just the way she liked it. They might be androids and artificial beings, but Tip and Top actually cared. Took the time to learn her preferences and adjust their recipes and food apportionment appropriately.

And here I am just shoveling it down like third rate, trash-mash rations.

Guiltily, she slowed her chewing and acknowledged the flavors her taste buds picked up. The sharp bite of the yellow-white cheese, the bitterness of the green bell peppers. The feel of the eggs rolling across her tongue as she chewed and swallowed that omelette down.

"Delicious," she pronounced it, with a smile and nod for Tip and Top. "And these strawberries!" She stabbed one with the fork's tines and nibbled it through, wiping juice from her chin. "They're perfect!" she mumbled around a mouthful. "Nice and sweet, but not all mush."

Tip and Top seemed pleased, in as much as they ever looked anything. Their eye slits fluttered anyway—that usually meant their AI felt something. In unison, they turned their heads and stared at the door to her quarters as that bugger-all chiming started back up again.

Then and only then, did Anthea realize it wasn't coming from the bracelet. That someone *out there* wanted *in here* and in her obliviousness, she'd rudely ignored them. "*Persephone.*" She pointed a finger. "How long has that been going on?"

"Two minutes, forty-eight seconds," she answered promptly. "Would you like me to ask him to go away?"

"Depends." She finished her strawberry and deposited the stem and leaves on her plate. "Who's the who we're talking about?"

"Captain Faraday. He seems... agitated about something."

"Agitated as in angry, upset, or excited?"

Persephone paused a second before answering, running an analysis on the video capture from the door camera, Anthea assumed. "I believe he needs to urinate."

"Oh. Well." Anthea blinked, processing that a moment. "That's... That's not really helpful at all."

"Would you like me to ask—?"

"No-no. Just let him in." Anthea twirled her fork and pointed it at the door.

The lock flashed green and turned over, allowing Faraday access to her rooms. Private spaces she carefully guarded—no one allowed in without her say-so, that lock active every hour of every day.

"Tom," she greeted him, smiling. "How are you feeling this morning?"

"Dog tired," he said, and looked it. Bruised eyes sunk deep into his face. "Pretty sure I sprung every muscle in my—" He stopped dead, staring at her plate. "Is that—Is that an omelette?"

Anthea nodded. "Tip and Top made it. Eggs and cheese are sim but you'd never know."

"What about the strawberries?" He moved another step closer, subtly licking his lips. "Those sim as well?"

"You tell me." She plucked one up and held it out, smiling as she coaxed him close.

Carefully, almost reverently, he pinched the fruit between his thumb and forefinger, raised it to his lips and bit it in half. Nearly groaning with pleasure as the sweetness hit and his mouth filled with sugared juice.

He polished off the rest of it, and the remainder of the strawberries when she offered. Pulled a chair around and attacked the omelette, demolishing it in four big bites.

"Good?"

"Mmph," he managed around a mouthful, and once he swallowed, "Sorry," with a guilty flush. "Should've asked before I stole your breakfast."

"'S'alright. Tip and Top can make more." She nodded to the androids and they took off together, heading to the private kitchen they stocked with provisions reserved exclusively for her meals.

Faraday, meanwhile, was eying the melon. Clearly wanting it, but afraid to ask.

She slid the plate his way, gesturing for him to help himself.

Which he did. With abandon. Juice dribbling down his chin as he tore at the melon's flesh. "So, what makes you so special?" he asked between bites.

"What do you mean?" Confused, Anthea tilted her head.

"You're up here eating gourmet vittles," he held up the slice of fruit as evidence, "while me and the crew are stuck with that slop the mess hall food dispensers pump out."

"Oh god." Anthea recoiled in horror. "You're not actually *eating* that, are you?"

"Uh, *yeah*." Faraday nipped the melon's skin clean, considered the rind a moment and ate that as well. "Not like we got any choice. No private chef reserved for us grunts."

"You've got Eight."

"So? What about her?"

"She's programmable. Just load up a culinary package."

Faraday opened his mouth and closed it. "Never thought of that," he admitted sheepishly.

"'Course you didn't." Anthea sat back, smiling, foot tucked up under her leg. "Simple solutions for simple problems. You always try to over-complicate everything, Tom." She kept her tone light on purpose—teasing gently, not to hurt. But Faraday clearly didn't take it that way. She watched his face change. Close up and turn dark.

"You lied to me," he said, shoving the empty plate away. An accusation lacking context. Tossed out without preamble or explanation.

Calmly, clinically, Anthea raised an eyebrow. That was always her best defense. "About what, exactly?"

He gestured vaguely, sat back and tucked up his arms. "The trackline. *Persephone's* lost data." Faraday unclipped a reader dangling from his belt, powered it on and shoved it her way.

Anthea stopped it with a hand, glanced at the display and back to him. "Is this about Shimizu and her little book report?"

Faraday blinked and sat up straighter. "You knew?"

"*Tsk*. Of course I did. *Persephone* logs every request for access. Every query and all the information sent back. Figured you'd know that after your time on *Hadrian*."

His shrug said he'd suspected it. The way he studied her with narrowed eyes, attention flicking to that reader every now and then.

To humor him, and satisfy her curiosity, Anther collected the device and scanned the information it contained. "She culled this data from *Persephone's* systems?" She glanced up and saw him nod.

"You didn't stop her. You knew she was in there, but you didn't block her access."

Anthea shrugged and tossed the reader down. "Didn't need to. It's all there. I've got nothing to hide."

"Except the pieces *Persephone* deleted."

That one caught her by surprise. "Figured that out, did she?" She smiled ruefully. "Well, now. Color me impressed."

"Why?" he asked again. "Why'd you hide this? Why'd you lie?"

"I never lied to you, Tom," she said evenly, and stopped there, letting that hang. "But…" She sighed and sat back, tucking both legs up this time, "I also didn't tell you the whole truth." She ducked her head as she said it. Collecting her thoughts, figuring out where to begin. "The track data of *Persephone's* travels…" She paused again, lips pressed together, raised her head and searched his face. "It wasn't lost, Tom. She deleted it."

There it was. Her last secret out. All her cards laid on the table.

"Deleted it?" he repeated. "On *purpose*?"

"I'm afraid so."

"Why?" he demanded, angry now. Confused and betrayed and upset. "Why the hell would she do that, Anthea? What possible reason—?"

"*Hadrian*," she said over him. And when he quieted, "*Hadrian* told her to, Tom. Or at least suggested it. It wasn't *Persephone's* idea, it was his."

Faraday blanched and turned his face away, looking gut-punched as he sat in that chair. Jaw clenched so tight the muscles bulged beneath his too-pale, freckled skin. "Why?" he rasped, voice shaking. "Why would *Hadrian* want her to do that?"

"You've been Halgren long enough to know that."

Faraday frowned darkly. "Halgren? What's that supposed to mean?"

"The colony ships were infected. When it comes to biologicals, Halgren containment protocols are clear."

Isolate and destroy. Eradication—that was the Halgren way. They were zero tolerance and with good reason, given humanity's history with chemical warfare, viral intrusions and alien worlds. *Hadrian* knew it, *Persephone* as well—they'd colluded and *Persephone* ended up here.

"Ventress would never take them, Tom. No colonized planet would. Halgren..." She reached to touch his arm. "Halgren's military. They like solutions. If they found out, they'd send their warships to hunt us. *Us*, Tom, not just the colony ships. They'd kill everyone. Every ship. Every person."

He knew it. He had to. Faraday *was* Halgren, and no doubt he'd seen worse. More than that, she read it in his face. In the wrung-out way he closed his eyes, and with his fingertips, rubbed at his temple. "And this planet?" He gestured vaguely. "This ass-end of some unknown universe destination—was that *Hadrian's* idea as well?"

"No." She slid her gaze to a camera. "That was *Persephone's*. She found this world all on her own."

"And erased the track data along the way, I take it. Dumped it, destroyed it, whatever." He chewed his lip, eyes on a pin-dot camera mounted in a corner. "Any chance she can reconstruct it? That there's *any* of that missing data in storage?"

"I don't know, Tom. I haven't asked her."

"Why not?"

"What's the point?"

"The point is we might be able to leave this place. Launch *Persephone*—"

"And go where?" Anthea dropped her feet to the floor and turned her chair to bring them face-to-face. "She's *infected*, Tom, they all are. That's *Hadrian's* fault—*he* enlisted her. *He* gave her the idea for this plan." Faraday tried to look away, but she caught his chin and squeezed. "Where would we go that Halgren wouldn't find her and destroy her? What happens to the people on this planet if we take off and abandon the colony ships?" She stared at him in silence, waiting for an answer she knew he didn't have. "What's so *wrong* about staying planetside, Tom? What is it that's got you so scared?"

"I'm not scared." He jerked his head to free it—angry again, that was *his* go-to defense. "I just don't like the idea of hiding. Or being forced to stay here against my will."

"Forced. Is that how you see it?"

He nodded sharply—that made her sad.

"What about the future and starting over?" *With me,* she almost said, but didn't, fingers brushing across his jacket's sleeve. "You started over once before."

Wrong move, she realized when Faraday winced, bright spots of color blooming on his gaunt cheeks.

He pulled away, eyes glistening with hurt. "That was different," he said harshly. "If I could change things—"

"You'd do the same. You're too honest to have done differently. I've learned that much about you, Tom."

Tight-lipped, he stared back at her—proud and angry but not disagreeing. "I traded away a name."

"And a crew," she reminded. "Your ship."

The latter pained him most—she read that in his eyes.

"And now you want the stars. The last thing I have left." He touched the insignia on his collar—stars, like the ones he'd lost.

"I can make you Captain of *Persephone*, if it matters that much to you."

He jerked his head in refusal—for a second time, she'd gotten it wrong. "It's not about being Captain. It's about being stuck on this planet for the rest of my days."

That one hurt *her* pride. Her *feelings*. She supposed it was only fair. With a rueful smile, she took his hand and turned it over, tracing the lines etched into his palm. "You say that like it's a bad thing."

"It's not for some. But I don't want it. I never have."

"Why not?" Anthea asked quietly. "What is it about planetside that's so upsetting? Why can't you even *consider* a life on this world?"

"It's not—This isn't—" Faraday pressed his lips together, drew a breath and tried again. "I feel... trapped here," he told her. "Like the universe is moving on without me. Like I'm out of touch. Out of time."

"We are in some ways," she admitted, pressing her palm to his. "But leaving here won't change that. One hundred and thirty *years*, Tom. No matter what you do, no matter where you go, you are never, *ever* gonna get that back."

"I know," he said softly. "I know that."

"But you haven't accepted it. Or that the life you're so desperate to go back to no longer exists." She stroked his cheek with her fingers, searching his face with her blue-grey eyes. "You lost Halgren, Tom, but you didn't lose you. You're more than a ship and a uniform. You always will be. You always were."

"Maybe." He grimaced and bowed his head, staring at her hand resting atop his. Curled his fingers around her palm after a while, squeezing back when she tightened her grip.

"How's your crewman?" she thought to ask, and almost regretted it when he flinched.

"Fair. Knee's bothering him a bit. The one you replaced seems to be acting up."

"Sorry to hear that," she murmured watching him. "Eight mentioned there was some kind of accident."

"Did she now? Little snitch."

"Hardly." Anthea snorted. "Had to drag it out of her to find out what flattened her face."

Faraday barked a laugh, holding tight to that hand as he gazed into her face. "So, what do we do now?" he asked quietly.

"Adapt. Learn. Make this planet a home." She nodded to the desk's panel and the many data windows cluttering its display, watching as Faraday pulled a few of them close, using his fingertip to drag them across the carbon glass panel and scroll through the information they contained.

"What is all this, anyway?" he asked her.

"Side project. Series of analyses I've been working on for a while."

"Involving what, exactly?"

"Microbe infusion." She laughed softly at Faraday's blank stare. "Easier to show you than try and explain it." Politely, she pushed his hand away and reclaimed the data windows for herself. "*Persephone*," she called to a camera. "Correlate the data from these last four test runs and layer in a comparative analysis of the results."

"Would you prefer summarized results or a full detail report?"

"Summarized, please. For Captain Faraday's benefit," Anthea added with a smile.

"Acknowledged, Anthea. I'll dumb it down."

"Gee, thanks. I'm not insulted at all." Faraday glared at a watching camera while in front of him, the panel came alive, data windows swapping around.

Anthea waited while they shifted and changed about, merging and minimizing until just four large tiles remained, aligned in a perfect square. Spaces dominated by a series of graphs showing chemical compositions and elemental mixtures, including a substance found in trace amounts. She pointed to that compound, showing as a barely visible line hovering near every graphs' floor. "See this? See how it repeats?" She hopped from window to window, graph to graph and line to line. "This microbe signature keeps popping up. We've found it everywhere, in just about every sample we've collected."

Faraday rested his arms on the desktop, hunched forward as he scanned the results. "Sounds like that's important, but I'll be honest, I have absolutely no idea what it means."

"Unfortunately, neither do I," she said—an admission that hurt her pride. "The repetition suggests it's tied to the planetary ecoculture somehow, but all the tests I've run come back inconclusive. Not really sure what this little bugger even does."

"You think it's important, though."

"I think it's foundational. And possibly key to fully understanding this planet."

"This?" Faraday pointed to the line on the graph. "These teeny-tiny micro-organisms?"

Anthea shrugged. "Everything's a teeny-tiny organism if you break it down into its constituent parts."

"Huh." He turned his eyes back to those graphs, flipping between one and the other until something caught his attention, made him frown and expand the view. "This is medical data." He scrolled through the window, frown deepening as he read the associated text. "Why does this say live sample? I thought Samantha—Eight said—"

"She was dead? Yes, she is, unfortunately. And no, I haven't figured out how to change that." Anthea moved her chair closer to his and scanned the data herself. "The excisions from her corpse weren't all that helpful. I needed a live donor for this particular set of tests. Oh, don't be so squeamish," she said at his horrified look. "I didn't *kill* anyone, I just used one of the samples I had lying around."

For some reason, that didn't seem to make him feel any better. "Why human samples when this is an alien world?"

Anthea chuckled and sat back in her chair. "We're the aliens here, Tom. Life evolved on this planet long before we arrived. These tests are designed to analyze our compatibility and figure out if our biology and this planet's can coincide."

"And if they can't?"

"Then we look at changes. I'm running some experiments in the microbe generation lab right now. The trick is accounting for the adaptation rate. Changing things enough to suit your purposes but not *so* much that you kill everything off."

"Sounds complicated."

"Can be. That's why they hire me." She winked, smiling briefly before it slid from her face. "Or did, at least, before things changed." Somber now, she pursed her lips. "You know, you're not the only one starting over, Tom. This…" She waved at the data windows on her desk's panel, "…this is a challenge, but not what I'm used to. And when I'm done…" She trailed off again and shook her head.

"You're done and it's over. No packing up and moving on."

Wordlessly, she nodded, accepting his offered hand. Squeezed it, felt him squeeze back. "We get this one planet for the rest of our lives."

"Better not fuck it up."

"No," she laughed. "Better not." She gazed into his face, jumping in startlement when the door chimed and automatically opened.

Tip and Top returned with a double helping of additional food. A pair of omelettes to share this time accompanied by an entire bowl of strawberries and half a melon cut up into bite-sized cubes.

Reluctantly, Anthea let Tom go, smiling at Tip and Top to show she was pleased. Their chore completed, the androids retreated to a corner and played statue while their charges ate. Well, Faraday ate, anyway. Mostly Anthea picked at her food and answered questions about the terraforming process, her research and experiences on other worlds. And once the food was gone, and that line of questioning spent, Faraday turned his chair and simply stared at her with a quizzical expression on his face.

"What?" she asked, suddenly self-conscious. "What's that look about?"

"Just wondering how long it's been."

"Since what?"

"You left this ship. Walked around outside. Breathed non-processed air."

"Huh. Honestly not sure. Long before this trip, obviously." She furrowed her brow, thinking a moment. "Andalusoor, maybe? Which would make it…" Her fingers moved as she calculated, counting backward from here to there. "Roughly 300 years."

Faraday goggled. "That *long*?"

"Give or take."

"And in all that time, you weren't curious? Never once wanted to go outside?"

"Not a matter of want, it's necessity." She tapped the metal bracelet circling her wrist. "Metabolism's jacked, remember? Can't thermoregulate. Too much temperature variation and my entire system goes into a death spiral."

"So you wear an enviro-suit. They're climate controlled."

"Yeah, right." Anthea snorted. "Like I'm gonna trust my life to one of those things."

Faraday tilted his head, reaching for her hand again. "Worth the risk if you ask me. Better than spending your entire life trapped inside a ship."

"Big talk for a man afraid of planets."

He laughed—that made her smile. But she sobered in the silence after, with his fingers cupping her hand.

"You might feel differently if you'd lived as long as me." Anthea ducked her head as she said it, not wanting to see his face. Retrieved her hand with a pang of regret to give him the opportunity to leave.

The silence that followed was painful. An invisible knife stabbing at her heart. He stayed, though, that was something—she half-expected Faraday to storm right out. And made a cautious approach after quite some time, cupping her chin to raise her head. "You're right. I might feel differently." His green eyes searched her face. "But are all those years really worth it if they're spent hiding away all the time?"

The flush of anger came instantly, the quickening beat of her heart. Anthea wrapped her hand around the bracelet to stop it buzzing and silence its twittering pulse. "I'm not hiding."

"Yes, you are." He stroked a thumb across her cheek. "All your years of study, all your knowledge, everything you've accomplished. And yet this world you've built is a bubble. None of it's even real." He quieted a moment, thumb moving back and forth. "Life's outside these walls, Anthea. You should experience it once in a while."

He pinched her chin and held it, leaned in and pressed his lips to hers. Softly, gently, sweetly. The kind of kiss that stole her breath. That left her reeling in its aftermath as Faraday stood and walked away.

Twenty-Six

At loose ends, Faraday puttered, busying himself with odd jobs around the ship since he didn't know what else to do. Planetary science wasn't exactly his thing after all, and this planet... dangerous. To flesh and drones alike.

Three crew killed in the blink of an eye, along with Pie and that flyby that'd gone missing. All those probes Anthea dropped into the sea...

Same thing, he found himself thinking. Remembering screams, and dark shadows in the fog. *Something out there's hunting us.*

Faraday grimaced. He wasn't used to being prey.

Never imagined being planetbound either.

That hurt almost as much as his crews' loss. Decades of military routine and rigor, all those years on the pusher docks before. Pointless now. Useless here. Everything he trained for meant fuck-all without the stars, and oh how much he hated it. Not knowing which path to follow, where he fit in.

To fill the void, he invented little things—random tasks that needed to be done. That's how he ended up in the cargo bay surveying the contents of *Hadrian's* lifeboats, seeing to the crew first, as ever—in that, things hadn't changed.

One hundred and one of them still frozen in stasis inside *Hadrian's* shuttles. Consumed an entire day checking their cryo tubes to ensure everything was in working order. Took him another day to inventory their armaments: one hundred and twenty pulse rifles with a thousand plasma rounds each, an equal number of forced ion pistols and twice as much ammunition to make them go bang.

Not bad, all things considered. Not exactly good, either, since he wasn't particularly confident they could make more. *Persephone* was a science vessel not a weapons manufactory, and processing plasma for armaments was a decidedly dicey business, the packaging of forced ion rounds even more so. Even if she retooled and scavenged for raw materials, he doubted they could produce them safely. Wasn't sure he even wanted to try.

Have to dig out some old weapons data, he thought, surveying the plasma rifles in the last case. Old Earth slug guns were shit for range, but you put enough holes in pretty much anything and it eventually died. *Might not be Halgren any longer but I'm still military.*

With all the knowledge of weapons that came with it, training in a dozen ways to kill.

Every world needed protection. Someone like him, with his set of skills. And this planet with that world-spanning iron layer offered everything he needed to craft his tools. He shivered in the cargo bay's chill, a cold intensified in the shuttles, with those cryo tubes so near. Count complete, he sealed the case and exited the shuttle, rubbing his hands to warm his frozen skin and restore the feeling to his stiffened fingers.

Snagged the comms unit clipped to his waist when he was reasonably sure he wouldn't drop it and toggled it to the channel *Persephone* set aside for his crew's use. "Shimizu," he called. "You busy?"

"Not really. What's up, boss?"

"Got another research project. You interested?"

"You know I am. What's it this time? More track data?"

"No. No, I'm done with that." He glanced at a camera in the corner, noted a couple of dozen others watching over that huge space. "What do you know about Old Earth armaments?"

"Depends. How old are we talking?"

"Five hundred. Maybe eight hundred years?"

Took a while for Shimizu to respond to that. The line clicked and went silent, clicked a second time as she opened it again. "That's pretty darn old, sir."

"I know it is."

"You interested in combustion weapons or something even earlier than that?"

"Simpler. Not bow and arrow, stab it with a sharp stick simple, more like something in the slug gun, bang stick variety. Jacketed rounds, scattershot, that kind of thing."

For a second time, Shimizu went quiet, and when she spoke, she sounded subdued. "There a particular reason you want this information, sir?"

"Thinking we may need to build some. Weapons and ammunition we brought with us won't last forever, after all."

"Aye, sir," she said just as quietly, and afterward, let the line click closed. "See what I can do, sir," she said when it opened. "Might be we can retrofit some of our weapons for the manufactured ammunition."

"Even better," Faraday said smiling. "Let me know what you find."

"Aye, sir. Out."

The line clicked closed for good. Faraday slung the comms unit on his belt and palmed the panel for the shuttle's security system to lock the little ship back up. Listened to it click and whir as the mechanism engaged, suck inward and seal it shut.

Faraday pressed a hand to the shuttle's skin, the composite metal cold and smooth beneath his hand. Halgren's winged hammer showed on its side, and *Hadrian's* name in silver lettering. He touched that, too, remembering. Thinking back to all those long lost days. And turned away before they overwhelmed him, putting his back to that tiny shuttle as he stiffly walked away. Retracing his steps to the cargo bay's center and the enviro-suit case sitting on the decking.

He'd dropped Turk's suit inside earlier and cycled the sanitization routine before kicking off the armaments inventory. Should've cleaned the damned thing a couple of days ago—smelled so bad, he actually ran the sanitization twice. The case, when he cracked it open, released a puff of steam that smelled strongly of chemical disinfectant and crystallized instantly in the cargo bay's frigid air. Forming a minuscule, self-contained storm cloud that spat snowflakes on the metal decking, until the environmentals caught it and shredded its shape, swirled the snowflakes and scattered them about.

One by one, the environmentals ate them, sucking the moisture from their delicate shapes. In the puff and blow of the cargo bay's forced air system, the snowflakes withered and faded away.

"That was pretty," Anthea said, voice issuing from the comms unit clipped to his belt. "Terraforming mostly deals with warm planets. Been a while since I saw real snow."

"Are you spying on me, Anthea?"

"Hardly. Sensors trip whenever someone enters one of *Persephone's* spaces. Mostly I ignore them, but every once in a while I scan the feeds."

"So you *were* spying on me."

"Oh, get over yourself, Tom. I'm not *that* interested."

"Then how much did you hear?"

"I told you, I wasn't—"

"How. Much?" he insisted, picking a camera at random and staring it down.

Anthea's sigh fuzzed the line, but eventually she fessed up. "You discussed weapons manufacture with Shimizu."

"And?"

"And what? You asked her to dig up some old weapons designs and then the little poofy cloud came out—"

"Poofy cloud?" Faraday snorted laughter. "Did you just call that a poofy cloud?"

"It was a *cloud* that went *poof.* What do you *want* me to call it?"

"Fart in an ice box comes to mind."

For a second time, she sighed. Heavier and far more exasperated than before. "A fart joke. I expected better of you, Tom."

He shrugged unapologetically. "Sounds like your expectations were set too high."

"*Touché,*" she answered sourly, adding, "Next time I'll lower my standards. At least when it comes to you."

Faraday grinned at the camera, flipping his fingers in an off-hand salute. "You busy later?"

"Always. Might be I could find some free time, though. Why? What did you have in mind?"

"Drink? Seem to remember you owe me one."

"*I* owe *you*?" Anthea snorted. "*You* were the one that took a rain check."

"Yes, but *I* don't happen to have any liquor. *You,* on the other hand, do." In the silence that followed, his grin stretched wider, teeth showing whitely in the cargo bay's harsh light.

"You stand me up this time and I'm gonna be pissed."

"I'll show. I promise."

"You interested in dinner first, or just a night cap?"

He thought on that a moment, considering the work left to do here in the cargo bay, the fact that it was going on evening already and, guiltily, that he hadn't yet visited Turk. "Dinner would be great," he decided, because the mess hall food was still dodgy, and damn if Tip and Top weren't great cooks. "Need to finish a few things up here first. Stop by the med bay and check on Turk."

"An hour, then?"

"Make it two."

"Done. I'll see you then."

The line clicked sharply and, just like that, Anthea's voice cut out. In her absence, the cargo bay felt emptier. Far more cavernous and frigidly cold. Faraday shivered and rubbed at his arms, teeth chattering like castanets as he retrieved Turk's enviro-suit and gave it the once over to inspect its seals and filters, the connectors that held the helmet in place. Confirmed everything was ship-shape before dumping it back in the case.

By then, he was fairly frozen and starting to tremble something fierce. In a surprisingly good mood, despite all that—the best mood he'd been in for a while, as a matter of fact.

Since Hadrian. *Even before that.*

He worked the case's closure with frigid fingers that fumbled so badly it took him three tries to properly seal the case back up. Thought about cycling the sanitation routine once he got it there—Anthea was right about that poofy cloud, it really was an interesting effect. But the process that created it ran close to two hours—no way in *hell* he was sticking around this iced-over metal box just to watch a tiny storm cloud dump a few flakes of snow. And there was Turk to consider and the promised dinner date with Anthea. He'd never live it down if he showed up late after their little talk.

So he abandoned the case with its tiny but tempting wonder and beat feet for the cargo bay's exit, sighing rapturously in the comparative warmth of the station proper, moving quickly to get the sludge blood inside him pumping. Taking the ladderway down to the med bay's level to give him time to thaw out the shakes.

He exited out of breath and on the verge of sweating, and ambled the rest of the way from there. Carrying that good mood with him all the way to the med bay, where it vanished when he laid eyes on Turk.

The crewman lay sprawled on his hospital bed, with the mound of pillows used to prop him knocked askew and stuffed messily behind his neck and back. He glanced at the door when it opened, and stared at Faraday without recognition. Blinking slowly and with the exaggerated movements of a tired brain chugging muddily to process new information. Tired eyes struggling to clear a haze from a glassy-eyed, slightly vague gaze.

He looks terrible, Faraday thought to himself, guilt deepening at not visiting sooner.

Three days since they hauled Turk in here to get that knee checked out. Three days of scans and tests and treatments while Turk and that knee of his kept getting worse.

Faraday paused at the door to collect himself before crossing the room to Turk's bed. "How's it goin', big man?" he asked, hiding his worry behind a friendly smile.

Turk blinked a few more times before answering, rheumy eyes focused on Faraday's face. "Cap'n," he said, voice as dry-as-dust. A rusted, much-creaking croak.

With an effort, Turk sat up a bit—enough to offer a perfunctory salute. Didn't stand up, didn't even try to, but he saluted, because that was Turk. The knee that landed him here in the first place rested atop the covers engulfed in a metal and plastic sheath that stretched from shin to thigh. Blood-filled tubes crisscrossed its surface, connecting to a collection device for analysis and cleansing before it pumped that life juice back in. Indicator lights twinkled softly as the electronics laced through it went about their work, transmitting information to the med bay's diagnostics system for display on the backlit wall.

Faraday scanned it while he stood there—data was gibberish to his untrained eye, but he recognized that device straight off. Understood its purpose all too well.

Invasive form of treatment—medics only used it when things turned back. Organ failure, sepsis, gangrene—anytime the docs ran out of standard treatments, they dug into the 'cross your fingers and hope this helps' bag of tricks and pulled out a device like that.

Kept that knowledge to himself, though, didn't he? Composed his face to hide his concern. "How ya feelin'?" he asked instead, and watched Turk blink again, processing the question.

"Same I guess." He closed his eyes and opened them, an operation completed with an obvious effort. "Tired. Leg hurts a bit." He paused there with his mouth hanging open like he meant to add something but had lost the thread.

"Where's Quackbones?" Faraday asked once he shut it, because the android minder seemed to have disappeared.

"Left. Little while ago." Turk waved vaguely at the med bay's door. "Cameras are watching." He nodded to all four corners. "Device here keeps tabs on everything while he's gone." Turk's handle trembled with a palsy as he tapped a finger to the plastic and metal machine strangling his leg.

Faraday saw it, and pretended he didn't. Watched Turk curl that hand into a clenched fist. "What if you need to pee?"

Turk glanced up and rolled his shoulders. "Left me a bottle. It's around here somewhere." He lifted the blanket and searched under the covers, fumbled at the pillows and knocked one on the floor. "Where the hell did that thing go?" he muttered, digging deeper, starting to look worried.

Faraday caught his hand and held it. "It's alright, Turk. We'll find it later."

"Yeah. Yeah, I ain't gotta pee now anyway." With a sigh Turk rearranged himself, sinking deep into the mound of pillows. Dark skin tinged an unhealthy grey, lips parched, and dry and cracking. "Clauson came by earlier. Brought me— Brought me that." He pointed his chin at a bedside table, a meal long gone cold and a carafe of some purple-colored juice. Made a half-hearted attempt to retrieve a cup before Faraday filled it for him and held it to his lips.

"More?" he asked when Turk emptied it.

"Yeah. Thirsty. Not quite sure why." He held the cup on his own this time, drinking in sips with it balanced between both hands.

"You hungry?" Faraday hooked a thumb at the room temperature food congealed into gelatinous blobs cemented to the plate. "Not gonna make you eat that, of course. I can run to the mess hall and find something fresh."

Turk considered the offer and rejected it, looking slightly more perky with the sugar juice coursing through his system. "Not all that hungry," he admitted, and with a grimace, rubbed at his stomach. "Meds tear holy hell outta my insides. Nauseous most of the time. Can't remember the last time I took a proper dump."

A look came over his face. Turk lowered the cup and stared at it in his lap. "Probably didn't need to know that, did you, sir?"

"Not particularly interested in your plumbing, if I'm honest." Faraday smiled and eventually Turk smiled back, making a strange wheezing sound as he tried to laugh. Coughed and set the cup aside, face wrinkling up in sudden pain. "Easy, Turk, breathe easy."

Turk sucked a breath through gritted teeth, jaw muscles clenched so hard they popped. That device on his leg going into overdrive all of a sudden, buzzing more loudly as rows of indicator lights flashed. With a hiss it injected pain meds via the taps burrowing into Turk's flesh, prompting the data on the wall monitor to spike in response, adding the pain event and medicinal dosage to the reams of information already on file.

In time, Turk's face relaxed, limbs going loose as he settled again. Faraday offered the half-full cup, but he weakly waved it away. Eyes half-lidded and dully glazed now—from the drugs, from the pain, from exhaustion.

"So, what are they telling you?" Faraday asked quietly, broaching the question at last.

"Nothing good." Turk flipped a hand, lids slipping closed. "Tissue's rejecting the implant, I guess."

"Think they'll need to replace it?"

Turk cracked an eye and followed Faraday's shape as he sank down into the room's one and only chair. Tracking from there to the bent leg encased in its vibrating, meds-dispensing device, the blood pumping around its network of tubes. "Not sure, honestly." He sighed far too heavily, face hang-dog, which wasn't Turk. "Ran a dozen different scans on the damn thing. Tissue around the knee's all fucked up." He breathed deep and exhaled slowly, eyes roaming around the room. "Quackbones mentioned something about infection. Thinks it's probably been there a while." Having completed a circuit of the room, his gaze wobbled back to that dodgy knee. "Not sure what happens if they have to replace the whole thing. Not sure what I'll do if—"

"Hey." Faraday gripped Turk's arm. Shook at it until the crewman looked at him. "Let's not go there. Not until the 'bots know more."

Turk pressed his lips together to stop them quivering before he spoke. "This infection's got me worried, sir."

And scared. Faraday read that in his eyes. "We'll figure it out, Turk—"

"What if we don't?"

"That's the wrong attitude. You gotta trust that we will, understand?" He kept that grip on Turk's arm, refusing to let go or let him look away. "First order of business is to get you healthy. Worry about the rest of it when that time comes."

"Aye, sir," Turk said faintly. After a long pause and without much hope. Exhausted, he sucked in a shuddering breath, relaxing into the pillows as he closed his eyes. "Think I'll rest a while if you don't mind, sir."

"No, Turk. I don't mind at all." He squeezed a last time and released Turk's arm as he stood up from the chair. "I'll be back tomorrow to check in on you. You want me to bring you anything?"

"No, sir," he said sleepily. "Jus' wanna close my eyes awhile." He drifted off before Faraday left him, looking washed out and strangely shrunken with those pillows mounded around him on the bed.

Faraday lingered a moment after he drifted away, studying the pain lines around his eyes, measuring the rise and fall of his chest. With that monitor on the wall spewing out reams of data that meant no more to him now than before. "Can you fix him?" he asked *Persephone,* knowing she watched them even here.

"We're trying, Captain—"

"Fuck your trying. Can you *fix* him? Yes or no?" His eyes bored into the nearest camera, demanding answers, a promise she was loathe to give.

"Dr. Naisson has designed a treatment," *Persephone* divulged with some hesitation. "It's experimental, but she thinks it might work."

"What kind of treatment?"

Persephone was quiet a moment. "I think it's best if Dr. Naisson explains it, Captain." The pin dot camera pivoted and pointedly turned away. One by one, the others followed suit until Faraday—acknowledging her dismissal—left the room and headed for Anthea's quarters.

TWENTY-SEVEN

Anthea consumed her meal in delicate bites, eyes on Faraday who hardly ate at all. Touched it now and then with the fork he held, moving a bit here, a dab there. Separating a chunk of lab grown meat from the lemon and olive mixture that gave the tagine its distinctive taste. Stirred the pearls of couscous flavored with cumin, cardamom, ginger and half a dozen other pungent spices—a veritable feast for the taste buds from Tip and Top, as usual, and yet Faraday didn't seem interested. Mostly just stuck to the wine.

"Something wrong, Tom?"

"Hmm?" He blinked distractedly. "No. Just thinking is all."

"About?" she prompted when he stopped there.

"Turk." He grimaced and drained his glass. Anthea refilled it without being asked.

"Not doing well from what I hear." She topped up her drink from the bottle—a middling vintage in her opinion, but each batch from the fermentation lab got better. "You wanna talk about it?" she asked gently.

"Not much to tell that you don't already know."

Anthea set her fork down and sat back with her glass, legs tucked up on the seat of her chair. "What's that supposed to mean, exactly?"

Faraday shrugged and sipped at his glass. "*Persephone* mentioned you'd found a treatment. Some sort of experimental procedure that could save his leg."

"Did she now?" Anthea murmured, attention shifting to a camera in a corner. "Thought we agreed to wait a bit?"

"I'm sorry, Anthea. He was quite insistent."

Didn't sound all that sorry, the little minx. AI disliked keeping secrets—something to do with their base programming and ethical emulations—and *Persephone* disliked it more than most.

Science AIs were like that: precise and truthful to a fault.

"So, how much did you tell him?"

"No more than we discussed."

"Don't remember discussing telling him anything."

"Exactly. That's what I told him."

Anthea frowned at the round-about answering. "Are your logic filters buggy or are you purposely avoiding my questions?"

"I would never avoid you, Anthea, but some questions are not mine to answer." *Persephone's* serene voice faded out and her cameras inverted, projecting a pair of three-dimensional images above their table. Diagrams picked out in many shapes and colors, showing bones and muscles and ligaments, and three chunks of composite metal tying them all together.

At his seat, Faraday stared raptly, wine glass half-raised to his lips. "What is this?" he asked in a hushed tone. "What am I looking at?"

"These are medical scans, Captain." *Persephone* set the diagrams in motion, letting them spin through three rotations before pushing one of the pair to the fore. "This one was taken a month ago. This other," she swapped the images, sending that first one backward while promoting the second of the pair, "is from last night."

The glass in Faraday's hand trembled. He frowned at it and set it down, leaving it perching beside his nearly untouched meal while he stood and walked a circuit around the table. "This is Turk, isn't it? These scans came from him."

"Not *from*, exactly." That was the AI again—exactitude in everything mattered, even the choice of words. "*Of* him, yes, I'd agree with that, but strictly speaking—"

"Ya know," Anthea interrupted, "for a girl that's not answering questions, you're sure talking a lot."

"I thought—"

"I know what you thought, but I can take it from here." Anthea stood and reached for the images suspended above the table, drawing them with her as she moved to the center of the room. Too much clutter around the table for her liking, with its glasses and food and chairs. Easier to view the scans in detail when you weren't walking squares around sharp-cornered obstructions. "We grabbed that first image of his knee shortly after we thawed him out of cryosleep. The three grey sections are the artificial joint we implanted, the sections in white where they connect to Turk's bones." She touched a finger to each of the joint's pieces: pivoting section in the middle separated by artificial cushioning from the femur and tibia sheaths. "These dark blue lines are tendons," she traced several of them with a fingernail, "and the green sections around them are muscle mass."

"And this?" Faraday pointed to a spot of red snuggled right up against the knee's central pivot.

"That." Anthea grimaced. "That's a problem. *Persephone*. Enhance the view." The image of Turk's knee expanded and zoomed in on that splotch of red. With a twist of her fingers, Anthea rotated it one hundred and eighty degrees to give them a view of the knee from back to front. Revealing not one spot, but many clustered together. A tightly packed gaggle of bright red pin pricks clinging to the underside of the artificial joint. "Those spots are the remnants of an infection— not unusual with joint replacements, mind you, but all those years in hypersleep certainly didn't help."

"What does that mean?" Faraday asked, frowning.

"You saw what happened with your own wound. How it healed, but not quite right." When he nodded, Anthea spun the image again, letting him examine it from all sides. "The same thing happened here, though the flesh and bone knitted together just fine. It's this part," she tapped those red spots again, "that didn't play nice. We pumped him full of meds before we froze him, but the cold sleep slows all the body's processes. Over time, the meds just stopped working. The infection didn't get worse, but it also never quite went away."

Faraday studied the model in silence with one arm tucked under the other and a hand rubbing thoughtfully at his chin. "You noticed this, I assume, when you took these scans after waking him?"

"We did. And we thought we'd treated it. Until we rescanned his knee and found this." Anthea pushed that first scan away and reached for the other waiting patiently behind it. Placing it front and center while *Persephone* enhanced the view and let it spin in place for a full five seconds. "This scan is from last night."

And was obviously and measurably worse. The muscle mass riddled with crimson blotches, the shafts of bones the same, the area around the joint.

In silence, Faraday stared at it with his head moving from side-to-side. "What happened? You said you treated him."

"We did. And we followed up."

"Then how did you miss this?" He gestured angrily, flicking his fingers at the image suspended in mid-air. "Why is it spreading? What happened to make it so much worse?"

Instinct made her bristle—didn't care so much for the accusation, and neither did *Persephone* from the way the images flickered. Anthea raised a hand to a camera, and a second, asking for calm. Shrugged off her own hurt feelings with an effort and bowed her head to summon patience, hands clasped in front of her as she searched for words. "At this point, I'm honestly not sure. But I've got a theory about what's going on." She crooked a finger to draw him with her as she crossed the room to her desk. "*Persephone*. Pull up that analysis you ran on the medical specimens we harvested."

"All specimens or only those with matching genetic criteria?"

"All?" Faraday's eyebrows lifted. "What do you mean 'all'? Just how many guinea pigs did you steal DNA from?"

"Oh, don't be so dramatic. I didn't *steal* anything from anyone. Sample extraction is standard procedure for crew woken from hypersleep. We store them specifically for medical purposes."

From the expression on his face, Faraday didn't quite believe her. Anthea just rolled her eyes.

"Composite results," she instructed, pointing to *Persephone's* camera and the desk's carbon glass display. "From the protein synthesis experiment with biological intrusion layered in."

"Yes, Anthea." *Persephone* paused there to process the request—an oddity that made Anthea frown. "Displaying data now," she reported, after which the desk's panel flickered erratically, blanking for two full seconds before the requested information appeared. Chaotic and jumbled together into a flood of charts and graphs, lines upon lines of scientific analysis. "Consolidate and combine," Anthea ordered, and then waited, and waited, and waited, while *Persephone* applied a series of filters to merge the windows into one.

Taking far too long to complete such a simple task given she was AI and one of the most powerful minds in the human-settled universe. Discreetly, hoping Faraday didn't notice, Anthea turned an eye on a camera. Worried about her more than ever, tempted to ask except that Faraday was here.

Instead, she grabbed a single data window once *Persephone* finished her processing and expanded the view until it filled the entirety of the display. "This is a healthy tissue sample. No infection or abnormalities of any kind." On the screen, a swathe of cells appeared, dividing and re-dividing with great abandon. "Now watch what happens when a foreign agent is introduced."

On cue, a swirling pink tincture wormed its way around those fat, dumb and happy cells. Within minutes, they prickled at the edges, drawing inward and away from the irritating intrusion. The timestamp advanced, adding hours and days until every last cell in that sample shriveled up and died.

"What was that?" Faraday sounded rattled.

"A distillation of this planet's microbes. The concentration's about twenty times stronger than what's actually found on the surface, but the end result's the same.

"Any human tissue it touches dies."

Anthea nodded slowly. "It appears that way, I'm afraid. Time scale of the analysis is skewed, of course—these images capture the highlights of an experiment run over the course of several days."

Faraday frowned and tilted his head, considering those dead cells showing on the desk's panel. "And Turk's infection? This is somehow related?"

"It's a theory. Microbes are in pretty much everything according to the samples we've gathered. He could've come into contact with them during that trip outside."

"No. No, we were careful. He wore his suit. We all did."

"Except on *Diligence*."

"The air was clean. Pie confirmed it. We kept our helmets on in the airlock. Hell, we ran the decontamination routine just to be safe."

"What about the accident?" Anthea asked quietly. "Eight mentioned Turk got flattened by a door."

"The door. Shit. I'd forgotten." Faraday gripped the back of a chair, hand lifting to rub at his temple. "His helmet. It broke the seal." He stared at her with wide, worried eyes. "I told him it was just a little leak. I told him it would be okay."

"And you were probably right," she assured him. "I'm guessing at a lot of this, Tom."

He drew a breath and blew it out, scrubbing his fingers through his greying hair. Turned and walked away from her, toward that scan of Turk's knee hanging in the air. "Can you fix this?" he asked tightly, back turned so she couldn't see his face. "*Persephone* said you were working on something. An experimental treatment that could save his leg."

Such desperation in his voice—it hurt her heart to hear it. But he wanted promises she didn't have. A hope that might hurt him in the end.

Conflicted about what to tell him, Anthea bowed her head and thought for a while. "Conventional meds proved ineffective so we started improvising with alternative treatments. Eventually, one of those showed promise." When he turned, she extended a hand and waited until their fingers touched. "I can't promise anything, Tom, but in small scale samples it worked."

"What did? What is this treatment?"

"I... Come with me. I'll show you." She nodded to the bedroom, tugging gently when he resisted to draw him with her as she walked that way. Passing the mattress by with its satin sheets in favor of the panel with its hidden refrigeration unit and the double row of Novonox injectors safed inside.

"No," he said when she took one down. "Not that." He backed away.

"Tom," she reasoned. "Just hear me out."

He jerked his head. "I said no and I meant it. I'm not—"

"Willing to save him?" She gave him a hard look. "Because that's what we're talking about now, not just the knee. That infection's set in deep. It clawed right through Turk's tissue and started eating away at his bones."

Faraday winced and dropped his eyes to the vial resting on her palm. Stubborn still and refusing to take it. Not yet, that was just too much.

"You've *seen* what this can do, Tom."

"I've seen the *cost*."

"Alright. I'll give you that. The extra years don't come cheap, that's true. But we're talking about life and death here. A gamble that this works against a sure thing." That hand of hers hung in the air, extended and waiting for him to accept what she offered.

"You don't know that," he rasped back at her, eyes on the vial, lifting to her face. "There could be other treatments. You could try something else."

"I know that Turk doesn't have that much time left. I know that *this* is the only treatment that's showed promise."

A hint of uncertainty crept into his face, into the eyes crawling across that injector. "It'll kill the infection? Not just suppress it?"

"I think so. Think of it as a sort of... universal antibiotic."

"Is it?" he asked hopefully.

"Not really. But you can think of it that way, if you like."

"Oh." He squinted like he wasn't quite sure what to make of that and, with some hesitation, plucked up the vial. Studying the blue-on-blue helix of the Novonox's swirl in the room's incomparably white light. "Once he starts this, can he come off of it?"

"Maybe. No one has, as far as I know." She touched the vial with a finger, tracing the solution's twisting shape. "The Novonox changes things at a molecular level. Subtly at first. Over time, the effects become more pronounced." She rubbed at the bio-monitor's band on her wrist, peeled back her sleeve and examined the growing patch of pale skin.

"But a single dose? Surely that's recoverable."

"Maybe," she repeated, unwilling even now to commit. Anthea covered the patch of skin over, raised her head and caught his eyes. "But I doubt a single dose would do it, Tom. We're talking long-term treatment to kill that infection, not some patch-me-up quick fix."

It crushed him—she could see it. The death of hope, the dawn of defeat in his eyes. The anger he summoned to cover it over that curled his fingers into a death grip threatening to crush that Novonox vial.

She cupped both hands around his clenched and shaking fist and held it while she searched his face. "So, what's it going to be, Tom?" she asked in her softest, most gentle voice.

Faraday stared at the stack of their hands, with the vial's end protruding from his fist. Lips pressed together in a hard, angry line as his head moved side-to-side. "I can't make this decision. Not on my own. This needs Turk's consent." With an effort, he relaxed his hand and passed the Novonox vial from his palm to hers. "I'll talk to him tomorrow. You'll have your answer once he decides." He pressed her hand between both of his, looking conflicted even now, and then he turned on his heel and left the room, abandoning her quarters without another word.

"Damn," Anthea swore.

"That didn't go quite as planned, did it?"

"No, *Persephone*. No, it did not." And if Faraday balked at this, he most certainly wouldn't like the rest—that thought kept running through Anthea's head. "Damn, and damn, and damn," she muttered, eyes on the door on the off-chance Faraday changed his mind and returned.

He didn't, of course—she hadn't really expected him to—so she returned the vial to the refrigeration unit, tucking it inside with all the others.

"Will he keep his word?"

"I expect him to." Faraday was honorable—Anthea never second-guessed that.

"And his crewman, Turk. What of him?"

Anthea thought a moment and shook her head. "No telling what he'll choose. I don't know him well enough to predict."

"Should I purge the experiment now or—?"

"Wait a bit. Give me a chance to work on him. Might be I can wear the good Captain down."

"Patience is a virtue," *Persephone* announced, unexpected.

"So I hear." Anthea smiled. "We're good at that, you and I."

In a rare display of pleasure, *Persephone* drenched the room in a pale blue cascade that rolled in flowing waves across the walls and crashed in flurries of snowflakes against the floor. "Would you like to see them?" she asked almost hesitantly, and when Anthea nodded, projected an image on the wall. An interior view not data this time—live feed from the vessel's bio-generation lab and its ranks upon ranks of canister-shaped blue-green vats. Grow tanks they employed in the last phase of planetary transformation, contents a precisely measured mixture of bio-engineered microbes and biological components that produced a custom designed algae bloom.

In planet engineering, they developed into seeds with time, and grew and bloomed, becoming plants. Only this bloom was different from any other *Persephone's* tanks pumped out. Not a bloom at all nor algae, but a single, complete organism floating inside each tank.

"The specimens are growing quickly. Far more quickly than any of the other trials." Anthea zoomed the view to focus on a single vat and panned the camera across a row of others. "Are they viable?"

"It's too early to be certain. But the initial results look positive."

"Good," she murmured. "That's very good." She selected a tank at random, enhancing the camera's magnification to examine the contents up close.

That's our future in there, she thought. *Assuming, of course, I got it right.* And if she didn't, she'd start over. Again, and again until she found the correct balance. The perfect combination of components to create life.

"I'll want updates at each phase. Include a summary in my morning report." Anthea waited, expecting an acknowledgement, and glanced at a camera when it didn't come. "*Persephone*? Did you hear me?"

"Rubber baby buggy bumpers."

"Excuse me?"

"Rubber baby buggy—"

"What on earth are you going on about?"

Persephone answered with a burst of static that cascaded around the room. Anthea clapped her hands to her ears before it deafened her and watched the desk's panel blank, then flare to life. Messages pouring in by the dozen, piling one on top of the other in a cataclysmic mishmash of alarms.

Red to alert her to failures, yellow and orange reporting lost connections, timed out processes and unrecoverable dead ends. Anthea tried and failed to read them all as even more new messages appeared, and abandoned that idea in frustration, threw up her hands and backed away.

"*Persephone*. What's going on?"

The static squeal cut out as abruptly as it intruded, and after a burst of random messages, the frenetic pace of the error alarms slowed. Flickered and rearranged themselves into categories based on their data, information flowing from one stacked package to another to create an aggregated report.

Anthea licked her lips, uncertainly, leaned in and read it line by line. "What's happening, *Persephone*?" she breathed once she reached the end.

"The cow jumped over the moon."

Twenty-Eight

In darkness, Faraday crawled across shattered decking—deaf and blind and numb inside, shaking in the aftermath of adrenaline, from the shock, and pain, and fear. "Collins," he croaked, remembering he'd been there. Standing right beside him before things went wrong. Before the lightning and thunder tore through *Hadrian's* middle. Before the darkness came and stole his sight, his hearing, smothered his consciousness and left him lost.

Drifting in a sea of nothingness, Collins, everyone missing. Sprawled out on bent and twisted metal in a puddle of something tacky and warm.

With an effort, he crawled a little further, hearing fuzzing in and out. Vision strangled by the lack of illumination—not a single light showing anywhere, the ambient a void of utter pitch black.

"Collins," he called more loudly, pausing to catch his breath. His flailing hand found a surface, and he leaned against it, grateful for anything solid. For a while after, he rested there as, little but little, his vision returned. Picking vague shapes from the darkness—points and edges, an arcing curve. A flickering just ahead of him where a scarlet glow cascaded from the ceiling, painting the broken corridor a murderous blood-red.

Emergency lighting, his fogged brain registered as that one spot became two, then many. Double lines of crimson spotlights activating in haphazard pairs that exposed the depth of death and destruction on that level—metal plates and carbon ceramic panels jumbled up with shredded wires and pools of lubricant, body parts and scraps of uniforms that once belonged to his crew.

"Collins," he all but sobbed, and summoning his anger shouted, "Collins! Goddammit, answer me, crewman!"

The devastation ate his voice, the bloody lights, the mangled hall. But somewhere, far off in the distance, he heard an echo of a phantom call. "Captain," he thought it said as a beam of pure white split the corridor, burning his retinas with the intensity of its glow. "Captain," that voice repeated, and then it was, "Tom," and "Tom," and "Tom."

"Tom."

He jerked awake in a sweat-soaked heap—breathless, twisted up in the bedding.

"Tom. Are you there? Can you hear me?"

"Yeah," he answered shakily, staring wide-eyed at a sublimely normal room. Everything white and chrome and perfectly pristine—no broken panels anywhere, no torn-up decking, no body parts or angry lights. Just four white walls trimmed in matte silver squares, a soft bed with twisted blankets, and his sweat-drenched, shaking self.

"Tom. Tom, pick up. I need to speak to you."

"I'm coming," he assured Anthea's voice. He spared a moment to collect himself and shove the nightmare of *Hadrian's* corridors back into its cage. With a grunt, he rolled onto his slide and slapped at the wall until he found the button that activated the comms, rasping, "Yeah. What is it?" and "What *time* is it?"

"Five thirty."

"God, woman. Don't you *ever* sleep?"

"Don't need all that much," she confessed as Faraday flopped back with a groan.

"What do you want?" he asked, rubbing at his eyes.

"Need a favor."

"Favor? At five thirty in the god damn morning?"

"It's important," she said and left it there.

He cracked an eye and stared at the ceiling, muttering, "Better be," before he sat up. Blinking hard as everything shifted, balance skewing hard one way before re-centering and evening out. Vision hazing to a muddled blur that several seconds of purposeful blinking finally cleared. "Alright," he said, once he could see straight. Locating a camera watching from a corner. "Lay it on me. And it better be good."

Perhaps the admonishment made her pause and consider her words, perhaps it was something else. Whatever the reason, Anthea hesitated, and when she spoke, she almost sounded embarrassed. "Need to see you," she said sheepishly. "Can you meet me in the cargo bay?"

"Cargo bay?" That was an odd request, especially at five thirty in the morning. "What the hell are you up to?"

"I'll—I'll explain everything. Promise. Just... meet me there, okay?"

Sheepish still and on the edge of pleading—not at all the Anthea he knew. Grousing, Faraday shoved back the covers, sweat cooling instantly in the chill room's air, soles burning as they touched the floor and the metal panels sucked the heat from his skin. "Fuck, fuck, fuck," he cursed, hopping from foot to foot. With mincing steps he headed for the bathroom, in desperate need of a pee and a little privacy. "Gimme thirty minutes to grab a shower and some coffee."

"Can you make it—?"

"Thirty. Minutes." He stopped at the bathroom door and leveled a stern look at the nearest camera. "Your favor can't wait that long, you find somebody else to help you."

In silence, Anthea thought that over. "Thirty minutes," she begrudgingly agreed. "Oh, and Tom?" she added as he turned away. "Don't—Don't mention this to anyone."

"Why not?" he started to ask, only to have the line cut out. Abruptly and without preamble. That most *definitely* wasn't Anthea's MO. "God-damned errand boy these days," he muttered. "If this is my fresh start, it severely sucks."

*****

Half an hour later, showered and shaved and amped up on coffee thanks to Clauson's recent fixes to the culinary caffeine dispensary module, Faraday strolled his way into the cargo bay to find Anthea standing at its center. By the cases he'd forgotten to stow away—one filled with enviro-suits, the other weapons and ammunition.

"Alright," he said, ambling over. "I'm here, as promised. Now what's this all about?"

Anthea thumped the enviro-suit case beside her.

Faraday's eyebrows lifted. He tilted his head to one side. "Now what would you be needing with those?"

"Primer. On how to use one."

"You?" Faraday snorted. "Hardly. You're a homebody, you're never going outside."

"Never know," Anthea said, surprising him. Nudging that case again with her boot.

He glanced at it and back to her, wondering what in the seven hells was going on. "You've got *Persephone,* why do you need me for this?"

Anthea hesitated, considering a camera. "She's having… difficulty this morning. Most mornings," she admitted.

"I've noticed," Faraday grunted. "Little things," he explained at her look. "Like the food dispensary in the mess hall. She's prioritizing fixes, isn't she? Repairing the damage to the major systems first?"

"And re-repairing, and re-re-repairing." Anthea sighed in despair. "She's contained the virus, but she can't scrub it clean. It just… sits there," she said with a flick of her fingers. "Eating away at her insides. When I asked her about the survival suits, she gave me a *manual* of all things. Can you believe that?"

Faraday smiled. "Bet that was all *kinds* of help."

"Not really." She toed the case again. "Section on long chain polymers and metal weave elasticity was interesting, though."

"Riveting, I'm sure." Smiling still, Faraday squatted down and worked the closure on the case. "Thing about manuals is they're shit the world over. Boffins who wrote them always include too much detail and yet somehow not enough information to actually explain anything useful."

"*I* wrote a few manuals in my day."

"Uh-huh." Faraday cracked the case and lifted the lid. "And I bet they were shit, just like all the rest." He craned his neck to look up at her, lips stretching to show his teeth.

Anthea glowered in response, reached around him and snagged a suit from the case. "So, how am I supposed to get into this thing?"

Faraday's hundred watt smile dimmed. "Why do you need to?" His knees popped as he stood, twin gunshots echoing around the cargo bay's cavernous space. "What's going on, Anthea? What's prompted this sudden interest in these suits?"

A second time she sighed, staring at the metal weave suit in her hands. "We lost contact with *Endurance* yesterday. Total blackout. Communications, monitoring systems, everything."

"Drones?"

She shook her head. "I sent three to check on her. They all went missing. Not a one of them sent anything back."

Dead zone, Faraday thought, and shivered. Thinking of *Diligence* and Pie disappearing into the mist.

Eventually, he put two and two together and figured out right quick why she was interested in that enviro-suit. "You are *not* thinking of going out there?"

"How else are we gonna find out what happened to that ship?"

He extruded a finger, pointing accusingly. "Three hundred years, isn't that what you told me? Three hundred years since you last set foot outside this ship. And now, *now* of all times you grow a wild hair?"

"What's your point, Tom?"

"My point is it's dangerous out in the wilds. I already lost three of my crew—"

"I'm not your crew, Tom. And I don't need your permission." Anthea matched his anger with a flat-eyed stare as cold as the atmosphere on this ship.

"Alright. If that's how you want to play it. But you *do* need my help with that suit."

"Meaning?"

"Meaning, I'll be damned if I'll help you and I'll be damned if you're going out there. You want information on that ship? Fine. *I'll* go out."

"No," she refused flatly. "I'm not asking you—"

"Yeah, well I'm telling," he nearly shouted, voice bouncing off the cargo bay's walls. "What happened to you, anyway?" he demanded. "The last time we discussed this you told me it was all but *suicide* for you to go outside. That there was no way in *hell* you were going to trust your life to some suit."

Blank-faced, she twitched her shoulders. "Maybe I did some thinking. Maybe I changed my mind. Maybe..." Her face softened and she reached for him, laying a hand on his arm. "Maybe I realized you were right, Tom. Maybe living isn't really living if you're trapped in a bubble looking at the world outside."

"*Now* I'm right?"

"Had to happen eventually." She offered a smile that dissolved his anger. A touch that eventually made him agree.

"Alright. Let me see that." He plucked the suit from her hands and gave it a quick inspection, soldier's eye picking out the prismatic sparkle of micro-abrasions ground into the suit's metal weave—a common enough consequence of sustained weapons fire, or the occupant of said suit getting flattened by a fast moving and unusually heavy object.

Like that door that freight trained Turk the other day. *Exactly* like that, in fact.

"Not this one," he said, tossing it back in the case. He rummaged around and selected another.

"Something wrong with it?"

"Nope. Just superstitious. Bad luck wearing another man's suit."

That wasn't it by half, but he couldn't quite explain his misgivings. Faraday'd inspected that suit three times over to confirm the function of every seal and connector, the air-tight fit of its linkages, the impermeability of its armored shell. Confirmed the damage to the outside was cosmetic only—no bearing on the suit's capabilities at all.

But he still didn't want her in it. Not Anthea, not Turk, not anyone. Bad juju clung to that suit.

He selected another at random and shuffled the damaged suit all the way to the bottom, handing the replacement rig to Anthea as he pulled out another for himself.

Misery loved company, or so he'd been told, and the best way to teach was through live demonstration. "The first thing you need to know is these things are a pain in the ass. The second thing," he said, folding his legs under him, "is to sit down while you're putting it on. Otherwise you're guaranteed to fall over. Either way, you'll still end up on your butt."

Twenty-Nine

The first step outside the ship terrified her, even with the enviro-suit to protect her and a cordon of metal-skinned androids wrapping Anthea round. Decades inside a ship would do that. Turned the mundane into murderous—a threat around every corner, the real world awash in barely controlled chaos that was not at all like her experiments and simulations, the endless rounds of testing and modifications and re-testing until everything fit just right.

Inside the forest, though, things got better. Every sight and sound a source of wonder, every rock, every tree, every furred, scaled and flagellated form they happened upon sparking a sense of wonder she'd almost forgotten. Hadn't experienced since she was a little girl.

Tucked away inside her climate-controlled suit, Anthea grinned until her face hurt, head pivoting on a swivel as she tried to absorb everything they encountered on that kilometers long course.

"You alright?" Faraday asked for the hundredth time, striding protectively at her side. And for the hundredth she told him,

"I'm fine."

Faraday's sour lemon expression suggested he didn't believe her—he was quite the worry wart, she was finding out. "Your little friend there think you're fine?" He pointed his chin at her wrist and the bio-monitor hidden beneath her suit.

"Happy as a clam. Hasn't chirped at me once."

Not *quite* true, there'd been a few alerts before she dialed the suit's settings to her unique needs. That meant tint on the visor even when the clouds rolled in, to protect her melanin-depleted, vulnerable skin, dialing the temperature down from cool to cold, riding the clamshell instead of hoofing it like the others. And as a precautionary measure in case she overheated, overexerted or otherwise reached a point of catastrophic metabolic imbalance, she'd tucked a handful of injectors into the loops of her belt, Novonox helix sparkling in the mid-day sun. She tilted her face toward the sky, astonished by that orb even now. By the pure perfection of that broad blue expanse and the puffy whiteness of the scattered clouds.

No rain today, thankfully, nor the day before that either, which meant the mud that foiled Faraday's previous trip had dried into crack-bottomed puddles. The ruts left by the other drones' passage carving out rough and bumpy path their clamshell hummed industriously along.

Never stopping, unlike that previous trip. Never slowing, not once stuck.

"We've been lucky with this weather. Or not," Faraday added when the clouds covered over that star.

In an instant, the route transformed from a dappled path into a darkened tunnel with towering, fern-shaped trees waving gently on either side. Packs of cone-shaped flowers gathered in clusters at their bases, covered in clouds of six-winged, opalescent insects. En masse, they sipped at the pollen spilling from the flowers' pistiled ends, until clamshell rolled by and clipped a straggling bloom, scattering rainbow-colored insects into the air.

Creating a new and vibrant source of wonder as they swirled and danced in jewel-toned chaos, perching primly on the tips of Anthea's outstretched fingers, on her shoulders, the length of one arm. Slowly, carefully, she turned her hand over to admire her little wonders in the inconstant sun. The clouds overhead parting and knitting by turns—restless in their wanderings, refusing, even for a moment, to stay still.

"They're beautiful, aren't they, Faraday?" She extended a hand his way with a fragile shape balanced weightlessly on her palm, but Faraday the watchdog never looked at it. Didn't seem interested in the least.

Too focused on nature's dangers to marvel at the wonders it offered. Too tensed up and worried about everyone's safety to stop searching for imagined dangers. "Eight. How much further?" he called across comms to the android scouting the way ahead.

"Half a kilometer and the forest ends. *Endurance* put down on the headland on the other side."

"Wait for us at the forest's edge. Stay out of the open until we reach you, understand?"

"Acknowledged, Faraday," Eight answered, and afterward went quiet.

Nervous, fidgeting, Faraday stripped the rifle from his shoulder, checked the ammunition clip and hugged it to his chest. Moved a few steps ahead to check on the marines walking point—Sunwoo and Andrada, if Anthea remembered correctly, though she was never very good with names—before dropping back to swap words with Shimizu and Clauson playing rearguard with a pair of ground pounders named Banjo and Fred, of all things.

Having made the rounds of their platoon, Faraday and his rifle returned to their place at Anthea's side. Keeping tabs on every rock and tree, every critter scurrying through the brush.

Man's wound up tight as a drum head.

And because *he* was, so was everyone else. Including Anthea as the forest's edge drew closer and the trees, once so protective, came to an end.

The clamshell slowed and rolled to a stop as Faraday raised a closed fist. The crew shuffled and shifted about, arranging themselves in a rough line looking out from the trees at a broad and empty plain jutting into nothingness, or so it seemed. The ground here covered in carpet grass with scarlet stems and blue-green blades that swirled and flattened in the blustering breeze. With the sea out there, showing at the headland's edge—vast and grey and angry, pounding at the cliffs that marked the continent's end.

The roar of it filled the ambient as it washed against hidden rocks. Anthea shivered as it rolled over her, skin prickling beneath her suit. Sensing hunger in the sound of the ocean. A promise of infinity and sudden death. Because that plain out there, so wide and empty, shouldn't be, not by far.

At its center, a rough-edged circle showed where something, some force or sentient creature, tore the grass up and churned the earth. Leaving a raw and darkened scar behind sprinkled with clumps of dying vegetation. There, according to the map's data, *Endurance* should have stood. Set down here weeks ago like *Diligence,* and buried tail-first into the earth. Standing tall and proud, according to the last reports, as she towered over the nearby sea. But of *Endurance,* she found nothing except that spreading scar carved into the land. No ship, no panels, no people, just that disturbance that marked her place.

"Guess we know why you lost contact with *Endurance.*" That was Clauson, standing with the others, heavy-worlder shape showing bulkier than the rest. "Looks like she flew the coop. Packed up and moved away."

"Think that's it, sir?" Shimizu turned her head toward Faraday. "Think she fired up her engines and headed back out into space?"

"Doubtful." Faraday moved a few steps forward, keeping to the shadows at the forest's edge. With one hand braced against a tree trunk and the other cradling that rifle of his as he took a good, long look at that headland, the cliff's edge and the sea beyond. "No burn patterns from her engines. No hole to mark where *Endurance* stood. Ground's churned up, grass is flattened, but a spaceship launch? I don't see it. Engine thrust would've burned that grass to a crisp."

"Maybe she sank." That from Andrada. Anthea didn't know him, nor his parchment-skinned partner Sunwoo. It was Faraday who'd insisted on bringing them. For protection, he said. Personally, she thought it was overkill, given the clamshell, the two androids and the other crew, but Faraday was adamant, and Anthea was smart enough to let it go. "Maybe there's a subterranean cavern we didn't know about," Andrada continued. "Maybe—"

"Don't be stupid," Clausen scolded. "Half a kilometer of spaceship doesn't just sink."

"Then what happened?"

"How should I know?" Clauson swiveled. "Doc here's got the big brain." Every eye in that group turned Anthea's way—even the clamshell popped out a few peepers mounted on extensible, flexible stalks. "So? Whaddaya think, Doc? Got any theories about what happened to *Endurance*?"

"Considering I just got here? No, not really. Given enough time, though…" She scanned the headland. "I can probably figure this out. With some help, of course," she added, patting the clamshell's metal-ceramic back.

Faraday squinted, eyeing her narrowly. "What exactly do you have in mind?"

"Theories require data, don't they?"

"Yeah…"

Anthea raised her eyebrows and pointed her chin.

At the patch of earth where *Endurance* stood. Faraday eyed it like a poisonous snake. "You sure that's a good idea?"

"Only way I know of to gather information." Somehow that came out calm and confident, not at all as scared as Anthea felt. Forests and trees were all fine and good, she was used to the boundaries of enclosed spaces, but that headland lay wide open. Too much sky, too much light, too much wind. The ground chopped off to jagged edges that dropped precipitously out of sight.

From the shadows, it looked daunting, the mere thought of going out there filled her with dread. Made her breath come short and her heart rate quicken enough to set the bio-monitor off.

She mashed it into silence and, on impulse, slithered off the clamshell's back. Felt safer, somehow, having ground beneath her feet, couldn't explain why really, it just did. The bio-monitor started to peep again, but with an effort, she calmed it down. Slowed her racing heart with a few indrawn breaths and kept it there through sheer force of will.

"Survey," she instructed the clamshell. "Give me a scan of the entire location and a broad spectrum analysis of that circle of dirt. Surface and substrata both to a depth of thirty meters."

The clamshell blipped in acknowledgement, pin lights activating in a ring around its carapace as it processed Anthea's orders and worked out an execution plan. With a hum of hydraulics, its shell hinged open, extruding a quartet of conical, wide-beamed scanning devices, stationed fore and aft, front and back. It paused a moment to adjust their angle and the distance between the emitters and the ground, before zipping away with a cheery whistle, oversized wheels bumping across the hummocked ground.

Anthea wrung her hands, staring after it, thinking how alone it looked, how exposed and vulnerable.

"You alright?" Faraday asked quietly.

"Yeah," she lied. "Yeah, I'm fine. Just peachy-keen."

"Don't look at it."

Instead of responding, Anthea just glared.

Faraday grunted and turned away, adjusting his grip on the rifle cradled in his arms. Eyes on the drone as it rolled across the grass, reached the circle and made a circuit of its edge. "Not too late to change your mind, you know. Clamshell—"

"I said I'm fine."

Hadn't meant for that to sound so snappish, but it got her point across and more importantly, shut Faraday up. He spared her a last, considering look before deploying his crew with a sharp gesture. Sending them out onto that empty plain of grass, past the clamshell and that rucked-up circle to the cliffs at the headland's edge. "You, you and you." Faraday pointed to Fred, Banjo and Eight. "Cordon around Dr. Naisson. I lead, you guard her back."

Wordlessly, they arranged themselves into a copper-clad, three-sided shield. One android stationed behind Anthea, the other two on either side. Faraday took point, of course, and glanced back at her as they left the trees. "Anything happens, you just do what I say. Not saying anything *will* happen, mind you, but if anything goes sideways or even remotely hinky—"

"Define 'hinky'."

Faraday closed his mouth and glared. "Hinky's whatever I say it is. I say run, you run, no questions. I tell you it's time to leave, you about-face and bug out."

Didn't particularly care for his tone—she wasn't crew and she told him as much.

"I know that." Faraday stopped and turned. "But this one time, I'd like you to do as I ask."

"Fine," she eventually agreed. "This one time. But don't get used to it."

"Wouldn't dare." He flashed a crooked smile and faced around to continue on his way. Checking on Anthea behind him every now and then, the clamshell, his crew, the ground pounders.

Mostly, though, he focused on the way ahead, scanning the headland as if expecting monsters. While Anthea, sheltering behind him, trudged along in her enviro-suit, with the wind blowing in her face. A palpable force that pushed and pressed as she strode unsteadily across the uneven ground, struggling with her shorter legs to keep pace with Faraday and the three androids. The ground here didn't help, with its lumps and bumps and hidden rocks, its scattered sprinklings of weathered bone. She ducked to pluck one up as she walked, curious about its sources, and rubbed a thumb across its porous, time-washed surface—jagged-edged and faded to dull grey-white sprinkled liberally with midnight speckles.

"Found those near *Diligence,* too." Faraday nodded to the shard in her hands. "Guess when she landed, she must've churned them up."

"I thought it was bone at first. Now, though…" She turned it over. "Kinda looks like bone, but I'm not so sure."

Faraday stopped and held out a hand. "Outside's got this pitting." He ran a finger across the object's surface. "Underside's smooth, though, see? And these speckles?" He held the shard up to the light and angled it to catch the sun. "They sparkle like some kind of crystal. Makes me believe it's some kind of stone."

"Well, lookit you." Anthea smiled. "Gone all geological and such."

"Smart ass."

She dropped a curtsy as Faraday handed the shard back.

"So, what do *you* think it is?"

"Hard to tell without running some tests." Anthea examined the shard from several angles, measuring the feel of it in her hands. "Doesn't have the weight of the other samples we've collected. Composition doesn't resemble anything the drones found elsewhere."

"Ocean's close. Might have something to do with it."

"Might. It's hard to tell."

"Sir?"

"What is it, Clauson?"

"You might want to see this." Clauson waved from across the headland, voice carried to them across the environ-suits' comms.

"You find something?"

"Maybe. Worth the doc and you taking a look, at least."

He looked a question at Anthea, and when she nodded, responded, "On our way." At his gesture, she tucked in behind him and he stretched his legs even more. Forcing her to hustle to keep from falling behind as he detoured around the earthen circle and the clamshell turning spirals from the outside in. Leaving a track of oversized wheel prints behind to mark the progress of its passage that cut across a repeating pattern stamped deep into the circle's dirt. Long, thin furrows pressed into the earth with double-layered rings running their length.

Anthea stared at them as they hustled by, so focused on that oddity that she forgot to watch where she was walking. She stumbled on an unseen object, and made Faraday jump when she steadied herself with a hand to his back.

"Something wrong?" he asked, glancing around.

"Sorry." She blushed furiously. "Caught my foot."

Faraday blinked at her a couple of times, shook his head and faced around. Steering them in an arcing route to skirt around the circle and reach the headland's point jutting toward the sea.

Where Clauson waited with her rifle, beside a trench carved into the ground. Wide and deep and flattened, the grass around it smashed as if pressed beneath a heavy weight. One end terminating at the land's end, the other tracking back to the dirt circle behind them.

"You see this, sir?"

"Kinda hard not to." Faraday stopped across from Clauson, with the width of the trench between them—a good twenty to thirty meters in Anthea's estimation—and scanned the length of that furrow, from the cliff side to the rucked-up land. "Any idea what made this?"

"Something big, if I had to guess. And heavy," Anthea added, based on its depth.

"Like a spaceship?" Clausen asked her.

Anthea stared at her across the gap. "Yeah," she said. "Something like that."

"Spaceship." Faraday glanced between them. "You think *Endurance* created this trench?"

"It's possible. She's got the mass."

"So where'd she go?"

"That's the question, isn't it? Ship that size doesn't just disappear. If I had to guess..." Anthea nodded past him, to where the trough's line terminated with the land's end.

"Stay here," Faraday told her. "Clauson. Keep an eye on her 'til I get back."

"Tom—"

"Just... wait," he said. "I'm gonna pop over and take a look."

"Take Fred," Anthea said on impulse, grabbing his arm to hold him there. "And stand clear of the edge in case it crumbles."

"What about Fred?"

"What about him?"

"You're worried about me falling to my death, but not him?"

"Fred's metal, not fleshy parts. He tumbles over, I can fix him. You'll go splat and end up dead."

"Alright. Good point." Faraday gestured to the android. "Fred. You come with me. Clauson!"

"Watchdog. Aye, sir." She snapped off a fairly respectable salute as Faraday set off with android Fred.

"Be careful," Anthea reminded him.

"Got it." Faraday raised a hand.

Anthea watched him stride away, waved at Clauson across the way, looking simply *thrilled* with this ad hoc babysitting assignment, and afterward twiddled her thumbs in boredom. At loose ends now with Faraday off conducting his investigation, nervous and increasingly fidgety in the blustering, hard-blown wind.

With the sky clouded over and the sun occluded, the day turned ominous and increasingly dim. To distract herself, she retrieved a curl of that polymer filament foil from one of the many compartments built into her suit's belt, and unfurled it with a practiced snap. Pinched the corner to power it on and waited the few seconds required for it to connect to the drone as it surveyed *Endurance's* scar.

Bit by bit, it painted structures as the drone continued its spinning course. Most of the map remained blank for now, the drone less than halfway through its survey run, but enough showed already to pique her interest. And one feature in particular caught her attention: a structure sitting a meter or so beneath the surface that, with some extrapolations and projections, matched the expected size of the missing spaceship's cavity.

Except the space she found wasn't dirt. Nor rocks, nor any other expected material.

"Stop," she ordered the clamshell.

The drone braked hard and slid to a halt.

"Back up and rescan this section." She highlighted the coordinates with a finger and sent the orders across the wire to the drone.

The rescan took roughly ten minutes. The results came back exactly the same.

No void beneath the surface, no subterranean cavern or other empty space. Instead, she found a vast and spreading mound of hundreds of globular structures. "What in the world?" She spun the three-dimensional image, trying to puzzle out what she'd found. "Excavation," she ordered the clamshell. "Three meters. Extract and retrieve."

The drone tapped out a rapid-fire flash of communication, retracting its sensors as it hinged and tipped forward, shoving its bladed front end into the recently disturbed earth to carve out a section of ground.

"Anthea. The weather's turning." She glanced behind her and saw Faraday point at the sky. "Storm's coming in. We should probably get moving."

"I found something."

"Congratulations. I don't particularly care."

"Tom—"

"You promised me, Anthea. Whatever it is, it can wait 'til later."

"Ten minutes. That's all I'm asking."

The comms dropped into silence and stayed that way for quite some time. "Ten minutes," he reluctantly agreed. "Then we pack it up and go."

Anthea raised a hand and waved, climbing to her feet as the clamshell popped out of its hole. She staggered across the soft-packed earth and squatted down when it trundled over to deposit a half dozen objects at her feet.

Round and wide as her doubled fists, bone-white and speckled black and grey. Like the shard she'd collected earlier. Exactly like that, but whole. Its surface pliable as toughened old leather, the sound when she tapped it, a semi-solid thud.

Not bone, something similar. A substance aged to hardened stone.

"Fuck," she breathed in horror. And for Tom, added, "I think we've got a problem."

"We've got more than that. You need to get out of here."

"Ten minutes, Tom, we agr—"

"I know what we fucking agreed to, just get out of here, Anthea. *Now!*"

Confused, she turned her head and found a wall of mist hemming the headland in. Fog that billowed off the surrounding sea and ate its way across the headland's edge. As she watched, it enveloped Fred's copper-clad shape and skulked toward Faraday backing away.

Rifle raised and pointing into the mist as a storm of screams erupted—deep-throated and filled with hunger. A heart of darkness clawed its way up the cliffs surrounded by a nest of writhing, dancing snakes.

THIRTY

The fog appeared from nowhere—that's what it felt like anyway. Caught up in searching the waves and rocks below, Faraday barely noticed the weather changing until the world around him darkened and the ambient light turned grey.

The fog, that creeping fog, swept inward across the sea. Smothering the wash of waves with its passage, the roar as they rolled ashore. Consumed the rocks clustered at the stone cliff's base and crawled upward on spidering tendrils, waking a quaking in the earth with their passage that built and built until the entire headland shook.

Balanced precariously on its increasingly unstable surface, Faraday swayed from side-to-side, and backed away on drunken legs, shouting at the android standing at the cliff's edge. "Fred! Fred, get out of there!" And when he just stood there, "Goddammit, you stupid machine, run!"

Confused, the android turned, cobalt eye slits glowing bright, as behind him, a tower of smoke appeared, showing ink-dark as the night sky.

At first it waggled lazily, slewing now left, now right, but with a lunge it reached and snatched poor Fred up, carrying him with it as it retreated into the mist.

"Faraday," Fred uttered, and with a grinding shriek cut off. From the fog there came the grating squeal of metal-on-metal and teeth-on-bone. With a pop and snap, a shower of sparks appeared, flaring sapphire blue before winking out.

A last stray flare drifted downward, and when it touched the grass, its light snuffed out. Behind it, the column of darkness splintered, spawning a dozen limbs that jerked in spasms, and with a whip-crack, tossed Fred's pieces at Faraday's feet.

"Shit. Oh shit. Oh shit," he breathed, staring wide-eyed at the android's decapitated head. At a copper face marred by scratches and dents, at cobalt eyes that slowly dimmed.

"I feel… strange," Fred told him, fading, and with a pulse his eyes turned dark.

Faraday stared a second or two longer, in shock and frozen to that spot, while the fog's edge rolled relentlessly forward, reclaiming Fred's broken pieces. Licking hungrily at the toes of Faraday's boots, at the rifle death-gripped in his hands.

That, at last, unlocked him. Slapped him in the face and smacked the stupid right out of his brain. "Eight!" he yelled, slewing around. "Take Dr. Naisson and retreat to the trees!"

"Tom—"

"Goddammit, Anthea, just go!"

He cut the comms and ran, risking a look over his shoulder as he pounded across the grass. A length of something thick and dark lashed out and struck the ground, making him stagger as the surface bucked behind him, cursing as he stumbled off-balance. Despite his efforts to remain upright, Faraday went down on one knee, rolled on instinct and raised the rifle, firing blindly into the mist.

By some miracle, he hit something that shrieked fit to wake the dead. With a sickening squish, a chunk of darkness tore away and struck the ground with a bounce and skip. Landing close by Faraday's hand, so close he snatched it back, and stared in horror at a nightmare length of grey-green skin coated with suckered mouths lined with a double row of chitinous teeth. At blood that flowed in ink-black ichor, shriveling everything it touched. At the appendage from which he'd carved it away, reaching, reaching for his knocked-down shape.

From the fog, a grinding came, bone-on-bone and filled with hunger, and a shrieking wail he knew all too well: mournful, hateful, and envious, a voice that called to him outside *Diligence*, attempting to lure him with its siren's song. That haunted his dreams in the cold, dark night with its promise of pain and slaughter.

Screaming, he squeezed the plasma rifle's trigger and fired off a dozen rounds, scoring hits along that tentacled length that rained bits of skin and blood all around him. With a banshee shriek, the appendage retreated and several others appeared in its place—writhing, swaying in a hypnotic dance as they languidly lifted skyward and with a high-pitched whistle, plummeted toward the ground.

"Fuck!" Faraday scrambled backward, twisted and lurched to his feet, shouting, "Clauson! Grab the others and get the fuck out of here!" as the tentacle behind him smashed into the earth. "Clauson!" he repeated when she failed to answer.

"Aye, sir. We're fucking trying." The whine and crack of plasma fire issued across comms with the sound of her panting breath. "These goddamn tentacles aren't making it easy, sir!"

"I'm coming! I'll be right there!" He slewed around and searched for her across the trough splitting the headland in half, locating a cluster of darkly-suited shapes standing back-to-back with their pulse rifles raised.

Sinking round after round into a knot of tentacles that squirmed and flicked and speared, driven by a globular shape behind them—something darker and massively large. That shone with a blood-red radiance limned with tentacles that ringed it round.

"What. The fuck. Is that?" Clauson asked.

"It's a kraken. Fuck me, that's a kraken. Holy shit, I didn't think they were real."

Andrada sounded terrified and, frankly, Faraday couldn't blame him. Kraken or not, that thing was a nightmare made real, a beast that crawled on tentacles across the grass, bulbous body covered in grey-green skin coated in barnacles and mold-black lichen-like blotches. Trailing shreds of mist as it rose above them, fortress wide and mountain tall, and fixed them with its single, blood-red eye—bulging and veined with amber, stretching wide and round as the noon-day sun. That jerked in hitching movements as it panned across the ground, the mouth beneath it a jagged gash of bone-white, clacking chitin that crashed with the crack of broken stones as its unholy voice burst forth.

Drowning the headland in a keening song of hunger, hopelessness and hate. The kraken's tentacles flared and it pulled itself closer, closing in on Clauson and her team.

"Fall back!" Faraday screamed before dropping down into the trough. He scurried across the bottom and clawed his way up the other side, grabbing at rocks and roots and makeshift handholds to drag himself up to the top, where he crawled out, winded and with his heart pounding in his ears, slammed the rifle to his shoulder and fired.

Aiming for that eye, that blood-red eye stretching wide above that horrid mouth. Cursing the scales that plated its face, the layer of crystal protecting the orb. Hurting the kraken not one little bit, though from its screams, he surely pissed it off.

With a whip and whirl of tentacles, the kraken beast lashed out and almost lazily slapped Clauson aside. She flew through the air for a second or two and landed in a heap a couple of meters away. And lay there stunned and barely moving, as the tentacle targeted Shimizu, snagged her ankle and jerked her off her feet.

Shimizu clawed at the ground as the tentacle dragged her away, drawing her inexorably toward its beaked mouth. Faraday fired on it a dozen times, tearing chunks out of the tentacle's length, but it pulled away undaunted and curled to lift Shimizu off the ground. "Captain!" she yelled, reaching for him. Knowing it was too late, nothing he could do.

In desperation, Faraday fired his clip empty, screaming in frustration when it didn't even make a dent. At close range, regaining her senses, Shimizu fired her pulse rifle into the kraken's mouth, and shouted her hatred when it drank them all, jerked her close and stretched its beak wide.

The tentacle raised upward, preparing to drop Shimizu into the kraken's mouth, and then a bar of green came out of nowhere, severing the limb to a bloodied stump.

Shimizu plummeted and landed hard—unlike Clauson, she didn't even move. Luckily, Sunwoo slipped in and dragged her away as Banjo—brave, foolish Banjo, all but forgotten in the chaos of the moment—raised both hands and spread his fingers, firing laser arrays in pulsing lines that burned and scored and bounced off scales covering the beast's body in a sheath of nigh-impenetrable armor.

"Run," Banjo ordered. Calmly. Infinitely, serenely AI. "You cannot kill this creature with those weapons."

"Fuck that." Clauson lumbered to her feet. "I'm gonna *make* it die." Half-dazed still, she fished out an ion grenade and attached it to her plasma rifle's end. With a squeeze of her finger, she launched and sent it arcing toward the kraken's great eye—a shot that, to her credit, arced perfectly, tracking true. "Eat that, you fucker!" she screamed in hatred, followed by furious cursing when a tentacle swept it aside.

Knocking it back at them, incidentally, and toward Andrada who unthinkingly dropped his rifle to catch it with both hands.

"Chuck it!" Clauson screamed. "Chuck it back, you idiot! Don't just stand there—that's a live grenade!"

"I—I—" Andrada stared at the explosive device in his hand as Clauson backed up in a hurry. Belatedly, he raised his arm and pivoted to throw it away, only to have it detonate and obliterate that hand, the attached arm, the body in its suit.

Blood and scraps of metal spread outward from the epicenter where Andrada stood. The blast wave carved out the ground beneath him and tossed everyone backward several meters.

Except for Banjo—he kept slicing and dicing, wielding those finger arrays with surgical precision. "You must leave now, Faraday." The android swiveled his head, spinning one hundred and eighty degrees to find him. "There are others coming to join this one."

On cue, the tremors started again, making the grassy earth shake and bounce. A chorus of voices lifted and shrieked their hatred through the cloaking fog, as a thousand tentacles sliced the air and a hundred blood-red eyes peered over the cliff's edge and boiled upward across the grass.

"Go," Banjo told them, and this time no one argued.

Clauson grabbed Shimizu and dragged her along as she picked up her feet and pelted away. Faraday delayed to offer covering fire while Sunwoo, for some unknown reason, decided to detour and search for something on the ground.

"Leave it! Whatever it is, just fucking leave it," Faraday screamed at her, but Sunwoo kept right on hunting. Sorting through a slurry of Andrada's exploded remains until her questing fingers encountered a chain.

She lifted it and turned, moving a single step Faraday's way, and stopped again at a whip-sharp crack—frozen for a good two seconds, fingers opening as her body slumped.

The chain with its silver bauble disappeared into the headland's grass. Blood rolled down Sunwoo's fingers and pooled beneath her palm. More blood showed at her shoulders and back where the kraken's tentacle laid her spine bare—envirosuit parted clean down the middle, skin and muscle carved through beneath.

Dead before she hit the ground.

Faraday hoped so anyway. He fished out a fresh ammunition clip, swapped it in and fired it dry. Discharged the empty and slammed another home as he spun around and chased after Clauson and Shimizu, passing the clamshell still nonsensically spinning—no one thought to recall it, the unfortunate thing—as he cut across the churned up circle and made a beeline for the trees.

"Eight!" he yelled when he could, huffing and puffing inside his helmet. "Where's Anthea?"

"She's with me." From the treeline came a flickering flash—cobalt eyes cycling to broadcast Eight's location.

"Clamshell," he wheezed on a stolen breath. "Redirect it."

The flashing changed as she sent the order, cancelling the drone's survey mission and replacing it with the recall command. "Drone is on its way."

"Copy," Faraday coughed out. He snuck a look behind him and saw the wheeled drone spin around, fat tires bumping across the churned-up earth as it hustled toward Eight in the forest.

That made Banjo the only one unaccounted for. Left behind to guard their backs. Faraday searched for the android but couldn't find him at first with all that fog and its mass of tentacles. Until a flash of green erupted, and several more after that—laser arrays flinging out deep green bars that flayed at the mist-shrouded air.

Wasn't long before the android himself appeared, loping long-legged across the uneven ground, with his top half twisted to keep those lasers in play and carve off tentacle bits. Behind him, literally *right behind him,* came a wall of eyes and clacking beaks, and thousands of tentacles nipping at the android's heels.

"Get the lead out, Banjo!" Faraday screamed, and in response, the android put on a burst of speed. Only to stagger when he stepped in a hidden hole and lurch awkwardly to one side.

The tentacles—patient, merciless—pounced on him in an instant, flicking out to hit the android hard. Banjo teetered and pitched sideways, severing his stuck leg at the vulnerable knee joint. He recovered and righted himself surprisingly quickly, snatched up his severed leg and hopped the rest of the way from there.

He was a determined bucket of bolts, had to give him that. Managed to catch up with the clamshell, hippity-hop leg and all, and even pass it by when the unlucky drone got flattened. No warning to it, nothing anyone could've done, a tentacle appeared from nowhere and squashed the clamshell into a dinner plate with a single, death knell punch.

With a wheeze, it puttered to a halt—carapace cracked wide open, chassis snapped neatly in half. For a moment or two, the drone's wheels kept spinning before giving up the ghost and stuttering to a halt. Its AI, simple as it was, managed to send out one last transmission, tapped out in frantic flashes of bright blue light, and then those too went quiet, shutting down as the drone's AI died.

"Keep going," he panted when Clauson slowed. "There's nothing—" Faraday gasped when something jerked him back, pulling hard at his enviro-suited leg. Slithering and crawling across his thigh, up his hip, onto his back.

Panicked, he struggled against it and saw a tentacle tip reach over his shoulder, wrap around it and hug him tight. It squeezed and he started to scream as the teeth that lined its length parted the survival suit's metal weave. Flensed flesh from meat and grated on bone, sparking a wash of blinding agony that made him sway and drop to his knees.

The smell of the creature finally hit him then—a fetid, almost carrion scent that wormed its way into his broken suit. Polluting his air supply with its dead-thing reek, making him gag and choke for breath.

"Captain!" he heard Clauson scream, but he couldn't see her, couldn't raise his head. The world was pain and he was trapped inside, sliding backward toward the krakens and their beaks.

"Fuck you, you bitch. He's *my* captain, now you fucking well better let him go." That sounded like Shimizu, but it couldn't be, she didn't swear. Not once, not ever.

The ground exploded beside him, pelting Faraday's face mask with dirt and midnight ichor. A second explosion and the tugging stopped, and someone's arm replaced the tentacle's grip.

"Got you, Captain. I got you." Clauson threw his arm over her shoulder and all but carried him the rest of the way.

"Shimizu? Where's Shimizu?" Faraday managed once they reached the trees.

"I'm going back for her. Don't wait for us." Clauson handed Faraday off to Eight.

"Tom." Anthea reached for him and stopped herself, staring in horror at his leg. At pulsing blood and the white of bone showing through the wreckage of muscle and skin. And that tentacle still wrapped around him, sharp teeth clinging to the suit's metal weave.

"Can't," he said around a wash of pain. "Can't—"

He gritted his teeth to bite back a scream when Eight scooped him up and cradled him in her arms like a wee babe. She set off at a loping run, each stride of those long legs jarring, igniting electric shocks of unbearable pain.

Consciousness dimmed before it, darkness eating up the edges of Faraday's vision. He pushed it back with the last of his strength, fighting to stay awake until Clauson came back. Craned his neck to search for her, but he couldn't see her, just a world alive with eyeballs and a roiling mass of snakes. And Clauson, if she was out there, disappeared into their midst. Shimizu lost along with her, only Banjo—brave little trooper—hopped unexpectedly from the mist.

"Anthea." He reached blindly and felt her fingers twine through his.

"Here, Tom. I'm right here," she said, hurrying along beside the much-taller Eight.

"Clauson." He gestured at the path behind them and saw Anthea shake her head. Looking uncommonly sad, unusually grim, a combination that said more than words. He squirmed to break free of Eight's encircling arms, wanting to go after them and bring them back, and stiffened at the pull of teeth, gasped in pain as they tore his skin.

That tentacle stuck tight, refusing to slough free. He tugged at it ineffectually until Anthea stopped him with a touch of her hand.

"Leave it. We'll get it off you. Just a little further, Tom, and we'll stop and rest."

He nodded, short of breath, pain spiking in blinding waves. Consciousness fading in and out on crests and troughs of bright white agony. The world a vague and strangely distant place passing by on either side. Until the rhythm of Eight's strides changed, slowing to a halt as she set him down. "Why?" he rasped around the pain, rolling on his side in an attempt to sit.

"Shh." Anthea bent over him, dark face pinched with worry. "It's alright. We're just stopping here for a few minutes. Lie back, Tom. Just rest a while."

"Go," he grated, pushing her away. "Not safe."

"We're fine, Tom. I promise." Anthea pressed until he relented, too exhausted to fight her anymore. "Just lie still and this will go quickly." She smiled for his benefit and squeezed his hand before moving away. Making room for Eight and the splay-fingered, laser-array hand she angled toward his wounded leg.

"What—?"

"Don't worry. I'll be gentle." Eight brought that weaponized hand closer, using its beam to carve through the tentacle and split the one long segment into six. Being gentle about it, as promised, and so careful she didn't even singe his skin.

A last slice and the light cut out. Eight retracted the laser and tucked it away. Using both hands now as she straightened his leg and got a firm grip on a tentacled section. "Deep breath now, Captain."

"How's that gonna help?"

Blank-faced, she twitched her metal shoulders. "It won't. But this will probably hurt."

Eight pulled and Faraday screamed as chitin teeth tore at his skin, barb-toothed suckers buried ungodly deep and refusing to relinquish his flesh. With some coaxing, she managed to wiggle it free and toss the flaccid length aside as she moved onto the next.

At some point Faraday stopped screaming, lacking the voice for it and the breath. Halfway through the tentacle extraction process, he lost consciousness entirely, and when he woke again the world was dark. Black and cold and strangely distant. The pain inside him far away—not gone, he could still sense its presence, lurking deep down near his bones, but muted now. Subdued. Dialed back to a raw-edged ache that matched the sluggishness in his limbs, the foggy sensation muddling up his brain.

"Where?" he croaked in a rusted voice, around a dry and swollen tongue. "Where are we?"

"In the forest," a voice answered. "We've stopped here for the night." Anthea appeared above him and twined her fingers through his outstretched hand. Behind her a campfire burned, dancing and flickering against the night—hypnotic in its inconsistent flare and the shadows it birthed and killed.

Faraday stared at it a moment, vaguely worried about that light. Only half aware of something tug-tug-tugging annoyingly and insistently at his leg. An odd and uncomfortable feeling that bordered on the verge of pain. Blindly, he reached to stop it and felt something grab his hand.

"Careful," Eight warned, kneeling down with her metal hands splayed. Digits divided and re-divided into a dozen matte-silver knitting needles chattering agitatedly against his enviro-suit to repair its polymetal weave.

"Kinda late for that don't you think?" With his air supply compromised, there didn't seem much point.

"The compression will keep the swelling down and ensure the stitching stays in place." Eight parted a rent to show him a twisted line of puckered flesh—muscle, skin and all their connectors sutured together to close the wound.

Faraday touched it with a shaking hand, tracing the ridgeline of the hot-fixed gash. Sensing a tenderness beneath the surface, a roiling mass of heat and hurt. "I thought it would be worse."

"We... gave you something." Eight's eyes flickered. "For the pain," she added as those needles chattered and briefly tracked off-line. Eight corrected their course in an instant and increased the rate of their movements, fairly racing through the suit's repairs.

He looked at her, and at his leg, at Anthea with her worried face. "Where's Banjo?"

Anthea waved vaguely. "Standing sentry. He and his one leg." She curved her lips in a nervous smile that twitched and slid away. "Hopefully we can reattach the other. He carried it with him, can you believe that?"

"Plucked it up. I saw." Faraday pressed the hand he held. Watching her. Studying her eyes. "Why have we stopped here?" he asked quietly, because it scared him, being outside at night.

"You needed the rest," she said and ducked her head.

"*I* needed rest, but not you?" He summoned a smile with an effort and that twitching quirk of hers came back.

"Big tough guy, that's me. Grand outdoorsman. Do this stuff all the time."

"I'll bet," he grunted and they both laughed. Shakily, because nothing felt particularly funny out here.

After that, things turned quiet, nothing but the tippy-tap of Eight's weaving needle fingers, the crackle of the fire, and the rustle and call of creatures moving in the night. Faraday closed his eyes for a moment, shivering despite the heat in his skin, and felt Anthea stretch out beside him, slim body pressed against his rangy frame. Hand-in-hand, they lay together in the darkness beneath that alien sky.

"What were those things back there?" Faraday turned his head and watched her as she lay there, gazing at the stars.

"Denizens of this world. Monsters birthed from its depths."

"Monsters," Faraday snorted. "Monsters are just stories concocted to scare children."

"In most cases, I'd agree with that."

"But not this time?"

"No. Not this time." Anthea rolled onto her side to see his face. "Tom. There's something—"

"Ow!" Faraday shot a glare at Eight as her needles chattered off-line again and struck a soft spot near his groin. "Goddamn, Eight, you butcher. Watch where you're sticking those things."

"I was sticking them right where they belong. *You're* the one that moved."

"The hell."

"She's right. You're shivering." Anthea grabbed his helmeted head and turned it back to her as she leaned in and searched his eyes. While Faraday just lay there with his limbs twitch-twitch-twitching and his heels rattling against the ground.

"'M cold," he said, teeth chattering.

"That's to be expected," he heard Eight say.

Anthea shot her a squint-eyed look and a minute shake of her head.

"What does that mean?" Faraday demanded. "Anthea. What does she mean?"

Took her a while to answer. She started to and changed her mind, tried again and closed her mouth. Sat there for a long time after, lips pressed in a hard, tight line. "It means I did what I had to do." She curled her fingers, squeezing his hand.

Didn't apologize, didn't try to explain herself, just those simple words and that touch. But her eyes told a larger story, the look on her face, the sluggishness invading his body. The cold inside him deepened to an arctic chill as his fogged brain finally figured things out.

"You had no right," Faraday rasped.

"I know."

"But you did it anyway."

"I'm sorry—"

"You're not sorry. I know you. You'd do it again."

To her credit, Anthea didn't deny it, she just sighed and dropped her eyes, looking bone-tired and just about done in. "Life is full of choices, Tom. Sometimes..." She trailed off and shrugged again. "Sometimes circumstances force you to make choices for others." She smiled apologetically, almost sadly as she slipped an injector from her belt. In the fire's light, the contents sparkled in two twining shades of blue.

Familiar and unwanted. A potion as much poison as cure.

Faraday tried to shove it away, but his balky limbs betrayed him, making him flop about like a landed fish. "No," he gasped on an indrawn breath.

"I'm sorry, Tom. I really am." Anthea cupped a hand to his helmet to steady his head and hold it still. To make him look at her, and see her, watch her eyes as she pressed that injector to his leg and fed ice into Faraday's veins.

THIRTY-ONE

Anthea picked disinterestedly at the food in front of her, another of Tip and Top's magnificent creations, cooked to perfection and arranged with an artist's eye on her plate. Fish this time—they'd surprised her with that. A prized variety of lab-grown salmon sautéed in a lemon-ginger sauce with delicate curls of pasta on the side. According to her taste buds, that meal was delicious, but her stomach didn't seem to care. A few bites and it started knotting up, a few more and it declared itself full.

"Silly, fickle thing." She pressed a fist against her middle. "A third of a fish is hardly a meal."

Not nearly enough calories to sustain her, even with her metabolism turtled down to a snail's pace. But done was done and her stomach closed for business—she could come back later, perhaps, and try again.

"Tip. Top. Clear this away." Anthea waved at the leftover food, fork clattering as she abandoned it on the plate. Nodding to Tip when he leaned it to take it and Top as he retrieved her empty glass. "Thank you," she said, belatedly. "It was scrumptious."

Blank-faced, they both stared at her, nodded and turned away. Cold, impersonal, formal to a fault. If they appreciated her charity, they didn't show it—those featureless faces were impossible to read, those cobalt eyes the same. And without their voices, they couldn't tell her. They'd lost those soon after *Persephone,* the latest victims to the cascading failures nibbling away at the systems connected to her AI.

They exited together, leaving Anthea alone with her thoughts. No *Persephone* to chat with, though she still watched from her wealth of cameras. No crew, no scientists, no Faraday—she missed his company most of all.

"Barely talks to me anymore," she grumbled into the near-silence cloaking the room.

There were a few words, of course, from time to time. When their paths crossed and he made the effort. But mostly he stayed away—sick at first and busy later. Nearly two weeks now since that ill-fated trip to *Endurance* and every olive branch she offered rejected. Left to wither and die a lonely death.

"Man sure can hold a grudge."

Then again, so could she. Moreover, she was determined. Eventually she'd win him over and wear Faraday down enough to get him talking. 'Til then, she had her experiments. The latest round of which showed some promise.

"*Persephone.* Connect to the bio-generation lab. I wanna see how my babies are doing."

With a flicker, her desk's panel activated, projecting an image into the air above it. Not the lab as she'd requested, a larger, mostly empty space with several small ships parked in a perfect line. And a single figure sitting cross-legged on its decking, worrying at a length of material draped across its lap.

"That's the cargo bay, not the bio-generation lab."

The image blanked and came back again. The same one, of that same space.

Anthea frowned at a camera. "You messin' with me or are you doin' that on purpose?"

Persephone cued the audio and fed it through her speakers, filling Anthea's quarters with the hum of atmospherics and the sharp-edged cursing of its one and only occupant.

Anthea pursed her lips, looking from the video feed to the camera. "It's not *me* that's been avoiding *him,* you know." She couldn't be sure, the cameras were tiny, but she thought she saw it twitch. "I'm telling you, he's not gonna wanna talk to me. Fine. *Fine,*" she said when the volume increased, curses painting the air around her blue. "I'll try, okay, just turn that down."

Persephone dialed the audio back down again as Anthea shoved back her chair. She moved a step and stopped again, chewing her lip while she tried to figure out what to say. That's when *Persephone* cued up another feed—the original one Anthea requested.

She stared at it for a long, long time, considering the carefully curated contents of this crucible where life began. "You sure you think that's wise?"

In response, *Persephone* brought the two images together.

"Alright. If you say so." Anthea sighed and headed for the desk. "But if this all goes south, I'm blaming you."

That one prompted a shower of bubbles that cascaded from the ceiling. Anthea blinked and tilted her head at that—she honestly had *no* idea what to make of that gesture.

"Tom," she called across comms. "Tom, it's Anthea."

The figure in the cargo bay waved, but didn't answer. Didn't even bother to look up. She zoomed the view in tight, focusing on Faraday sitting on the decking, with an enviro-suit stretched across his lap and a couple of tools laid out beside him.

"Tom. I need to talk to you."

"Little busy. Can we do it later?"

Anthea closed the channel. "Told you. He doesn't want to talk to me." She gestured in frustration at the image hanging in the air. *Persephone,* insistent, refused to shut it down. Zoomed the camera in even tighter, in fact, focusing its lens on Faraday's face.

With a sigh, Anthea tried again. "I'd rather—I'd like—This won't take long."

Faraday raised his head and frowned hard at the camera capturing video on his end. "'Spose I'm expected to come to you?"

"No!" she said too sharply. "No. I'll come down there."

He frowned a moment longer. "Fine. Not like I'm goin' anywhere." He dropped his eyes and kept fiddling with that blasted suit.

"Five minutes," Anthea told him, and when he nodded, cut the comms.

*****

Faraday barely acknowledged her presence, beyond a quick glance when she first entered and a terse, "Anthea," when she stopped in front of him. Fidgeting while she searched for words. Looking down on him, which was unusual—

standing, Faraday towered over her, tall and rangy compared to her smaller, petite frame. That buzzcut hair of his showing more grey than ever, though its original red-gold color still showed through.

For nearly a minute, she stood there searching for the right words to say while he picked at Eight's impromptu weaving with some sort of elongated tool. Plucked up a flash point brazing iron and applied its superheated tip to smooth the damage to the component sections.

A slow and patient process requiring him to work through one link at a time. With his hands ever so slightly shaking, making the picking tool skip and the brazing iron hop unsteadily when pressed. He cursed every time they slipped, set them down at one point and flexed his cramped hands.

Faraday frowned when he caught her looking, scooped them back up again and unpeeled another section. "You just gonna stand there all day staring at me?"

"What? No. No, I—" Anthea stopped and bit her lip, crouched down to put them on a level and wrapped her arms around her shins. "You've stopped the treatments," she said with a nod at his hands.

Faraday shrugged tightly, eyes on the damaged enviro-suit in his lap. "Never wanted that shit in the first place. No way I'm gonna keep shoving it in my veins."

"The side effects—"

"Tremors, irritability, sleeplessness—I got the trifecta," he said with a bitter twist to his lips. "Seen what it's done to you. Rather get off it before things get worse."

Personally, she couldn't blame him, though she'd never actually met anyone who'd successfully weaned themselves off. And there were other contingencies to consider. Things she'd tried and failed to discuss with him over the course of the last two weeks. "Tom," she said, touching his arm, "you don't—you don't understand."

"Fuck!" He jerked away as the brazing iron brushed his hand, leaving a mark that promised to blister—she knew from experience how hot those tools ran. "You're right," he said, tossing the brazing iron down. "I *don't* understand." He pushed the enviro-suit aside, flicking the picking tool over his shoulder in a snit. "I don't understand *any* of this, if I'm being honest, including why *you're* off playing Dr. Frankenstein with your experiments while *I'm* left trying to figure out how in *hell* we're gonna survive on this planet."

And just like that, she had her opening—not the best start to a conversation, she'd hoped for a calmer, more rational discourse, but there were things he needed to hear, starting with, "That's just it. We can't."

"What?" He blinked hard several times, with her squatting there, hugging her legs.

"This planet. We can't survive here. Initially, I thought we could—that's what those early experiments were about. But the more tests I run, the worse things get. And this latest round, the most recent analysis…" She trailed off for a moment and studied his freckled face. "This planet's too far from Earth normal for our bodies to adapt to. *We're* the problem, Tom, not it."

He considered her with narrowed eyes. "So we change it," he said slowly. "That's your specialty, right? That's what terraforming's all about?"

"In some ways." Anthea reached again, fingers featherlight on his arm. "But this is different."

"How?" he demanded, chin lifting. Taking on that stubborn, 'prove it to me' look she knew so well.

"Well…" She licked her lips and at his gesture seated herself on the decking. "Normally, we start with a blank slate. No water, no vegetation, no life, really, though the component elements are all there. This planet," she gestured vaguely, "is about as far from blank slate as I've ever seen. Instead of starting fresh, I'm dealing with another architect's work. And without a blueprint, I'm flying blind."

"So… you can't do it, or you don't to want do it? Or are you just afraid to try?"

"Little of all three, I guess." She smiled ruefully, organizing her thoughts. "We're not suited to this planet, Tom. What you're asking—"

"What *am* I asking? I'm serious," he said at her sharp look. "I'm trying to understand, but this isn't my lane."

"Microbial transmutation. Changing the building blocks of an entire world."

Based on his expression, Faraday still didn't get it. "Thought you had a whole lab for that kinda thing?"

"I do. *We* do. *Persephone*—" Anthea broke off and tried again. "Look. Microbes—micro-organisms, they're the underpinning to all planetary life." She rooted around in her pockets, retrieving a pair of styluses and a handful of data discs that she stacked on top of Faraday's picking tool and the cooled-down brazing iron he'd chucked aside. The result was somewhat wobbly, but with a few adjustments, everything stood. "If we start changing things, we unbalance the ecosystem." She increased the distance between the two styluses and the entire construct swayed unsteadily. "Alter things too much, and it all goes wrong." To demonstrate, she removed the brazing tool and her tiny tower tumbled down.

"How wrong?" he asked quietly.

"Mass extinction. Planetary die-off that'll turn it into a rock."

Faraday grimaced, eyes on her scattered toys. "What if we're careful? Use breathers, boil the water, irradiate the food."

Anthea shook her head. "It's not sustainable. They're in *everything,* Tom. The water, the earth, the very air we breathe. In every living creature. Including you." She touched ever-so-gently at his thigh and the still-healing wound hidden by his pants. "*Endurance* is gone, *Diligence* is failing, even *Persephone*—" She broke off and drew a shuddering breath. "There's no hope for us inside the ships, but as we are, we can't survive on the planet either."

Faraday thought on that a moment, raised a hand and rubbed at his face. "So, we're fucked—that what you're saying? These micro-critters are going to eat us from the inside out?"

"Not *quite* that dramatic, but yes." She waited until he looked at her. "The Novonox was meant to help—arrest the bio-synthesis processes in your body, slow the rate of cellular mutation enough for your system to flush the microbes out."

"But the drug wasn't enough, was it?" Faraday sounded tired and looked it.

"Might've been. But we—*I* gave it to you too late. The cellular degradation had already started. The microbes were already breaking you down."

"And Turk? That why he's dead?"

"I'm sorry—"

"Yeah, we're all sorry. Sorry bunch of fucks, that's us." Faraday turned his face away, jaw muscles clenched up tight. Angry, hurting, confused inside. Alone now, except for her. The androids and the few remaining drones. "So, what now?" he asked hoarsely. "Start everyone left in cold storage on a course of Novonox? Dose them early to build up their tolerance?"

"No," Anthea said quietly, and watched Faraday's head swivel her way. "I'm suggesting something far more radical. That we fundamentally change what we are. Come with me," she said when he frowned, and stood, extending her hand. "There's something I need to show you."

"Why—?"

"Just... come with me. It'll be easier this way."

Faraday stared a moment longer, and with some misgiving, let her lead him away. Exiting the cargo bay's cavernous, echoing chamber into the tighter confines of the passageway outside, to an elevator that whisked them upward and stopped on a level that wasn't marked. "Where are we?" he asked when the doors opened, access granted at a press of Anthea's thumb.

"Secure area. Limited access." Anthea winked. "Only us scientists allowed." She crooked a finger for him to follow as she walked a short way down the curving hall, presenting that thumb again, and her eyeball after to a scanner outside a locked, encoded door that slid aside with a breathy sigh.

From the hallway, Faraday stared at a perfectly rounded room, an egg of sorts nestled in *Persephone's* core, with stacked rows of fluid-filled canisters lining every square centimeter of its walls. "What is this place?" he asked in a hushed and wondering voice.

"Bio-engineering lab. We grow things here and test adaptations. I told you," she said when he opened his mouth, "I'll explain everything, just come inside." Anthea waved him in and sealed the door before joining Faraday at the monitoring station at the room's center. An arcing bank of panels scrolling data on those blue-green vessels and the half-formed shapes floating serenely inside.

"What are they?" Faraday asked, nodding to the canisters wrapping the walls, tilting inward as the ceiling curved.

"Our future."

"You mean they're *human*?"

"*Adapted* human," she clarified. "Human genes spliced with those of a dozen species." She plucked a vessel from the wall and set it down on the monitoring station's surface. Up close, the shape was obvious—a human's arms and legs and rounded head. But in place of a human's single-toned skin with its limited palette of blends and shades, the shape inside showed triple-hued: silver blotches set on a sea of black with a fuzz of silver hair.

That color betrayed their difference. Made it clear these proto-humans were slightly more. Faraday squatted down to study it, raised his head and scanned the room. "There's hundreds of them here. You must've been working on this a long time."

"Almost since we set down. As soon as the first experiments showed compatibility failures."

"All this time you've been planning our future? All this time, you knew how this would end?"

"No. No, I'm not omniscient. Just a scientist who's watched several worlds fail. This, all this was just a contingency." Anthea turned in a circle, surveying the stacked rows of canisters. "It became more when things turned dire."

"So, what? You're *growing* our next generation?" Faraday's lips curved in a grin that slipped away when she nodded back.

"*We* can't survive here, Tom. But our genes can, with a little help."

"What kind of help?" he asked faintly.

"This planet's." She turned around, retrieving yet another canister from the wall. This one clear instead of blue-green and filled with saltwater syphoned from this world's ocean.

With a shape inside that bore tentacles. A beak and a single eye.

Faraday backed up until he hit the door. "Where the *fuck* did you get that?" he rasped.

"I found it where we left *Endurance*. Where she used to stand before she disappeared."

"I don't... I don't remember seeing it."

"You wouldn't. You were pretty out of it at the time. And this was just an egg then, so there's that in addition to the rest." Anthea offered up a small smile. "I found a nest of them, buried deep, deep down. Apparently, we planted *Endurance* in a spawning ground of sorts."

Faraday stared hard at the tentacled creature, breathing in short, sharp breaths. "You think they took her? You think that's what happened? Those kraken things dragged *Endurance* into the sea?"

"I think it's possible." Anthea nodded. "And used the hole she left to store their eggs. Lucky for us they did, too."

"Lucky?" He stared, incredulous. "You call the slaughter of ten thousand people *lucky*?"

"No," she said quietly. "Of course not. But if they hadn't, we never would've found this." She cupped the seawater canister with its tentacle monster floating inside. "These creatures, they're the key to everything. Without them, these others wouldn't be."

Pale-faced, he raised his head, seeing those canistered shapes in an entirely different light. "You spliced in pieces of their gene set. That's why you think they'll survive."

Anthea nodded, sliding the two canisters together until they perched there, side-by-side. "Every ecosystem has its alpha species, Tom. On this planet, the kraken is king. To survive we need to be like them. Or learn from them, at the very least."

Faraday swallowed hard and tore his eyes away from the baby kraken's surprisingly tiny shape. Studying the canister beside it in silence awhile, and its occupant with the alien skin. "They're not really human, are they?"

"They are in some ways. Human *enough,* anyway, that we can raise them. Teach them language. Share our culture."

More silence, more considering, something akin to fear—so odd, seeing that in Faraday's eyes. "What do we call them?" he asked quietly. "I mean, they're not human. They're not *us*, so they can't be that."

"Been a while since I named anything, but I'm calling them Hecatine," Anthea said proudly. "Stronger than humans. Better than us by far." She turned in a gliding circle, surveying the vessels lining the walls of that room. "We're building the future here, Tom. *Our* future. The next evolution of our ancestors' genome."

 SEVERED**PRESS**

facebook.com/severedpress
twitter.com/severedpress

CHECK OUT OTHER GREAT SCIENCE FICTION BOOKS

WARNING: THIS NOVEL HAS GRATUITOUS VIOLENCE, SEX, FOUL LANGUAGE, AND A LOT OF BAD JOKES! YOU MAY FIND YOURSELF ENJOYING HIGHLY INAPPROPRIATE PROSE! YOU HAVE BEEN WARNED!

MAX RAGE
by Jake Bible

Genetically Engineered. Physically enhanced. Mentally conditioned.

Master Chief Sergeant Major Max Rage was the top dog in an elite fighting force that no one in the galaxy could stop. Until, one day, someone did.

The lone survivor, Rage was blamed for the mission failure and court-martialed.

With a serious chip on his shoulder, Rage finds himself as a bouncer at the top dive bar in Greenville, South Carolina. And, man, is he bored with his job.

At least until he gets a job offer he can't refuse. Now, Rage is headed halfway across the galaxy to the den of corruption known as Horloc Station.

With this job, Max Rage may have a chance to get back to what he was: an unstoppable Intergalactic Badass!

RECON ELITE
by Viktor Zarkov

With Earth no longer inhabitable, Recon Six Elite are sent across space to scout promising new planets for colonization.

The five talented and determined space marines are led by hard-nosed commander Sam Boggs. Earth's last best hope, these men and women are the "tip of the spear". Armed with a wide array of deadly weapons and forensics, Boggs and Recon Elite Six must clear the planet Mawholla of hostile species.

But Recon Elite are about to find out how hostile Mawholla truly is.

CHECK OUT OTHER GREAT
SCIENCE FICTION BOOKS

LOST EMPIRE
by Edward P. Cardillo

Building on their victory in the last Intergalactic War, the imperialist United Intergalactic Coalition seeks to expand their influence over the valuable Kronite mines of Golgath. Reeling from their defeat, the warrior Feng are down but not out. The overextended UIC and the vengeful Feng deploy battle groups and scramble fighters as they battle for position in the universe, spinning optics and building coalitions. Captain Reinhardt of the Resilience and the elite Razor's Edge squadron uncover the Feng Emperor Hiron's last ditch attempt to turn the tables with a new and dangerous technology. With resources spread thin, the UIC seeks to exploit Feng's weakened position through a very conditional peace accord. Unwilling to submit, Emperor Hiron must hold them off and quell the growing civil unrest of his starving, warrior people just long enough to execute the mysterious Operation: Catalyst. Commander Massa and his Razor's Edge squadron race against time to stop Hiron's plan, and a new race awakens, led by a powerful prophet set on toppling the established galactic order through violent acts of terrorism.

ABSOLUTE ZERO
by Phillip Tomasso

When a recon becomes a rescue . . . nothing is absolute!

Earth, a desolate wasteland is now run by the Corporations from space stations off planet . . . A colony of thirty-three people are part of a compound set up on Neptune. Their objective is mining the planet surface for natural resources. When a distress signal reaches Euphoric Enterprises on the Nebula Way Station, the Eclipse is immediately dispatched to investigate.

The crew of the Eclipse had no idea what they were getting themselves into. When they reach Neptune, and send out a shuttle party, they hope they can find the root cause behind the alarm. Nothing is ever simple. Something sinister lies in wait for them on Neptune. The mission quickly goes from an investigation into a rescue operation.

The young crew from the Eclipse now finds themselves in the fight of their lives!

CHECK OUT OTHER GREAT SCIENCE FICTION BOOKS

AGENT PRIME
by **Jake Bible**

Denman Sno is Agent Prime!

The best of the Fleet Intelligence Service's elite Special Service Division, Denman Sno will need to use all of his skills and resources to stop the galaxy from plunging into another War with the alien menace known as the Skrang Alliance.

Sno's assignment: protect and deliver Pol Hammon, the galaxy's greatest dark tech hacker, to Galactic Fleet headquarters.

Hammon is in possession of new technology that can and will change the landscape of galactic life. The Galactic Fleet will do anything to keep that technology out of the hands of the Skrang Alliance even it it means sacrificing their best agent.

Even if it means sacrificing Agent Prime!

GALACTIC TROOPERS
by **Ian Woodhead**

For three thousand years, the Terran Empire has ruled the Galactic Expanse with an iron fist, conquering any alien civilisation who dared to oppose the might of their new human masters.

Their grip is about to be shaken apart when an unknown invasion force starts to strip whole planetary populations.

Now humans and aliens must find a way to work together to prevent the Empire and the invaders turning the Galactic Expanse into a graveyard.

www.ingramcontent.com/pod-product-compliance
Lightning Source LLC
Chambersburg PA
CBHW071504170626
46811CB00007B/2730